TRIUMPH IN DUST

IAN ROSS has been researching and
writing about the later Roman world
and its army for over a decade.
He lives in Bath. Visit his website:
www.ianjamesross.com, or find him
on Twitter: @IanRossAuthor.

TWILIGHT OF EMPIRE

War at the Edge of the World

Swords Around the Throne

Battle for Rome

The Mask of Command

Imperial Vengeance

Triumph in Dust

IAN ROSS

TRIUMPH IN DUST

TWILIGHT OF EMPIRE VI

First published in the UK in 2019 by Head of Zeus Ltd

9 7 5 3 1 2 4 6 8

A catalogue record for this book is available from
the British Library.

ISBN (HB): 9781784975333
ISBN (XTPB): 9781784975340
ISBN (E): 9781784975326

Typeset by DivAddict Solutions

Printed and bound in Great Britain by
CPI Group (UK) Ltd, Croydon CR0 4YY

Head of Zeus Ltd
First Floor East
5–8 Hardwick Street
London EC1R 4RG

WWW.HEADOFZEUS.COM

When the wall was broken through, when the elephants
pressed in,

When the arrows showered, when men did valiant deeds,

Then there was a sight for the heavenly ones.

Ephraim Syrus, *Carmina Nisibena*

THRACIA

CONSTANTINOPLE

•NICOMEDIA

BITHYNIA

PON

GALATIA

ASIANA

•EPHESUS

LYCIA

ISAURIA

RHODES

CRETE

GORTYN•

CYPRU

MEDITERRANEAN

THE EASTERN PROVINCES
OF THE ROMAN EMPIRE
A.D. 336

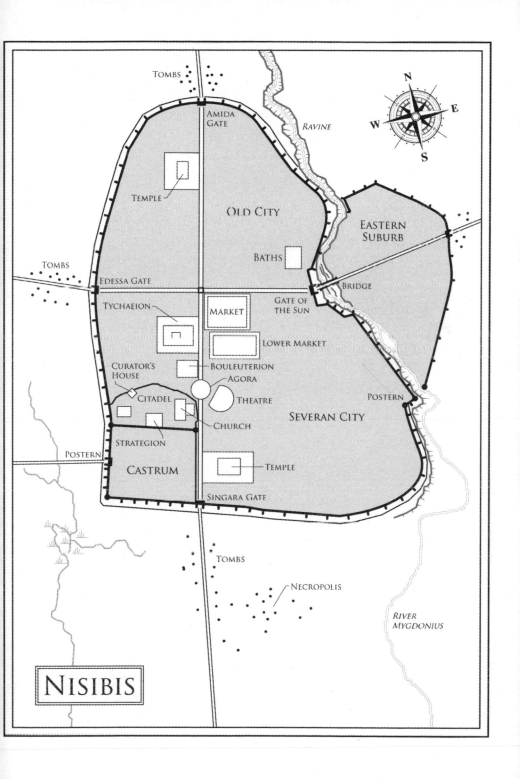

NISIBIS

HISTORICAL NOTE

Following the defeat of his rival Licinius in AD 324, the Emperor Constantine has reigned for twelve years over a united Roman world. Under his patronage, Christianity continues to gain in strength and influence, while followers of the older religions increasingly feel that the traditional ways of Rome are dying.

But the emperor himself is getting old, and facing new challenges. In the east, Shapur II, the young and vigorous King of Persia, disputes Constantine's claim of protection over the Christians living within his domains. In Armenia, a state allied to Rome, the king has converted to the new faith, adding fuel to the simmering fires of Persian resentment.

Now, as Constantine reaches the thirtieth anniversary of his rule, the ancestral enmity between the two great powers threatens once again to break into open war.

PROLOGUE

Constantinople, July AD 336

'Leva!'

At the word of command, the purple silk drapes rose smoothly upwards, drawn by hidden cords. A stir ran through the men gathered in the great hall of the summer *consistorium* as they saw the figure of the emperor enthroned on the dais before them. As one, civil ministers and military officers, priests and eunuchs, all in their gorgeously patterned court garments, sank to kneel on the marble floor. Only the bodyguards of the Schola Gentilium remained standing, lining each side of the hall with their shields grounded and their silvered spears upright. The assembly rose to their feet, lifting their hands in salute to the emperor and crying out the acclamation in unison.

'*Constantinus Augustus, eternal Augustus! God gave you to us! God save you for us! Your salvation is our salvation!*'

Twice, three times, then four times the shout went up, echoing back from the high panelled ceiling. Then the honour guards that flanked the dais banged the butts of their spears, and all fell silent.

Seated on the throne, Constantine set his jaw and stared, unblinking. He was sixty-three years old, but still he held himself stiffly upright, his stern face impassive beneath its mask of powder and cosmetics. The weight of the jewelled diadem on his head sent runnels of sweat down his brow, and his shoulders ached beneath the heavy hug of his gold-embroidered cape.

Flies circled lazily in the beams of sunlight from the tall windows of the apse, and smoke rose from the tripod braziers on either side of the throne, fogging the air with cloying incense. Letting the silence stretch, Constantine studied the faces of the men assembled before him. He saw avarice and awe, reverence and resentment. Someone near the back of the hall stifled a cough.

They think this is easy.

But ruling an empire was no easy task. It was a stern duty, a labour of Hercules, and he felt it in his aching bones. Thirty years on the throne: the lavish games and shows of his *tricennalia* had only just been concluded. Thirty years, and every one harder than the last, with fewer rewards. Had he not done enough? He had brought peace to the Roman world, crushed his enemies and reunited the empire. He had built this great city of Constantinople, dedicated in the name of the One True God. He had raised the Christian faith from persecution to glory, and filled the empire with magnificent churches. He had been generous too; so much gold had flowed from his hands that he doubted there was a single citizen who had not been enriched by his largesse. He had done all that, but still it was not enough. Always the same restless ambitious fury he had known all his life, driving him on, forbidding him happiness. What more could God ask of him? When would he be granted peace?

He had slept badly the night before, troubled once again by vivid dreams. They were the most terrible dreams, the ones that came to him at the darkest hour of night, when those he had destroyed returned to him. He saw again the proud faces that he had thrown down. Maximian, Maxentius, Licinius. Whispering to him in their anguish. *Remember me. Remember me.* His own wife, his own eldest son... *Remember me when you confront your God. Speak my name at last, and despair...*

'Majesty?'

Constantine flinched, irritated that he had let his mind wander. He focused once more on the scene before him. A eunuch knelt beside the throne. 'Majesty,' he said again in a sibilant whisper. 'The ambassadors of the King of Persia?'

Tightening his lips slightly, the emperor raised a finger from the arm of his throne. At his signal, the *Magister Admissionum* climbed to the lower step of the dais, raised his gold staff of office, and cried out in a voice that echoed down the hall.

'Let Vezhan Gushnasp, the envoy of Shapur the Second, King of the Persians, and those who accompany him, be called!'

A sonorous note from the water organ in the side chamber, and a file of white-uniformed Protectores entered through the far doors of the hall. Once they had formed up in a double row facing the central aisle, the Persian delegation followed them in from the vestibule.

Constantine had kept the Persians waiting for nearly ten days now, all through the celebrations of the tricennalia, and had been happy to do so. Let them witness the might of the Roman Empire, he thought. Let them marvel at the passions of the crowd, the glory of the imperial salutations. Let them see everything, and take word of it back to their upstart king in Ctesiphon. He had already seen the inventory of the official gifts: ten gold-embroidered carpets, six saddles panelled in ivory and set with gemstones, eighteen peacock-feather fans, a couch made of elephants' tusks... the list went on. Constantine was unmoved by it; he was satiated with luxuries. Now the men who had brought those gifts all the way from the royal court on the Tigris stood before him.

Vezhan Gushnasp, the chief envoy, had a bone-white face and pointed black beard; he wore a gown of gold-worked crimson silk and a tall white hat. Not daring to glance up at the dais, he advanced slowly between the ranks of soldiers until he reached the disc of purple marble set into the floor. Then, with a crumple of silk, he prostrated himself full-length, touching his forehead to the stone. Constantine hid his smile; he rather liked this Persian form of genuflection. Perhaps, he thought, he should introduce it to the Roman court as well? His sons would like that, he knew; they had a taste for the obsequious.

Getting to his feet, the ambassador walked slowly forward to the foot of the dais. Climbing the first two steps, he prostrated himself once more. Reaching out with one hand, he took the trailing hem of the emperor's purple robe and touched it lightly to his lips. Then he shuffled backwards from the dais, stood up, and retreated to the purple disc once more.

'The letter from the King of Persia, sublimnity,' the eunuch beside the throne whispered, proffering a sealed roll of parchment on his silk-veiled palms. Constantine took it, moving only his forearm and keeping the rest of his body immobile. He raised the scroll, tapped the royal seal against his mouth and then laid it aside once more; there was no need for him to read it, and he knew very well what it would say. Another slight signal.

'Let the envoy of the King of the Persians speak!' the Magister Admissionum declared.

Vezhan Gushnasp raised his eyes for the first time, and a thin smile showed though his beard.

'His Immortal Mazda-Worshipping Majesty, Shapur the Second,' the envoy cried, 'King of the Iranians and the Non-Iranians, of the Race of the Gods, Brother of the Sun and Moon, Master of the four corners of the World, bids his brother, the Great Constantinus Augustus of the Romans, greetings and good health.'

Constantine tightened his grip on the arms of the throne. It was not mere hubris that had caused him to delay the audience with the Persians. He had wanted to wait until the festivities were finished. For this meeting, he would need all his fury, all his assurance. Already he could feel his blood beating faster, stirring the ashes of his heart. But he kept his expression blank, his voice mild.

'And how is my brother the King of Persia?' he asked. 'In good health too, I hope?'

'By the grace of the ever-loving Ahura-Mazda, the king prospers.'

'I rejoice to hear it. And why has the king sent this new embassy to us so soon?'

'Majesty,' the envoy said, drawing himself upright and tipping back his head, 'it has come to the divine ears of my sovereign, the all-powerful King Shapur, that certain devotees of lies have been spreading rumours about affairs in the east. Rumours, majesty, that may upset the understanding and concord between the great nations of Rome and Persia, which bestride the world like twin colossi, illuminating the hearts of all men like two great lamps burning with the fires of truth...'

'Enough!' Constantine declared suddenly. 'I know very well why you have come here, Vezhan Gushnasp.' The foreign syllables left a sour taste on his tongue, like dirt. 'You were last here two years ago. Do you remember what I said to you then?'

'I seem to recall, majesty...'

'Two years ago, you came to us with a request from your king that Rome supply him with a certain quantity of iron ore. To make weapons to defend his eastern border against barbarians, so you said.'

'A request your majesty was generous enough to grant.'

'I did! And I told you why I granted it. I knew that your king was enlarging his army, and needed iron to equip his troops. And what did I tell you? *It does not accord with the honour of Rome that her soldiers fight enemies who are inadequately armed!*'

'Your majesty has a commendable sense of humour!'

'It was no joke,' Constantine said quietly. Seldom had anyone commended his sense of humour. 'For a long time we have heard the pleas of the followers of the true religion within your master's domains,' he went on, 'telling of the persecutions directed against them. We have informed your master that all Christians are under our protection, and he has promised us that he will alter his course of action.

'And yet,' he said, raising one finger towards the ceiling, 'only a month ago, we received news from the east that your king has stirred up sedition in the kingdom of Armenia, and raised a rebellion to depose our ally, King Tigranes, a pious monarch and a follower of the Christian faith. Not only that, he sent his own troops into Armenia to seize Tigranes and his family, and then to *burn out his eyes with hot coals*!'

His voice had risen to a shout. Now Constantine swept his robe around him and stood up, striding to the edge of the dais. He saw that the envoy was trying hard not to quail before him. The rest of the assembly stood in stunned silence. Many would not have heard the news from Armenia; doubtless the Persians' had hoped that the emperor knew little about it either. If so, they had hoped in vain.

'Are these mere *rumours*?' Constantine shouted, raising a clenched fist. 'You cannot deny them! How does your king account for these atrocious crimes?'

'Majesty,' said the envoy, fanning his hands in a placatory gesture, 'there may have been certain regrettable acts, carried out by over-zealous servants of my sovereign, but...'

'Be silent!' Constantine commanded. He thrust his chin forward, staring down at the envoy. Behind the mask of fury he was savouring this moment. Nobody knew what he was about to do; he alone held the fate of the world in his hands. He felt the heat of power surrounding him, the aura of invincibility like a golden penumbra cloaking his ageing body.

'You will return to your king,' he said gravely, 'and tell him of our displeasure. You will tell him that unless he returns the family of King Tigranes to power, and pays a full compensation for the unholy mutilation of that monarch, *and* withdraws all Persian troops and Persian supporters from the kingdom of Armenia, he can expect the full irresistible might of the Roman army to be directed against him.'

He paused, staring down at the assembly. Many among them appeared shocked now, even nervous. Others, he was glad to see, were barely concealing their smiles. The envoy Vezhan Gushnasp had grown even paler, struggling to contain his affronted anguish.

'Majesty,' he said in a strained voice. 'The world is held in a delicate balance... a most delicate balance. Far be it from me to suggest a course of action to one so exalted, but surely any differences can be solved by moderate means...'

'You have heard my words!' Constantine declared. 'Now go, and take them back to your master. And tell him this too – if he wishes for more Roman iron then he will get it. *In the hands of Roman soldiers!*'

'Get this thing off me,' he said as he walked, fumbling irritably with the massive jewelled brooch that secured his robe. Two eunuchs hastened to obey, drawing the cloak from his shoulders as the emperor paced through into the private chamber adjoining the audience hall. Rid of robe and diadem, Constantine eased himself down onto a chair and waited while the slaves removed his purple leather shoes. Only then did he take up the cup of wine set ready for him on the circular table and swallow three long draughts.

'Majesty,' the Praetorian Prefect said, bowing his head as he followed the eunuchs into the room. The Master of Offices and the Superintendent of the Bedchamber trailed behind him; all of them looked similarly perplexed.

'Majesty,' the prefect said again. 'Are you entirely sure that it was wise to dismiss the envoys so abruptly?'

'Of course I'm sure,' Constantine snapped. He placed the cup back down on the table, pleased to notice that his hands were admirably steady. 'Arrange for the diplomatic gifts to be returned as well.'

'But surely the Persian king can never agree to these demands? It amounts, in effect, to a declaration of war. Surely it's not too late to have the embassy recalled – after such a salutary shock, no doubt, they will be more pliable? Unless, of course, you genuinely intend war with Persia?'

'Yes I *genuinely intend war with Persia*,' the emperor said, raising his voice. He felt his neck swelling with anger. 'What part of that statement do you fail to comprehend?'

His ministers exchanged glances, and again Constantine felt that pulse of absolute power, absolute certainty. It was almost dizzying; he took another drink.

'Besides,' he said, setting the cup down, 'I was instructed to do this by God himself. In a dream.'

'Ah,' the prefect said, abashed. 'Well, in that case... perhaps we might convene a meeting of the imperial council...?'

Yes, yes, Constantine thought. They would talk and offer their guidance, their quibbling objections, couched in the usual extravagant praise. But he had made his decision, and made it publicly. He had cast the dice. Too long had he endured the provocations of the Persians. Too long had he sat on thrones and listened to men talking, the endless whittling words of legal experts and fawning courtiers.

They thought he was too old, he knew that. Maybe they thought he would retire one day soon, like Diocletian before him, who had gone off to his seaside villa to grow cabbages. Most of them were probably already making their plans for the approaching succession, gambling on which among his squabbling sons would make the best candidate, which of them would be best placed to capitalise on his death. The thought of a full-scale military campaign at this stage threw all of their plans into the air. *Good*, Constantine thought. *Let them live in the moment for a change!* He would die as he had lived, with the reins of power firmly in his grasp.

And war, surely, would be a balm to his soul. Two years before, he had watched as his cavalry slaughtered the Goths on the snowy banks of the Danube, and had felt only anger at the senseless waste of manpower. But the Persians were different: they were the ancestral foe of the Roman people. Every emperor had dreamed of crushing the might of Persia, and a few had attempted it. The dream of Great Alexander, the ultimate conquest. Yes, Constantine told himself, this was his true destiny: he would carry the proud standards of Christianity eastwards, beyond the Euphrates and the Tigris. In the name of God he would destroy the kingdom of Iran-Shahr once and for all. That would be his finest achievement, his gift to mankind and to the heavens.

And if he did that, surely God would forgive him his crimes.

Surely he would dream no more of the mocking dead, of the wife and son he had condemned and then erased from history. War had lifted him to supreme power; war would be his legacy. All the blackness of his soul would be scoured away by the blood of his enemies. Then, and only then, could he undergo baptism, and meet his God with a pure heart.

'We have, I think, an established set of plans for a campaign against the Persians?' the Master of Offices was saying.

'Updated every year,' the prefect replied with a shrug. 'As circumstances change. But mobilising the eastern armies and preparing them for full-scale war would take a considerable time... Financing it would be difficult too; the provinces are still recovering from the effects of the Syrian famine eighteen months ago, and most of our tax-gatherers have no effective way of increasing their surpluses...'

'Find a way,' Constantine snapped. 'There's always gold, if you know where to look.'

'Presumably, majesty,' the Master of Offices said, 'your second son, the Caesar Constantius, would be taking command of the proposed campaign, as he's already based in Antioch?'

'I'll be taking command myself,' Constantine said. 'My son is brave and confident, but he has no experience in these matters. I, on the other hand, have been leading armies all my life. He will be my deputy. And I want the armies mobilised for war by the opening of the campaign season next year.'

'The harvest in Syria and Mesopotamia is in late May and June, majesty,' the Master of Offices said, exchanging a glance with the prefect. 'We would need to wait until then in order to have sufficient fodder and supplies, even with direct requisitioning. But if we could delay until later, perhaps, after the summer... a campaign in winter would be quite feasible...'

'No!' Constantine shouted, pounding his fist on the table. 'We attack next summer, as soon as the harvests are gathered in! Everything must be ready by then. Delay any longer and Shapur will think I'm weak and timid. He'll have time to muster a force to oppose me.'

'Then, majesty, you would need to appoint somebody to prepare the eastern troops, I think – if, as you suggest, the Caesar Constantius is inexperienced, and our current government in the east is largely civilian. Could we consider our options for a suitable senior commander, perhaps?'

Constantine frowned, then glared at them. Already they were conspiring to steal his glory! But he knew what they were up to – every one of his ministers had military men among his clients and followers, eager officers they would push forward for the new senior position in the east. He could not allow that – he would make his own decisions, and not let them snatch control away from him.

'I will nominate a commander myself,' he said quietly, dropping his chin to rest on his knotted hands. He frowned deeply, thinking – there were plenty of capable officers in the

army, but fewer and fewer as the years went by. Not many
that he could trust. Not many that would be free of the web of
patronage and favouritism that enveloped the imperial court.
No, he needed a soldier of the old school, somebody who knew
his job and would be impervious to the flatteries and temptations
of high office. Where now were the soldiers he had known in his
younger days, those brave and capable officers who had led his
armies to victory after victory?

Old, he realised. Or dead, or retired to comfortable oblivion…
For a few long moments he pondered, sensing his grip on the
situation slackening.

A name came to him, unbidden. A name he had not even
considered for many years. He was tempted to dismiss the idea;
it was eccentric, perhaps dangerous – but the suddenness of his
intuition felt startling. Had God prompted him? He had known
such things. And perhaps, he thought… perhaps it was not such
a bad idea after all?

'You have a suitable officer in mind, majesty?' the prefect
asked with a guarded frown.

A slow smile tightened Constantine's lips, and he raised his
head.

'Yes,' he said. 'Yes, I believe I do.'

PART ONE

PART ONE

CHAPTER I

Dalmatia, August AD *336*

The three men walked in file, down the path through the pines to the edge of the sea. Still early, and the land was in shadow, but the morning sun was bright on the calm blue expanse of the bay. One of the three stepped onto the shelf of rock that jutted above the water; from here he could see the little island, less than a stade out from shore. He kicked off his sandals, and felt the warmth of the previous day through the soles of his feet. The water below him was deep and clear, translucent blue-green over a bed of white stones. Stripping off his tunic, he passed it to one of the slaves behind him and stretched his arms above his head.

Aurelius Castus was sixty years old, but his body was still solid and heavy with muscle. His tanned flesh was scored with the pale tracery of old battle wounds, his silver-grey hair and beard shorn in a military crop. The first sun caught the crown of his head, and he closed his eyes and breathed in, filling his chest with cool air and the scents of the pines, the dry earth and the sea. He exhaled slowly, drew another breath, then took two steps forward and dived.

Crashing down into the water, he kicked up from the seabed and back to the surface, gasping at the shock of the cold. A few sweeping breaststrokes carried him clear of the rocks, then he struck out for the island in a powerful front crawl. Occasionally he glanced towards his destination, although he knew its position by heart. It was not much of an island, just a hump of rocks jutting from the sea, crowned by a dry fringe of scrub; the smallest and closest of the group that stood just off the end of the peninsula. Salt water stung his eyes, and he felt the sun on his shoulders and the back of his head.

These morning swims had become a routine for him. Two or three times a week this summer he had swum out to the island and back, just as he had done nearly every summer for the last decade. It was not only necessary exercise; the ritual cleared and focused his mind. The sense of repetition was a welcome echo of the life he had known in the army. For a while each day, as he swam, he could forget himself. He could forget his aged and battered body, his scarred face and mutilated left hand. He was no longer Flavius Aurelius Castus, *comes rei militaris*, retired general of the Imperial Roman Army. His life held no victories, and no deaths. No dishonour, and no disgrace. Instead he felt only the symmetry of his body in the water, the stretch and flex of muscle and the action of breath, the steady living flow of the sea all around him.

For ten years he had known this. Ten years of peace, contentment and security: he never failed to thank the gods. There were times, certainly, that he missed his old life: the blood-rushing thrill of battle and the fierce comradeship of the legions. But he fought down such memories. If they pressed too hard, he had only to remember how close he had come to losing everything.

Halfway out from the shore he slackened his stroke, let his legs sink and rested, treading water, rising and falling with the sea swells. When he turned his head to the right he could see the cove at the head of the bay, a mile distant but clearly visible. He picked out the white colonnades of the villa's front portico, the red tiles of the roof, the land rising behind it in olive groves and orchards to the wooded hills, all hazed by the morning sun. Yes, he thought, fate had been kind to him, after everything. He had a home, lands and wealth, a family, and he was married to the woman he loved. To have risen from nothing and to have gained all this seemed a rare blessing.

A slight tremor in his chest, and the faint twitch of what could be a cramp in his leg. Every year this morning exertion drew more from him. When would he grow too old for this? Not yet, Castus told himself. He flexed his limbs, then kicked forward once more towards the island.

Twenty more strokes. He was close now, his strength undiminished. This far from shore the sun was hot on the water, glaring bright whenever he opened his eyes.

He dipped his head, and something struck him a hard blow on the chest. Pain engulfed the muscles of his left arm, sudden panic driving through him like black lightning. He was sinking, sucking in water as he gasped. Had he collided with something beneath the surface? Or had some creature risen from the depths and rammed into him? But the water was bearing him under, his mind numb, his limbs powerless. The punch had come from within, he realised... *from his own body*. Choking, he felt his lungs contract and knew that he was about to die.

For a few long moments the confusion and shock stunned him. Blood beat in his head, a muffled thumping in his ears, and the last air burst from his mouth and rushed in streams of bubbles around his face. He had a sudden clear image of his corpse being dragged from the sea, the sorrow of his loved ones... Then fury gripped him, a desperate savage desire to live. From deep inside, he summoned the energy to kick out at the heavy water, to stretch his right arm upwards, as if he could grasp the surface and haul himself up. He was thrashing, pressure all around him and his heart like a lifeless rock in his chest.

With a crash of water he burst back into glaring light and air. He filled his lungs, then let out a shuddering cry. The pain had faded to a throbbing ache, but he had never felt so weak, never so alone. He caught a glimpse of the island, and it seemed stades away from him. Willing himself to slow his breathing, to relax the panicked clench of his muscles, he concentrated on treading water and keeping his head above the surface.

He was alive; he had survived somehow, though he knew he should be dead. What had happened? What god had struck him? With a rush of shame he remembered his comfortable thoughts of only moments before, and they seemed like fatal hubris.

Trying to move as slowly and calmly as possible, he began to push forward again through the water. A relaxed breaststroke, but still he felt the grinding pain in his muscles, the fluttering anxiety in his chest, and the cold nausea rushing through him. At any instant, whatever had almost crippled him could strike once again. Waves buffeted at his face, and he sucked water as he felt the strength pouring from his limbs.

Finally, with a grim sense of victory, he saw the rocky flank of the island ahead of him. A few more strokes, and he could drop his legs and feel shingle grating between his toes. He hauled himself up from the water, feeling the weight of his body pooling inside him. Stumbling, he scrambled between the rocks and the rasping scrub bushes along the shore, then eased himself down to sit. The morning sun burned in his eyes.

Trembling, choking on air, he sat and waited for the nausea to pass. The left side of his chest and his arm still ached, with a strange burning numbness that he had never experienced before. The distance back to land appeared vast; he should attract the attention of his slaves, call for a boat to come out to the island. But at once the thought felt shameful. If he showed such weakness, it would be the end of him.

Now the immediate terror had passed, Castus felt a sense of glazed wonder at his escape from death. Had his life been preserved only for it to be snatched from him on the return swim? He had never entirely believed in fate, or in divine control over mortal lives. But the idea that his survival was a matter of chance alone was dizzying.

Already he had been on the island for far longer than usual. He could see the two slaves on the shore standing beneath the pines, peering across the water, and he waved to them. He was relieved that neither appeared to have noticed his moment of pain and panic. With a sense of gathering dread he got to his feet, then scrambled down the side of the rock and waded back into the water. Tremors of fear gripped him as the sea rose around his chest.

Pushing away from the shelving seabed he began to swim, the same slow cautious stroke, keeping his head up. His left arm felt weak, but he could move it. His chest was tight, his muscles burning. With every movement he expected the explosion of pain from inside him.

The journey was gruelling, and took an age. As he drew closer to the shore he felt the fear mounting as his blood flowed more rapidly. But he kept to the same pace, only breaking stroke as he neared the shelf of rock. He stretched out his arm, and one of the slaves reached down and helped to haul him from the water.

'Slow today, dominus!' the slave said with a grin.

'Tired,' Castus managed to reply through clenched teeth. 'Slept badly last night.'

The sun was hot along the shore by now, and Castus stood upright, breathing deeply as the other slave sluiced the salt from his body with a flask of fresh water. He took the flask, drained the rest of the water in three long swallows, then scrubbed himself dry with a rough linen towel and pulled his tunic on.

'Go on back ahead of me,' he told the slaves. 'Got a bit of cramp.'

They nodded and turned for the path; if they suspected what had happened they gave no sign of it. Castus wondered how he must look. He half expected his face to be leaden grey, his limbs marbled. Once the two slaves had vanished from sight up the path between the trees he leaned against the trunk of a pine, willing the sickness to pass. Violent shudders ran through him, and he felt as though he had been kicked in the chest by a horse.

Resisting the urge to slump down at the base of the tree, he flung the damp towel across his shoulder and began to climb the path. After a few paces it curved to the left, following the line of the shore. It was a mile back to the villa, and Castus knew every step of the way. Even so, he moved carefully, pausing to rest at times, wary of exerting himself. As he walked, the feeling of wonder at his survival returned to him. He had stepped up to the threshold of death; he had sensed the darkness beyond. If the gods had not meant him to die, he thought, then perhaps what had happened had been a warning. He could die in his sleep and know nothing of it. The realisation of how complacent he had become was stunning.

But the familiar path along the wooded shore calmed him, and restored his spirits. Morning sun slanted down through the trees, waking the life all around him. Birds sang, and insects whirred in the shafts of light. Halfway back to the villa, Castus stepped off the path into a shaded grove. There was a low mound in the centre, scattered with the dried petals of flowers. Pulling himself up straight, he touched his brow reverently. Months had passed since he had last turned aside to visit this place. It was a tomb, and the mound held the ashes of a young man that Castus had once saluted as emperor.

Caesar Crispus had been the oldest son of Constantine, and would have been his heir if cruel fortune had not ended his life. Accused of treason and adultery, and condemned to death by his father's order, Crispus had taken poison. Castus had been there with him at the end, just as he had been with the emperor's wife Fausta, the lover of the young Caesar, when she too had died. The tragedy of those deaths had almost been eclipsed, for Castus, by the doom that had very nearly fallen on him and his family.

Again the cold tremor from inside him, the whisper of mortality. Crispus and Fausta had both died, and he, Castus, had survived the accusations of treason, the disgrace, and lived to grow old in comfort in this forgotten corner of Dalmatia. The world had asked nothing more of him; could he ask any more of the world?

Marcellina was already sitting out in the front portico by the time Castus returned to the villa. He saw her as he climbed the steps to the boat dock, and at once straightened his back again and tried to compose his features. But he could tell as he approached that she had some idea of what had happened to him; even if the slaves had said nothing, his wife had always been keenly intuitive of his moods.

'Good swim?' she asked as he paced across the portico to join her. She was trying not to let her concern show, but he noticed her slight frown and the deeper note of enquiry in her voice.

'Got a bit weary towards the end,' he said, shrugging. He had no wish to alarm her any further. She took his hand, with a light pressure that sent a ripple of emotion through his body. Quickly he leaned down and kissed her.

'You smell of the sea,' she told him, smiling.

Marcellina had grown up in the wild borderlands of north Britain; even after so many years, the sea and the warm Adriatic sunlight filled her with joy. She was a couple of years short of fifty, but looked much younger still. Her face only showed the lines of age when she smiled; her hair was lightly shot with grey, but often she coloured it with henna. Standing beside her in the morning shade of the portico, Castus felt more powerfully than he had for years the sense of calm peace that she evoked in him, a sensation he had seldom known in his life before they met. *And how close I came to losing all this*, he thought.

'I'll take my breakfast in my chamber, I think,' he said. He still did not trust himself not to betray the fear of what had happened during his swim. 'Could you tell them to bring it in to me?'

She nodded, then relaxed in her cane chair and closed her eyes. The ease of their life together was a rare blessing, and always had been.

Pacing through the vestibule, Castus entered the cool pillared courtyard at the heart of the house. A figure stepped out from the far doorway, a stout and swarthy man with a mossy black beard and a sword-scar across his face.

'Dominus,' the man said with a wry salute. 'Ready for our fight later? Today I'm going to drop you in the dirt – the gods told me so in a dream!'

Castus hid his grimace. 'Perhaps not today, brother,' he said.

Pharnax was from Numidia, and had fought as a professional gladiator for twelve years, until the sport was banned by imperial order. Now Castus employed him as a bodyguard, weapons trainer and sparring partner. At one time they had trained every day, out in the dusty yard behind the slaves' quarters, Castus countering the ex-gladiator's more flamboyant style with the familiar *armatura* sword drill he had perfected in the army. But every year their practice sessions became fewer.

'You insult me!' Pharnax declared, spreading his hands in mock disgust. 'Soon I'll have only your little girl to fight. And you, old man – you'll just be keeping me around for my conversation!'

'Save your strength,' Castus growled. 'You'll need it to pick yourself up after I knock you down tomorrow.'

He slapped Pharnax on the shoulder as he left the courtyard, then walked on through the darkened outer room and into his chamber. Castus had always shared a bedroom with his wife, but this small cell at the rear of the house was his own private domain. Sunlight beamed down through the window grille, falling across the table with its piled scrolls and tablets. Castus remained as scrupulously tidy as he had been during his days in the legions, but with nowhere else to go the contents of the room seemed to multiply in profusion.

In one corner stood an armour rack, the gilded and burnished muscled cuirass displayed upon it gleaming in the angled light. Below it was a folded scale corselet, and on the shelf above stood a row of three helmets, together with Castus's eagle-hilted *spatha* in its tooled red leather scabbard and his broad military belt. Years had passed since he had worn any of it, or the embroidered tunics and padded arming vests stored in the chests and cabinets along the far wall. Now he took one of the helmets from the shelf, brushing away the film of dust from the bowl. He caught his reflection in the curve of polished metal, and glanced away quickly. Inside, the leather lining was still stained with the sweat of some distant battle. From the back of his mind, Castus could summon those scenes clearly. The fog of dust; the swirl of bodies in combat. The noise of ringing iron and screaming trumpets, and the glory of hard-won victory. Never again would he know such things; he felt the loss of it now.

One of the slaves came in with food and drink on a wooden platter. Placing the helmet back on the shelf, Castus seated himself beside the table and sipped from the cup of watered wine, then dipped the hard bread in olive oil and chewed thoughtfully. Left to his own tastes, he still kept to the old army diet, familiar all his years.

Yes, he thought, this was his life now: the ritual of the morning swim, the weapons training with Pharnax, then walking or riding in the hills. Pleasurable hours with Marcellina and their daughter. He had a few acquaintances in the town of Salona, and several times old army friends had made the lengthy detour to the villa, to sit and drink wine with him and relive the days they had once known. It was enough; he told himself that. But still the sense of loss itched within him. The fear that had gripped him earlier when he felt himself plunging towards death rose once more. A cold sense of mortality.

Soon all this too would be gone.

Enough. He had never been prone to idle thoughts, and already he was beginning to feel recovered in mind and body. Finishing the last of his meal, he took a scroll from the table and scanned through it until he found the last passage he had read. Literature was a new discovery for him. Marcellina had always loved reading, but Castus himself had been illiterate as a youth and had found the written word alien until very recently. Now he made the effort whenever he could: not the poetry and philosophy that his wife so enjoyed, but sober prose histories that spoke of things he could understand. Turning the scroll to the light, frowning and muttering the words quietly to himself, he began to read.

A movement from the far side of the room caught his eye, and he let the scroll drop. Hs daughter stood in the open doorway, perched on one leg and leaning against the frame.

'Aeliana!' Castus said, smiling. 'You slept late?'

The girl just pursed her lips. She was nine years old now, and becoming wilful in her attitudes. Crossing the room, barefoot on the tiled floor, she pressed herself against his shoulder so he could kiss her cheek.

'What are you reading, Papa?' she asked.

'Titus Livius. It's all about the ancient days of the Romans.'

'Is it good?' she asked, peering dubiously at the words on the scroll.

'I like it. It talks about battles and military campaigns. Things I know well – though I doubt Titus Livius did! I can picture the scenes as I'm reading. But it's very old, written in the Latin of hundreds of years ago.'

'Older than you?' Aeliana said with a mischievous grin.

'Hard to believe, I know. But yes.'

'Hylas said you looked ill after your swim,' she said, her expression only shifting slightly with the change of subject. 'Are you better now?'

'Much better. It gets tiring being so very old, y'see. You'll find out one day.'

She held a cool palm against his brow. 'Well, you don't have a fever. But you should rest, I think.'

Castus hugged her tight, kissing her again. 'Oh, you're my doctor now, hmm? Well, I promise I will.'

Soon enough, he knew, his daughter would want to leave this place. She had lived at the villa all her life, excepting brief trips to Salona and once to Rome when she was only an infant. It was all she had known, and she was happy, although it would not be long before she would want more from life. The world was huge, and Castus had seen most of it. Even he felt his contentment to be stifling at times.

Marcellina's other children, his stepdaughters, were settled into their own lives now, with children of their own. Sabinus, Castus's son by his first marriage, was serving with the imperial bodyguard, the Corps of Protectores. Castus had not seen him for over eighteen months, and the few brief messages he had received told him little he did not already know. But the world had moved on, he was forced to admit; both Sabinus and the women of his family were Christians now, just like the emperor himself. Recently, Castus had heard that even the Goths beyond the Danube were turning to the new faith. Here in this forgotten enclave on the Dalmatian coast, he felt like an inhabitant of an age that had passed.

'Can I go with Pharnax in the boat later?' Aeliana asked, breaking into his thoughts. 'He's just going around the promontory to the village and back. Please can I?'

'Well...' Castus said, considering.

Before he could say more, a sound came from the courtyard outside. An unfamiliar voice; the scrape of studded boots on tile. With a hand on his daughter's shoulder he urged her to remain in the chamber, then he got up and went outside.

There was a stranger waiting in the courtyard with Pharnax

and a couple of the door slaves. A young man in the cloak and uniform of an imperial courier. As Castus appeared he straightened, and gave a very correct military salute. He must have left Salona before dawn, Castus realised, and ridden hard to arrive here so early.

'Excellency,' the courier said, and held out a slim tablet. Even from several paces away Castus could make out the imperial seal. He took the message, then signalled to the slaves to take the courier to the kitchens and give him food and drink.

'What is it?' Marcellina said, pulling a silk shawl around her shoulders as she walked in from the portico.

Castus just shook his head, turning the tablet in his hands. He could feel the warmth rising to his face, the tremors running up his spine. The message came from Constantinople, he could tell, from the imperial court. He had received nothing like this for a decade, ever since he had been ordered to resign his commission and retire into private life.

Breaking the seal, Castus opened the tablet and read the words scored into the wax. Then he took a deep breath.

'I am ordered to Constantinople,' he said, exhaling. 'To present myself before the emperor.'

Marcellina took the tablet from him and seated herself on the low wall between the garden pillars. She read the message quickly, then laid it down beside her. 'Can they do that? Can they give you orders like that? You left the army years ago – you don't have to agree to their demands now...'

Castus could give no answer. Sensations rioted through his mind: amazement, then affronted anger, then a dark foreboding. But there was another feeling too, one that he could not deny. He felt now that he had been waiting for this moment for many years. The appearance of this message, so soon after his close encounter with death, seemed too much of a coincidence not to be significant. He felt the intricate strands of fate tightening around him. This time he could not disbelieve in them. *Perhaps*, he thought, *perhaps life is not over quite yet.*

Marcellina stood up again, and placed her hands on his shoulders, gazing at him. 'Look at me,' she said. Castus could see the concern in her eyes. 'Is there any way you can refuse this?'

'None. The courier'll report that the message was delivered and that I read it. I have to go, at least... That's the only way I'll discover what this is about.'

'You *know* what this is about,' Marcellina said, anguish in her voice. 'Constantine needs you for some warlike scheme or other, something nobody else has the experience for – or nobody else wants. He'll order you away to some distant place where your life will be in danger... Why else would he summon you out of retirement, after what happened ten years ago?'

Castus cupped her face in his hands, kissing her brow. 'It might not be like that,' he said, trying to sound reassuring. 'He wouldn't be sending me off to war, not after so long.'

Marcellina let out a groan, pulling away from him. 'Have you really forgotten everything?' she cried. 'Or have you forgiven it so soon? Constantine *killed* his own wife and son, and would have *killed you too*! He threatened us all. A man like that has no care for you, no sense of humanity at all... I can't believe you're so willing to do what he commands!'

'I'm not!' Castus said, hearing the growl of anger in his voice. 'I forget nothing, and I forgive nothing. But this... I can't just refuse. It's in my blood – I at least have to find out what it's about...'

'Oh yes, I can hear it in your voice already,' Marcellina said quietly. 'All these years I've thought you were done with soldiering, that you'd left all that behind you, all those things that could have killed you. But you're like one of those old warhorses that can't help responding to the sound of the trumpet. You *want* to go, don't you? You want another chance.'

He knew he should deny it, but they both knew that it was true. In the few short moments since he had read the message, Castus's mind had begun to race, his blood to flow faster. The weakness he had experienced that morning, the sense that life was done with him, had been dispelled.

His wife had dropped to sit on the wall again, pressing her brow into the heel of her hand. 'If the emperor sends you away somewhere,' she said. 'Then I'm going to find you there. Even if it's the furthest steppes of Scythia or the far end of the Nile. And our daughter's coming too. I'm not letting you return to that life without me, do you understand?'

'Of course,' Castus said. It would be difficult, but in truth he was glad of her obstinacy. He had to be reminded that he was no longer a young man, and had much to lose.

Marcellina was gazing at him again, and he could see the hurt in her eyes, the deep anxiety.

'You're sick, aren't you?' she said. 'This morning, when you came back from your swim, I could see it. You looked like death, husband.'

With an effort of will, he sat down beside her, embracing her. 'I can't deny it,' he said. 'But I've recovered now, and after a few days' rest I'll be fit to travel. I'll go to Constantinople, find out what the emperor wants with me, then I'll send a message back here to you. We can decide things from there onwards.'

Marcellina pressed the hem of her shawl to her eyes, dabbing away tears. Of sorrow or of anger, Castus could not tell. Perhaps both. Then she took his hand and kissed it.

Ten years, he thought. Ten years of peace.

Was that all the gods would grant him?

CHAPTER II

'You have not, I think, visited the Great City before, excellency?' the notary said, seated beside Castus in the open two-horse carriage as they rattled along the wide colonnaded main street of Constantinople.

'I visited it several times,' Castus replied. 'Back when it was called Byzantium.'

He was not in the best of moods. The previous evening he had arrived at the outskirts of the city, after journeying for nearly a month across Macedonia and Thracia. Much of the way he had travelled on horseback, or on foot, trying to build his stamina to its old levels. But the exertion had worn him down, and the distances had allowed plenty of time for his initial enthusiasm to shift into resentment and foreboding. He missed Marcellina and Aeliana badly, and the thought that he might not see them again for many months was painful.

'This central avenue is called in Greek the *Mese*,' the notary was saying, flourishing his hand at the colonnades to either side. 'Broader and grander than any in the empire, so they say! And when we reach the Augusteion you'll see wonders... Ah, but this is the Forum, and the Column of the Sacred Augustus.'

The carriage had entered a broad circular plaza, surrounded by double-storey porticos. Castus estimated that the Thracian Gate of the old city must have stood here – no trace of it, or the old walls, now remained. In the centre of the plaza stood a tall column of purple marble. Gazing up, shielding his eyes against the bright morning sun, Castus made out the gleaming golden figure at the column's head.

'Sol!' he breathed, and touched his brow reverently.

'Ah, no,' the notary said with an embarrassed smile. 'Although the statue does wear the radiate crown of the sun god, it is in fact a portrayal of our Most Sacred Emperor. The base of the column, you know, contains several very holy relics. Among them the remains of the original loaves that Christ used to feed the five thousand! They were brought here from Jerusalem by the emperor's late mother, the Sainted Augusta Helena.'

Helena. Castus frowned at the name. He had known Constantine's mother, and knew that she had been principally responsible for the accusations against Crispus and Fausta. The news that she was now regarded as some sort of divine figure was disconcerting.

But the city was impressive, even if Castus was loath to admit it. He had last been here shortly after Byzantium had surrendered to Constantine's besieging army. Back then, this whole area had been covered by military camps and siege works, amid the ruins of the orchards and villages that had stood here before that. Much of the ground inside the new walls was still a construction site, with tall brick apartment blocks and towers of scaffolding filling the residential zone. To either side of the central avenue, Castus caught glimpses of more building work, and even of poorer buildings, shacks and hovels, clustered behind the proud façades. Constantinople would be the greatest city on earth, some people claimed; already they were calling it the New Rome. But Castus had seen the Old Rome, and was not convinced.

Moving on from the circular forum, the carriage continued down the slope and slowed to a halt beside a pillared monument – the 'Golden Milestone', the notary called it. Here they dismounted from the carriage and walked the last distance to the palace on foot. Huge buildings rose on all sides, with the dark blue waters of the Bosphorus visible beyond. The notary was already pointing out the Hippodrome and the Church of the Holy Peace, the Zeuxippus Baths and the Golden Basilica. It was still early in the day, but like most of the rest of the city the streets and porticos were thronged with people; the celebrations of the *Ludi Romani* had just commenced, and huge numbers of spectators had flocked in from the surrounding countryside. After many years living in rural seclusion, Castus had grown unfamiliar with crowds, and to be surrounded by so many people put him on edge.

At the end of the colonnaded street stood a great gateway, where soldiers of the Schola Scutariorum stood guard in full armour. The façade above them was adorned with marble statues and gorgon heads, with a large painting over the arched gate showing four golden figures, the largest jabbing a spear into a snake that writhed beneath their feet. The Christian symbol was painted above them.

'The image of the Sacred Augustus and his sons, the Caesars,' the notary explained, 'trampling the serpent of evil and casting it into the sea...'

The snake represented Constantine's defeated rival, Licinius, Castus guessed. He had served in that campaign himself. But the emperor's three surviving sons by Fausta had been children at the time; only the eldest son, Crispus, had played a major role. Now he, like Fausta herself, had been erased from history, and it was forbidden even to speak their names. Swallowing down sour memories, Castus followed the notary in through the gates of the palace.

In the marble-panelled entrance hall, as large as a basilica, they waited while a steward ran to announce their arrival. Standing stiffly, Castus gazed around him at the host of others waiting in the hall. Anxiously he rubbed at his smooth chin. That morning he had shaved off the beard he had worn ever since leaving the emperor's service. He was wearing his best tunic and breeches too, his finest cloak flung across his shoulder and secured by a jewelled brooch, but it was civilian attire. Without a sword by his side, and the broad military belt at his waist, he felt almost naked. Ludicrously overdressed too, although compared to most of those around him his clothing appeared almost drab.

'Excellency.' The inner doors had opened, and a pair of white-uniformed Protectores had marched forth to conduct him into the palace precincts. Without another word to the garrulous notary, Castus acknowledged their salutes and then followed them.

Passing through the entrance hall, they led him between the hulking flanks of barrack buildings, the quarters of the Scholae, and down long colonnaded walks. To either side spread ornamental gardens, courtyards, statues and monuments. The morning clamour of the city faded, and the only sounds were footsteps on marble and mosaic, and the plash of the water fountains.

Finally, at the far side of a shaded courtyard, the two guards led Castus into the vestibule of what he took to be the main audience chamber. An official met him there, an *admissionalis* with a jewelled brooch the size of a dinner plate securing his cape. The air smelled strongly of incense, and the hush had an added heaviness, as if the walls were padded with velvet.

'Excellency,' the official said, inclining his head. 'The Most Sacred Augustus will receive you in half an hour, during the First Audience. After that you will be granted a private interview with His Clemency. You recall the protocols of approach to the Sacred Presence?'

'Of course,' Castus said in a gruff mumble. He recalled all too well the turgid formality of the imperial court. He recalled too the last time he had been ushered into the presence of the emperor: that terrible day in Rome, when he presented Constantine with the news of his son's death, and narrowly avoided the same fate himself. Surely it was madness to have returned, even on imperial orders?

As he waited, he looked around him at the others in the vestibule: many peered back at him in frank curiosity, but his scarred and weathered features, and his expression of glowering distaste, caused them to avert their eyes quickly. Castus felt his mood of unease shifting to angry black resentment. Marcellina had been right; he should never have come here.

A boom from the inner chamber as the doors swung back, and the sonorous voice of the herald echoed from the high ceiling. Castus joined the other men as they filed through the doors and into the vast audience chamber. The purple drapes still hid the dais and the throne in the apse at the far end. In silence they assembled, and waited once more, as the incense wafted around them.

Then a word of command, the drapes rose, and there was the emperor seated upon the high throne, flanked by guards. At once the whole assembly dropped to kneel on the marble floor. The words of the imperial acclamation rang out; Castus just mumbled them in the back of his throat.

For what seemed a very long time, he stood in a daze of anticipation and discomfort. At last he heard his name and titles called, and strode forward. Eight long paces, and he saluted and dropped to kneel once more. There was no word from the throne. He got up again, one hand flat on the floor to help him rise. As he did so, he risked a glance upwards, and his breath caught. Constantine sat rigidly, his face a whitened mask beneath the heavy jewelled diadem, but the paint could not hide the hollowed cheeks and sunken eyes. He could have been an embalmed corpse.

Returning to his place at the rear of the hall, Castus waited through several lengthy droning speeches, most of them panegyrics of praise for the emperor's justice and generosity, and pleas for assistance from the representatives of various provinces and cities. His mind fogged; the incense in the air made him want to sneeze. Then, at last, it was done. The emperor stood upright, raised his right hand in benediction, two fingers extended, then turned to leave. As he did so, Castus caught the glance that Constantine sent in his direction. The very slightest nod. As the renewed chants of praise rang from the assembly, the drapes fell once more.

'This way, if you please,' a sibilant voice said. Castus turned – the figure at his elbow was a eunuch. 'The emperor will see you now.'

Letting the rest of the crowd drain from the hall behind him, Castus followed the eunuch through a side door and down a narrow passage. A pair of Protectores made a perfunctory effort at checking him for concealed weapons. Then one of them pulled aside a damask curtain and opened the door beyond.

The emperor of the Roman world was sitting at the far end of the small chamber, in a whitewashed apse with windows that looked out over the Bosphorus. Eunuchs fussed around him, wiping the caked cosmetics from his face with dampened cloths. Constantine waved them away as Castus entered, then took a gold cup from the table beside him and drank deeply.

'That's all I do these days, you know,' he said. 'Sit in that hall and listen to strangers telling me how wonderful I am. It's exhausting. After a while I start to wonder whether I might not be so wonderful after all. Then again,' he said, fixing Castus with a narrowed gaze, 'I'm sure that you, for one, would agree with that assessment.'

Castus clamped his jaw and said nothing. From this distance, and in clear daylight, he could once again recognise the emperor he had known for so many years. But the marks of age were plain to see: the slackened flesh webbed with wrinkles, the drawn tension around the jaw. Constantine had removed his golden cape and heavy jewelled headgear, but he still appeared to be wearing a wig, dyed in dark russet and threaded with gold.

Another sip from his wine cup, then the emperor inhaled sharply and stood up, peering at Castus with his jaw jutting. 'How long's it been?' he said.

'Ten years, majesty.'

'Feels like it, eh? It shows, too. You look like an old man! Can you still swing a sword?'

'I've never had any difficulties with that.'

'Hmm,' Constantine said through his nose. Clasping his hands at the small of his back he stalked around the room. Castus remained standing as the emperor circled him.

'I remember the last time I saw you,' Constantine said. 'You do as well, I'm sure. We've had our disagreements, you might say.'

Disagreements, Castus thought. A fine way of putting it. After their last meeting, the emperor had ordered him imprisoned on a charge of treason – a charge Castus had narrowly avoided. He had hated Constantine then, and had never been able to excuse him for condemning Crispus and Fausta and then covering up his crimes.

'Such things are in the past,' Constantine said quietly, as if he had read Castus's thoughts. 'The river of time washes away everything in the end, does it not? I trust that sufficient years have passed for any dishonour to be forgotten. Yours… or mine.'

Castus felt his neck stiffen. It was as close to an admission of guilt as the emperor was ever likely to give him. *But the dead stay dead.* Nothing could be forgotten, nothing forgiven, and they both knew it.

'I've travelled a long way to get here, majesty,' he said. 'What do you want of me?'

Constantine returned to face him, standing barely an arm's length away. The emperor was wearing perfume, but Castus could smell the reek of old wine-sweat rising through it. 'Very well,' Constantine said with a brief smile. 'I need an experienced military commander. Somebody who understands soldiers, and soldiering. I believe you may retain a sufficient sense of duty to consider my proposal.'

A proposal then, not an order. Castus gazed back at the emperor, into his harried eyes, and realised that Constantine was nervous. Was he worried that Castus would refuse? He could do that, yes... but how easy it would it be to turn down the master of the world?

'Sit, why don't you?' Constantine said. He clicked his fingers, and one of the eunuchs lingering at the margins of the room hurried to bring a folding stool and set it beside the table in the apse. The emperor returned to his chair, and Castus sat opposite, fists braced on his knees.

'What do you know of the situation on our eastern frontier?' Constantine asked, swirling the wine in his cup.

'I've been avoiding current affairs, majesty.'

Constantine pursed his lips. 'The Persians, you know, have long been testing our resolve. Their young king thinks himself my equal, and longs to reverse the terms of the treaty his grandfather agreed with Galerius. He goads me... Already he's arranged a revolution in Armenia, the overthrow of our allies there. This impious whelp has dared to persecute Christians in his domains, when he knows that all followers of Christ are under my protection!'

He banged the cup back down on the table, his eyes blazing and the colour rising to his cheeks. Castus remembered the emperor's fits of anger well.

'As you know, I have always been a lover of peace,' Constantine said, calming himself. Castus suppressed the urge to smile. No living man, surely, had been less pacific. 'But some things cannot be endured. I have decided, with a heavy heart, that these provocations cannot be allowed to stand. The glory of the Roman name, and the glory of God, demand action. In the early summer of next year, therefore, I intend to lead a full-scale military campaign against the Persians, to humble their ambitions and liberate the believers from their oppressions.'

'You intend to lead it yourself?' Castus asked quietly.

'Of course! We may be old, you and I, but we are not decrepit!'

Castus shrugged. The emperor was three years older than him, but he could make no argument.

'As you may know, my son rules in Antioch, as Caesar of the East. My second son, Constantius.'

Your third, Castus thought.

'He is a fine boy, and has passed the age of manhood, but he has little experience in command, and little knowledge of the complexities of military affairs, or of discipline.'

Constantine paused, glancing at Castus. 'Your own son is there too, I think,' he said. 'Sabinus? He serves with the *Protectores Domestici*, docs he not? My officers speak well of him.'

Castus felt a jolt in his blood. He had not known that Sabinus was in Antioch; his last letter had come from Egypt. The chance to see him again, perhaps even to serve beside him, was a potent lure.

'But our eastern army is not in the best condition, and has not been for many years,' Constantine went on. 'As you know, the former emperor Licinius withdrew the best troops from the eastern frontier for his battles against us at Adrianople and Chrysopolis. Few of those men returned. In recent years I've been obliged to stiffen the Syrian field army with detachments drawn from the Danubian legions. But much remains to be done, to prepare for war.'

A training and administrative job then, Castus thought. Hardly a glorious task. 'What position would I hold?' he asked.

Constantine sat upright, squaring his shoulders. 'I propose,' he said, 'to promote you to the rank of *Magister Equitum per Orientem.*'

Master of Cavalry in the East: not a title that Castus had heard before. The emperor was quick to notice his uncertainty.

'It's a traditional post, one of many I've lately revived. You would not command merely the cavalry, but the entirety of our military forces in the eastern provinces. Your only superiors would be the Caesar and the Praetorian Prefect of the East, his eminence Flavius Ablabius. Your task would be to inspect the state of the troops and their officers and prepare them for the coming campaign, and you would have full authority to make any improvements you decree.'

Castus peered out of the window, considering. 'What about after that?'

'I intend to travel to Antioch in mid May of next year,' the emperor said, 'and take command of the army, with my son Constantius as deputy. At that time you could either choose to lay down your own command, with full honours, or continue to serve in an advisory capacity. Either way, you would be promoted to the Senate of this city, with proconsular rank. I would grant you permission to remain on your estates if you so chose, although your family would of course be ennobled for posterity.'

Nodding slowly, Castus drew a long breath. For so many years he had believed the army was behind him. Only memories remained, whether bitter or sweet, to console him for all he had lost. The chance to relive those days, to know once more the life of the legions, the authority of high command – and with his son beside him too – was intoxicating. But it would be a hard job: caretaker for another man's army, with all the gritty work of marshalling men and equipment, and none of the glory. Misgivings fought with temptation.

'Why me?' he said at last. 'I've been out of the army for years, and you've got other senior commanders in your service still. What about Gratianus, or Polemius? What about Saturninus?'

Constantine sniffed, shrugging. 'Gratianus proved unworthy of high office,' he said sourly. 'I appointed him commander of the forces in Africa, but he disgraced himself with corrupt practices. Polemius is a decent soldier, but he lacks initiative.

And Saturninus was grievously injured in the recent Gothic war on the Danube. A lance wound to the, uh... to the groin. He still lives, though in great pain, and he is barely a man. No. You, Aurelius Castus, are the one I choose for this task.'

But there was more to it, Castus knew. The commanders he had mentioned had been friends of his at one time, but there were plenty of other officers, younger men, in the army. Already he could guess the truth. The emperor needed a man free from connections, somebody from outside the circles of power. Either that, he thought, or nobody else wanted the job.

'You hesitate?' Constantine said. 'I don't blame you.' He sat forward in his chair, meshing his fingers beneath his jaw. 'You can believe what you like about me,' he said. 'And about past events as well. I'm not asking you to do this for my sake, but for the sake of the empire we both serve. For the undying glory of Rome. This will be my last campaign. If I survive it, I intend to be baptised in the holy waters of the River Jordan, just as our saviour Christ was baptised. Then I shall await death in a state of purity. But I need a victory. And for that I need an army that can fight, and win. So I'm offering you a last command as well. A last chance for us both, eh, before we meet our end?'

He smiled suddenly, and in his eyes Castus caught a strange yearning. It was almost hideous to behold, but he realised that the emperor was alone, totally alone here at the heart of his power. Could it be, after so long, that Constantine considered him to be a friend?

With a dull shock of surprise, Castus found that he pitied this man.

'And what if I refuse?'

The emperor tightened his lips, his expression darkening. Clearly he was not used to men speaking to him so frankly. Then he grinned. 'You've already come all the way here,' he said. 'If you had any intention of refusing, you'd have stayed at home with your wife!'

CHAPTER III

'Consider, then, free will,' the voice said from within the curtained doorway. 'Do we truly possess it, when our liberty is constrained by, ah… by external forces, by the threat of violence or the demands of law? In the union of soul and body we are capable of choosing both evil and good actions, but – *ahem* – as Plato says in the *Timaeus*, our spirits perceive the ideas implicit in true being…'

Castus leaned a little closer to the curtain, frowning. The language was Greek, but the accent was the Latin of the western provinces. Yes, he thought, he knew that voice: this was surely the place he sought.

Three hours had passed since he had landed at the harbour of Rhodes, and he had spent all that time asking questions and following vague directions. The two marines who had escorted him from the liburnian galley *Neptune* doubtless wondered what their newly appointed *strategos* thought he was doing. They stood idly in the shade of the market portico, hardly bothering to conceal their disinterest. One of them was shaking a pair of knucklebone dice in his palm.

'Wait here,' Castus told them, and pushed aside the curtain.

The room beyond was dim and dusty, and still resembled the storage chamber it must once have been. Rows of benches were drawn up facing the far wall, most of them empty. Four youths, sullen-looking boys in their teens, sat slumped on the remaining benches, a couple scratching idly at the tablets in their laps, the rest staring into space with an attitude of truculent boredom. Castus stood in the doorway and said nothing. Flies whirled in the sour air.

'So, what we call freedom,' the voice went on, 'is merely the power of obeying our true nature, and from that obedience all good actions must proceed...'

The man at the far end of the room was wiry and grey, a threadbare philosopher's cloak flung across his shoulders. His beard was ragged and his hair had receded to a wild fuzz around his bald scalp. He spoke with a halting, distracted air, his free hand rising and falling, his gaze darting about the margins of the room. For several long heartbeats he did not notice Castus at all.

'And so, just as the soul has exchanged the peace of eternity for the fast-flowing river of time, we can – *ahem* – choose to direct and discipline our intellect towards a union with the Absolute. As Lucian says of Demonax, the free man is he who lives without hope and without fear, and only the free man can be truly happy...'

Castus shook his head, smiling. He had first encountered Musius Diogenes over thirty years before, in the legion fortress at Eboracum. The former schoolteacher had been a conscript to the Sixth Legion; he had never been the most eager of soldiers, but he was stubborn and courageous, and had a sharp mind. Castus had employed him for many years, first as his secretary and then as the head of his military staff. Diogenes had taken his discharge at the first opportunity, intending to set up a school of philosophy, and since then Castus had received only a few brief messages from him, sent from Nicomedia, Tarsus and Ephesus. The last one had come from Rhodes, but that had been over a year ago. Yet here he was.

'Our master, Plotinus,' Diogenes said, clearing his throat once again, 'expands on this last point in the ninth book of the fifth

Ennead...' He paused as he noticed Castus standing at the back of the room. Awakened from their torpor, his students turned on their benches and peered, startled. Castus was plainly dressed, but his broad military belt and brooch, the gold torque at his neck and the silver eagle-hilted spatha at his side proclaimed his status.

'But that, I think, can wait for another day,' Diogenes said quietly. 'Away you go now, and tomorrow be sure to tell the absentees that they must attend!'

The class broke up with noisy haste, the four youths filing past Castus and out through the door with curious sidelong glances. When the room was cleared, the two men stood in silence. Diogenes stared at Castus.

'Either I am experiencing a phantasm,' he said warily, 'or you are once more in the army.'

Castus managed a look of stern authority for a few moments, but could not keep it up. He grinned, took four long strides across the room, and embraced his old friend.

'So,' he said. 'You hope for nothing and fear nothing, eh. Are you happy and free?'

'If only, brother,' Diogenes replied with a wry smile. 'Although if freedom lies in simplicity, I have that at least!'

Sniffing, Castus gazed around the room at the cracked plaster and the cobwebs. From the corner of his eye he noticed the smudged charcoal drawing on one of the benches: a cruel little caricature of Diogenes himself as a wild-eyed stalk sprouting wiry hairs. Coughing quietly, he sat down on the bench and placed his hand over the drawing.

'I'm supposed to have a dozen students,' Diogenes was saying, plucking at the hem of his cloak. 'As you saw, few of them bother to turn up. Oh, they're decent enough. But their fathers are rich merchants who want a bit of classical education for their offspring, and they're intolerable! They treat me like one of their own slaves. When I think of the things I've seen and done, it grieves me.'

Castus could only shrug, ashamed on his friend's behalf. Diogenes might play at being a philosopher, but he was still an army veteran. Civilians would never understand these things.

'You're visiting Rhodes for some time?' Diogenes asked, raising an eyebrow.

'I'm only here briefly,' Castus told him. 'There's a galley down in the harbour, taking on stores and water, and we sail at dawn tomorrow. But I've got a few hours free – join me for a cup of wine?'

'An inspired suggestion,' Diogenes said, turning to gather an armful of scrolls and tablets. Castus carefully erased the charcoal drawing with the heel of his hand, then led Diogenes to the door.

'You find me, I'm afraid, in straitened circumstances,' Diogenes said as they walked out into the fresh air of the agora portico.

'Looks it. If you don't mind me saying so.'

The two marines playing dice against the wall snapped to attention as Castus appeared, then stared with unconcealed disdain at the ragged figure of Diogenes. But they fell into step quickly enough as the two men walked across the agora.

'Well, I've known better,' Diogenes said. 'In Ephesus I was doing quite well for myself. I married, you know. Sweet girl, a widow, but I fell into a dispute with her relatives. A question of money, very embarrassing – I made some unwise investments. Then some of the Christians in the city had the temerity to accuse me of teaching banned literature, and even of practising sorcery, of all things! I was obliged to leave with some celerity...'

Castus let him talk as they continued downhill, following the broad stepped street that descended to the harbour. The two marines marched along behind them at a discreet distance. He knew that Diogenes was alight with curiosity about his unexpected arrival, and what might have brought him here; he also knew that the other man was holding back his questions for now. But it grieved him to see his old friend brought so low.

'I confess, brother,' Diogenes said with a sigh, 'these recent years have been a disappointment. I am, it seems, neither as clever nor as respectable as I might have imagined. But this is a poor time for the intellect, overall. These days I find myself agreeing with Seneca, who said that the end of all philosophy is to teach us to despise life...'

Castus had heard enough. He paused suddenly in the middle of the street, halting Diogenes with a hand on his shoulder. 'Very well then,' he said. 'Hear me out. I sail tomorrow for Antioch, to take command of the armies in the east. The emperor has commissioned me to oversee the condition of our troops...'

'The *emperor*?' Diogenes broke in, with a frown of dismay and a quick glance at the two marines standing idly nearby; he had never held Constantine in high regard, and the events of a decade ago had only cemented that impression.

'I've been allocated an official military staff, of course,' Castus said with a dismissive shrug, 'but I'd prefer to have a man with me I can trust, as private secretary. You know my methods, and I know your capabilities. You wouldn't be on the army payroll, but I'd pay you from my own funds. If you accept, you'd need to be ready to leave immediately.'

'Immediately...?' Diogenes said, peering around himself at the sunlit town he had called home for the last three years. Seagulls cried overhead, and the few passing people in the street remained carefully disinterested. 'I don't know,' he said. 'All that I possess is here, little though it is... If I simply left it...'

'No need to decide right now,' Castus said. 'You haven't had lunch yet?'

Diogenes shook his head, not hiding his pinched expression. Castus guessed that he had not eaten properly in many days.

'There's a taverna down on the docks that has good fish,' he said. 'Good wine too, they say. We could take a private room there and talk it over.'

'Perhaps,' Diogenes said with sudden enthusiasm, 'we could make it a very long lunch? We have, I think, a number of important matters to discuss...'

The fifty-oared *Neptune* slid out of the harbour of Rhodes at first light. By the time the sun was high the galley was hauling across the open sea. Diogenes had stood at the stern railing as the island fell away to the west, but now he was gazing forward, into the east and the promise of a new future. As Castus had expected, he had not taken much persuading; the previous evening he had closed up his academy, leaving a sign by the door suspending classes indefinitely. With the last of his money he had paid for a decent haircut, and Castus had advanced him a little more to buy some respectable clothes. It was pitiful, even so, to see the meagre possessions that Diogenes had brought from his lodgings. The sailors and marines aboard the galley still regarded him with lingering suspicion, but the news that this eccentric figure was a military veteran, and had taken a wound at the battle of Chrysopolis, granted him a small measure of respect.

It also appeared that Diogenes, in his wanderings, had kept himself far better informed of affairs in the empire than Castus himself had done.

'So there are *four* Caesars now?' Castus asked, baffled. 'I thought Constantine has only three surviving sons?'

'He does,' Diogenes said. They were sitting by the shelter at the stern of the galley, just behind the steersman. 'The younger Constantine rules as junior emperor in Gaul, Constans in Italy and Constantius in the east. Their father presides over them all.'

Castus remembered meeting all three once, when they were still children, the youngest a baby in the arms of his nurse. Strange to think of them holding imperial power now.

'But a few years ago,' Diogenes explained, 'the emperor promoted the son of his half-brother Flavius Dalmatius to the same rank. Now this young man – Flavius Julius Dalmatius – rules the Danube provinces. Both he and his father distinguished themselves in the recent war with the Goths; the Caesar Dalmatius is a favourite of the army, so they say.'

'So Constantine intends to split the empire four ways?' Castus asked, leaning on his fist. 'Just like Diocletian did once.'

'So it seems. I suppose he must think that it would be more stable that way. After, of course,' Diogenes added quickly, 'he passes on to his eternal rest...'

Both men glanced towards the stern. Iovinus, one of the Protectores assigned to Castus's retinue, was lingering at the railing, peering across the waves at the distant coast of Lycia. No doubt, Castus thought, Iovinus or one of the other members of his military staff would have been ordered to report back to Constantinople on the progress of the mission, and his own behaviour. Important to avoid saying anything that might sound disloyal to the wrong ears.

Even so, the division of the empire sounded like a dubious scheme; had Constantine really involved this young Flavius Julius Dalmatius to provide a balance between his ambitious sons? Maybe it would work, Castus thought, although all his experience in the last thirty years suggested that such men would seldom agree to share power. Constantine himself was proof of that.

But it was a beautiful day, with a light breeze and the sun sparkling on the water, and the pleasure of travelling once more soon drew Castus's thoughts from the tangled concerns of imperial politics. He raised his head, and saw his own purple draco banner waving from the flagstaff above him. Another six or seven days' voyage would bring him to Antioch, and then the real work could begin.

He had already written to Marcellina, telling her to wait until the spring before coming to join him in the east. She would not be happy about the arrangement, but it needed to happen that way. He felt once more the sharp ache of separation. It would be many months before he saw his wife or Aeliana again. But the emperor had been right; Castus had made his choice when he had first seen the message, back home at the villa. Marcellina had been right too, though: he knew he should not have accepted, but he was a soldier and he could not resist the call to arms. It was in his bones, and always had been. He would be pushing himself hard in the coming months. Harder than was wise, certainly. Was he really just a fool, tempted by the promise of power?

Over the creak of the oars and the rush of the waves he heard a dry rasping sound from beside him.

'What are you chuckling about?'

'Merely the absurdity of our situation!' Diogenes said, breaking into a grin. 'Here we are, two old men setting out to confront the might of the Persian Empire!'

And the emperor back in Constantinople made three, Castus thought grimly.

'I have a premonition, you know, that I will not return from this trip.'

Castus laughed in surprise. 'Nothing like beginning with a light heart!'

'Oh, I don't mean that in a morbid way. Everyone must die sometime – to live forever would be against nature. What could be better than to spend one's last days seeing wondrous sights and strange new places? No – I thank you for this opportunity, brother. Already I feel my spirits lifting! But I know I will not be coming back this way again.'

Castus dropped his hand and trapped his thumb between his fingers in a warding sign against bad luck. He was glad of his friend's good humour. But he prayed that he was wrong.

Nearly forty years had passed since Castus had last seen Antioch, but at first glance the Metropolis of the Orient did not appear to have changed a great deal. The regular grid of streets and avenues spread from the banks of the green Orontes to the dark slopes of Mount Silpius, and on an island formed by the branching river was the new city, site of the imperial palace and Hippodrome. As the light galley that had brought him up the river from the seaport of Seleucia Pieria approached the wharf nearest the palace, Castus felt transported back to the time when he was a young soldier in the Second Herculia legion, fresh from the Persian campaign.

Evening was coming on, and the air carried the distinctive odours that he recalled so well: the sweet-sweaty aroma of smoke, dust and spices, mingled with the raw sour smell of drains. How young he had been when he last came to this city, Castus thought. But the past was gone. He was no common soldier now, but a high imperial official soon to be burdened with duties, confined by protocols, and doubtless pestered by intrigues.

The palace at Antioch had been built by Diocletian, and like many of that great soldier-emperor's constructions it followed the plan of a military camp, albeit on a massive scale. Castus at once felt at home as he passed between the barracks of the bodyguards and the offices of the notaries and the imperial ministries, and entered the central courtyard before the audience hall. But even here there were changes: as he entered the palace, he had seen the vast octagonal shell of a new church, still under construction but soon to be one of the grandest buildings in the city. He put that out of his mind as he dismounted from the carriage that had brought him from the docks, and made his way deeper into the palace, towards the residential quarters that lined the riverbank.

'Magister! Welcome to Antioch!' the Praetorian Prefect declared, clasping Castus by the shoulders and rising on his toes to kiss him on both cheeks. They were in the reception room of the prefect's wing of the palace, the lamplight gleaming off marble and mosaic, and three wide arches opening onto the outer portico that stood high above the river. The evening breeze whispered in across the polished floor.

'Please, sit – you must be weary after your long journey.'

Castus had spent most of the last ten days sitting down, aboard ship or carriage, and felt far from weary. But he followed the man to a pair of facing couches. The prefect made a slight circling gesture with a raised finger, and the slaves ran to fetch refreshments.

Flavius Ablabius was the most powerful man in the eastern provinces; including the Caesar Constantius, some said. He had a striking appearance, short and pot-bellied, with powerful arms and hands covered with coarse black hair. Castus might have taken him for a stevedore rather than a bureaucrat. His voice was deep and rich with the accent of his native Crete, and he wore a jewelled Christian monogram as a pendant, set with enamelled portraits of the emperors.

'I'm sorry to say the Caesar is not currently here,' Ablabius said. 'He left ten days ago for a trip to Damascus, but he should be returning very soon. Your son Sabinus is with his retinue.'

Castus fought down the swell of disappointment. He had learned of the Caesar's absence already, but had been hoping to meet Sabinus as soon as he arrived.

'We've prepared suitable quarters for you and your staff within the palace precincts,' Ablabius went on. He was speaking in Latin; Castus was fluent enough in the demotic Greek spoken in the east, but the prefect seemed eager to demonstrate his *Romanitas*. 'You also have a public audience hall and offices in the forum of the main city. However, you'll hear about all that later. For now, please do relax and rest. The baths are heating and everything you might desire is on hand!'

The slaves returned, bringing cups of wine and a dish of warm honey cakes. 'Do try one of these cakes,' the prefect said with a smile. Castus had the absurd impression he had made them himself. Usually he was very good at judging men by their attitudes and appearance, but Flavius Ablabius appeared inscrutable. He took one of the cakes and tried a piece.

'Bit sweet for my tastes,' he said, dropping the rest back onto the dish. The honey gummed his fingers.

Ablabius grinned, highly amused. 'Excellent!' he said. 'A true soldier of the old model! Too many here are sadly corrupted by luxury. But as for you – well, your reputation precedes you!'

'What reputation would that be?' Castus asked, his guard rising suddenly. He was aware that many people must know of his connection with the deaths of Crispus and Fausta ten years before.

'Oh, your military reputation, of course!' But the prefect's smile said plainly that he had implied more than that. 'And, may I say,' he went on, 'a man of your capabilities is certainly what we require here in the east, in our current situation.'

Castus just nodded, wary of flattery. He was already far too experienced in the insincerities of court life. But there were things he needed to know; better to hold back his misgivings until he could determine friends from enemies.

'What's your assessment of this *current situation*?' he asked. He had been briefed before leaving Constantinople, but wanted the views of those closer to the scene.

Ablabius let out a long and eloquent sigh. 'As you know,' he said, 'the King of Persia, Shapur the Second, is still a young man. Not yet thirty. But he's vigorous, and eager to assert himself. He's been king a long time – he was proclaimed as such before he was even born…'

'Is that possible?' Castus asked with a frown.

'It is! The crown was placed upon his mother's swollen belly while he was still in the womb. This did mean, of course, that we had little trouble from the Persians for a long time, with the king still an infant. Nearly two decades of peace on our eastern frontiers.'

'But now?'

'But now Shapur is a man, and things have changed. About ten years ago, when he first came of age, he dismissed his more cautious advisors and began to see himself as a warrior monarch. He made war first upon the *Saraceni*, the Arab brigands of the desert. Then, more recently, he turned his attentions to Armenia. Now it seems he wishes to try his strength with us, and avenge the humiliating defeats of past ages.'

'And what *is* his strength?' Castus asked, swirling the wine in his cup.

'Considerable. Going on current intelligence, Shapur can summon an army of somewhere between one hundred and fifty to two hundred thousand men.'

Castus whistled quietly. The field army based around Antioch numbered only eighteen thousand; the emperor's own forces in Thracia and at Constantinople were thirty thousand strong, and the *duces* who commanded the frontier armies had around sixty thousand between them, in theory at least. Even if every Roman soldier in the eastern provinces were gathered for battle, the Persians would still outnumber them.

'But most of the Persian troops are peasant levies,' Castus said.

'True enough. Although overwhelming numbers can win wars, as you doubtless know. And Shapur has his noble cavalry, his *Aswaran*. His bodyguard too, and a great many mercenaries. His troops have been fighting in Armenia and on his eastern border, while ours have known little but perfect peace for over a decade.'

'Which is why I'm here,' Castus said flatly.

'Which is why you're here!' Ablabius replied, smiling. 'But it's not only our soldiers who lack experience,' he went on. 'Increasingly, we see officers, even senior commanders, who have never served in the ranks. Never stood in the *line of battle*, one might say, or breathed the dust and sweat of the common man.

That's why we need *you* here!' He narrowed his eyes. 'You and I are quite similar, I believe.'

Castus frowned. 'We are?'

'My father was a sausage-maker, you know,' Ablabius said, flexing his ringed fingers. 'As a child I swept the floors of a taverna in Gortyn, and later served drinks in a brothel. You probably look at me and see a perfumed, self-satisfied bureaucrat – and you'd be right in that assessment. But everything I have, I have gained by the sweat of my brow and the work of my hands!'

Castus hid his surprise. He had heard that the Prefect of the East came from humble origins in Crete, but never knew how humble. Whether he had gained so much by honest labour alone was another question.

'But there are others here, you know, who resent the likes of us,' Ablabius continued. 'Men who are born to wealth and power guard it jealously, and disdain those who have risen by merit and industry. Some of these men even mutter that our Sacred Majesty is unwise in promoting the deserving over the heads of those whose only recommendation is their parentage. Such men may seek to undermine us, or work against us.'

'Who are these men?' Castus asked in a low growl.

Ablabius smiled again, and nibbled a honey cake. 'You'll meet them soon enough. One of them is the governor of the eastern diocese, our *Comes Orientis*, Domitius Dracilianus. He's away on a trip to Edessa, but he too will return soon. A difficult man. Until your appointment he had control of the field army in the east, and was not happy about the change of command. Strangely, he claims to be related to you – or to your son at least.'

'My son?' Castus's frown deepened. The name had sounded familiar.

'Dracilianus is related to your first wife, I think. Which makes your son his second cousin, or something of that nature. The family trees of our senatorial clans form a tangled orchard...'

Of course, Castus thought. His first wife Domitia Sabina had been a daughter of the Roman aristocracy; he had met her cousin, Domitius Latronianus, several times and openly detested him. There had been one more cousin as well, Lepidus; he had conspired against the emperor during the Italian campaign, and Castus had killed the man himself. The thought that another member of the powerful Domitii family held office in the east, and that he would have to work with him, made Castus curse under his breath.

'I mention this only as a warning,' the prefect said. 'I'm sure you are more than capable of ignoring the insults of such men and doing your job. And I wish you the best of luck in it. Let us be allies, if we can, in the endeavours ahead?'

'Fine,' Castus said, after a grudging pause. Ablabius extended his hand, and he clasped it in the gesture of concord. Allies they might be, for now – but never for a moment, he told himself, should he trust this man.

CHAPTER IV

Castus had arrived in Antioch looking for a fight, although he had not admitted it to himself at the time. As he approached the largest of the military camps on the broad plain to the west of the city, he suspected that he might have found one.

'What are those men doing standing in the field?'

He reined in his horse, the rest of his retinue and bodyguard halting behind him while the Protector Iovinus rode over to the sentry at the roadside. Rutted fields of dry stubble spread on either side of the road, which ran straight towards the dark line of the camp fortifications. Squinting in the morning sun, Castus peered at the row of figures that stood outside the perimeter entrenchment. Eight dejected-looking men, all with hair cropped in the military style. But they appeared to be wearing women's dresses, long garments of thin gaudy cloth that trailed around their ankles.

Iovinus returned. 'Soldiers under punishment, dominus!' he said. He was grinning at first, but when he caught sight of Castus's scowl his face fell.

'Under whose orders?'

'General Valerius Mucatra, Comes Rei Militaris,' Iovinus said. 'He's in command of the field army detachments here.'

'And where is this General Mucatra?' Castus asked quietly. He had sent notice of his arrival hours before, and would have

56

expected the commanding officers to meet him at the camp gates, but when he looked up the road he saw only a small party of cavalry waiting to receive him.

He nudged his horse forward, and the rest of his retinue formed up around him as he rode towards the camp. Castus had brought only a small bodyguard with him from the city, with Diogenes and the chief members of his military staff. But with his standard-bearer, trumpeter and herald riding in front, his little retinue should be enough to proclaim his authority to anyone he might meet. He knew he would need to assert that authority soon enough.

The field army of the east was stationed around Antioch, both in the camps and billeted in the city itself. Castus knew what people had always said about the eastern armies. The balmy and pleasure-loving atmosphere of the Syrian cities was supposed to sap the fighting spirits of soldiers, making them indolent and cowardly in battle. Corruption was rife here too, gnawing the heart out of discipline, morale and efficiency. Or so the stories went.

As the trumpets cried and Castus rode in through the gates and along the broad central avenue of the camp, he feared that that those stories were entirely justified. While many of the troops were assembled to either side of the avenue in good order under their standards, just as many were massed in shambling groups, their officers nowhere to be seen.

There were plenty of good soldiers in the field army, he knew: detachments of the Seventh and Tenth Gemina legions among them. The Tenth had been under his command at the battle of Chrysopolis, and many of the older men in the Seventh had marched east from Spain with the legion twenty years before. It was easy to pick out these veterans: tough weathered-looking men in their middle years, their equipment clean and bright, their formations solid. But there were far too many new recruits, men who knew nothing of the army and appeared to have little conception of discipline. As Castus rode slowly along the avenue, he could not help noticing the large numbers of civilians mingled with the troops, staring like idlers at some public spectacle. Women and children too, and the tent lines beyond them looking more like a bazaar than a military encampment. He set his jaw, breathed deeply, and rode on.

Valerius Mucatra was waiting outside the command tent at the heart of the camp, his tribunes and staff officers arrayed to either side of him. He was a short man, but solidly built, with a shaved head and a thick black beard, and his heavy eyebrows bunched into a frown as he watched Castus approaching. As the herald announced the arrival of the Magister Equitum per Orientem, the assembled officers raised their arms in salute. But meeting him here, rather than at the gates, was a clear gesture of disrespect.

Castus was mounted on the largest and most powerful horse from the palace stables. He was dressed in his gilded muscle cuirass and plumed helmet, his red general's cloak pinned with a solid gold brooch inscribed with the emperor's name. He returned the salute, then eased himself down from the saddle, careful not to betray any signs of the aches in his back and thighs. He knew they must already regard him as an old man; no need to add detail to that impression.

'Magister,' Mucatra said, touching his brow as Castus strode towards him. 'We weren't expecting you to come out here so soon.' His voice carried a distinct Thracian accent. Castus took off his helmet and tucked it under his arm; then with the briefest glance at Mucatra he walked straight past him and entered the tent. With a baffled frown, the army commander followed, his officers at his heels.

Under the canvas, a spartan selection of basic furnishings stood on the straw matting. Mucatra was soldier enough in that respect at least. Castus turned on his heel and faced him. 'There are eight men standing outside your fortifications, dressed as prostitutes. Why?'

Mucatra looked startled by the abrupt question, but only briefly. 'They disobeyed orders,' he said with a shrug. 'I'd expressly cancelled all leave, but they went into the city on an errand and did not return for a whole day. In the brothels no doubt, so it seemed apt!'

'And you thought that humiliating them would make them better soldiers?' Castus growled. He had given enough punishment in his time, but mocking men, and in the sight of civilians too, was different. 'They'll desert at the first opportunity. And the dignity of the army suffers.'

There was a pause as Mucatra digested the accusation. Then he drew a breath, nostrils flaring, and pushed out his chest. This was a confrontation now, with the assembled officers and the men of Castus's staff as witnesses.

'The Comes Orientis, his excellency Domitius Dracilianus,' the commander said slowly, 'has given me authority over these troops and their discipline. You might take the matter up with him, perhaps.'

I will, Castus thought, *as soon as I find him*. 'My authority comes direct from the emperor,' he said. 'The Augustus has charged me with making this army ready for war, and I intend to do so. The discipline of your men is disgraceful.'

Mucatra's face reddened, and Castus could see that he was struggling to contain his wrath as the words struck home. 'My men will be ready for war when the time comes,' he said at last, grinding out the words. 'Presently the nearest Persian is hundreds of miles away on the far side of the Tigris!'

'The job of a soldier is to be ready for war at any moment,' Castus said in a low voice. 'Your officers and men may think they have an easy winter ahead. They do not.'

He turned as he spoke, glaring at the assembled tribunes. Few could meet his eye, but he saw many angry glances pass between them. *Be careful*, he told himself. *You're out of practice.*

'I have served in the army for over twenty years, *excellency*,' Mucatra said, squaring his shoulders. 'From what I hear, you've spent the last decade in civilian life. Many things have changed since you last wore the belt.'

'Men don't change,' Castus replied. He stared down at the Thracian, guarding his anger. 'You were at Chrysopolis, yes?' he asked.

Mucatra nodded tersely. 'I was a staff tribune,' he said, and hesitated.

'In the army of Licinius, wasn't it?' Castus went on, in a mild tone. 'Were you wounded in the fighting?'

'I was not.' Mucatra was visibly seething now, his face dark red. 'But I have served Constantine loyally ever since that day. I will accept no accusations to the contrary!'

'None intended. But tell me this – how many times have you fought in battle?'

Mucatra could not answer.

'How many times have you led men in a charge against an enemy shield wall? How many night marches have you made through hostile country? Have you ever stormed a fortification at the head of your troops, and been first across the enemy rampart?'

From the corner of his eye Castus could make out Diogenes trying to suppress a smile. He had said enough already, but a spur of anger drove him on.

'How many men have you slain in battle? How many wounds do you carry on your body? How many cities have you seen sacked and burned by a conquering army? Have you faced down a charge of cataphracts or *clibanarii*? Well?'

Mucatra coughed a scornful laugh. 'No man alive has done all that.'

Castus said nothing.

Silence from the other men in the tent, and the moment stretched long. Finally Mucatra dropped his gaze and exhaled loudly.

'I'll return in three days,' Castus said. 'I'll want to see a full parade of all the troops under your command, in battle order. In the meantime, you'll give my private secretary the codicils of commission and service records of all the officers of *ducenarius* grade and upwards.'

He left the tent with a sense of nervous exhilaration. He had gone much further than he had intended with Mucatra, but if he was to command these men then he must first control them. The general would be a bitter foe, he knew, and would take a long time to get over his humiliation. So be it.

Returning to his horse, he made a show of checking the tack and bridle while he waited for Diogenes and the other members of his staff. Then, when all were assembled, he gripped the saddle horn and heaved himself up. A sudden stabbing ache in his chest, a wave of nauseating pain down the left side of his body; sweat burst on his brow, but he managed to haul himself into the saddle and sit up straight. His head was spinning, the light crashing around him.

It was nothing, he thought. A passing muscle cramp. But he could feel his heart thudding against his ribs. Inhaling, clenching his jaw, he composed his features and rode out the last swells of pain. He caught Diogenes' anxious glance, and turned away. Nobody else appeared to have noticed anything.

Clearing his throat, he raised his arm and gave the signal to move.

Flavius Julius Constantius, Caesar of the East, returned to Antioch four days later, as the first cold breezes of October brought a foretaste of the coming winter. Castus had expected the young emperor to receive him in the grand audience hall of the palace, but he was directed instead to a garden court in the residential wing.

The Caesar was exercising, running laps of the courtyard

with his bodyguards jogging along behind him. Watching from the upper portico, Castus studied the nineteen-year-old ruler of the east with an appraising frown. Constantius did not have the physique of an athlete: he was tall, but his torso appeared stretched and tubular and his legs short and bowed. His complexion was dark, and he wore his hair long at the nape, in the fashionable Germanic style. He completed another lap, legs pumping, then slowed to a halt and braced his arms against a pillar. One of his attendants stepped closer and whispered, pointing to the gallery where Castus stood waiting. Constantius glanced briefly upwards, then left the courtyard.

Moments later a *silentiarius* appeared, bidding Castus to follow him through the passage and out to the broad pillared river terrace of the palace. Castus knew that his first encounter with the Caesar had been intentional; he understood what message it was intended to convey.

The terrace stood high on the river wall: five hundred paces of colonnaded walkway with a view out over the curve of the Orontes and the wide flat lands beyond, all the way to the dark line of the Taurus Mountains on the horizon. Constantius was already waiting there when Castus arrived, still dressed in his short tunic, a linen towel around his neck. He remained standing between the pillars, watching the small boats on the river below as Castus knelt before him and gave the salute.

'Flavius Aurelius Castus,' the young man said in a thin high voice. 'You come to us highly recommended by my father.'

'Glad to hear it, majesty.' Castus stood up and assumed a parade stance. He was aware that the Caesar had not once glanced in his direction.

'Although I am surprised,' Constantius said briskly, turning from the pillars. He rubbed the sweat from his face with the towel, then flung it aside and clicked his fingers. A slave brought a stool for him to sit. Castus recalled the boy's father doing something similar back in Constantinople.

'Surprised?'

'Yes!' Constantius said, sitting down. 'While I would not question my father's wisdom, it does seem strange that the eastern armies should need a dedicated senior commander to oversee their training and preparation. I've inspected them myself, and their qualities are obvious. I've trained with them myself too, both cavalry and infantry. Our troops are the finest that the empire has ever produced. I don't see that your position here is entirely justified.'

Castus inhaled slowly, trying not to tighten his jaw. The last five days in Antioch had revealed the scale of the task before him. Diogenes and the *numerarius* of his military staff were at that moment working through the accounts and muster rolls of the field army units, and had already found an alarming number of discrepancies. But it was not Castus's job to challenge the young emperor; not so soon, at least.

'Surely the Augustus meant no slight on our troops,' he said, squaring his shoulders. 'But a campaign on the scale he's intending takes a lot of work.'

'Oh, true enough,' Constantius replied, gazing at the river again. 'Humbling the might of Persia is no easy undertaking. But it can be done – and perhaps it should have been done before now.'

With a pinch of unease Castus realised the implication of his words. Clearly, he thought, Constantius had wanted to lead the attack on Persia himself. It galled the young man that he must wait for his father to come and take over, and that another officer had been installed to keep him away from direct command in the meantime.

But now Constantius appeared struck by another thought. He rubbed at his chin. 'I'm told you knew my mother,' he said. 'And you were with her when she died. Is that true?'

Castus's discomfort climbed higher. He had indeed known Fausta, far better than he could ever dare admit. And he remembered all too vividly the moment of her death, in the overheated baths of the Sessorian Palace in Rome. But Fausta, like Crispus, had been erased from history: could her son really support that? He had only been a boy of nine at the time, and Fausta had never been the most maternal of women, but surely it had marked him deeply.

'I was honoured to meet your mother a few times,' Castus said carefully. 'And, yes, I was present when she died.'

'A tragic accident, so they tell me. My grandmother, the Sainted Helena, always refused to speak about it. I wonder if there's anything more you could tell me?'

'Nothing, majesty. An accident, true enough.' How could he say more, when even speaking Fausta's name was a crime?

But with the mention of the Caesar's mother, Castus noticed his resemblance to her. He had some of his father's mannerisms, but Fausta showed in his colouring, the way he narrowed his eyes, the petulant set of his lips. Did the influence extend to his character as well? Castus hoped not. A combination of Constantine's ruthless lust for power and Fausta's suspicious and devious intelligence could be truly dangerous.

'I suppose you must also know that I'm aware of your connection with my late stepbrother as well,' Constantius said, idly studying his fingernails. 'We should all be careful, I think. Those around you tend to come to bad ends!'

'So what did you make of the Most Blessed Caesar?' Diogenes asked, speaking from the corner of his mouth.

Castus took his time replying. They were in the main armoury hall of the imperial *fabrica*, out in the northern suburbs of Antioch, and the noise around them was immense. The air shivered with the sound of beating hammers, the roar of the furnaces, the hiss of quenched iron. The air in the long pillared hall was dense with steam and charcoal smoke, and reeked of hot metal. This was the first occasion since Castus's meeting with the Caesar the previous day when he could speak without risk of being overheard, but even here he was cautious.

He picked up a newly forged sword blade from the stack on the bench beside him, holding it by the tip and naked tang and angling it to the light. The edges were still blunt, but the dark swirl of the hammered iron showed good craftsmanship.

'He's younger than he thinks he is,' he said, leaning closer to Diogenes. 'Hungry for power too, although it sits awkwardly on him. His head tells him he can rule; his heart knows he's not ready for it. For now it's all play-acting. But he doesn't care much for me, that I know.'

Diogenes was nodding slowly. 'You think he could be troublesome? I mean...'

Castus cut him off with a quick sidelong glance, then placed the blade back on the bench and walked on down the hall. He had already asked himself that same question several times: Constantius resented his position, and the power that came with it, but would he really try to undermine an authority that came directly from his father?

'And through here, excellency,' said the superintendent of the armoury, 'we have the helmet workshop.'

In the side aisle of the next hall, a row of men were bent over wooden workbenches beating, shaping and riveting plates of iron into helmets. At the far end, other men were hammering out the decorative sheeting that would cover the bowls; the best helmets, those destined for the guard troops and the officers of the field army, were plated in gold, silver and polished bronze.

Castus strolled down the aisle, overseeing the work with approval. Only as he reached the far end did he notice the tall young man in the uniform of the Protectores, waiting by the rack of finished helmets. For a couple of heartbeats he did not recognise him.

'Sabinus!' he cried, breaking into a grin, then took three long strides and threw his arms around his son.

Flavius Aurelius Sabinus was twenty-five years old now, taller than his father and almost as broad in the shoulders. He was handsome too; his appearance reflected more of his mother's aristocratic Italian and North African heritage than Castus's own blunt and brutal features. He returned the embrace, then pulled back with a bashful half-smile.

'Excellency,' he said, 'I received an order to transfer to your staff.'

'Of course you did!' Castus said, gripping his son by the shoulders, 'I wrote it myself! And there's no need to call me that, you know – I'm your father.'

'And also my commanding officer,' Sabinus replied quietly, flinching slightly.

Castus's grin slipped. It was glorious to see his son again; he had been impatiently awaiting their meeting ever since he had heard of the Caesar's return to Antioch with his retinue. But in all that time, and all the days that preceded it, he had never once considered how Sabinus himself might feel about the reunion. He had never considered that the young man might be uncomfortable, even embarrassed, by the new arrangement. He saw now that he had been foolish.

'But I give thanks to God for your promotion,' Sabinus said with stiff formality. Then he turned to Diogenes, and Castus could not help but notice how much warmer and more genuine their greetings appeared.

The business at the fabrica was quickly concluded – Castus ordered that production of body armour and helmets should increase by a third, and more armoury workers should be drafted in to meet demand; he would make another inspection in ten days to check progress. As he moved towards the arched doorway of the hall, Sabinus paused and drew him aside.

'Father, I'm very grateful for the transfer,' he said quietly, 'and happy to see you again too, of course. But, please – I have to ask that you treat me just the same as the other men on your staff. Already I've heard the others talking...'

'Yes, yes,' Castus broke in tersely. 'They suspect favouritism. Always happens. But don't worry about that – I requested you because I need capable men around me that I can trust. And I know you well enough to believe you fit that description.'

'Thank you,' Sabinus said. For a moment Castus feared he was about to salute, but he dipped his head instead.

Together they walked towards the sunlight and clean air of the courtyard. There was much that needed doing that day, and Castus hoped that he would have the opportunity soon enough to rebuild his relationship with his son, once the awkwardness of their initial meeting had worn off. With a sour pang he remembered that there would be an imperial banquet at the palace that evening: he would be the guest of honour, seated beside the young Caesar. Yet more formality, and more guarding of his words and gestures. The sooner he could conclude his business in Antioch, he thought, the better.

'Aurelius Castus!' a voice cried as he emerged from the hall. 'Excellency – so glad to meet you at last!'

Castus squinted into the sunlight with a scowl of annoyance; he wanted no further meetings today. The man crossing the armoury courtyard towards him wore an urbane smile offset by the coldness of his hooded eyes. He was middle-aged, but his neatly cropped hair had already receded from his bald scalp. His tunic and cloak were of deep blue, plain but expensively fashionable, and his only jewellery was a gold medallion portrait of the emperor, worn as a brooch. Slaves and attendants trailed him.

Domitius Dracilianus, Castus realised, trying to ease his scowl as the man approached. Governor of the Diocese of the East.

'Forgive me for my absence when you arrived here, dominus,' the Comes Orientis said. 'I was in Edessa, and set off as soon as I heard the news.'

Castus submitted to the embrace of greeting. There was something restless and very sharp about the man's expression, he noticed, although his eyes remained unnervingly stony. A clear resemblance to Castus's first wife too, and to Sabinus.

'Cousin, good to see you again,' Dracilianus said, embracing the young Protector. 'You have a fine son, excellency,' he said to Castus.

'I know,' Castus replied, squaring his shoulders. He glanced at Sabinus, who still appeared uncomfortable in his presence.

'But I'm glad I had a chance to meet you before the banquet this evening,' Dracilianus said in a more confidential tone. 'I wanted to speak with you – in some privacy, if that would be possible?'

Castus shrugged. There were horses waiting to take him and his staff back to his headquarters in the palace, and he did not have much time to spare. 'If you make it quick,' he said.

He gestured to Diogenes, who inclined his head and moved towards the horses. The rest of the staff followed behind him. 'Sabinus – stay with us,' Castus said.

Placing a palm on Castus's shoulder, Dracilianus led him a short way along the armoury portico, with Sabinus pacing behind them.

'As you know, I've been in command of the military forces here for several months,' Dracilianus said, 'but I'm a civilian, of course, and know little of the military life. Your presence here is a great help. I'll retain control of the logistical and supply side of things though, and if you need anything more I'd be glad to assist.'

He paused – they were out of earshot of the men waiting by the fabrica gates now. 'I must say, it's fascinating to meet you,' he went on. 'I've heard a lot about you over the years.'

'What have you heard?'

'Oh, merely stories,' Dracilianus said with a light shrug. 'My cousin Latronianus in Rome used to talk of you, of course. I'm afraid he probably didn't leave a good impression. Not the most flexible of men. But still I consider that we have a family connection.'

Castus exhaled, trying not to frown too obviously. He had never wanted any connection with the Domitii family.

'And then, naturally,' Dracilianus said, beginning to pace once more, 'there are the honours you've won in battle. There are few military men alive today, I would think, who have your experience. Our Most Blessed Caesar may seem a little headstrong, but I assure you that he knows how vital you are to the military situation here.'

Castus peered at the man from the corner of his eye. It was hard to know if he was being entirely serious, or just trying to appear loyal. Dracilianus gave a quick secretive smile. *He knows everything*, Castus realised. Doubtless he had already spoken to his ally Mucatra too.

'I believe you're a follower of the traditional religion?' Dracilianus went on, dropping his voice. 'That's good. There are far too many Christians in the administration for my tastes – it helps to keep a balance.'

Glancing back, Castus saw that Sabinus was still following close behind them, appearing not to be listening.

'It's the faith of our emperor,' he said, 'and of our Caesar.'

'Well, yes,' Dracilianus replied, smiling again. 'Although there are some who hope to profit by the association. You've met the Praetorian Prefect already, I suppose?'

'Ablabius? Yes. Why?'

'He's probably already insinuated things about me,' Dracilianus said, a note of spite creeping into his voice. 'Probably given you the tale of his rise to wealth and glory as well. That man's gained his current position solely with the help of a lot of waxed tablets and a very moist signet ring! He is entirely amoral, and has the convictions of a windsock. I'm afraid he's also been engaging in secret communications with Flavius Dalmatius, the father of the Caesar Dalmatius.'

Castus halted, turning to face Dracilianus. 'They're secret, but you know all about them?' he said.

'In my position it helps to remain informed. There is, of course, nothing directly treasonous about Ablabius's correspondence; he's too clever for that. But many of us suspect that he favours Dalmatius over Constantius, and perhaps even intends to set himself up as regent over all the Caesars, in the unfortunate event of our Augustus passing away...'

'I'm a soldier,' Castus broke in. 'I have a military job to do, and I intend to devote myself to that. I'm not interested in getting involved in any of your palace intrigues.'

Dracilianus stared back at him, his eyes glazed and lifeless. 'But you already *are* involved,' he said. 'Here we both are, talking privately together... Plenty of people to see us, and you can wager that there are spies among them, ready to report our meeting to the prefect. Soon he'll know of our conversation, although he won't know what we talked about. Will you be the one to tell him?'

'And you came all the way out here just to stage this little drama?'

'Oh, I'm just being friendly,' Dracilianus said. 'And I do have your best interests at heart. But you should be very careful in Antioch, excellency. This city is a nest of scorpions!'

CHAPTER V

Long after nightfall, Castus sat slumped on the couch in his private chamber. At least he had survived the banquet; he had eaten as little as possible, and drunk even less, but even so it had been a trial. He felt his stomach roil, and let out a low belch.

'They say that the eastern provinces inspire refinement in the manners,' Diogenes commented wearily. 'With you, it seems to be having the opposite effect.'

'Just expressing my inner self,' Castus said, and took another sip of watered vinegar wine.

'Ah, humour! There's hope for you yet, perhaps.'

Castus coughed a laugh. 'So,' he said. 'What else?'

Diogenes was seated on the far side of the room, a stack of tablets on the table beside him in the light of a triple-branched bronze lamp. A couple of fat moths battered and flicked around the flames.

'These records suggest,' Diogenes said, picking up one of the tablets, 'that over half the officers of the field army owe their positions to recent appointment, and have no previous military experience. Most seem to have purchased their commissions or gained them via patronage, although it's impossible to be sure. But I'm reliably informed that the tribune of the Fourth Equites Cataphractarii bought his codicil of appointment from the *Primicerius* of the Sacred Bedchamber, for thirty *solidi*!'

Castus snorted. 'I'd forgotten your talent for sneaking around.'

Diogenes appeared affronted. 'The quest for knowledge takes many forms,' he sniffed.

Castus raised a palm in apology; he had meant no offence. As for what Diogenes had discovered, he knew that such things had always happened in the army, even in his day, although the abuse seemed to be endemic here in the east. 'Selling smoke', it was called. And with so many senior positions occupied by political appointees, there was little chance for deserving men from the ranks to rise in the military hierarchy. Already he had made some changes: he had dismissed the absentee tribune of the Tenth Gemina, and promoted one of the *ordinarius* centurions to temporary command of the legion in his place. Flavius Barbatio was a proper soldier, a blunt-featured Pannonian who reminded Castus of his own younger self. No doubt he would make a decent *praepositus*, and in time Castus might get him a permanent commission as tribune.

But corruption in the army seemed a bottomless pit, and rooting it out would take months. Already he had received complaints from citizens at the rapacity of the army requisitioning agents and the abuses of the troops billeted upon them. Some soldiers had taken to charging entire villages protection money, and even fighting off the tax-collectors on behalf of their new 'clients'. Castus rubbed his jaw and grimaced ruefully. Truly he had been given a job nobody else wanted.

'At least you seem to have made yourself the most unpopular man in Antioch,' Diogenes said. 'The Caesar and his officials resent your authority, the army officers resent your promotions, the soldiers hate your discipline and the city people hate the new grain tax you've imposed. Not bad after less than a week. If we keep this up, our only friends out here might be the Persians!'

'Oh, they'll have reason to hate me too, soon enough.'

'At least we're allowed to *kill* the Persians...'

Castus smiled. Antioch was a fractious city, and rioting seemed a regular occurrence. He hoped it would not come to that, whatever additional burdens he had to place on the people here. His concern was more for the higher levels of government; sitting in the banqueting hall that evening, he had been all too aware of the currents of mistrust, even open hostility, flowing between the guests. Plenty of it directed his way too. He knew how to build an army, but without a united government to back it up his preparations would be useless. Still, he thought, all that would doubtless change once Constantine arrived in early summer next year. Once he himself had done all the hard work.

'Get some sleep,' he told Diogenes. As a civilian, the secretary had not attended the banquet, but he was yawning and red-eyed from his administrative work. Nodding his thanks, Diogenes collected the tablets and departed.

Alone, Castus got up from the couch and paced a circuit of the room. He was tired too, but his digestion was troubling him, and the nagging anxieties of the day as well. He slapped at one of the moths around the lamp, but it fluttered out of his reach. The far door was open, the archway giving access to the upper portico of the building's internal courtyard. Hoping for fresher air, Castus pulled aside the drape. The lamplight flickered his shadow over the wall as he stepped outside.

The moon hung over the rooftops of the palace precinct, and from somewhere nearby Castus could hear the voices of soldiers, singing a barracks song he remembered from his youth. The great water clock above the Gate of Hours sounded, twelve ringing notes. Castus leaned heavily on the railing between the portico pillars, staring down into the darkness of the courtyard. Not for the first time, he wished that Marcellina were already here with him. A silent prayer for her safekeeping, directed to the black sky above. But it would be months before she joined him in Antioch. In the early spring, once the weather cleared, he would set off on a lengthy tour of the frontier districts; there were troops garrisoned in cities and fortresses all across Syria and Mesopotamia, and he would need to visit every one. Only then, once he returned to Antioch, could he expect to see his wife again. He felt the weight of his duties heavy on his shoulders, and the ache of separation.

Voices rose from the courtyard below him. Sentries, Castus realised, guarding the lower chambers of the building. For a while he ignored them – just two men, speaking quietly together in Greek as they passed the long hours of darkness. But then one of the men spoke again, and his words caught Castus's attention. Frowning, he suppressed a slight guilty shudder – he had never cared for those who spied or intruded on others. Then he took four quiet paces along the portico, until he stood directly above the sentries, and leaned across the railing.

'And he was there, the old man himself?' the first voice asked.

'He was the one! He gave him the poison with his own hand. So Metrophanes was saying. Whether it was on the emperor's orders or not, he was the one that killed… *you know who…*'

Castus felt his stomach clench, and he gripped the railing tighter. He knew all too well what they were talking about. It was true that he had given Caesar Crispus the poison that had killed him, more than a decade ago. What else had the soldiers heard about him? Metrophanes was the numerarius of his military staff, his chief accountant. Castus had been aware that stories of what had happened years before might have leaked out, however much the emperor had tried to suppress them. But the realisation that his staff, his own men, were discussing his role in it all was painful.

The old man, he thought. So that was what they called him now!

He wanted to shout down to the sentries, demand that they explain themselves. But that would just make things worse. Swallowing his shame, his bitter anguish, Castus paced silently back along the portico and into his chamber. No doubt, he thought, one of those men that had attended the banquet earlier had been responsible for circulating the rumours about him, to undermine his authority. Once stories like that took wing, he knew, it was almost impossible to trap them. Any attempt he might make to deny them would only make things worse.

Sighing with disdain, he dropped back onto the couch. Better to let people judge him by his actions, rather than trying to fight rumours. Wearily he picked up the wax tablet and stylus from the side table. He had been trying to compose a rough draft of a letter to Marcellina, telling her what had happened since his arrival. But writing had never come easily to him, and the scrawl of unconvincing platitudes scratched onto the wax just sounded clumsy when he read them back to himself. Communication had never been one of his strong points. With a grunt of irritation he reversed the bronze stylus and rubbed out the words with the flat end, then dropped the tablet back on the table. Sleep, he thought, he needed to sleep. And tomorrow...

A tapping at the inner door broke into his thoughts. Castus stood up. A muffled voice from the hall outside.

'Come in!' he called.

The door opened and two soldiers entered the chamber. 'Dominus!' said the first, saluting. 'A message from the Praetorian Prefect – he wishes to speak to you.'

'At this hour?' Castus muttered, baffled. Did Ablabius want to discuss something that had happened during the banquet earlier? Clearing his throat to hide a yawn, Castus picked up his cloak from the couch and stepped towards the far corner of the room to fetch his sword and belts.

The lamp flame twisted, a moth-shadow passing against the light. For a heartbeat he felt the warning breath up the nape of his neck, the sudden intimation of impending danger. Then he turned and looked back at the archway that led onto the portico. A third man stood in the opening, wearing a hooded cape and carrying a drawn sword.

Castus froze; ice poured through his veins. Three against one, and he was unarmed. The lamp glow lit the face of the man in the archway: his expression was blank, but in his eyes was a killing determination. Castus saw him glance quickly at his two accomplices by the inner door; one of them stepped to the side, blocking Castus's path to his sword. Then the man in the portico arch lifted his blade with both hands and charged.

Shock and dread pinned Castus for a heartbeat. Then his fatigue was gone and the power of instinct alone flowed through him. Bunching his cloak around his left forearm, he snatched up the bronze stylus and launched himself towards his attacker; as the man stabbed with the sword Castus blocked the blade with the bunched cloak, shoving it away from him as the steel sliced into the wadded wool and gashed his arm. Then he slammed his other hand up under the man's jaw, driving the pointed bronze spike of the stylus through the soft flesh at the top of his throat.

Hot blood streamed down his arm and spattered over his chest as the man reeled against him. Castus stepped back, thrusting the attacker's body aside as he turned and sending him sprawling across the mosaic floor. The man's feet kicked as he died, blood spurting, the stylus still jutting obscenely from his neck.

Pain from his gashed arm, but he fought it down. The other two men were closing in around him, swords drawn, but moving far more cautiously now. *Fools*, Castus thought, *they should have used knives in this confined space*. He felt a sudden flare of hope.

The man on the floor still clasped his sword in a death grip; if Castus stooped to grab it, one of the other men would strike. The two who confronted him now were nervous; he could see that. They had expected this to be easy. But their nerves could make them reckless. He watched their eyes and their open mouths, the blades in their hands.

'New to this?' he growled. 'I've been killing men since before you were born.'

The man on his right drew a quick breath between his teeth and edged forward, raising his sword. Castus took two steps back until he felt the edge of the table against his hip. He reached behind him, seized the bronze lamp from the tabletop and then flung it across the room at the swordsman. The man cried out, flailing his arm as hot oil sprayed and the lamp snuffed out. Darkness engulfed them all, the after-image of the arcing flames flashing against Castus's vision.

But he knew this chamber far better than his attackers. He stepped quickly to his left, reaching out until he felt the wall. Stretching his hand down, he found the curved edge of the low side table with his fingertips, grasped one of the legs and whirled it up before him. The other swordsman was already advancing, unsure in the darkness, slashing his blade through the air. Castus paused for two heartbeats, then swung the table at him. The blade hacked into the wood and stuck fast; Castus dragged it aside, then smashed his fist into the man's face.

Three steps to the left, into the pitch darkness near the door, and Castus reached down and found the hilt of his own scabbarded sword. He pulled it upwards, shaking the scabbard free, then levelled the blade and struck. A heavy jolt up his arm as the steel bit, and the second man went down.

The third attacker was somewhere in the middle of the room. Standing quite still, Castus could make out his shadowy form against the moonlight through the portico archway; he could hear the man's rapid breathing as he turned in gathering panic. From somewhere outside the room came the sound of shouts and hobnailed boots crashing up stairs.

'Surrender,' Castus said quietly.

The man let out a gasping cry, spinning on his heel. Then he raised his blade and lunged at the darkness. Castus stepped aside quickly, then punched the pommel of his sword into the man's forehead. The attacker dropped sprawling on the tiles.

Light flared from the portico arch, and Castus blinked and shielded his eyes, squinting as he made out the two sentries from the courtyard below, brandishing a flaming torch. A moment later, the inner door burst open. Sabinus rushed into the room, armed but still dressed in his sleeping tunic; Diogenes and more soldiers were at his back. There was a body just outside the threshold too: the sentry that had been guarding the door, his throat slashed open.

Castus stood in the sudden illumination. Blood freckled the walls and covered the floor, and the whole room stank of it. Already he could feel his legs beginning to tremble, the sickening cramps of delayed shock twisting in his gut. He thought he would pass out, or vomit. But he forced himself to stand straight, still gripping the bloodied sword.

'You took your time,' he said to the two soldiers in the portico archway. They were stunned, staring at the bodies on the floor, the smeared and spattered blood. With dulled disappointment Castus noticed that the third attacker, the one he had struck, had managed to drive his own sword up below his ribs. He was dying slowly, a pool of gore spreading from his twitching body. No surprise, Castus thought: the man would have known that he faced long and brutal torture and execution if he were taken alive.

'Brother,' Diogenes managed to say, with an appalled gulp. 'You haven't lost your talent for slaughter, I see.'

Castus grinned fiercely, then raised his hand and let the sword drop to the floor.

For the first time in months, he felt truly alive.

CHAPTER VI

'I'd always *assumed*,' Diogenes said as he rode, 'that Syria would be sunny and warm. At least I'd hoped it might be, once we got out of Antioch...'

Winter had passed in blizzard cold and whipping sleet, ice-edged winds howling from Mount Silpius, and then a drenching rain that brought floods down the stream beds and clogged the streets of Antioch with mud. It still felt like winter now, as Castus and his small retinue rode eastwards across the Syrian plain. A cold stinging drizzle was turning the road to a glistening mire that muddied the horses to knee and hock.

'Wait a few weeks and it'll be sunny enough,' said Egnatius, the tribune commanding the mounted escort. 'Pretty soon you'll be grumbling about the heat, I'd put money on it!'

Flavius Egnatius had a quick grin and the build of a natural cavalryman. He was leading forty-eight troopers of the Equites Armigeri; together with the members of Castus's military staff, his officers and the slaves, the column made up nearly eighty men, with twice that many horses and baggage animals. An impressive array, although the very minimum possible; Castus had brought no wheeled transport, nothing that would slow him down on the muddy roads or in the desert's dust. He would move fast, only announcing his arrival at the last moment in the cities and fortresses along the route. At least, that was the plan.

They had left Antioch at the end of February, just after the official celebrations of the emperor's birthday. Finally, Castus thought, he had escaped the constricting grip of the imperial court, all the grinding administration and management, the queues of petitioners and the relentless military training, that had worn at his nerves since he first arrived in the east. Now, after five long months, he was free, with an open road ahead of him. But as he turned in the saddle and glanced back, he saw only a line of identical-looking riders in drenched brown capes and hoods, the heavy-laden camels bringing up the rear looking particularly woeful under the persistent rain.

At least some of his party were still in good spirits, several days out from Antioch. The numerarius Metrophanes, a plump round-faced Athenian, was even singing as he rode. He had a good voice too. Castus had not forgotten that Metrophanes had been spreading rumours about him, back when he first arrived at Antioch. Probably, he thought, many others had done the same.

He was more concerned about the *Primicerius Officiorum*, the head of his military staff. Claudius Sollemnis was a thickset Gaul with a suspicious frown. Capable enough, but Castus sensed that the man disapproved of him. Five months of working together had done nothing to change that, but Sollemnis gave no real cause for complaint either. And Castus had enemies enough already without seeking for more.

Unsurprisingly, the three men who had attacked him the previous autumn had never been identified. Castus was sure they were soldiers from the garrison, paid to murder him, but nobody was willing to claim any association with the dead. The prefect's investigators had identified a cabal among the officers Castus had demoted or threatened with discharge; conveniently, all the suspects had killed themselves before they could be questioned. But the real culprit, Castus knew, could well be higher up the chain of command. The thought that the men could have been acting on the orders of the Caesar himself, or his closest advisors, had added an even greater sense of oppression to the preceding months: Castus had gone everywhere armed, and accompanied only by men he believed he could trust. Whoever was behind the attack could well strike again, but next time they would be far cleverer about it.

At least the news of the attempted murder had caused enough sensation in Antioch to drown out the other rumours about him. The story that the Magister Equitum had fought off a band of attackers in his own chambers had gained him a certain grim celebrity in the city. The rumours had grown more elaborate over the following months, and Castus heard them repeated back to him: there had been five assailants, or eight, all of them heavily armed. He had killed them all using only a stylus, or beaten them to death with his fists... At least, Castus thought, people respected him now. Feared him a little too, perhaps. He was no longer *the old man*.

The column was passing through an area of low rolling hills, with orchards of bare trees stretching away on either side of the road. A monotonous country under the low grey sky, and the scattered villages, all similarly muddy and uninviting, did little to improve the view. As he rode, Castus thought back to the last letter he had received from Marcellina.

We will leave for the east around the kalends of March, and should be in Antioch by the middle of May. Three months, he thought, before he would see her again. In his own letters he had not mentioned the attempt on his life; he would wait until he could tell her in person about that. *Do not worry about us – we will journey by easy stages. But be careful yourself – I pray for your safekeeping, husband. Your road will be far harder than ours.*

True enough, he thought.

The highway he was following now stretched across Syria, through Hierapolis to the Euphrates, then on across Osrhoene and the wide plains of Mesopotamia, all the way to the city of Nisibis and the distant Tigris. The vastness of the lands he had to cover was daunting: as he reached the crest of a low hill Castus could see the countryside rolling away southwards to the horizon. Beyond that horizon was the open desert, vaster still. And somewhere out there was the Persian frontier, and the battleground of the war to come.

Once, generations past, the Roman domain had ended at the banks of the Euphrates. But successive emperors had pushed their borders eastwards, beating back the Persians and claiming a great swathe of territory all the way to the Tigris. Now this territory formed a massive northern salient, centred on Nisibis and extending beyond the Tigris into the foothills of the mountains. If the Persians wanted to invade, that would be way they would come. Their armies would cross the river and sweep across the Mesopotamian plain, crushing the cities and fortresses in their path, all the way to Syria. They had done just that, back in the distant days of the emperor Valerian, and sacked Antioch too.

But Constantine's planned invasion would take a different route, striking south-east from Syria down the Euphrates, directly into the heartland of the Persian realm. Castus had studied the route itineraries and the illustrated plans, the troop rosters for all the field armies and frontier units. He knew the emperor wanted him to draw as much strength as possible from the Mesopotamian garrisons to build up the expeditionary force on the Euphrates. But he could not afford to weaken them too much. Those garrisons were the only guard against the possibility of a Persian flanking attack from that direction.

With a twitch of irritation, he shrugged the thoughts from his mind. He had several days of travel ahead of him before he reached even the Euphrates. The rain was easing off, but his hands still felt numbed as he gripped the reins, and his horse's heavy gait on the muddy road was beginning to wear at his thigh muscles.

'We'll rest at the next milestone,' he called to Egnatius, who signalled back to the troops that followed him. They rode a little way further until they saw the whitewashed stone at the verge, then walked their horses off the road beneath a stand of dripping plane trees.

There was one extra rider who had accompanied the column since Antioch, and Castus was glad of his presence. He had first met the exiled Persian prince Hormisdas twelve years before, on the eve of the battle of Chrysopolis. Hormisdas had been a guarded and overly polite young man in his teens then, only recently escaped from captivity to seek sanctuary in the empire. Now he was aged about thirty, round-faced and stout, dressed in Roman military style but still with his Persian moustache and elegantly curled hair. He could almost have looked foppish, but Castus had seen the man on the practice field, and knew he was an expert horseman and a fierce fighter. Of all the men that Castus had met in the palace at Antioch, Hormisdas was the only one he truly liked or trusted; he knew a great deal about Persia too, and the Sassanian king's army, and Castus was glad of the opportunity to learn more about his opponents.

Most of the time, however, it had been Diogenes quizzing the prince.

'But is it true,' the secretary was asking as they dismounted under the trees, 'that in the Zoroastrian beliefs of your people evil was created by the anti-god, who somehow... generated it from himself?'

'Buggered himself, you mean!' Egnatius called. 'That's what they believe, isn't it, prince? Your devil buggered himself, got pregnant and gave birth to evil!' A few of his troopers joined in the laughter.

Hormisdas was smiling too, with a refined sort of condescension. 'It must sound an outlandish concept to your Roman ears,' he said. 'But truly this is what our priestly *mobeds* tell us. Ahriman, Father of Lies, must certainly have created evil from somewhere, no? For how else can the evil we see in the world exist?'

'Many great philosophers have grappled with that same problem,' Diogenes mused, 'although seldom have their ideas been so, ah, colourful…'

'And your people wash their faces in sheep's piss!' Egnatius said, grinning as he rubbed down his horse. 'Isn't that right? Every morning and every night they do it!'

Hormisdas spread his palms, still smiling. 'Again I cannot deny it,' he said. 'And yet, you know, fresh urine is an excellent purifying agent. It may seem disgusting to you cultured Romans, but I assure you that many of your own practices would seem quite vile to the devout Mazda-worshipping sons of Iran-Shahr!'

'And how do they seem to you?' Castus asked. Odd, he thought, that he had never once doubted this Persian's loyalty to Rome.

'I have been a guest in your emperor's domain for many years,' Hormisdas said, assuming a grave expression. 'I respect Rome, and I respect your customs. If, with the help of the gods – and of your emperor too, of course – I regain my rightful place on the throne of Iran-Shahr I will be a different man. I will purify myself and worship the holy flame five times a day as the mobeds direct. But you have a very good saying, I think – to every country its own custom. And when you are in Rome…'

'Act like a Roman!' Egnatius declared, and tossed his wineskin to Hormisdas.

They remained three days at the town of Beroea, and by the time the column moved onwards the weather had cleared. Black clouds still barred the sky to the north, but the landscape around them was different now. The road crossed areas of scanty cultivation, then passed through wide tracts of arid stony wasteland. Across the plain rose strange rocky mounds that might once have been settlements. The desert felt much closer here, Castus thought as he rode; he could feel that great emptiness, like a pressure in the air.

Just after midday the column passed another group of riders coming in the opposite direction, mounted on camels and small ponies. The riders drew off the road to let the Romans pass: when Castus glanced at them he saw that the men were wrapped in coarse blankets pulled up over their heads as hoods. Beneath the hoods their faces were thin and dark, their eyes fearless.

'Saracens,' Egnatius said, noticing Castus's attention. 'There's quite a number of them settled in the area to the south of here.'

'I thought the Saracens were nomads?' Castus asked as they rode on.

'Most of them are, strictly speaking,' the tribune replied. 'But some choose to settle inside our frontiers for parts of the year. The open desert's their country, and they have little regard for borders.'

'But they're on our side?'

Egnatius shrugged, with a wry smile. 'With them it's hard to say! Many of their clans have pledged allegiance to the emperor, and we promote their chiefs to phylarchs in our service. But there's another lot that fight for the Persians – often we suspect that the division between the two isn't as strict as they might pretend!'

Castus glanced back warily at the riders they had just passed, who were already moving off in the other direction. 'Not a people to trust, then?'

'I wouldn't,' Egnatius said. 'Though some would. They're thieves and brigands for the most part. They range like birds of prey over the entire desert, seizing whatever they can find. But they're also the finest light cavalry on earth!'

'Some would, you say?'

Egnatius nodded. 'There's an officer called Lycianus, for one. We'll meet him at Nisibis with any luck. He commands a unit of Saracen irregulars, and swears by their honour. Speaks their language; knows most of their chiefs too. He's a strange sort of man himself though. You'll see soon enough!'

They stopped for the night at the village of Beseletha, a huddle of houses strung along the road, surrounded by orchards and melon beds.

'You know, you really are taking Spartan virtue very seriously with your arrangements,' Hormisdas said, lounging on a threadbare dining couch in the central chamber of the rough *mansio*. 'When the Praetorian Prefect tours the provinces, he always takes with him a full Schola of mounted guardsmen, six carriages, the best cooks from the palace, together with a troupe of dancers and a full orchestra to provide music while he eats!'

Castus was not at all surprised. He doubted that Ablabius felt the luxuries were necessary, but the prefect clearly loved the outward appearance of authority. 'You shouldn't listen to music while you eat,' he said. 'Gives you indigestion.'

After their simple meal was concluded, he sat for an hour playing *latrunculi* with Egnatius. The grid of the board and the polished black and white glass playing pieces had a simple clarity that Castus enjoyed, and the strategic thinking focused his mind. Even so, it was frustrating that Egnatius beat him every time they played.

He sighed heavily as the tribune trapped his final piece between two of his own. 'Another game?' he asked as Egnatius cleared the board.

'I'm for my bed, dominus,' the tribune said, yawning as he stood up. 'Besides,' he said with a brief salute, 'I prefer not to ask too much of fortune!'

Once the tribune had left, only Sabinus remained in the chamber; he was seated on the far couch, drying and polishing his sword and scabbard. Castus smiled; he too had always been sure to clean and maintain his equipment, instead of leaving the slaves to do it.

'Play a round with me?'

His son glanced up, raising his eyebrows, then slipped the blade back into the scabbard. 'I'd rather be excused, Father,' he said. 'There's a rider leaving for Antioch at dawn, and I'd like to send a letter with him.'

'Who are you writing to?' Castus asked, more sharply than he had intended.

Sabinus was already on his feet. The slightest pause before he replied. 'Just friends,' he said, in a halting tone, and tried to smile. 'I do *have* friends, you know!'

'Of course,' Castus said with an abrupt nod. He gave a gesture of dismissal, and Sabinus left the room.

Alone, Castus stared down at the empty grid of the game board. Five months, and he had still not established anything beyond a formal relationship with his son. Sabinus was determined, it seemed, to preserve the distinction of rank between them. Once, Castus thought, his son had been close to him. But now he was a man, and had his own life. He still wondered sometimes if Sabinus was embarrassed by his presence, even angered by it.

With a growl of displeasure, Castus set the pieces back on the board and began shifting them around, attempting to play against himself. A question came to him: who were these friends of his son's in Antioch, and what was he telling them? At once he tried to suppress the thought, but already it was turning in his mind, spinning remorselessly into suspicion. No, he told himself, he could not allow himself to think like that. If he started to suspect even his own son... But he had noticed that Sabinus was devoted to Caesar Constantius, just as he had been devoted to Crispus as a boy. A terrible sour premonition rose in him. Who better to act as a spy than his own son, after all? He snatched up a handful of playing pieces and squeezed them in his fist, as if he could grind the glass to powder. He could not believe it. *He must not.*

*

Thunder the next morning, and the clouds pressed down like a black iron lid over the plain as the retinue rode onwards towards the city of Hierapolis. Castus had slept badly, racked by guilt and suspicion; he shrugged off Egnatius's attempts at conversation, ignored the ongoing debates between Diogenes and Hormisdas, and rode in grim silence.

It was mid-afternoon, the thunder still growling and lightning flickering away across the drab desert to the south, when Castus saw the two scouts galloping back down the road towards the head of the column. He sat upright in the saddle; one of the men was holding the corner of his cloak bunched above his head. *Enemy in sight.*

'Persians!' the scout cried as he approached. 'Persian cavalry – lots of them – up in the village ahead!'

'Impossible!' Egnatius said, but his hand was already on his sword hilt. Then the second scout confirmed the report of the first.

Castus made a calming gesture, but he felt the shock of the news chilling his blood. They were still fifteen miles from Hierapolis, well to the west of the Euphrates; the Persian frontier lay hundreds of miles away. Surely the scouts were mistaken?

Or perhaps not. Could it be, Castus wondered as the initial shock turned to dread, that the Persians had launched a surprise attack towards Antioch, and this was the vanguard of their force? Even a raiding party, if it had penetrated this far, was surely much stronger than the handful of troops in Castus's retinue.

Fighting down a shudder, he unpinned his cloak and slung it over the saddle behind him, then took his helmet from its leather bag. 'Close up,' he said quietly. 'No signals – but I need every man ready at my command.'

Egnatius saluted, and passed the orders back down the column. Castus glanced at Sabinus, and caught his grave nod.

Then he shook the reins, nudged with his heels, and moved forward at a trot.

He could see the village on the horizon now. Just a low cluster of buildings beside the road, orchards around it and a line of cultivation that followed a stream bed. Then he saw the figures against the skyline: mounted men, fanning out to block the road. He heard the thumping of massed hooves as Egnatius's men closed into a wedge formation. The line of riders up ahead remained motionless, merely watching as the Roman force approached.

'Persians, sure enough,' said Egnatius, moving up on Castus's left. By now they could see the glint of the riders' horse trappings, the bright embroidery beneath their dun-coloured riding coats. Some wore tall, silvered helmets. 'But what are they doing here?'

Castus shook his head, frowning. There was something uncanny about the Persian riders; they appeared unconcerned, almost relaxed. A dozen spanned the road, with the same number again waiting to either side. At his command, Castus knew, the wedge of armoured horsemen behind him could blast straight through their thin cordon. He raised his hand, slowing his horse to a walk.

Hormisdas was riding right behind him. 'I'd not think less of you if you stayed back,' Castus told him.

'There is no war between our peoples yet,' the Persian replied. 'Besides, you might need a translator!'

Little more than twenty long paces between them, and Castus drew his horse to a halt. From this distance, he could make out the weaponry of the Persians. No spears or lances, but every rider carried on his hip a long straight sword with a curving ornamental hilt and a bow cased on his saddle. And every man had the hilt of his sword tied to the scabbard with a red silk cord.

Egnatius rode forward a little further, the standard-bearer following him with the long purple tail of the draco flapping in the damp breeze.

'Clear the road!' the tribune cried. 'Clear the road, in the name of his excellency Flavius Aurelius Castus, Magister Equitum per Orientem!'

As Egnatius spoke, Castus saw another rider coming from the direction of the village. A tall man on a high-stepping black horse; the Persians on the road parted as he turned a brisk circle and took up a position at their centre.

'Magister,' Hormisdas said in an urgent whisper, leaning from his saddle. 'I recognise that man; he is a *wuzurg*, a great noble. Be careful. His name is Zamasp. He's dangerous.'

Castus gave the prince a curt nod, not turning his head. His eye was drawn first to the newcomer's mount. He knew little about horses, but this was certainly the most magnificent animal he had ever seen, glossy black and powerfully muscled, like an equine statue come to vivid life. The bridle and trappings were adorned with gold ornaments and blue silk tassels. Compared to the Persian nobleman's horse, Castus's own solid gelding resembled a draught animal.

But the rider was almost as impressive. Zamasp sat straight in the saddle, not even touching the reins but controlling his mount with the pressure of his knees. He wore a long coat of deep blue silk worked all over with silver embroidery, with the glint of scale armour showing beneath. His hair flowed in black ringlets over his shoulders, his beard was cut square and his broad heavy moustaches were curled up into points like the tusks of a boar. Black kohl rimmed his deep-set unblinking eyes. But he glanced only briefly at Castus.

'You have a piece of filth attached to you, Roman,' he said in fluent Greek, gesturing towards Hormisdas. 'You should shake it off, then wash thoroughly.'

Castus heard Hormisdas growl deep in his throat, but the prince made no answer. Zamasp's finger brushed lightly at the silk cord tying his scabbard; Castus did not doubt that he could free his weapon quicker than sneezing if he wanted to. The black horse tossed its mane and stamped the dirt, then circled once more.

'You heard the tribune, Persian,' Castus said. 'Dismount your men and get off the road, or we'll ride you down.'

From the corner of his eye he could see Sabinus moving up to cover his left. The troopers of the Equites Armigeri had formed a line behind him. Somewhere in the distance the thunder rolled again.

'I think not,' Zamasp said. His horse tossed its head and pawed the road. 'We are the escort of his excellency Vezhan Gushnasp, emissary of His Majesty Shapur, King of Kings, to the court of your emperor. Under the terms of the treaty between Rome and Iran-Shahr, we are entitled to accompany him, to protect against brigands and other such... *inconveniences*.'

'There are no brigands here!' Egnatius called. 'And you should have Roman troops escorting you!'

'Alas!' Zamasp said, spreading his palms. 'Our Roman escort was slow and lazy. We were obliged to leave them on the riverbank.'

Castus nudged his horse forward a few more steps. He noticed the Persian shift in his saddle, his hand straying closer to his sword once more.

'You've got an envoy with you?' Castus growled. 'Where is he?'

'If you wish to prostrate yourselves before his excellency Vezhan Gushnasp, my men would be honoured to conduct you to him.'

'I don't put my face in the dirt for anyone,' Castus replied. 'Bring him out here, or I'll consider you raiders, or spies.'

Zamasp leaned back in his saddle. His hooked moustaches twitched. He moved his hand away from his sword, fingers spread. 'As escorts to the envoy,' he said, 'we have diplomatic status. Also, as you see, our weapons are tied. We come... in *peace*.' He said the word with a smile, as if he considered it a joke.

'You're no threat to us, Persian. We outnumber you two to one.'

'And one of my Aswaran is worth five of your troopers. So?'

'You have a strange idea of diplomacy.'

Zamasp laughed suddenly, appearing genuinely amused. Then he sat forward in the saddle and peered at Castus.

'So this is the great general that the emperor of Rome sends to confront us?' the Persian said. 'What is your name again? Festus...? Crestus?'

Castus breathed in, careful not to show his anger, then walked his horse forward a few more steps. He could feel the big gelding growing restive, the horse's heavy muscles flexing.

'I confess I'm disappointed,' Zamasp went on. 'I was expecting a more formidable figure. Instead I see an old man with the face of a peasant, who speaks Greek like a rather stupid schoolboy. Is this really the best that Rome can do?'

'Enough of your abuse, Persian!' Sabinus cried, riding forward to join Castus. His hand was on the hilt of his sword.

Instinctively, Castus reached out and took his arm. 'Stay back,' he said quietly.

But Zamasp had caught the gesture. His smile grew broader. 'You have a hot-headed young friend there, general,' he said. 'A handsome one too. I see you're keen on him! So it's true what they say about you Romans and your *fancies*?'

Castus clenched his back teeth. He could sense the bristling anger of the men behind him. The Persian must know that his goad was biting; he appeared to be enjoying himself. But Castus could see the tension in his man's body, his hard steady eyes; he was ready for combat at any moment. The big gelding blew angrily and tossed his head as Castus walked him forward again. The two battle-trained horses eyed each other, heads pressed back and chests out.

'Summon your envoy here now,' Castus said. 'I'll talk to him, not to his bodyguard.'

A scream came from the field to the left of the road. Castus glanced quickly: running figures, a galloping horse. Some of the slaves from the baggage train must have gone to collect water at the stream and met the Persians there. He glanced back, and caught the movement of Zamasp's hand unlashing the cord from his scabbard. With a kick of his heels, he pushed the gelding forward.

Zamasp grabbed for his reins as his horse shied. Too slow; Castus's gelding had lashed his head forward, biting at the black animal's neck. The Persian swept his sword free, fury creasing his face as his mount reared and spun, dancing on its hind legs. At once every rider behind him had snatched the bow from his case and nocked an arrow; every trooper of the Equites Armigeri had his spear raised.

'Peace!' a voice shouted in Greek, then in Persian. 'Put down your weapons, I beg you!'

From the direction of the village a figure was approaching fast, mounted on a grey pony. The envoy, Castus guessed; the man was still wearing a sleeping tunic under his cloak.

Zamasp walked his horse backwards, retying the cord on his weapon. Castus glared at him, then slipped the spatha back into his scabbard and turned to the approaching envoy. A slave was running behind the newcomer, carrying a palm branch on a pole.

'Magister,' the envoy said, bowing his head and spreading his hands as he joined Castus. 'I apologise for any misunderstanding! The *hazarbed* Zamasp sought to give no offence.'

Zamasp said nothing. Clearly, Castus thought, whatever the supposed difference in status, the military commander was the dominant one here. A couple of the Persian riders had dismounted and were attending to the wound on the neck of their leader's horse. Zamasp sat in the saddle, arms folded; the horse pawed the ground, looking almost insulted.

'We've heard nothing about any Persian embassy crossing our

frontier,' Castus said, frowning at Vezhan Gushnasp. 'You claim you left your Roman guards at the river – why?'

'An unfortunate delay, magister,' the envoy said in faultless Latin, regaining his composure now the threat of immediate violence had receded. 'We are waiting here for our escort to catch up with us, in fact.'

Castus noticed Zamasp's disdainful shrug. Clearly the Persians had intended to ride all the way to Antioch unescorted, and demonstrate the laxity of the Roman defences. He scowled, fighting down his anger, and looked back at the column behind him: he was unwilling to detach any of Egnatius's men to watch over the Persians, and did not doubt that Zamasp would find a way to lose them if he did. But he could at least send a rider to warn the commander of the next Roman garrison.

'And I cannot understand,' the envoy went on, 'why you were not informed of our presence! As you know, I visited the Augustus Constantine in the summer of last year. My king, His Mazda-worshipping Majesty Shapur, is eager that I should speak with your emperor again, and attempt once more to dissuade him from the reckless course of war.'

'Reckless?' Castus said, and snorted a laugh. He had heard in Antioch about the last Persian visit to Constantinople. More likely, he thought, King Shapur was just playing for time. And some of his nobles were less inclined to wait for the commencement of hostilities.

'Your emperor wants to try his strength against us, as everyone knows,' Zamasp broke in. The envoy shot him a warning glance, but the Persian commander ignored it. 'You are lucky that the King of Kings is a lover of peace. Others among us are not.'

'So many people talking about peace these days,' Castus said quietly, shaking his head. The black-rimmed eyes glared back at him. To either side, the two groups of armed riders waited in formation, watching each other.

'Remove your men from the road,' Castus said, turning to the envoy. 'You will remain here in this village until I send a replacement guard to you from Hierapolis. My garrison commanders will be instructed to treat you as hostile invaders if you go any further west without a proper escort.'

'Your emperor would surely not be happy for an embassy from his brother monarch to be delayed like this,' the envoy said warily.

'My emperor would not be happy for armed Persians to be wandering about Syria on their own either,' Castus replied with a twisted smile. 'You might get lost, or fall in with bad company!'

For a few long tense moments Castus thought that the envoy would refuse, or that Zamasp and his men would ignore the envoy's instructions. But at last the orders were given, and the Persian riders moved off the road and back towards the village just as the first rain began to fall. The envoy Vezhan Gushnasp departed with a fulsome bow, and only Zamasp remained, still in the saddle, watching as the Roman column filed past him in the falling rain.

Castus sat opposite him, Sabinus and Egnatius flanking him, until the last of the Roman baggage train had moved away up the muddy road towards Hierapolis. He was glad to see that the village was a miserable-looking collection of hovels; doubtless the Persian envoy and his men would have an uncomfortable wait there.

'If your emperor once again fails to see the virtues of reason,' Zamasp called from the far side of the road, 'then we may meet again, under less diplomatic conditions.'

'I'll look forward to it,' Castus called back.

'You should not. It will be a sad day for you.' Zamasp circled his horse on the verge. 'I would not kill such an old man – no! I think I will cut off your hands and feet and send you crawling home to your emperor.'

Castus heard Sabinus draw a sharp breath. But the danger had passed now – these were only words.

'But that one, your handsome friend,' Zamasp said, pointing at Sabinus. 'Him I will kill. And after I have killed him, I will have the skin peeled from his corpse, dyed and stuffed with chaff, and displayed on the wall of our greatest temple, as my people once did to your Emperor Valerian. And you will watch, helpless, as I do it.'

He sat for a moment more, staring at Castus through the rain. Then, with the barest movement, he turned his magnificent horse and spurred into a gallop, back towards the village behind him.

PART TWO

CHAPTER VII

Constantinople, March AD *337*

'*Hosanna!*' the voices around her cried. '*Blessings to the King! Blessings to the one who comes in the name of the Lord!*'

Through the lattice screens of her litter, Marcellina saw a waving forest of greenery filling the street. Palm fronds and olive branches. The people carrying them, calling out the blessings, were dressed in long white unbelted tunics, men and women alike bare-headed and many of them barefoot too. It was the Day of Palms, the beginning of the Paschal week, and Constantinople was thronged with devotees.

'I never knew there were so many Christians in the world!' Aeliana said. The girl was sitting opposite her mother in the cramped confines of the swaying litter, gazing out with wide eyes.

'Nor did I,' Marcellina said quietly.

Pharnax was walking alongside. The scarred ex-gladiator was watching the crowd too, raising an arm now and again if any of the palm-wielding worshippers got too close. He had insisted on accompanying her and Aeliana into the city, sticking close to them as he had done throughout their journey from Dalmatia.

'Leave them,' Marcellina told him. 'They mean no harm.'

Pharnax nodded, but did not appear convinced.

They were nearing the heart of the city now, the great plaza called the Augusteion. Marcellina had never been to Constantinople before, and the crowds and the huge buildings on all sides felt oppressive. A light drizzly rain was falling, blurring the distance into mist. She had received the message the evening before, granting her permission to attend morning mass in the Church of the Holy Peace, in the presence of the emperor himself. It was not a permission she had requested, or one she desired, but as the wife of the Magister Equitum per Orientem she supposed she had certain obligations. Besides, she was curious. After all these years she had still never seen the Emperor Constantine in person.

The litter came to a halt as the bearers eased it to the ground. Marcellina glanced out, and saw the façade of the basilica rising before her, the walls and gateway of the pillared forecourt surrounded by armed guards and silentiaries of the imperial retinue. Climbing from the litter with Aeliana, she stood for a while staring around her at the host of richly dressed worshippers converging on the church. She felt dowdy and provincial in their company, and pulled her shawl across her head. From within the church she could hear the sound of chanting.

Marcellina had called herself a Christian for many years, although her faith was personal, almost philosophical. She had seldom attended a church service, and preferred reading poetry and literature to religious texts. Cut off in an isolated corner of Dalmatia, she had almost believed that Christianity was something she had invented for herself, a quieter and deeper faith than the ancient religions, the distant and implacable gods of earth and sky that her father had worshipped, and her husband still revered. But seeing her faith proclaimed so loudly and boldly here in the imperial city was a shock. It had not been the first.

Two nights before, she had stayed at a mansio on the Perinthus road, and shared her dinner table with a pair of bishops, also travelling to Constantinople for the Paschal celebrations. One of them had been a follower of Arius, the other a supporter of Bishop Athanasius, and very soon they had fallen into dispute and violent argument. As the wine flowed, they had hurled abuse at each other – *'Pervert! Heretic!'* – and would have come to blows had the mansio slaves not separated them. Marcellina had found it a chilling and depressing display. Her Christianity was deeply felt, but she feared it had become just another excuse for men to fight one another. And the world needed no more excuses of that sort.

'Mother!' a voice said, and Marcellina saw her daughter Maiana hurrying through the crowd, with her husband Laurentius. They embraced, and then Aeliana stretched up on her toes to hug her half-sister. Maiana was Marcellina's second daughter by her first husband, and she had been living in Constantinople for the last five years. She had prospered, clearly; she was expensively dressed, and rather more plump these days, but looked happy.

Laurentius, Marcellina's son-in-law, was a handsome man with a self-satisfied air. He had recently been promoted to ducenarius of the Corps of Notaries, mainly due, Marcellina suspected, to his wife's connections. Even after his disgrace and retirement, Castus's reputation still counted for something at the imperial court.

'Mother, can I come with you into the church?' Aeliana asked, tugging on her hand. 'I want to see the emperor.'

'No, you must stay out here with Maiana. Pharnax will look after you.'

The bodyguard was attracting nervous glances from the passing crowd, but appeared entirely unmoved. Pharnax had spent most of his life looking intimidating.

Taking her son-in-law's arm, Marcellina walked with him through the gateway into the church courtyard. The guards merely glanced at her invitation with its imperial seal.

'We hear encouraging reports from Antioch,' Laurentius said, 'about your husband.'

'Do you?' Marcellina asked. She had heard only sparingly from Castus since his departure, and she had little idea of what he had been doing in the east.

'Oh yes, he's getting on well! He seems to have managed to terrify most of the army and half the court. He'll have them all in fighting shape very soon, no doubt.'

'Why should he want to terrify them?' Marcellina asked with a slight smile. She knew that many people found her husband imposing. Many people underestimated him too, taking his size and his brutal appearance as evidence of stupidity. Few, she suspected, saw him as he really was, and as she knew him to be.

'Best way to get things done, I suppose!' Laurentius said, shrugging awkwardly. 'Besides, there was that attack on him last autumn – that would give anyone a reason for resentment...'

'What attack?' Marcellina said sharply. She was still trying to smile.

'Oh, dear, you didn't know?' Laurentius whispered with a disingenuous frown. *Idiot*, Marcellina thought. 'Yes, he was attacked in his quarters by several men. But don't worry, he fought them off – killed them, in fact! Some army matter, they say, although obviously it leaves a bitter taste...'

Marcellina made a sound of agreement. She was not surprised that Castus had mentioned nothing about the attack in his letters to her. What could she have done, save worry even more that she did already? But it pained her all the same. She knew her husband was in danger – he had seldom been far from it – but to be thrown back into such peril after so many years of safe retirement seemed unjust. The sooner she joined him in Antioch, she thought, the better for them both.

'Who are those men?' she asked, hoping to distract herself.

'Them? Persians,' Laurentius said. 'The white-faced man is the envoy of King Shapur. They won't enter the church, of course, but they're permitted to stand in the courtyard.'

'Who's the taller man behind him, with the curving moustaches? He looks... vicious.'

'I don't remember his name,' her son-in-law said. 'The chief of the envoy's bodyguards, I think. Come – let's go inside.'

After the damp grey daylight, the darkened interior of the basilica resembled a vast cavern. Bodies packed the aisles, and the air was fogged with cloying incense, but when Marcellina glanced upwards she saw the high vaulted ceiling glowing with paintings of birds and flying angels.

Laurentius led her through the press at the doors, and then she left him and shuffled to her designated position in the women's section, near the back of the hall in one of the side aisles. From there, Marcellina could peer between a couple of pillars and, if she angled her head, see the high altar in the distant apse. Priests, presbyters and deacons flanked the apse, and the Bishop of Constantinople stood before it, reading from a codex.

'*Blessed is the one that comes in the name of the Lord,*' the bishop intoned:

'The True Word against the Lie,

The Saviour against the Destroyer,

The Prince of Peace against he who stirs up war...'

A loud cry from the doors, and at once a rustling stir ran through the crowd. Everyone in the church was sinking to their knees, some even prostrating themselves on the marble floor.

'The emperor!' the woman beside Marcellina hissed as she knelt.

Marcellina dropped to kneel beside her, feeling the blast of clean air from the open doors, the almost palpable wave of awe filling the room as the emperor passed along the central aisle. As she heard his footsteps get closer she risked a glance upwards. Constantine was pacing slowly, and his heavy court robes were so stiff with embroidery that he appeared to be gliding. His jowled chin was tucked down against his chest, his large beakish nose aimed at the floor, and he looked as though he was scowling.

This is the man, Marcellina thought, *I have despised for over a decade. This is the man I can never forgive. The man who put his own son to death; the man who raised up my husband, and then tried to destroy him... This is the man.*

Constantine passed out of sight, taking a place somewhere near the front of the hall, close to the altar. The congregation rose, and soon the massed verses of the Psalms filled the cavernous space.

'Who may ascend the mountain of the Lord?

Who may stand in this holy place?

The one who has clean hands and a pure heart...'

Lulled by the echoing voices, the heavy scents and the warmth of the bodies all around her, Marcellina let her mind drift. She would remain in Constantinople for the rest of the Paschal week, and then move on. The road ahead crossed Bithynia and Galatia, Cappadocia and Cilicia. A long road and an exhausting one, all the way to Antioch. Would Castus be there when she arrived? Would he be safe, unharmed...?

Abruptly, Marcellina became aware of the sound of coughing from the front of the basilica. Others appeared to notice it too, and the chant faltered. The coughing continued, then turned to a hacking gasp. Leaning forward between the pillars, Marcellina stared towards the apse, and her eyes widened. It was the emperor, she could now make out. Constantine himself, bent forward and racked by coughs, the eunuchs and guards rushing to attend him.

Whispered words spread through the congregation as the last chanting died. The bishop was glancing anxiously towards the emperor, who had managed to stifle his coughing fit but was still gasping, his back heaving. At an imperceptible signal, the guards around the emperor marched swiftly towards the basilica doors, lining the aisle. Constantine was already making for the exit, flanked by eunuchs who supported his elbows, and another who dabbed at his mouth with a linen cloth. In a great wave the congregation sank to its knees, and Marcellina knelt with them.

But just as the emperor neared the far doors he was struck by another fit of coughing. Marcellina glanced up quickly, and in that instant she caught sight of Constantine as he turned his head in her direction. His face was dark red, his chin flecked with blood and spittle.

And in his eyes was a look of stark, mortal terror.

CHAPTER VIII

The raucous crowing of a cockerel roused Castus from troubled sleep.

His mind was still whirling: in his dream the deep water was surrounding him, panic thrashing in his chest, his consciousness shrinking as he felt death dragging him downwards. He shuddered, then winced sharply as he opened his eyes to the sunlight angling from the high window. Somewhere outside, the cockerel let out its harsh cry once more.

He was in Nisibis, he remembered, in his sleeping chamber in the Strategion. The sea was hundreds of miles away, and he was alive.

Keeping his eyes tightly closed against the daylight, he struggled to raise himself from the mattress. His head felt poisoned, and there was a stinging pain behind his temples. Was he sick? Then he remembered how much he had drunk the night before. Years since he had been so reckless in his cups. He had sat up late after dinner, drinking with his military officers; a welcome release at the time, but now he felt foolish for it. Yawning until he felt his jaw click, he scrubbed at his scalp with his knuckles. He shouted – it sounded more like a dog barking – and Vallio, his slave orderly, bobbed his head around the door.

'Water,' Castus croaked, raising his head.

Vallio returned almost immediately, bringing an earthenware jug of cool water, a bowl and a cup. Castus splashed his face, then drank deeply. Levering himself upright, he managed to stand and stretch his arms above his head. Flashes of hot colour danced in his skull.

'Outside,' he said, then pulled on a tunic and lumbered across the room towards the door.

The Strategion of Nisibis stood on the southern edge of the citadel mount, the only area of high ground in the city. It was usually the residence of the *Dux Mesopotamiae*, the commander of the military forces in the province, but for now it was Castus's temporary home. The complex was built in the local style: around a central courtyard garden of ornamental palms were rooms with thick mud-brick walls, small high windows and vaulted ceilings to provide cool shade in the long summer months. That may be the case, Castus thought, but for all the faded paintings on the plastered walls the chambers still felt like the inside of a tomb.

Passing through the vestibule, he stamped up the steps to the flat roof. Awnings provided shade, and there was the faintest whisper of a morning breeze. Groaning, he eased himself down onto a stool and waited while the slaves brought more water and a dish of bread and olive oil.

Castus had arrived in Nisibis two days before. After leaving Hormisdas at Edessa, he had journeyed up into the Armenian foothills to survey the new defences of the town of Amida and the upper Tigris valley. Descending once more to the fertile Mesopotamian plains, his party had entered a different season; the warm sunlight and clear blue skies of springtime were a blessing after the long months of cold and gloom.

Nearly forty years had passed since Castus had last visited this place. He had been a legionary then, serving in the army of the Emperor Galerius, who had camped his troops outside the city of Colonia Septimia Nisibis. Castus had remained in camp and not entered the city itself, but he had heard a lot about the place. Half a dozen times over the centuries, he knew, Rome had swallowed Nisibis up and spat it back out again, and while it was a Roman city now it had never seemed truly a part of the empire.

To the south of the citadel mount, the ground dropped to the level expanse of the military *castrum*, built over a hundred years before by the deified emperor Septimius Severus. That same emperor had rebuilt the walls, extending them to encompass the castrum and the new city district that spread away eastward to the bank of the river Mygdonius. Chewing on the hard bread, Castus gazed over the camp. Birds of prey were circling above the parade ground and the regular lines of barrack buildings; kites, Castus guessed from their broad wingspan. The sky was already deep blue, and the sun getting hot. Beyond the wall the green cultivated land stretched to the flat horizon.

He had spent much of the previous day down in the camp, reviewing the troops and meeting with the dux, Romulianus, and the other military officers. Three thousand men were garrisoned here, of the First and Sixth Parthica legions, with the same number based at the fortress of Singara, four days' march south-east on the edge of the open desert.

'I want to send half your legionary and cavalry strength south to Circesium on the Euphrates,' Castus had told the dux the day before. 'They'll wait there with the other frontier detachments and join the imperial field army in two months' time.'

Romulianus had made no immediate response, but Castus could see that the man was not happy. He had expected as much, and continued: 'The remainder of your force,' he said, 'will remain here to guard the fortifications. Nisibis is the bulwark of our north-eastern frontier. If the enemy try to send a force through Mesopotamia to outflank our advance on the Euphrates, they'll need to break the defences here. With the force remaining to you, you'll have enough men to stop them.'

'I understand,' Romulianus said. He was a dry-looking, unsmiling man with a stubbled jaw, who held himself with an impatient stiffness. 'But I had hoped,' he added, 'that I might be permitted to join the field army myself. I have capable subordinates here, if it's just a matter of holding the position. I believe my abilities would be better used in a more active role.'

Castus sucked his cheek. He knew that the task he had given to Romulianus and the other frontier duces lacked obvious opportunities for glory. But neither did his own. 'No,' he said, in a tone that forbade further argument. 'Your place is here. The defence of the eastern frontier is critical, and I need a man with the rank and experience to take full command. And,' he went on, lowering his brows, 'to take full *responsibility*. You are to hold the cities and fortresses and prevent anything getting past you, nothing more. The enemy may try to draw you out with raiding parties or feint attacks. Resist them. You don't have the strength for a field battle. Am I clear?'

'Clear enough,' Romulianus had said, unable to conceal his disappointment.

And with any luck, Castus thought as he sat beneath the awning, the dux and his men would have nothing to do but stare at an empty horizon. The emperor would be leading over sixty thousand men down the Euphrates, and the Persians would surely need all their forces to oppose him. Or so the plan went. Castus touched his fingers to his lips and raised them to the sky: *May the gods be good...*

The sound of a cleared throat behind him, and Castus turned to see Sollemnis, the chief of his military staff, waiting by the stairhead. The Gaul appeared more than usually sullen, although he was always so taciturn it was hard to be sure. Castus gestured for him to approach.

'Today's reports, dominus,' Sollemnis said. 'One from Barbalissos detailing the provision of river barges, another from

Soura concerning your appointment of Quintianus as the new commander of the field detachments there...'

Castus grunted. Even trying to nod made his head hurt. He rubbed at his brow with finger and thumb.

'And a confirmation of today's meeting with the *Curator Civitatis*, Vorodes,' Sollemnis went on, shuffling his tablets, 'together with several written appeals from members of the council...' He appeared almost to be relishing the scrupulous detailing of all the correspondence.

'Yes, yes,' Castus said, a little too loud. 'There's time enough for that later. Leave me for an hour or two.'

Sollemnis adopted a pinched expression, then bowed curtly and retreated.

'Brother,' Diogenes said, stepping from the stairs as Sollemnis made his departure. 'You've only just risen? The day is long advanced!'

'I'd have risen a lot later still,' Castus said, grimacing, 'if that fucking cockerel hadn't woken me up.'

Diogenes widened his eyes, feigning a puzzled look. 'Ah, yes!' he said. 'An extraordinarily rowdy fowl. Perhaps we could order it to be executed for disturbing the dignity of the Magister Equitum?'

Castus scowled at him. He was in no mood for levity. But once the idea had worked its way into his fogged mind he was forced to laugh. He ate a little more bread, washed it down with water, and began to feel restored. Diogenes had strolled to the edge of the roof. Trumpet calls drifted from the southern gate, and the sound of shouted orders from the barrack lines.

'Can you believe,' Diogenes said, 'that I spent over an hour yesterday debating with a gymnosophist from the banks of the Ganga? I swear that neither of us had a word of any language in common, but in some miraculous way I seemed to understand everything he said, and he likewise!'

'You amaze me,' Castus replied flatly. 'Where did you find this... gymnosy...'

'In the agora, of course. I was observing discreetly, as you instructed me to do. Brother,' he declared with enthusiasm, spreading his arms to the morning sky, 'I'm so glad you brought me east with you! All those years I wasted in classrooms, sifting the dry dust of received knowledge... Out here I feel my intellect nourished as never before! In fact, for the first time in my life I'm starting to feel truly philosophical...'

'What I meant,' Castus said patiently, 'was that you should observe the people, the city, try and find out something useful. Not that talking to strange foreigners in imaginary languages isn't useful to somebody, I suppose...'

'Yes, well,' Diogenes said with a slight sniff. Shading his eyes, he gazed down at the castrum, the circling birds, the angle of the city wall. 'What would you estimate the perimeter distance of the walls to be?' he asked in a speculative tone.

'Of the whole city? No idea. Must be a few miles, I'd say.'

'Three thousand, four hundred and forty-one double paces,' Diogenes said. 'Which is just over three miles in total circumference.'

Castus stared, bemused, a piece of bread raised his hand. 'How in the name of Hades do you know that?'

'I paced the distance myself,' Diogenes said with a rather preening smile. 'Earlier this morning, while you were sleeping off the effects of your, ah, *military symposium*. I woke a couple of hours before dawn, and as it was cool I thought I'd take a brief walk. But once I'd got up onto the ramparts I found the exertion quite beneficial.'

'I see,' Castus said, impressed despite himself. 'Learn anything else?'

'The walls are thirty-six feet high on average, ten to twelve feet thick, mud-brick on a rubble core – you can see they've been repaired in places. Towers every hundred paces or so. The defences are strongest to the west, north and south, of course: there's a lower fore-wall on those sides, with a dry moat beyond it dug down into the bedrock.'

'And to the east?'

'The walls over there stand directly on the bluffs above the river. It's little more than a stream at the moment, though I'm told that now the meltwater's started coming down from the mountains the level should rise dramatically. But the bed's deep, and the bluffs are high, so only a single wall is required. The suburb on the far side of the river only has a rough perimeter defence, although I didn't get over there to study it further.'

'You did well,' Castus said. Diogenes was trying to conceal his glow of pride.

'Well, since you're paying me,' the secretary said, 'and I have an enquiring mind, I thought I may as well do something you might appreciate...'

Castus shrugged down a stir of guilt. It was true that he had been giving Diogenes little to do; his official staff handled most of the administrative work. But he had mainly brought the secretary along for company, and because he knew he could trust him. To act as an advisor too, although he would admit that to nobody.

'I'm meeting the city leaders today,' he said, waving away a persistent fly. 'You heard anything about them yet?'

'Not much,' Diogenes replied. 'The curator, Vorodes, is one of the wealthiest men in Nisibis, so I hear. He's also High Priest of Baal Shamin. So, a follower of the traditional gods, unlike his Christian colleague Dorotheus, the *Defensor Civitatis*. The two of them detest each other, naturally.'

Castus gave a wry grimace. Clearly the religious divisions in the city were reflected in the leading citizens; he reminded himself that he needed to preserve his neutrality here. Drawing a deep breath, he stood up – a little too quickly. His head reeled, and pain stabbed behind his eyes. Rubbing at his temples, he stared out into the sunlight.

It was going to be a long day.

Three hours later, his hangover had still not shifted. He was getting used to the dull gnawing sensation at the back of his skull, but the curator Vorodes was doing little to ease his sense of fatigue.

'Thirty years I've served this city, excellency,' the curator said, raising an emphatic finger, 'and now my son too has a seat on the Boule. I'm told that in the west men try very hard to avoid the duties of city council service, is that true? Here in the east, we still consider it the greatest of honours!'

Flavius Septimius Vorodes, Castus thought to himself, must have been very young indeed when he first became a councillor; he looked barely older than forty now. A tall man, dressed in the Persian style of baggy white trousers and tunic, he had a clipped beard, a smooth olive complexion and a look of lively intelligence in his dark eyes. Vorodes radiated the kind of confident assurance that Castus had encountered often in the very rich. He was eager to impress though. Whether that was due to genuine pride in his city, or some deeper anxiety, Castus was in no mood to determine.

'My family first gained Roman citizenship in the days of the deified Severus,' the curator went on. 'Back when Nisibis first became a *colonia*. But all of us regard that status as an inestimable blessing. See there, the statue of the great man himself, with Diocletian on the opposite side of the steps.'

Nisibis was laid out in the familiar grid of streets, with two broad colonnaded avenues, like the ones Castus had seen in Constantinople and Antioch, meeting at the centre beneath a four-sided processional arch. But Vorodes had arranged to meet him outside the Tychaeion, the temple of the city's presiding deity. Castus had Sabinus with him, and two of the Protectores, Iovinus and Victorinus. The curator was accompanied by a dozen bodyguards and as many slaves, who formed a cordon all around them. They stood at the base of the steps, gazing up at the statues of the emperors and the huge ornamental façade of the Tychaeion beyond.

'Some of our more passionate Christians campaigned to have the statues removed,' Vorodes said in a hushed voice. 'The image of Diocletian particularly – they regard him as a persecutor and an oppressor, as you know. But since they refuse to enter the precincts of the temple anyway, except for public meetings, it seemed an obtuse argument.'

They climbed the steps, and Castus almost gasped with relief as they passed into the cool shade of the temple. Together they gave sacrifice before the image of the city Tyche – only wine and a pinch of incense, as blood sacrifices were banned by imperial order. The emperor's new religion, Castus thought sourly, had succeeded in imposing its will here too.

'You've got a lot of Christians in Nisibis?' he asked as the two of them were descending the steps once more.

'Oh yes,' Vorodes replied. 'We have a saying here. Out of every ten people in the city, one is a soldier, another is a Jew and another a foreigner. Of the rest, three are Christians and three follow the old gods.'

Castus counted quickly on his fingers, frowning, and reached the stub on his left hand. 'What about the tenth person?'

'About the tenth person,' Vorodes said with a smile, 'nobody knows, and nobody asks!'

Despite his instinctive distrust of civilian officials, Castus found that he liked the curator. He sensed a forthright honesty in the man, although he did not doubt that could change under pressure.

'The Christian bishop's a powerful man here then?' he asked.

'Iacob, yes,' Vorodes replied, his smile fading. 'You might say his voice is as loud as the whole council combined. A strange man. He eats no meat, you know, and drinks no wine, and he seldom bathes. I asked him about that once, and he told me that those who've been washed in the blood of Christ need no further washing... He dislikes women too. I do wonder, myself, why somebody should devote so much time to thanking and praising their God when they deny themselves all the good things of the earth!'

'I should speak to him,' Castus said.

A flicker of dismay passed across the curator's face, quickly erased. 'Are you certain that's necessary?' he asked.

Castus nodded. In truth he would rather do nothing of the sort, but if the bishop was a person of influence in the city he needed to determine his loyalties.

'Well, you must visit him in his church then – he refuses to leave its precincts so soon after their Paschal festival... But here we have the main granaries...'

All around the margins of the Tychaeion courtyard, behind the porticoes, were long buildings with massive buttressed walls. Inside, the curator led Castus and his party along pillared aisles lined with huge clay storage jars.

'Enough grain can be stored here to feed the whole city, fifty thousand mouths, for four months,' Vorodes explained with a swell of pride. 'And we can fill to double the present capacity once the harvest's gathered in. There are cisterns beneath the city, cut into the bedrock, holding sufficient water for the same period, on a limited rationing. Anyone attempting to reduce the city by thirst or hunger would be in for a very long wait!'

'Strong walls too,' Castus said as they emerged once more into the sunlight.

'Yes,' the curator said. 'But do you know the real strength of Nisibis, excellency?' He glanced at Castus, eyes narrowed.

Castus shrugged, shaking his head.

'Do you mind walking a short distance? No? Then follow me...'

They left the temple precinct and crossed the wide central avenue, the curator's bodyguards pushing a way through the crowd. They were attracting a small throng of followers now, men and a few women calling out to Vorodes, or even to Castus himself, with petitions of grievance. Both men were content to ignore them.

On the far side of the avenue they passed between the stalls in the portico and through a pillared gateway. The crowds were thicker here, and Castus sensed Sabinus and the two Protectores drawing closer to him, watching the faces around them. He felt a warm prickle of anxiety himself; since leaving Antioch he had relaxed a little, but now the threat of an attempt on his life was once more possible. Keeping his hand on his sword hilt, he followed Vorodes through the gloom of the gateway and out again into the sunlight.

'Welcome to the *wazar*!' the curator declared. 'Or the emporium, you might say.'

Castus had seen markets all over the empire, but seldom had he encountered a scene like this. What at first seemed a formless chaos of packed bodies emerged, as Castus moved slowly through it, into an intricate network of stalls and trading pitches: a town in miniature. Some of the stalls resembled large shacks or tents, others were a mere blanket spread on the ground.

Vorodes led him through the centre of the market, between towering stacks of amphorae and bales of cloth, stalls selling everything from ceramics to fish sauce to camels and slaves. There were entertainers too: dancers and singers, and high above the heads of the crowd a child walking on a stretched tightrope. Smoke drifted from charcoal fires and incense burners, and the air was rich with spices, mingling with the stink of dung and human sweat. And everywhere was the sound of commerce: the clink of coin, the rapid gestures of negotiation, the hustle of profit. Yes, Castus thought, *this* was the strength of Nisibis.

'As you know, excellency,' Vorodes was saying over his shoulder, 'Nisibis is one of only three cities where trade is permitted between the Persians and the empire, and certainly the most important. And via the Persian domains, we have traders coming from much further away. Sogdiana, Transoxiana, Gedrosia… other places you've perhaps never even heard of!'

'Hm,' said Castus. He had never heard of Transoxiana, or Gedrosia either. An array of mirrors in silvered bronze and smoked glass caught his reflection, and he looked quickly away.

'The caravans arrive in the eastern suburb, on the far side of the river,' the curator explained. 'There are lodgings for them there, and other… *amenities* for travellers. Their goods are checked by the customs agents, and they pay the usual tax of an eighth part of the value. We take a portion of that, and the rest goes into the imperial coffers. Only then can they cross the river, enter by the Gate of the Sun, and sell their goods here. So, you see, everyone profits!'

Castus turned his attention to the crowds once more. Sure enough, in one glance he could pick out men from all across the empire; and many of the faces and costumes were alien even to him. But all had been drawn here, to this crossroads of the world's commerce.

'And here,' Vorodes said, leading Castus up a short flight of steps into the cool shade of a portico, 'is the finest of all our emporia.'

The stalls here looked more permanent, and Castus noticed the grim-faced men standing guard all around them. The wares displayed in this part of the market were only for the wealthiest buyers.

'Look,' the curator said, lifting a bolt of cloth from one of the tables. 'This is the real thing. All the way from Seres, across the deserts of Bactria. You'll seldom find silk this fine in Rome.'

The cloth flowed in a liquid wave as Vorodes unrolled it. A shimmer of green and gold, like sunlit oil on water. The curator passed it to him, and Castus felt the brief caress of the silk across his scarred hands. Only one woman he had ever known had worn cloth of such quality, and she had died in a bathhouse in Rome. He stepped away, suppressing a shudder.

'Take it, please,' Vorodes said. 'A gift, from the Boule of Nisibis. For your wife, perhaps?'

Castus smiled tightly and shook his head, passing the silk back. He knew a bribe when he saw one.

'You must be keen to maintain good relations with Persia then, I expect,' he said. 'If the borders close, so do your trade routes.'

'Indeed they do,' Vorodes said, dropping the bolt of silk back onto the table with a brief gesture to the merchant. 'War is the enemy of all our prosperity!'

They walked together along the portico; Castus noticed that the curator's slaves were clearing the route ahead of them.

'I know it's not my place to ask,' the curator said quietly, 'but, as you can see, the situation between the emperor and the King of the Persians concerns us directly. I appreciate that you can't disclose anything of your plans, or the emperor's, but I wondered if you could give me, in confidence, any assurance that this city would not be directly affected by... whatever those in Constantinople might be discussing?'

Castus stopped, turning quickly on his heel to confront the other man. Vorodes blinked, but held his ground.

'What's discussed by the emperor is no business of yours, citizen.'

'Indeed not. But all of us know of recent events in Armenia. We know of the embassies sent by the Persians, and of the haste with which they returned. We've known only peace here for nearly forty years, excellency. If that's about to change, it would be pleasant to get some forewarning.'

Pleasant it might be, Castus thought. But any reassurance that Constantine was not planning an advance through Nisibis to the Tigris would be as good as an admission that the emperor would direct his troops down the Euphrates instead. And such information could no doubt be valuable to the enemy.

'The emperor has the wellbeing of all citizens at the forefront of his mind,' he said, picking the words with care. 'He is, as I'm sure you know, a great lover of peace.' It was an atrocious lie, but he could say nothing more.

Vorodes led him out of the gateway at the far end of the silk portico, around the flank of a public bath and back to the central colonnaded avenue. He seemed resigned to the fact that Castus would tell him no more about the plans for the coming war.

'If you still intend to pay a visit on Bishop Iacob, strategos,' the curator said, 'then best do it soon. He usually retires to pray in the middle of the afternoon.'

'I'll do that,' Castus said.

'But be careful. I have little time for the Christian faith, but the bishop is said to be a man of great power. A sort of sorcerer, you might say. He once cursed a group of women washing clothes in the river – they were partially naked, I believe, and refused to cover themselves – and caused all of their hair to fall out. And then he cursed a Persian merchant, for some fault or other, and the man exploded like a statue struck by lightning! Or so people say, at least.'

Castus raised an eyebrow. But he clasped his thumb between his fingers all the same, as a warding sign against evil.

'But I would be honoured if you came to my house for dinner this evening.' Vorodes smiled. 'If you have time, of course. I'd like to reassure myself that you haven't gone bald, and you are, shall we say, still all in one piece!'

CHAPTER IX

Nisibis was a city of temples. Besides the grand Tychaeion opposite the market, there were huge edifices dedicated to Baal Shamin and Beth Samas, to Sin and Tar'atha and Na'bu. The names were alien, but Castus recognised them all the same: Jupiter and Sol, Luna, Venus and Mercury. Gods he knew well, wearing the masks and costumes of a different land.

By contrast, the fifteen or so Christian churches in the city appeared rather modest. Even the synagogues of the Jews and the fire temple of the Zoroastrians were larger and more splendid. Only one – the Church of the Saviour – was impressive in size. That was Bishop Iacob's stronghold. And that was where Castus would have to go to find him. At least, he thought as he approached it along the colonnaded central avenue, the church had a commanding location. Built on the eastern flank of the citadel mount, the broad entrance steps and plain-looking face of the basilica loomed over the crowds in the agora below like a rebuke.

Climbing the steps, with Sabinus and the two bodyguards behind him, Castus kept his back straight and his chin up. He was a representative of the emperor, and of the might of the Roman army. Churches did not intimidate him, and neither did sorcerer-priests who could make men explode. So he told himself as he strode across the paved atrium court at the head of the steps, towards the massively carved main door of the basilica.

A cluster of either worshippers or beggars hung around the atrium and the doorway; it was hard, Castus thought, to tell the difference. They shrank away from him as he approached, several making pious gestures against evil. Castus snorted a laugh at the irony; now he was the bringer of ill omen! At the doors he halted, cracking the tip of his staff down on the paving. It occurred to him that he had never before entered a Christian church.

'What do we do?' he whispered over his shoulder to Sabinus. 'Do I just... walk in?'

'The church is open to all, Father,' Sabinus replied quietly. 'I'll go in first if you like. But we cannot enter carrying weapons.'

He stepped past Castus, slinging his sword baldric from his shoulder and passing it to one of the guards that accompanied them. Shrugging down his annoyance, Castus did the same. 'Make sure you don't lose it,' he said through his teeth.

Just inside the door, Sabinus wetted his fingers from a stone basin and touched them to his brow; Castus refused to repeat the gesture.

The inside of the basilica was dark after the noon sunlight, but as Castus's eyes adjusted he saw the brilliantly coloured mosaics covering the walls, the vaulted ceiling, the floor underfoot. He scanned the pictures, and saw crowds of people with strange blank faces moving in procession, animals being herded into a boat, terrified soldiers overwhelmed by the rushing sea...

'Enemy of Christ!' a voice declared in heavily accented Greek. 'Commander of the host of Satan! Persecutor of the faithful! You dare to enter God's house with innocent blood on your hands?'

Castus turned, and saw that one of the beggars from the doorway had followed him into the basilica. He was old – surely a decade older than Castus himself – with a perfectly bald head and a white-stubbled chin, and wore a rough brown cape with a grey tunic beneath.

'I've never persecuted any of your faithful, bishop,' Castus said, realising the man's identity. 'I never had the opportunity.' He heard Sabinus hiss through his teeth.

'You were a follower of the impious Diocletian, the God-hating Galerius?' the bishop said. 'You still venerate them, yes, as they burn in hellfire, and suck upon the teats of Satan?'

Victorinus, one of the Protectores, took a step forward, his hand moving instinctively towards the absent hilt of his sword. Castus waved him back. Cocking his head, he gave Iacob a twisted half-smile. The bishop appeared more absurd than offensive. Hard to imagine such a man having any real power. Although appearances were deceptive.

'You're welcome to your bigoted views, priest,' Castus said. 'But save your energy. The emperor I serve is Christian, and so is his son.'

Now it was Iacob's turn to laugh. An unsettling sight; his teeth were crooked and blackened. 'Yes, God has lifted the lamp of truth above the Palatine itself! We rejoice that our Augustus's heart has been filled with the Lord's love... So may Christ banish all falsehood. But what of his son, the Caesar? Is it true that he has sympathies for the heretical beliefs of Arius, whom the Almighty caused to explode on the toilet for his detestable sins?'

Castus grimaced, bemused. 'He's a Christian, as everyone knows.'

'So he doesn't favour the insane idea that Christ was somehow *made*, as a pot is made on a wheel, by God Almighty, out of some inferior substance?' the bishop said, stabbing the air with his finger and almost gnashing his teeth in his fervour. 'That the Son is a mere demiurge, rather than a being coexistent and eternal...? Or are you uninformed about the doctrinal controversies of our Church?'

'Do I *look* like I'm informed about the doctrinal controversies of your Church?'

'The Caesar is orthodox in his beliefs,' Sabinus said quickly. Their voices were echoing in the darkness of the basilica.

'Aah? Let us hope so,' the bishop said.

Turning to face him squarely, Castus hooked his thumbs in his belt and stuck out his jaw. 'I care nothing for your religious disputes,' he said in a low tone. 'But I'm told you're a person of influence in this city. I need to know that you'd use that influence wisely in a time of war.'

'Oh, have no fear of that, strategos,' the bishop said with a cracked smile. 'The Persians are the confirmed enemies of the Church, and all Christians hate them for their persecutions. You'll find no greater supporters of Rome in this city than my congregation. If you're looking for those who might prefer a new master, you should think of looking elsewhere.'

'Who do you mean?'

'Those who would find it hard to enter the Lord's kingdom. And those whose ancestors sinned against the light. And those who worship in the empty sepulchres of demons! Those are your enemies, strategos.'

Castus had heard enough. But as he was leaving the church, another man came hurrying up to him. A younger priest in a long tunic of clean unbleached wool. 'Excellency,' he said, bowing his head, 'please excuse the bishop. The holy father Iacob was fasting for many days over Pascha, and he struggles to contain his holiness...'

'Quite all right,' Castus said curtly. 'You can tell your bishop that I found the meeting very instructive. Let's both hope we don't need to repeat it, eh?'

It was only as he was marching up the slope towards the Strategion that he thought to ask Sabinus what the old bishop had meant by his last remark.

'In the holy texts, Christ said that the rich would find it hard to enter heaven,' Sabinus explained with an embarrassed shrug. 'They would be the members of the city council, I expect. The Jews sinned against the light by condemning Jesus. And those in the empty sepulchres would be the followers of the traditional religions.'

Castus snorted. 'Doesn't leave us many people to trust then, does it?' And in the dusty air he could almost hear the bishop laughing at him.

'And so you survived your meeting with our fearsome priest?' Gidnadius, the *Praeses Mesopotamiae*, asked. 'He didn't try to curse you, transform you into an animal, anything like that?'

'Nothing like that,' Castus told the governor. They were reclining on the couches in Vorodes's rooftop dining chamber. The curator's house stood on the northern slope of the citadel mount, close to the Strategion. Three of the chamber's walls had wide arches opening onto the roof garden, framing views across the city, the line of the walls and the open country beyond.

'In fact,' Castus went on, 'I suspect all the ranting is a sort of defence. He seemed more eager to warn me than curse me.'

'Interesting,' Vorodes replied, but said no more.

'He was insulting,' Sabinus broke in. 'The bishop, I mean. Eccentrics like him give the faith a bad name.'

'Then you shouldn't linger too long in the east, young man,' the governor said. 'Eastern religions are amazingly devoted to eccentricity!'

The dinner was more relaxed than Castus might have feared, and after a long day pacing the hot streets it was pleasant to recline on silken couches and sip chilled white wine. Slaves stood around the margins of the room with feather fans on long bamboo poles, waving the flies away from the table, and a cooling evening breeze flowed through the open archways.

Jewelled silver incense holders shaped like scorpions flavoured the air with their smoke.

Castus felt on edge all the same though, and tried to say as little as possible. Luckily Gidnadius, despite being a smug and fussy little man, was garrulous enough, praising the qualities of the various wines, the roast lamb in spiced apricot sauce, the asparagus and cucumber salad, even the pickled eggs. He quizzed Sabinus too about affairs at the palace in Antioch; clearly he was anxious to escape from Mesopotamia himself, and to rise in the imperial hierarchy.

Vorodes was a suitably gracious host. His son Barnaeus sat beside him; already a council member at barely sixteen years old, the boy was content to listen and say little. But the curator's wife had also joined them for dinner, and Castus found his attention far more drawn to her. Aurelia Sohaemia was a woman of around forty, dressed in a simple gown of plain white silk, a scarf draping her head and ivory bracelets on her bare arms. Castus had seen her before, he realised, in the crowd when he first entered the city. She had been dressed in the local style then, the towering beaded headdress and gauzy veil across her face and shoulders almost concealing her appearance. But he recognised her all the same. Her long features gave her an Arab or Persian look, and she could almost have appeared mournfully grave, but when she glanced in his direction Castus caught the quick intelligence in her eyes, the spark of warmth.

Gods, he thought to himself, and tried to concentrate on his food, and the conversation between Gidnadius and the others at the table. For over six months now he had been surrounded almost exclusively by men. The Caesar's court in Antioch was an entirely male domain, and in his travels since leaving the capital Castus had encountered only a few female slaves and matronly wives of officials. Every time he glanced up he seemed to catch Sohaemia's eye, and felt his blood quicken. *Don't be a fool*, he told himself. *Don't be an old fool, after all this time...*

When the meal was done, Vorodes called three musicians to entertain the guests with plangent melodies on the Armenian harp. As they played, Castus raised himself from the couch and went to the wide opening that led to the roof garden outside. Plants stood in terracotta urns, and the air smelled of herbs and blossom. The sun had set but there was still plenty of light in the sky; the mountains along the northern horizon stood out clear and black. The lines of the city walls were plain to see, the double ramparts and towers picked out by sentry fires. Within their circuit spread the tight-packed streets and houses of the city itself, a landscape of flat roofs in the low evening light, with the pillared shapes of temples and the domes of bathhouses rising between them. From this vantage, Castus could see almost the entire city as far as the northern gates. He heard distant chanting, dogs barking, the lowing of camels. The air had that characteristic smell of the eastern provinces, a dusty smoky yellow-brown scent. Dung fires and spices, Castus assumed. Something else too, a hint of musk and rosewater...

With a start he realised that the curator's wife had joined him on the rooftop. Sohaemia had a shawl around her bare shoulders, although the air was still warm. She stood close beside him, miming a shudder.

'My husband has already asked if you could tell us more about the emperor's strategy,' she said. Her voice was low, slightly husky. Castus could not tell if she was being deliberately seductive. 'I know,' she went on, 'that you cannot give us any details. I respect your discretion.'

When he had seen her glancing his way in the dining room, Castus had assumed that the curator had instructed his wife to charm him. Now he realised that things were the other way around. Of the two of them, Sohaemia was in charge here; she had told her husband what to ask in the market that day.

'I don't direct the emperor's intentions,' Castus said. 'I just prepare the ground. I'm more a steward than a military commander.'

She laughed lightly, though her nose. Then she half turned towards him, watching his profile as she spoke. 'Our lives here are very delicately balanced,' she said. 'You look at this city before you, and you see – what? Wealth, stability, commerce? Strong walls, a confident populace? All those things are here, but none of them can guarantee safety. Everything we have gained, everything we love and value, can be snatched from us in an instant. You military men, emperors and generals, you think of the armies and the campaign plans, the chances of victory and defeat. But out here we have to live with the consequences. So we have to plan for every eventuality. Armies bleed lands and cities alike, strategos. And wars kill more than just soldiers. You understand what I mean.'

Castus was trying not to look directly at the woman beside him, but he felt the intimacy of her presence in the gathering darkness. 'From what I know,' he said, almost in a whisper, 'you need not fear. Constantine won't direct his armies this way.'

He heard her exhale. She touched him on the shoulder, then pressed her palm against the muscle of his chest. 'Thank you,' she said. For a long moment she held the touch, then she went back inside.

Hours past midnight, and Castus lay sleepless on his mattress, staring into the darkness. Somewhere above him a moth was flitting around the ceiling, battering its wings against the walls. Had he told the curator's wife too much? Strictly speaking, he decided, he had. Had he done it purely because he desired her? Once again yes.

With a low groan he rolled onto his side and pulled the corner of the blanket over his head. The chamber was hot and airless, and he could still hear the moth fluttering about. He thought of Marcellina. She would be in Constantinople by now, he guessed, or even on the road eastwards already. Another couple of months, sixty days at most, and he would see her again. He missed her badly; how stupid he had been, he thought, to feel attracted to another.

In all his life, Marcellina had been the only woman to understand him, and see him for who he truly was. Castus had loved his first wife, Sabina, in a tortuous sort of way. But whatever affection she had returned had always been tainted by bitterness. Then there had been the Frankish slave, Ganna. And the emperor's wife Fausta too, whom Castus had almost hated and almost loved. Beyond them: a barbarian woman in the wilds beyond the northern frontier, an army prostitute in Britain, and a few more elsewhere. Now he came to think about it, Castus thought, he had been quite absurdly chaste.

All the more reason not to be misled now.

Sighing with annoyance, he sat up on the mattress and threw off the blanket. He had no idea of the hour; some time had passed since he last heard the calls of sentries from the military lines. The sky was already lightening with the coming dawn.

And somewhere on the far side of the hill the cockerel began to crow.

CHAPTER X

They were a day's ride north of Singara when they entered the desert. Since leaving Nisibis their route had taken them first through the fertile well-irrigated lands along the Mygdonius River, then across an expanse of scrubby fields and rough pastures. Now, quite suddenly, all signs of cultivation, and of civilisation, had fallen away. Castus and his escort rode across a vast ochre-grey plain of stone and dust, scored by dry ravines, and the horizon stretched empty and flat in all directions. It was the harshest and most alien landscape he had ever encountered.

'What do you see out there?' said Lycianus, the scout commander who had joined the party before they left Nisibis. He waved his arm at the emptiness.

'Nothing,' Castus replied as he rode. He wanted to spit, but his mouth was too dry. The air felt saturated with fine dust, and the sun filled earth and sky with heat. He twisted in the saddle, hot leather creaking beneath him, and narrowed his eyes. 'Nothing at all.'

Lycianus made a rasping sound that might have been a laugh. 'That's the way it looks, eh?'

'You see things differently?'

'I don't,' Lycianus said. 'But *they* do.' He pointed to the pair of slim dark horsemen who rode ahead of them. Lycianus had twenty of his own men with him, to act as scouts and foragers.

Equites Saraceni Indigenae, they were called: irregular cavalry recruited from the desert peoples. They wore no armour, just simple unbelted tunics and blanket cloaks, but each rider carried a bow and a long slender lance, and they looked more than capable of using them.

'And what do they see, these Saracens of yours?'

'They see, dominus,' Lycianus replied, 'a landscape as full and flourishing as the plains of Pannonia.' He gave a thin smile. 'They know every stone and every wadi. They read the sky and the wind. They know the good camping grounds, the places where a man can draw water from the earth, or find fodder for his horses. They know the places of battle, and the lines of retreat. The places sacred to the gods, and those haunted by demons!'

Castus sniffed, and rubbed his tongue over his teeth. Squinting again, he stared into the emptiness and tried to imagine it as something more than a wilderness. He could not. Granted, here and there he could make out clusters of dry thorny scrub in the crevices, even a few wiry clumps of tamarisk showing pinkish in the surrounding drabness. But there was nothing more. The hoof-beats of their horses crunched, loud in the surrounding stillness. A hot wind plucked twists of dust from the stony ground. This was a hostile place, he thought, a malevolent place. Lycianus's mention of demons caused his shoulder blades to tighten.

He was riding with the vanguard of the column, as usual. Behind him the line of men and horses and camels stretched away into the pluming dust. It was easy to see why so many Roman armies had been beaten by the Persians and their nomad allies in this land: this was cavalry country. Any infantry force caught out in the open here would be surrounded and annihilated. Mysterious, Castus thought, why anyone would want to fight over such a desolate place.

Lycianus himself was a mystery too. How old was he? Castus could not tell. Perhaps fifty. A big man though, almost as big as Castus himself, and a fine horseman, with a look of tightly controlled power about him. His skin was burned almost as dark as the men he commanded, but his eyes were pale blue and his sandy hair bleached the colour of old ivory.

Before Lycianus had joined them, the tribune Egnatius had told Castus a little more about the man. He was not a native of this country, but came originally from Moesia on the Danube; he had joined the army under Galerius, and fought in the Armenian war as a trooper of the Scutarii under Maximinus Daza. A few years later he had been captured by the Saracens, and had spent nearly ten years as their prisoner. The experience served him well; by the time he was released he knew the language and culture of the desert peoples fluently, and had made important allies among them. Lycianus had risen fast in the army since then. Now he held the official rank of praepositus, but his actual role was harder to pin down. He ranged widely with his irregulars, all across the sweep of the desert frontier, and seemed to have little regard for military hierarchy.

A useful sort of officer, Castus thought, although a difficult one to manage.

By that evening they were in sight of the great barren ridge that screened Singara, and as the sun dropped they made camp below the northern slope, near the ruin of an old mud-brick *castellum* crumbling into dust. The scouts found tamarisk and thorn bushes for a fire, and as the light turned the flanks of the ridge to glowing copper-red they slaughtered a pair of gazelles they had brought down with their bows. Castus sat near the fire and watched the Saracens casting the chunks of meat into the embers to roast. Sabinus was with him; Egnatius and Diogenes too. Lycianus returned from his tour of the piquets and took a seat on the blanket beside them. Weary from the hot day's travel, and lulled by the cool of evening and the smoke of the fire, for a long time none of them spoke. The slaves brought roasted meat, with bread and wine. Diogenes alone refused it; he had long ago given up eating flesh, for philosophical reasons that Castus did not even try to understand.

'How many different tribes of Saracen are there?' Diogenes asked at last.

Lycianus stared at the fire, unblinking. In the gathering darkness the camels roared as they were hobbled, and the troopers laughed and talked quietly as they ate their evening meals.

'There are many tribes,' the scout commander said. 'As many as the birds in the sky, some say, and almost as many kings to rule them. But until recently they were all gathered under the rule of the Banu Lakhm, based at Hira, an oasis town far to the south.'

'You've been there?' Castus asked.

'Oh, yes,' Lycianus said with the flicker of a smile. 'I spent some time there. The Lakhmids paid tribute to the Persians, but while King Shapur was only a boy they became very independent. Too independent, the Persians thought. So, a dozen years ago, when Shapur reached manly age, he led a great campaign against them and conquered Hira. Many died, and many more were taken captive.'

'He forced an alliance on the survivors?' Sabinus asked, dry-voiced.

'Some of them. Others wouldn't agree to it. So Shapur made an example of them.'

They waited in silence for Lycianus to say more. Night had fallen now, and the flames of the fire had died down.

'You see those long lances that my men carry?' Lycianus asked. 'Well, Shapur took each of the Saracen prisoners who would not submit to him – there were thousands of them – and he drove one of those lances through the muscle of their right shoulder, piercing them front to back. Many of them died of the wounds. Those that did not would never use a weapon again.'

Castus shuddered, feeling a sympathetic ache in his chest. Chewing at the half-raw gazelle meat, washing it down with vinegar wine, he tried not to imagine the scene. He had known many atrocities in war, but nothing so creative in its cruelty. 'Better just to kill them,' he said.

Lycianus shrugged. 'Maybe so,' he said. 'But it was a terrible act, a fearsome act. The Saracens regard such things with awe, you see. Awe and respect. *Dhu'l Aktaf*, they call Shapur now – the Piercer of Shoulders.' He gave a mirthless rasp of a laugh.

'But I understand that they're divided in their allegiances,' Diogenes broke in. 'Why do some still fight for the Persians? And which of them fight for us?'

'There was a young prince of the Lakhmids who escaped the slaughter at Hira,' Lycianus said. 'A man called Imru al-Qays. He rode west across the desert and joined his mother's people, the Azdites of the Banu Tanukh. Very soon he gained power over the Tanukhids, and proclaimed himself king of all the desert Arabs between Syria and the borders of Egypt. He was a great man, Imru al-Qays...'

'You knew him too?' Castus said.

Lycianus nodded. 'He was... a friend, you could say. A friend and client of Rome too. The Augustus Constantine gave him the title of phylarch, military commander of all the Tanukhids and their allies, and he served us well. He even became a Christian!'

Sabinus made a choking sound as he ate, and gulped heavily. 'There are Christians among these barbarians?'

'Quite a few,' Lycianus told him. 'On our side at least. They had a bishop as well, although I don't know what happened to him. Imru al-Qays died eight years ago, and left his realm to his three sons by his second wife. Sadly the sons soon fell to fighting among themselves. One, the eldest, rode back east and submitted to Shapur, who made him King of the Lakhmids at Hira. The other two warred for a long time. One killed the other, and took the title of phylarch, but he died less than a year ago. A scorpion in his shoe, so they say.'

'So who rules the Tanukhids now?' Castus asked. It was an important question. Just as Nisibis and the Tigris fortresses guarded the north-eastern flank of the Roman domain, so the Tanukhid Saracens protected the desert routes south of the Euphrates. Their allegiance would be vital in the campaign to come.

'Imru al-Qays had another son, by his third wife, a young princess of the Azdites,' Lycianus said. 'But his older sons never accepted her, and the boy was only born after his father died. There are many chiefs among the Tanukh who would set themselves up as regent until he comes of age to rule. But you'll meet them soon enough, dominus!'

'When?'

'Around the time of next month's full moon, if all goes well,' Lycianus told him. 'Plenty of ground to cover before then.'

The fire was dying down, and Castus stretched out and pulled a blanket over himself. Lying on his back, he gazed up at the brilliance of the stars, hazed here and there by smoke. A sense of emptiness came over him, as if the spirit of this desolate land had seeped into his blood. What was he doing here, so far from the place he called home? Why was he journeying through this empty landscape, this violent and demon-haunted world of alien peoples and strange gods? He should be far away, with Marcellina at his side...

As he drifted towards sleep he heard the voices of Lycianus and the others still sitting beside the glowing embers.

'But why are they so addicted to war and strife, these people?' Diogenes asked. 'It seems to me that this land is broad and empty enough for any number of Saracens to wander at will.'

'You don't understand them,' Lycianus said. 'Few people do. *I* do, a little. They have a fierce regard for freedom, and a sense of honour that would leave the proudest Roman in the dust.'

'But what are they fighting for? There are no cities out here, few enough places that you could call, well... *places*. Their allegiances seem to shift like the sand. What drives them to these endless feuds?'

'What drives them?' Lycianus said, and Castus could hear the smile in his voice. 'The most important thing they know. Something they prize above all else, above even honour. The thing they call *tha'rr*.' The word was a guttural sound in his throat.

'What's that?' Sabinus asked quietly.

'Hard to translate,' Lycianus told him. 'But we would probably call it *revenge*.'

Singara, Castus soon decided, was surely one of the hottest, dustiest and most flyblown garrisons on the entire Roman frontier. The fortress stood on rising ground below the great ridge, with the open desert stretching away to the south. More than three thousand men were based there, from the First and Sixth Parthica legions, a couple of cavalry units and a *numerus* of Gothic *auxilia*, and Castus pitied every last one of them. But the walls were strong, the fortress well provisioned, and after three days inspecting the troops and giving the officers the same orders he had given to Romulianus at Nisibis, Castus was glad to be on his way again.

The road ran south-west across the arid plain, towards the valley of the Chaboras River, which would lead them down to the Euphrates. It was an old road, little more than a track, but for the first few hours Castus picked out the weathered milestones still marking the distances. One of them still bore a faded inscription, naming the emperor Severus Alexander.

But a little further the milestones were gone, the ridge of Singara had sunk below the northern horizon, and there was nothing but bare sand and rock in every direction. Somewhere to the south, only a few miles away, lay the effective limits of the Roman Empire. No wall or ditch marked it, no river or natural boundary. The power of Rome just faded into the empty dust, and somewhere beyond that dust the realm of the Sassanid Persians, Iran-Shahr, began.

'Scorpions,' the orderly Vallio said, riding behind Castus. 'Scorpions and flies. Flies and snakes, and nasty little spiky bushes. That's all there is here… Why'd anyone want to live in such a ghastly place as this?'

'Some find it beautiful,' said Diogenes in a dubious tone.

There was a kind of beauty to it, Castus had to admit, especially in the evenings and the early morning, when the light played across the barren land and the sky glowed luminous blue. But it was an inhuman beauty all the same, and in the heat of midday it was hard to appreciate. Sweat was pouring off him as he rode, soaking his clothes. He had taken to wearing a thin scarf draped around his head, as he had seen the Saracens doing, but the sun reflected up from the stony ground and glared in his eyes all the same. He lifted his canteen and sucked a mouthful of warm water, sulphur-tasting from the springs at Singara, then swilled his mouth and spat.

'Why is that crippled mongrel following us?' Egnatius asked, riding up alongside. Castus looked back: a rangy-looking dog with three legs was hopping along the verge of the road, tongue lolling.

'It's been following me since we were in Singara,' Diogenes explained. He was apparently oblivious to the heat, although he was sweating profusely, and his bald head was reddened by sunburn. 'It appeared hungry, so I fed it, and ever since it won't leave me alone! But I've come to rather like it – a most intelligent creature. I think I might observe it, for philosophical purposes.'

'Certainly it's got some notion of where it's next meal's coming from,' Egnatius said. The dog looked up at him with a hopeful grin.

'Keep it if you want,' Castus told Diogenes. He had never been fond of dogs. 'But it's not getting any of our rations... And put something on your head before the sun boils your brains!'

Through the heat of noon they continued south-westwards. It was late afternoon, the light glaring in the faces of the riders, when Lycianus came galloping back to join Castus. 'Dominus,' he called, swinging his arm to the southward. 'Company!'

Castus tugged the reins, slowing his horse as he craned up in the saddle and stared in the direction of the scout commander's gesture. An empty horizon, bare grit and stones. 'What am I supposed to be looking at?' he said through his teeth.

'Dust,' Lycianus replied.

'I can see that!'

'No, the cloud, there on the horizon. Many horses, so the scouts say, perhaps camels too, moving parallel to us.'

Squinting, face bunched, Castus tried to make out some telltale smudge in the air. But the faint eastern breeze was carrying the dust of his own baggage camels and cavalry horses up along the column, and compared to that the southern sky appeared clear. Just a slight discolouration of the blue, he thought, a yellowness just above the horizon. Sabinus rode up to join him with the other two Protectores; Egnatius was close behind.

'A Persian patrol, do you think?' Sabinus asked.

'Maybe. Could just be roaming tribesmen,' Castus said, almost to himself. 'Or a merchant caravan, perhaps...'

'No merchants use this route, dominus,' Lycianus told him. 'And if they did, they'd be up here on the road with us, not wandering about out there in the open *qafr*. The Sassanids don't tend to range this close to our frontier either.'

'So what are they?' Castus snapped.

'We'll know soon enough,' Lycianus said, glancing at the position of the sun. 'If they're friendly, they'll send a party over to greet us. Probably ask to share our camping ground. Custom of the desert. If not...'

The scout commander appeared more annoyed than surprised, Castus noticed. Perhaps, he wondered, Lycianus blamed himself for not noticing the new arrivals sooner. 'How far to the next fort?'

'That'd be Praesidium Qatna, on the Chaboras. We could reach the river by nightfall if we rode hard, but we'd tire the horses, and our column'd be spread out along the road. Easy target. Riding in the dark's out of the question in this rough country. So we'll have to camp for the night, better sooner than later. Whoever's out there'll make their move before long, for good or ill.'

Castus was still staring at the horizon, expecting to pick out a line of horsemen dark against the glowing sky. He looked back at the column behind him. Egnatius had left small parties of his Armigeri troopers at various forts and cities along the road from Antioch, but he still had thirty with him, and with Lycianus's Saracens that gave Castus fifty armed horsemen. More than enough, he guessed, to deter any but the most ambitious desert raiders.

'Order your men to find us a camp ground,' he told Lycianus. 'We'll set up our perimeter before nightfall – no tents, in case we need to move quickly – then let's see what our friends out there want to do.'

They rode on in silence, every man in the column turning to scan the southern approaches as news of the interlopers spread among them. Lycianus told some of his men to keep a close watch in the opposite direction too, just in case.

'It's strange,' he said to Castus a while later. 'It's not been thirty days since the spring equinox. The tribes always keep a truce for a month either side of it.'

'A truce?' Sabinus said, and snorted a laugh. 'How very civilised!'

'In honour of the goddess, Al-Uzza,' Lycianus explained, turning to Sabinus. 'Who we would call Lucifer, the morning star. I'm afraid plenty of the Saracens are still idol-worshippers, as you would put it!'

Castus shot him a glance, frowning. He had already determined that the scout commander had no love for Christians. 'So, what?' he growled. 'They're not supposed to fight anybody?'

'Maybe they're Christians out there?' Sabinus said with a grim smile.

'Or maybe they've been told that *we're* Christians,' Lycianus replied. 'Or Romans, anyway, and somebody's promised them a good bounty for our heads!'

They camped for the night on a broad expanse of flat sandy ground, just off the road, with a dry watercourse choked with thorn bushes marking one flank. The ground was too hard to dig trenches, but Castus ordered the troopers to cut the bushes and sharpen the spiny tips of the branches, setting them as a rough barrier on the other three sides of the position. On Lycianus's suggestion, he also ordered fires lit around the perimeter, with sentries stationed between each one. Then, with the camels hobbled and the horses tethered in lines, Lycianus sent a party of his men out on a patrol to the south to try and discover who was shadowing them along the horizon. They returned as night fell, with nothing to report; whoever it was out there in the open desert had melted away ahead of them, and they had seen nobody.

'Ah well,' Castus called, 'maybe we'll have a quiet night of it after all!' A couple of the troopers grinned back at him, but few appeared convinced.

He remained awake until after midnight all the same, pacing the perimeter with Egnatius. The wind was picking up, booming in from the blackness of the desert laden with dust and fine sand. Sparks flurried from the watchfires, the camels moaned and roared and the horses stamped and whinnied. Castus pulled his scarf up over his mouth and peered into the darkness. He had a tent-party of Armigeri troopers armed and ready beside their saddled horses, in case of sudden alarms. Was he being too careful? Perhaps so, he thought; but something about the groaning wind, the whipping sparks from the fires and the dust steadily dulling the stars overhead set his nerves on edge.

Sabinus came to relieve him, yawning and rubbing the grit from his eyes. Castus clapped a hand on his son's shoulder, squeezing the muscle. 'You have command,' he said quietly, then stumbled towards his sleeping mat.

He washed his face and mouth with water, then lay down and tugged the blanket over himself. It was already full of fine sand, and he cursed as he shook at it.

'Dominus?' said Vallio, appearing from the darkness. 'Would you like to use the silk to cover yourself? It'll protect you from the dust.'

'Silk?' Castus mumbled irritably. 'What silk?'

'Your silk, dominus. In your baggage.'

Vallio moved away, then returned with a heavy bolt of cloth in his hands. Castus felt it, and his irritation flared into anger. 'How long have we been carrying this?' he demanded.

'Since Nisibis. You bought it there, I thought?'

'I did nothing of the kind!' Castus growled. Who had slipped it into his baggage before he left the city? The curator, or his wife Sohaemia? Clever of them anyway. A parting gift, perhaps, or a last bribe.

Suddenly he laughed. 'Take it away,' he said. 'No point in spoiling it with dust, eh?'

Lying down again, he rolled until the blankets covered him. He could give the silk to Marcellina, he supposed, when he met her in Antioch. That at least was a pleasing thought. He smiled, and a moment later he was asleep.

CHAPTER XI

The attackers came in the blackness before dawn, with the dust-laden wind behind them. A scream from the darkness, a drumming of hooves on stony ground, then the first riders were leaping in across the thorn hedge, blasting through the sleeping camp as the cries of alarm shattered the stillness.

Castus was awake at once, his mind sharp as he grabbed for the sword lying beside him. Blindly he stared into the gloom; the darkness was filled with whirling dust and smoke, the milling shapes of men and horses and the flicker of arrows. Stumbling to his feet, he drew his sword; pointless to try and find his horse, and he fancied his chances better on foot in this chaotic murk. Around him men yelled and screamed, horses kicked and reared, and all sense of direction was gone.

'Protect the strategos!' somebody was yelling. 'Protect the magister! Shields – *now*!'

Figures ran from the gloom, dismounted troopers forming around him, shields raised. Vallio appeared, lugging Castus's own shield. The standard-bearer was with him, and in moments Castus stood at the centre of a knot of men. The fight swept around them in the turmoil of gritty dust. Arrows banged into the shield boards; one of the troopers gave a stifled cough of pain as he fell.

'Father!' Sabinus cried, pushing his way into the defensive ring. 'Father, we didn't see them coming – they walked their horses past the piquets and we only heard them when they broke into a gallop!' An arrow whipped past his head, and he flinched.

'Get your shield up,' Castus snarled. 'Protect my back.'

A charging horse veered from the dust, lit briefly by the embers of a fire. Two men flung spears, and Castus saw the rider turn in the saddle and shoot before spinning his horse and riding clear. The beating of hooves, and two more horsemen rode past; they wore unbelted Roman tunics this time.

'We're going to kill our own men in this darkness!' a biarchus of the Armigeri shouted.

Horns wailed, and somewhere in the dirty fog Castus heard the noise of blades rattling against shield rims. The wind was beginning to thin the dust now, and in the faint pre-dawn light the shapes of the surrounding encampment were becoming clearer. Castus was breathing hard, his heart running fast. From along the eastern perimeter he could hear the shouts of the sentry parties: all clear.

The raiders had vanished as quickly as they had appeared, leaving bloody destruction in their wake.

'They knew what they were doing,' Egnatius said, scrubbing a hand across his scalp. His hair stuck up in spikes, sweat matted with dust. 'Feint attack from the west, then a main strike from the south and rode straight through us. Testing us, I'd say.'

Castus nodded. 'What's the damage?'

'Four of my troopers dead and five more wounded, though none too badly. We lost three of the slaves, and two of Lycianus's piquets killed before the attack. Oh, and one of yours is in a bad way too.'

Castus found his son kneeling beside the body of his fellow Protector, Victorinus. The man had been speared as he struggled up from his blankets, a grievous wound in his belly. He still lived, but pain convulsed his features and blood leaked steadily from his wound, blackening the dust around him.

'It was my fault,' Sabinus said, standing as two of the Armigeri troopers tried to staunch and bind the wound. 'I'm sorry. It was my fault – I was in command. I should have seen them before they attacked…'

'Quiet,' Castus said gruffly. He grabbed his son by the nape of his neck and squeezed. 'It was a well-planned attack, and if anyone's to blame it's me.'

'Will he live?' Sabinus asked quietly, angling his head towards the fallen man.

'Not for long. Give him wine if he'll take it, then load him and the dead men onto the baggage camels.'

Metrophanes had been injured too; the plump little numerarius sat on the ground, face pale, fumbling as he tried to wrap a linen bandage around the arrow gash in his upper arm. He looked more shocked than badly hurt. As Castus approached, the wind took the bandage and whipped the end of it away into the dirt. Castus knelt beside the man, tying the linen quickly.

'Thank you dominus,' Metrophanes said, voice quavering. 'I'm sorry… I've never been wounded before.'

'I don't need you for your bravery,' Castus told him. 'Can you still use your arm?'

The man nodded.

'Then get your horse saddled; we're moving.' Diogenes' three-legged dog came hopping by, nuzzling the bloodied ground, and Castus nudged it away with his boot.

'Dominus,' Lycianus said, striding through the windblown grit. 'You should see this.'

A group of soldiers stood around another downed man; one of the attackers, at least, had not survived the raid. As Castus approached, the soldiers kicked at the corpse, spat upon it, jabbed it with spears.

'Stand away,' Castus ordered. Then he dropped to kneel beside the body. The man was young, barely more than a youth, with a downy moustache and long hair bound with a rag. He wore a quilted linen doublet and a loincloth, both stained with blood. Flies were already massing around his eyes and mouth.

'Lakhmid, probably,' Lycianus said. 'Saracen certainly. But this is Persian.' He tugged a dagger in an inlaid scabbard from beneath the body.

Castus got to his feet, rubbing the dirt from his palms. The sun must be up by now, he thought, although it was screened by the mass of dust in the eastern sky. Only a dull reddish glow filtered through, turning the desert the colour of dried blood.

'You know they weren't just raiders?' Lycianus said quietly.

'I know that. Somebody knew we were here.'

'Somebody knew *you* were here, I'd say. Only the chance of killing or capturing the supreme Roman commander, the Magister Equitum per Orientem himself, would cause a band of desert nomads to attack an armed military camp!'

Castus frowned grimly. He had been thinking the same thing. He had been careful to keep the details of his movements as secret as possible, but the officers at Singara knew where he was going, and many others too. But no, he thought: there would not have been enough time for a spy at Singara to summon these attackers. Nisibis then... Angrily he shook his head. Knowing who had betrayed them would not help him now.

'They have Persians leading them, you think?' he asked Lycianus.

'Possibly. But they're still out there – I sent a couple of scouts to patrol and they reported enemy horsemen spread out to the north and east of us. No idea of numbers. They're waiting till we move, then they'll hit us again.'

Castus was peering to the eastward; he could see nothing of the enemy, but the sky was a brown wall. 'That looks dirty,' he said.

'Dust storm, coming this way. Maybe an hour till we feel it.'

'Can we reach Qatna any faster?'

Lycianus frowned, considering. 'If we head south along this wadi we'll get to a dry plateau. Due west across that and we'll reach the fort. Three hours, maybe four, if we move fast.'

'We'll do that,' Castus said. He strode across the camp to where Egnatius was marshalling his Armigeri troopers. 'Get them mounted up,' he ordered. 'Every man in body armour and helmet, ready to fight. We ride in close formation, baggage camels at the centre, fast as we can but steady – don't let any gaps open between us.'

Egnatius saluted and gave his orders. Heaving himself into the saddle, Castus rode over to join Lycianus again. The scout commander sat motionless on his horse, staring into the approaching brown murk. He mumbled something under his breath.

'What was that?' Castus asked.

'Arab saying,' Lycianus told him, smiling grimly. '*War is the mother of dust.*'

They knew the enemy were out to their left, and as they rode every man was hunched in the saddle, sheltering behind his shield rim and peering over his shoulder every few heartbeats, alert for the first galloping assault. Ahead of the storm the air was clearer, and the sun glared on the broken ground, the dry stones along the lip of the wadi, the tangled twists of thorn and tamarisk. Lycianus took the lead, guiding the column at a steady trot, while Castus rode with his staff at the head of the main body of cavalry, his standard-bearer at his back carrying the purple draco whipping in the breeze.

Only an hour since sunrise, and already the day was getting hot. Sweat was pouring from beneath Castus's helmet, soaking the rag he had tied across his nose and mouth. The metal of his cuirass burned to the touch, and a river of liquid flowed down his spine to pool above his waistband. He glanced across his shoulder and saw Sabinus close to his right. Metrophanes rode behind him, cradling his injured arm. Diogenes was carrying the three-legged dog on the saddle before him, its head poking out from the folds of his cloak.

'There they are!' Egnatius called. Castus turned his head sharply, and saw the shapes of men and horses appearing from the haze of glowing dust across the eastern plain. They looked like ghosts at first, a line of them riding parallel to the Roman column, then took more solid form as they drew closer.

'They're trying to get ahead of us,' Sabinus cried. 'They want to surround us!'

Lycianus had seen it too; already he was quickening his pace. The rest of the column followed him, the horses breaking into a canter. The air was saturated with dust; Castus felt it gritting in his throat. The saddle pounded beneath him as his horse laboured over the rough ground.

'Turn your shields!' one of the soldiers yelled. 'Archers!'

Sure enough, shafts were dropping between the horses. Castus glanced to his right, and saw another body of Arab horsemen riding up on the opposite flank, shooting from the saddle. Still at long range for now, the arrows arcing. Lycianus's men were already shooting back.

Up ahead, the wadi opened to a dry stony riverbed, clear of bushes. Lycianus turned to the right, leading the column up the dry bluffs above the river towards the flat ground of the plateau. As the camels laboured up the slope, Castus turned and saw the main body of the enemy veering in pursuit, riding straight for their rearguard. Then they were onto the plateau, and their pace increased. Ten miles of flat open country to the Chaboras, and the shelter of the fort. Castus could feel the wind at his back, pushing him onwards. This was a race now.

Screams from the right; the sudden change of direction had brought Egnatius's troopers smashing into the thin screen of enemy horse archers. Castus saw a Lakhmid rider brought down by a lance, his horse collapsing beneath him in a fountain of dust. He was yelling at his men to keep moving, keep formation, but the damp rag across his face muffled his words. Furious, he tore it away and breathed dust instead.

'Coming up fast on the left!' Sabinus shouted. Castus risked a look: sure enough, the enemy vanguard had crossed the dry river and were already outpacing them.

'You see him?' The sound of Sabinus's voice was almost shredded by the wind.

Castus stared, his eyes stinging. One of the riders wore a tall pointed cap and a scale cuirass; his horse trappings were hung with flashing gold ornaments and tassels of red and green.

'Persian?'

'Could be,' Castus yelled back. 'He's leading them anyway!'

The next moment, a pall of wind-driven dust rolled across them, eclipsing the sunlight and plunging the mounted men and the galloping horses into dim brown shadow. Castus dipped his head, eyes tight shut, feeling his horse shudder and flinch. Sand hissed in his ears, and through it he heard Sabinus's cry of warning.

'They're coming!'

The enemy riders had veered again just as the first wave of the dust storm hit them; now they came charging out of the racing brown fog, straight into the flank of the Roman column as it buckled in confusion. Castus saw horses all around him – his own men, massing to protect him. But the Arab horsemen had broken their line; arrows cut in from both sides, and then all cohesion and direction were gone.

Castus had his sword in his hand, but the dust was blinding him and he could barely control his horse. Terror drove through him; he would die here, lost and confused in the middle of a dust storm... A javelin flashed past, and he felt his horse shudder beneath him as an arrow scored its flank. No sign of Sabinus or Egnatius. He gritted his teeth, dug in his spurs and pushed forward, deeper into the swirl of the melee.

A pony appeared out of the dust, galloping hard, the rider leaning back in the saddle and then flinging a spear. Castus leaned just in time, and the missile darted past him. A heartbeat later and the pony crashed against the side of his horse, the Arab in the saddle slashing at him with a short sword. Castus aimed a clumsy cut across his body, but the enemy rider was still pressing his left flank. Spurring his horse forward, Castus reached out with his crippled left hand and seized the man by the neck of his tunic, dragging him halfway out of the saddle. But the Lakhmid pony was still galloping alongside, the man gripping tight to the saddle with his knees. He hooked his arm around Castus's body and started stabbing the short blade into the small of his back; Castus felt the point denting the plate of his cuirass. He punched the man's head with the pommel of his sword, but still the attacker's grip would not slacken.

'Just fucking *die*!' Castus snarled.

He managed to get the blade of his sword round in front of him, pressed the point into the side of the man's neck, then thrust across the saddle. The Arab let out a gargling scream as the blade went in. He clung on for a moment more, then Castus kicked him clear and rode on.

Only ten paces' visibility in front of him. Vague shapes of horses and men plunging in close combat. The blown sand and dust scoured his face as he stared around him. A figure ran from the murk: Metrophanes, his horse gone, the bandage trailing from his wounded arm.

'To me!' Castus bellowed, pulling on the reins. The plump numerarius almost tripped and fell as he stared back in fright, then he recognised Castus and stretched out his arm. Castus seized him, dragging the man up behind him in the saddle as his horse blew and shied.

'Dominus, here!' A biarchus of the Armigeri was leading a riderless horse. Between them they wrestled Metrophanes across into the saddle.

Was the dust clearing? Castus risked a glance behind him. Through stinging eyes he saw the shapes of the desert he had just crossed, the bodies of the dead and injured strewn on the ground, a camel galloping free, spilling baggage. Two or three men on foot, running or limping: his own men or the enemy's, it was impossible to say.

And a horse with green and red tasselled trappings, a rider with a raised lance, galloping straight towards him.

Castus managed to turn his own horse just in time, wheeling the big gelding to get his sword towards the attacker. He saw the lance jab at his face, and slashed with his blade to knock it aside. The Persian rider pushed with the shaft, almost shoving him out of the saddle, then let the lance drop and swept out his sword.

The two horses circled, necks weaving and legs kicking. The Persian aimed a blow and Castus rolled, letting the blade glance off the back of his cuirass. Then he stabbed, leaning forward in the saddle. The Persian reared back, too slow, then cried out as Castus's sword jabbed him beneath the arm, above the edge of his scale armour. Not deep, but enough to wound him.

Castus felt a spearhead slam into his back. His cuirass stopped the blow, but the force was like a hammer to the base of his spine. He pitched in the saddle, almost sliding off, seeing the Lakhmid horseman on the far side of him turning and angling his weapon for a second strike. His sword had jolted from his hand and was dangling by the wrist-cord, and the Persian officer was closing in on his right.

Dust exploded around them, Sabinus and two mounted troopers plunging between Castus and his assailants. Slumping in the saddle, Castus saw his son hack at the Persian officer, a single blow almost cleaving the man's shoulder. He raised himself, hissing a breath through his teeth, and the pain punched up into his chest.

'Father, are you wounded?' Sabinus cried, seizing the bridle of his horse.

'No,' Castus managed to say. 'No – just bruised, I think… let's go!'

He could barely feel his arms as he recovered and sheathed his sword. No idea of direction, or any real notion of his surroundings. Castus concentrated on staying upright, remaining in the saddle and keeping close behind his son.

They rode onwards, with the stormclouds rolling dark plumes all around them. Lycianus appeared with two of his men, and reported that the enemy attack had been driven off. 'They're still out there, dominus, hanging on our flank,' he said. 'But with their commander down I don't know if they'll risk another attack.'

'How far to the fort?' Castus said through his teeth.

'We could see it by now if the air was clearer!'

Slowing the pace, they took time to regroup. Six riderless horses, and another three men missing. It could have been worse. Forming up, they rode onwards with Lycianus in the lead. Another fifty paces, then a hundred. Then, quite suddenly, they rode clear of the dust and into clean bright air and sunlight. The storm still towered at their backs, but up ahead of them was Praesidium Qatna, a foursquare mud-brick fort with towers at each corner, surrounded by a straggling village and patchwork of fields along the riverbank beyond.

Castus wanted to sob in gratitude. Instead he ordered the trumpets sounded and the standards raised.

Moments later, the gates were open and the ragged column was riding through the arch and into the central courtyard of the fort. Castus slid down from the saddle, took a waterskin and sluiced the dust and sweat from his scalp and face. Then he stood with teeth clenched, arms raised, as Vallio cut away the straps of his cuirass and prised the dented metal plates off his body. He shouted in pain as he lowered his arms again, then felt the relief flooding through him.

The courtyard was packed with men and animals, camels milling and shaking dust, troopers unsaddling and rubbing down their sweating horses, others attending to the wounded and the bodies of the dead. Castus sat on the broad coping of the well while the slaves hauled up more skins of water. His whole torso felt bruised, his spine and chest aching fiercely. But he was shaken too, weak inside with the sensation of delayed shock and fear. *That should not have happened.* He was supreme commander of the Roman army in the east, by the emperor's command, and he had almost thrown his life away in some chaotic desert skirmish. A swell of nausea rose in him and he swallowed it down, then drank water to hide his nervous discomfort.

'You're the Magister Equitum?' said a dark-skinned man with curly greying hair, shoving his way through the throng. He appeared dubious of Castus's identity.

'I am,' Castus told him, squinting. 'And you are?'

'Flavius Philippus, excellency,' the officer replied, and saluted. 'Praepositus commanding the garrison detachment of the Twelfth Palestinian Cohort.'

'What are the enemy doing, praepositus?'

'Not much,' Philippus replied. 'My sentries reckon there's between one and two hundred of them out there, but they've mostly retreated to the east now. We're more than strong enough to fight off any attempt they might make on the walls.'

'Have they come in that sort of number before?'

'Never!' the officer said, wide-eyed. 'I've been here five years, and all we've seen is occasional raiding parties, bandits and the like. The *sarakenoi* have never attacked us – they flee from our patrols.'

Castus stood up with a grunt of effort. The praepositus led him up the steps to the rampart, Castus leaning heavily on

Sabinus's shoulder as he climbed. On the walkway above the main gate, they peered out across the desert to the east. The dust storm was passing now, the air clearing in its wake, and the enemy horsemen were disappearing with it. A few still lingered at the margins of the plain, lit strangely by the sun against the dark sky, but soon all had vanished below the horizon.

'Think they'll be back?' Sabinus asked.

Castus frowned, leaning forward onto the wall. If he put his weight on his hands, his bruised spine didn't ache so badly. 'Not for a while, and perhaps not at all,' he said. 'From here down to Circesium we'll be following the Chaboras. No more open desert until we're on the far side of the Euphrates.'

He muttered a quick prayer, and touched his brow. With the luck of the gods, he thought, the riders that had ambushed them would not keep up their attack now their leader was dead.

'Thanks for getting between me and that Persian,' he said to Sabinus. 'I think he had me there.'

'I couldn't see what was happening,' his son said with a diffident shrug, staring at the desert. 'I just acted on instinct...'

Castus cuffed his shoulder. 'You saved my life,' he growled quietly. 'Now accept my thanks.'

Sabinus gave a taut smile. Clearing his throat, Castus looked to the east once more. He remembered what Lycianus had said to him at dawn, and knew now that it must be true. Only the chance of killing or capturing him had led the desert tribes, usually so cautious, to attack such a strong target. The Persian officer leading them must have received good intelligence of his movements. A spy, or an informer, Castus thought. At least now he knew that he had been betrayed.

And from now on he would be ready for anything.

CHAPTER XII

Forty days later, eighty miles west of the Euphrates, Castus sat on a low dais in the shade of an awning, waiting for the barbarians.

He had already been waiting for some time. At Circesium he had delayed for ten days, and at Palmyra for ten more, and for all that time Lycianus was sending his scouts and messengers out into the surrounding wilderness to make contact with the chiefs and minor kings of the Tanukhids and their allies, summoning them all to the assembly. Now, finally, the day had come.

Out beyond the margins of the camp, beyond the troops of Legion I Illyricorum waiting in formation in the boiling sun, and the scrubby fringes of the palm groves that surrounded the oasis to the south, the open plain was a scene of activity. Castus could see what looked like vast numbers of camels and horses, herds of goats and figures on foot, all of them milling in the shimmering distance. Far away, towards the sand dunes that lined the horizon, dark tents were going up as the various tribal retinues made camp. And approaching, slowly and steadily from the wavering heat of mid-afternoon, came the chiefs and kings themselves.

'Why do we have to go through this charade with these brigands?' Sabinus asked. He was standing just behind Castus's stool, dressed in his cuirass with his helmet under his arm.

'Why not just send them their orders? They're supposed to be our allies.'

'That's not the way the tribes do things,' Lycianus told him, standing on Castus's opposite side. 'They have their treaties with us, but those treaties are made with individuals, not states. Your father here is a representative of the emperor, so commands their respect. A messenger could never do that.'

'And why do we need the respect of barbarians?' Sabinus asked quietly.

'We don't,' Castus said tersely. 'But we need them to do what we want and keep our southern flank secure. And for that, it helps if they respect us.'

'Otherwise they could just melt away into the desert,' Lycianus said. 'Or even change sides, who knows?'

Yes, Castus thought, the Saracens could well do that. But he needed their compliance; they were the last piece of the strategic plan that he needed to assemble. The ides of May had come and gone; now everything else was prepared. The troops in the field army camps around Antioch were ready to march, the frontier commanders knew their orders and had contributed their detachments; the flotillas of supply barges were already congregating at Barbalissos and Soura on the Euphrates.

And, only the day before, Castus had received notification that the emperor had finally set off for the east himself. Constantine would be in Antioch by the end of the month, ready to take command and lead the invasion of Persia. And at that point Castus's task would be done. He had received a letter from Marcellina as well, telling him that she had just reached Antioch. The thought of laying down his command and returning to civilian life was bittersweet, but he was coming to relish it. Sitting here in his full regalia, the red general's cloak around his shoulders, his repaired cuirass gleaming, surrounded by bodyguards and officers and the awesome symbolic might of

Roman power, he longed more than ever for the easy comforts of home.

A blast of trumpets broke into his thoughts. The troops lining the approaches tightened their ranks, spears glittering and standards raised, as the rather shambolic array of camel riders covered the last distance to the ring of tents and pavilions. The eight chiefs dismounted, slaves brought dishes of water for them to wash their hands, and then the Saracens were conducted through the cordon of guards and into the shaded area beneath the awning where Castus sat waiting for them. Each of them bowed deeply as he stepped onto the matting, then they settled themselves before him, sitting cross-legged. Their followers and attendants clustered behind them, fanning the flies away from them with palm-frond whisks.

'Someone's missing,' Lycianus whispered, leaning closer. 'Could we wait a little longer?'

Castus shrugged, irritated already by the lengthy delays, the gathering heat, the protracted solemnity of the occasion. Slaves were moving around the half-circle, offering cups of fresh water – the desert Arabs, Lycianus had explained, did not drink wine.

These Saracens of the Tanukhid tribes appeared far wilder than the men under Lycianus's command. Wilder too, Castus thought, than the Lakhmid Arabs who had attacked him in the desert east of the Chaboras. While some of the chiefs wore tunics of Roman pattern, most of their followers wore only a pair of rough blankets, one around the waist and the other thrown across the shoulders. Their exposed skin was burned dark by the sun, and their hair was long and either matted into ropes or bound with a simple headband. They carried broad straight swords of hammered iron, long lances and bundles of javelins. Some of them appeared to be wearing Roman-pattern army boots, which they took off as they entered the shade. But Castus was drawn most to their faces; they were lean, raw-boned and hawkish, and each had a look of ferocious pride and disdain.

But there was something else in their attitude, and it took Castus a while to spot it. Several of them would not meet his eyes, and all appeared guarded and evasive.

'We've waited long enough,' Castus said, swatting a fly from his face. The troops waiting outside would need to seek shelter from the sun very soon. 'Welcome them, in the name of the emperor, and tell them what we require of them.'

Lycianus took a step forward. But before he could speak, the sound of voices came from the bright dusty sunlight outside. Castus sat up, squinting into the glare.

Another camel was approaching, a group of Arab riders on light ponies escorting it. The newcomers moved through the cordon of soldiers, the camel advancing almost to the edge of the tent enclosure. The chiefs beneath the awning had shuffled on their haunches, turning to face the new arrival.

Mounted high on the camel was a young woman in a saffron-coloured linen tunic. The animal sank to its knees, and the woman stepped down from the tall saddle, her attendants rushing to assist her. Castus watched her as she walked towards the shelter of the awning. She was in her early twenties, he guessed, and her round face had a rather hard expression, belied by her very large kohl-rimmed eyes. Her black hair was braided and piled on top of her head, and she wore a heavy gold ring around her neck with a large medallion; Castus could just make out the portraits of the emperors, and a Christian symbol.

'Who's she?' he said from the corner of his mouth.

Lycianus let out a slow breath. 'Her name is Hind,' he said.

The woman walked into the centre of the half-circle of seated chiefs. They shuffled aside, making space for her, and one of her attendants brought a folding stool for her to sit on, facing Castus. The woman had not smiled; she appeared not to have blinked.

'She's another of their chiefs?' Castus asked in a whisper.

'She's the widow of Imru al-Qays,' Lycianus said, leaning closer. 'Their last king… I haven't seen her for years.'

By the tone of his voice, Castus guessed that it was not a happy reunion.

And now he saw the attendants bringing another figure into the shade of the awning, a boy of about seven or eight years old, dressed like his mother. This, he guessed, would be the posthumous son of Imru al-Qays. The sole surviving heir to the King of the Tanukhids. Several of the chiefs muttered what sounded like greetings, although Castus could hear the hostility in their voices.

'This isn't good,' Lycianus said, beneath his breath.

Castus frowned a question at him – Lycianus had not mentioned this woman Hind to him before – but now the assembly of chiefs had fallen silent and turned to face him. The woman in the centre was sitting very straight, hands folded in her lap and her head tipped back, gazing at Castus with a frank and disconcerting directness.

'As before,' Castus said to Lycianus with weary patience. 'Greetings, in the name of Constantine Augustus and the Caesar Constantius, and give them the speech...'

He and his officers, together with the *Dux Phoenicis* who commanded the troops in the province, had agreed the wording the day before. The Saracen leaders would be told of the forthcoming war between the Emperor of Rome and the Persians, and asked to renew the treaties, the *symmachia*, agreed by their forefathers. The speech took quite some time, the fluid vowels of the Arabic language blending into one another.

Castus sat still, barely listening as he studied the faces of the chiefs. Some nodded; others appeared wary. But the woman, Hind, sat upright and unmoving. The boy sitting beside her fidgeted. There was an impressive assurance in her attitude, Castus thought, all the more striking as she was the only woman in an assembly of men. He had a sudden memory from long ago. Another barbarian woman he had known, whose presence had been as commanding. Cunomagla had been a chieftainess of the Picts in northern Britain, and Castus remembered her well. She too had had a young son, and desired to rule in his name. Apprehension stirred in his gut, mingling with fascination. This woman Hind was not as impressive in appearance as Cunomagla had been. And set beside Marcellina, or even the wife of the curator of Nisibis, she could almost have appeared plain. But there was a bold fervour in her unblinking stare, the way she tipped back her head and confronted Castus and his officers.

Lycianus finished his speech, and Castus gestured for the gifts to be presented. Fine swords, forged in Damascus of Roman cavalry pattern – one for each of the chiefs. The soldier presenting them hesitated before Hind, glancing back at Castus, who nodded. One for her as well.

'Is it usual for the Saracens to be led by women?' he asked Lycianus in a whisper.

'Sometimes,' the scout commander replied, speaking equally quietly. 'But this one's very young, and inexperienced. Some of the other chiefs don't trust her. They don't care for her religion either.'

Castus snorted a quick laugh. 'I'm with them on that,' he said.

One by one the chiefs raised their right hand and recited what Castus took to be their names and an oath of allegiance. Now only Hind remained. She raised her hand.

'I am Hind bint Amr al-Hawari, wife of Imru al-Qays, mother of Nu'man, King of all the Tanukh,' she said in heavily accented Greek. Her voice was high and nasal, rather harsh, but she spoke clearly. 'It gives me great joy to swear friendship with Rome. My people too are joyful. Soon we will behold the blessed face of the Holy Emperor Constantine and his son! Joyfully we will spill the blood of Rome's enemies!'

Castus blinked, nonplussed. 'You speak Greek very well, *kyria*,' he said.

'Yes! It was taught to me by the most holy Pamfilos, our bishop, who was carried to heaven by Almighty God.' She raised her hand, one long finger pointing at the sky. 'We give praise to Great Jesus that soon a new bishop will be sent to us by the Most Blessed Emperor!'

Castus cleared his throat, trying to hide his surprise. A couple of the other Saracen chiefs were mumbling what sounded like complaints. One raised his hand towards Hind, crying out something and then gesturing towards Castus.

'They don't like her speaking in Greek, I take it?' Castus asked Lycianus, switching into Latin.

'They think she's trying to set herself above them.'

'Enough!' Castus commanded, raising a palm. The chiefs fell silent. The shadow of a smile crossed Hind's face.

He had been intending to end the assembly at that point – already he was longing for the mosquito-haunted cool of evening – but before he could speak again Castus saw one of the Saracens setting a silver bowl on the matting. An attendant poured liquid into the bowl from a greasy-looking goatskin bag.

'What's that?' he asked.

'Fermented camel's milk, dominus,' the Dux Phoenicis said, leaning closer and pulling a sour face. 'The Saracens drink it to seal their alliances.'

'I can drink it for you, if you like,' Lycianus added.

'No,' Castus said. He had delegated enough authority to the scout commander already. 'Bring it here.'

The chiefs nodded their appreciation as Castus took the brimming bowl. It was decorated with scenes of cavorting nymphs – a previous diplomatic gift, he wondered, or a raider's plunder? – but the liquid inside was thick and yellow-white, scummed with floating globules of fat. It smelled atrocious.

Holding his breath, Castus raised the bowl and sipped from the rim. He tried not to gag as the thick greasy liquid filled his mouth; it tasted of rancid butter, with a hint of stale urine. He gulped, then puffed his cheeks and forced a smile. The Saracen chiefs grinned back at him, several of them muttering low cries of congratulation. His guts were still roiling as the bowl passed between them, each taking a drink and passing it on. Hind drank last, swallowing heavily and then licking the rime of milk and fat from her lips.

'Well, that went smoothly enough,' Egnatius said as the chiefs made their departures. 'And now our desert flank is secure.'

'Easy for you to say,' Castus told him. 'You didn't have to drink camel's piss!' He took a cup of wine from a slave and swigged heavily, but the sour greasy taste would not leave his mouth.

Striding to the edge of the awning's shade, Castus watched as the Saracen chiefs mounted their horses and camels. Each had brought a small retinue of warriors; most were milling about in noisy confusion, calling out and gesturing, eager to return to camp. Only those that accompanied Hind had the look of true fighters. Stern and silent, they waited while their mistress mounted her camel with her son behind her, then, at her shout of command, they swung into the saddle with spears in hand. *Those*, Castus thought, *are the men I would want beside me in a battle.*

'Why are our troops acting so strangely?' Sabinus asked, frowning. Castus noticed that several of the soldiers of Legion I Illyricorum, drawn up around the meeting site, were turning away as Hind and her entourage passed. They made quick gestures against the evil eye, and some covered their groins.

'A superstition,' said the Dux Phoenicis with an embarrassed smile. 'Some of our local recruits believe that the Saracen women have the power to curse with their eyes. They believe that the curse can make their... I'm sorry, it's quite ridiculous... can make their genitals wither and drop off!'

Castus barked a laugh. 'Let's hope our enemies believe the same!'

Lycianus appeared beside him with one of the camp slaves. 'Excellency,' he said in a low voice.

Castus turned, raising an eyebrow.

'A message, from the woman, Hind,' Lycianus said. 'She wants to meet with you in private, alone, in her tent this evening. The messenger said she has something important to tell you, but wouldn't say any more.'

'Something important?' Castus repeated. He'd had enough of important matters for one day. 'What do you think?'

'I suspect,' Lycianus said darkly, 'that she wants you to give her the title of phylarch over the Tanukhid tribes, the same title her husband once held.'

Castus pursed his lips. 'Not sure if I have that power,' he said, then glanced sharply at the commander. 'You don't think it'd be wise – why?'

Lycianus took his time replying. 'Many of the other chiefs distrust her,' he said. 'She's said to be insane, or possessed by a demon. I didn't mention this before – I never thought she'd show her face again – but there were rumours that she was behind the assassination of the last king, her own stepson.'

'Hm,' Castus said, pondering. 'Scorpion sting, didn't you say? Easy thing to arrange. But if she has some important information then I should talk to her at least. I'll be sure to wear some stout boots when I do.'

Evening was coming on as Castus, with his officers and bodyguards, rode down to the Saracen encampment. The low sun turned the surrounding desert a glowing shade of rose, and made a blue haze of the smoke from the cooking fires.

Each of the chiefs, Castus noticed, had pitched his own camp. Each had his cluster of black goat-hair tents, surrounded by herds of camels and goats, horses and guards. But the space between was thronged with wandering tribesmen. Some rode horses bareback, some danced or sat in circles chanting and singing. A few of them had thrown off their blanket garments and walked stark naked in the cool of evening, but all kept their weapons with them. As Castus and his men rode by, the purple draco standard before them, the Saracens raised their spears and cried out in greeting. '*Rome! Rome!*'

There seemed little order to the encampment, but a small boy ran ahead of the horsemen, guiding them to Hind's tent. It was larger than the others, a huge humped black structure like a pavilion, guards squatting all around it in the sand, cradling their spears. A fire of dry palm fronds smouldered outside, the smoke driving away the mosquitoes.

Castus dismounted, but ordered Egnatius and his six Armigeri troopers to remain in the saddle. Sabinus and Lycianus followed as he marched towards the tent. The scout commander had retained his misgivings about the meeting, and was looking more than usually tight-lipped and grave.

'Just one thing, dominus,' he said as they walked. 'If she has a spear inside the tent, you must leave at once. It means she intends to marry you.'

'*What?*' Castus exclaimed, brows creased. He had never known Lycianus to tell jokes; the officer appeared entirely serious.

'Only temporarily, of course,' Lycianus added. 'It's a custom of theirs.'

'Barbarians!' Sabinus muttered.

There was an armed bodyguard outside the flap of the tent door, a massive bearded man carrying an unsheathed sword, his bare chest running with sweat. As Castus approached he barred the way, held up three fingers and shook his head. Then he held up one finger and nodded. No translation was required.

'Father, I can't let you go in there alone,' Sabinus said urgently. 'It might be a trap.'

Castus sucked his cheek. 'If you hear me shout,' he said, 'you have my permission to chop this guard's head off and rescue me. Either from death or from marriage!'

With obvious reluctance Sabinus stepped back, and the guard moved away from the tent door to allow Castus inside.

Stooping through the opening, Castus straightened and blinked. The interior of the tent appeared pitch black after the evening sunlight outside. Then, as his eyes adjusted, he saw the lamp hanging from the central pole, the mats and rugs spread on the ground, the haze of smoke filling the air.

And in the centre of the tent, Hind standing completely naked with her hair unbound.

His throat tightened and he looked away quickly. From the darkness he heard a stir of quiet laughter. Steeling himself, he forced his eyes back to the woman in the lamplight. She was standing with one foot raised on a low stool, a slave girl kneeling before her, shaving her pubic mound with a bronze razor.

'Welcome, strategos,' Hind said.

Castus swallowed heavily. It was very hot and close in the tent, and sweat prickled his brow. He knew at once that the woman had contrived this meeting to disconcert him. She was trying to intimidate him, to make him quail with embarrassment, or debase himself with undignified lust. He forced himself to stand steadily, meeting her eyes, trying not to glance downward too openly. The slave finished her work and shuffled away on her haunches.

'Kyria,' he said, in as sober a tone as he could manage. 'Your messenger said you had important matters to discuss.'

'Indeed yes,' Hind said. She paused, pushing her hair back from her shoulders. Then she spread her arms, and two more slaves drew the long linen tunic over her head. Clothed, she seated herself upon a stool.

'Your chiliarch, Lykianos, has told you many stories of me, yes?' she asked. 'He says I am mad, a monster, a murderer, yes?'

'He mentioned that many of your people don't trust you.'

Hind made a dry spitting noise, lips pursed. 'My people are not fond of leaders. They love freedom too much! But sometimes they need to be led. When there is war. And war is coming, so you say.'

'War is coming,' Castus said quietly.

He had known, from the first moment he saw this woman, that she had a shrewdness and bravery far beyond her years. How much of that was just self-assurance, he could not tell. How much, indeed, might be a kind of demonic possession he did not want to ask himself. But he sensed no madness in her. Instead he sensed a commanding fervour and a steely ferocity. With a jolt of surprise, he realised that he had last seen such a combination in the Emperor Constantine, in his younger years. No doubt she was also capable of vindictive rage, but such a quality could be as useful in war as it was harmful in peace.

'My husband Imru al-Qays,' Hind said, 'was phylarch of the Tanukhids, by order of your emperor. Now, if there is war, we need a phylarch again to lead us in battle. I want you to give me that title, give me the insignia of command.'

'Would the other chiefs agree to follow you?'

Hind gave a derisive snort. 'I would compel them!' she cried, with such savage emphasis that Castus had no trouble believing her.

'Your chiliarch,' she went on, 'does not want me to have this title. He hates me, that is why. He was a close friend of my husband, and loved his sons. One of his sons in particular he loved. But now two sons are dead and the third is gone to the Persians, and *my* son is the true successor. Let me command in his name, and I will reap the Persians for you.'

'Tell me why I should trust you,' Castus said slowly.

Hind smiled, and gestured to one of her slaves. The woman approached, head bowed, and raised her hands. In her palms was a twist of thin leather, coiled like a crude scroll. Castus took it, frowning. One side was rubbed white, and tiny letters were inked all across it. Peering in the low lamplight, Castus tried to read the words; they were in Latin script, numbers and letters muddled together, but he could make no sense of them. Hind herself, he guessed, could not read – and none of the Saracens would be able to understand Latin.

'Where did you get this?'

Hind smiled more widely, showing her white teeth. 'My people travel across all the desert,' she said. 'Often they stop travellers. To ask for... presents. Tolls, yes! Some days ago, they found a rider in the deep desert, travelling fast towards the Persian lands. He had that, hidden in a secret place. Very much he wanted to keep it!'

Castus grimaced, not wanting to imagine what the Saracen robbers must have done to the lone messenger to extract his secret from him. He looked again at the rough scroll, bringing it close to his eyes, sure that if he squinted at the scrawl of tiny letters they would somehow form into intelligible words.

'Keep it,' Hind said. 'I think maybe it is important for you?'

'It could be.' Castus tucked the scroll into his belt. 'My thanks to you.'

'So,' she said. 'Now you know I help you. You will help me, yes?'

Castus understood. Whatever the fractious nature of leadership among the desert tribes, the title of phylarch, awarded by the greater power of Rome, was worth more than any petty sovereignty. With it, Hind's power over the other chiefs would be uncontested, unless they wanted to rebel against Rome altogether. He paused, weighing his options. But he knew that he had already made his decision.

'I can grant you only this,' he said, standing upright and hooking his thumbs into his belt. 'The emperor himself, or the Caesar, must agree this title, but I will report to them that I find you worthy of it. And I believe that they will heed my words.'

Briefly Hind closed her eyes, and a look of blissful contentment passed across her face. Then she was wide-eyed again, glowing with ambition. 'I trust your words,' she said. 'And I will trust you.'

She stood up, turning, and Castus bowed to her as he prepared to leave.

'You are very old,' Hind said abruptly, glancing back over her shoulder. 'Is the emperor as old as you?'

'Older,' Castus said with a wry grimace.

'But he can still fight? And so can you?'

'I can only speak for myself. Yes. I fought against your Lakhmid cousins in the desert only a month ago.'

'The Lakhmids are a nest of infected rats!' Hind snarled. 'Soon we will slay all of them, and their Persian masters. The Persians are insects – *zzzt! Zzzt!*' She darted her fingers in the air. 'And we will swat them!' she cried, clapping her hands together.

'I look forward to it.'

'That is good,' Hind said, and turned to face him once more with an appraising glance. 'I am pleased,' she said, 'to meet a man who has such qualities. And it is rare to find such an old man who can look at a woman with desire, and still control himself. Are you married?'

'Yes,' Castus told her, feeling his face darken. 'My wife is in Antioch, and I'll be with her very soon.'

'May God speed your journey,' Hind said with a shrug. 'Your son, is he also married?'

Castus blinked. 'Not yet,' he said.

Hind gave another wide smile. 'Then I shall look for him on the battlefield! As I shall look for you, Aurelios Kastos.'

'You managed to evade marriage then?' Sabinus asked as they mounted their horses.

'More or less,' Castus said. 'Actually I think she's more interested in you.'

Sabinus coughed and looked away. Laughing to himself, Castus thought back over the strange meeting. Already he was starting to question his promise to Hind. Would the emperors agree to what he had suggested? He had not yet considered how Constantine or his son might greet the idea of a warrior queen leading their Saracen allies. With a sour pang, he remembered some of the things the emperor had said in the past about women. But surely barbarians could be allowed their differences from civilised peoples?

He had not spoken to Lycianus since leaving Hind's tent. The scout commander appeared to have guessed already what had happened, and was keeping silent about it. *So be it*, Castus thought. *But may the gods grant that I was right.*

As they rode back through the encampment, a sudden burst of shouting came from nearby. Castus tightened his reins, his horse twitching at the noise, and reached for his sword. Egnatius had already circled three of his troopers around to either flank. Peering into the gathering evening twilight, Castus made out a crowd of men surging towards one of the fires, all of them yelling and brandishing their weapons. But the shouts were joyful, enthusiastic. Two of the men carried something slung between them on a pole.

'Hunters,' Lycianus said. 'They must have been down in the ravines beyond the palm groves.'

They rode closer, keeping together. The two men had dumped their burden on the ground, and the others swirled around it, still letting out cries of jubilation. As the horsemen approached, the mob parted, gesturing; in the light of the fire Castus saw a dead animal, tied by its paws to a long pole. It was a lion, and a big one. The hunters shouted, raising their spears to the moon that hung full and pale above the eastern horizon.

'They're praising Al-Uzza,' Lycianus said. 'This is an omen, they say.'

Castus leaned in the saddle, studying the dead beast. A male, he noticed, but it had only the faintest ruff of a mane. Its flanks were stippled with old scars.

'What sort of omen?' he asked.

'The death of a lion means the death of a king,' Lycianus said. 'The King of the Persians, maybe?'

'Maybe,' Castus said in a low voice. But he was thinking of other kings. Old kings, and perhaps old leaders too. He fought down a shudder, feeling the breath of premonition.

Then the dust rose in the firelight, and he turned his horse away.

CHAPTER XIII

He found Diogenes the following evening, shortly after his arrival back at the praetorium of the legion fortress in Palmyra. The secretary was sitting in the shade of the portico behind the baths of the headquarters building, scratching lines in the dust with a stick. His three-legged dog was sitting beside him, turning its head from side to side as it watched. Just for a moment Castus feared that his friend had gone mad, and was trying to teach the animal to read. The secretary had remained at Palmyra with a headache when Castus rode out to meet the Saracens two days before; perhaps the sun had boiled his brains?

'What do you make of this?' Castus asked, once they had exchanged greetings. He took the leather scroll from his belt pouch.

Diogenes peered at it, curious. He held it at arm's length, then brought it close to his face. Then he turned it the other way up and exclaimed, '*Ah!*'

'Is it written in Latin? My reading's not too good, but I can't make anything of it.'

'No problem with your reading, brother,' Diogenes said. 'This is written in code.'

Castus nodded, relieved. 'Looks like some kind of list – can you work it out? I've shown it to nobody else, so keep it to yourself.'

'I'll see what I can do,' Diogenes said with a studious frown. 'But at first glance it doesn't appear an impossible conundrum.'

For most of the next day Castus had little time or energy to consider the scroll and its mysterious message. He spent several hours in the private chambers the legion prefect had set aside for his use, going through his correspondence with Sollemnis and Metrophanes, and composing the official reports on the treaty with the Saracens. One for the emperor, another for the Caesar, and a third for the Praetorian Prefect Ablabius in Antioch. The day was insufferably hot, the sun glaring through the slatted shutters, and Palmyra seemed populated by an infeasible number of fat black flies, which settled on every surface. It was shortly before nightfall, as Castus returned to his quarters after a long cool bath, that Diogenes found him.

'Dominus,' the secretary said with rare formality, falling into step beside him as he walked along the corridor towards his chamber. 'There's something we need to discuss with some urgency.' Diogenes had a tight and anxious expression, and Castus felt the kick of blood in his chest.

'Clear the room,' he said, as he entered, to the slaves and clerks who still lingered over their work. Once all were gone and the door firmly closed he gestured for Diogenes to sit and poured him a cup of watered wine.

'I apologise that this took me so long,' the secretary said quickly, drawing the leather scroll from inside his tunic. 'The code was quite simple, as it happened – a basic substitution of letters. I was overthinking the matter, I suppose, looking for greater complexity. But I believe we can safely say that the message is not the work of a master cryptographer!'

'So?' Castus asked him. 'What does it say?'

Diogenes spread the scrap of rolled leather on the tabletop. 'This column,' he said, tapping it with a gnarled finger, 'gives a list of all the military units either currently or shortly to be at Circesium and Soura on the Euphrates. This second column provides their full strength in officers and men, horses and camels. The side column here details the boats and barges collected for supply on the river.'

Castus drew a long breath, widening his eyes. His heart seemed to have slowed suddenly. 'So that means...?'

'That means, brother, that we have a big problem!'

Light-headed, Castus sank down onto a stool. He took a long swallow of wine. For a long time now he had known that somebody was giving information to the enemy – somebody well informed of his own movements, for a start. But he had never suspected that information this specific and detailed was being sent to the Persians. And with that information, the enemy would be able to estimate the plans for the forthcoming campaign with considerable accuracy. He muttered a quick prayer of thanks to the gods that it had not reached its destination. But could there be more like it?

'May I ask where you came across this item?' Diogenes asked.

'A woman gave it to me,' Castus said thickly. He saw Diogenes raise his eyebrows. 'It was found,' he said, 'on a messenger in the desert, heading for Persian territory.'

'Could this messenger be questioned?'

'I doubt he's in any condition to tell anybody anything,' Castus said. He pressed the heel of his hand against his forehead, cursing. If only he had known the importance of the scroll, he could have asked Hind more about it. Asked to speak to the Saracens who found it – interrogated them, even. Who had been carrying it, and where had it been found? But knowing that would not help him now.

'These details,' Diogenes said quietly, running his finger down the inked list again. 'How many people would have had access to them?'

'A few. Not many. Maybe a supply clerk at Soura, or somebody in the *officium* of one of the provincial commanders...' But even as he spoke, Castus knew that the treasonous message had been sent by somebody much further up the chain of command. Perhaps, he thought with gathering dread, by somebody on his own staff.

'Leave this with me,' he said, taking the scrap of leather and rolling it tightly between his fists. 'There's nothing more we can do about it tonight.'

When Diogenes had gone, Castus sat for a while in the gathering twilight, not lighting the lamps. He sipped warm wine, tapping the rolled leather against the edge of the table. Then he went to the window, threw open the shutters, and gazed out into the night. No coolness to the air, just the same solid heat. The sky was black and sprayed with stars, the huge moon glaring its light over the flat roofs of the barracks and the town, the perimeter wall and the flat grey desert beyond. Grimly Castus pictured silent messengers galloping across those dark and dusty plains, carrying further treasonous messages that would disclose all his plans and preparations and spell ruin for the Roman army.

Irritably he shook the image from his mind. He was tired, that was all. Four days more and he would depart Palmyra for Emesa, the last stop on his lengthy tour. After that, a return to Antioch and a reunion with Marcellina and his daughter. But with Constantine too, and the Caesar Constantius. The thought of seeing those men again did not gladden his heart. Perhaps, he thought, he really could just walk away from all this. Lay down his command and give up the army once more. It seemed the best thing. Life was worth so much more than the service of the emperors could provide.

A knock on the door, and a sound of a voice. Castus turned from the window, called out permission, and the doorkeeper stepped into the room. Egnatius followed behind him, throwing back his cloak.

'Excellency,' the cavalry tribune said, saluting. He appeared baffled by the darkness in the chamber. 'My apologies for disturbing you at this late hour.'

'Yes?' Castus said wearily.

'I thought you should see this.' Egnatius waited until the door was closed behind him, then advanced to the central table and placed a tablet upon it. 'Two of my men were on sentry duty at the Emesa Gate. They stopped a provisions merchant as he was leaving – it seemed a strange hour for him to be setting off – and gave him a thorough search, as you'd ordered. They found this tablet concealed in his baggage.'

Castus felt immediately alert, his mind focusing. His hands trembled slightly as he lit the lamp. To have a second secret communication fall into his hands so soon was surely a gift from the gods. But he could be certain of nothing yet.

'Tell the doorkeeper to summon Diogenes,' he said, picking up the tablet and breaking the seal. He studied the wax, disappointed not to see the same cryptic sets of letters and numbers he had seen on the leather scroll.

'Looks like Greek,' he said, and passed the tablet to Egnatius.

The tribune frowned deeply, angling the tablet to the light as he peered at it, then shrugged. 'I can't read Greek myself,' he said. 'Just a blur to me!'

The two men were sitting at the table drinking wine by the time Diogenes appeared. The secretary had obviously been asleep, but was wakeful enough now. He took the tablet, bent his head over it, then gave a dry chuckle.

'No codes here at least,' he said. 'But the content is interesting. It concerns you.'

'Me?' Castus said.

'Indeed so. The writer of the message believes that you've exceeded your authority in dealing with the Saracens. He claims, I am afraid to say, that you show signs of weariness, advanced age and confusion, and lack the stamina for command decisions!'

Startled, Castus could make no reply. Then he slammed his fist down on the table. 'Bastard!' he growled. 'Who wrote it? And who's it for?'

'That I can't say,' Diogenes replied, still studying the tablet. 'There are no names, and no sign of a destination. Presumably the messenger knew where to take it.'

'I have the merchant in the cells,' Egnatius said. 'We'll soon wring the truth out of him!'

Struck by a thought, Castus took the rolled leather scroll from his belt pouch and tossed it down beside the tablet. 'Is the writing the same, can you tell...? I mean, did the same person write both messages?'

'I know what you mean,' Diogenes said with an irritated nod. He scrutinised both documents, taking his time. 'Hard to be sure, but I think not.'

Castus exhaled. Presumably one of the messages might have been copied by another hand. Or perhaps the traitor used a scribe...? He was still fighting down the insult of the second message.

'However,' Diogenes declared, sitting upright suddenly, 'I strongly suspect that whoever wrote on the tablet here also wrote *this*.' His eye had fallen on one of the stack of documents on the table. Taking it, he held it close to the light, glancing repeatedly between it and the tablet. 'Yes, yes... the Greek characters are formed in the same idiosyncratic way! The shape of the *kappa* here, for example... a very eccentric oblique downstroke...'

'You're sure?'

Diogenes sat upright again, red-eyed. 'As I say, I can't be sure. But it seems likely. Who wrote this other document?'

Castus took it from him and glanced quickly at it. A slow dark fury rose through his body. He turned to Egnatius.

'Take four of your men,' he growled. 'And bring me Claudius Sollemnis.'

It was past midnight when the prisoner appeared, and they were all assembled to meet him. Castus stood behind the table, flanked by Egnatius and Sabinus, as the two cavalry troopers who had dragged Sollemnis from his bed stamped into the room. Sollemnis himself hung between them, still bleary and dressed in his sleeping tunic. He appeared confused by the sudden arrest. The taciturn Gaul was either shamming, Castus thought, or he was genuinely innocent.

The leather scroll lay upon the table, opened to show the inked message. Castus watched carefully as Sollemnis glanced at it. No sign of recognition in the man's eyes. Then he threw the tablet down on the table. This time Sollemnis responded; his jaw dropped, and the breath appeared to rush from his body.

'Talk,' Castus told him.

Sollemnis swallowed heavily, then composed himself. He drew back his shoulders and looked Castus in the eye. 'I was following the orders I was given,' he said.

'*Whose* orders?' Egnatius demanding, taking a step forward.

For a moment the prisoner gave no answer, glancing warily between the men who confronted him. 'The orders of the Praetorian Prefect, his eminence Flavius Ablabius,' he said.

'So you're his *spy*?' Sabinus said with an outraged scowl.

'He's the emperor's most senior officer in the east!' Sollemnis exclaimed. 'And I am a loyal servant of the emperor.'

'But why?' Sabinus broke in. 'Why should the prefect need this?'

Egnatius stifled a laugh. 'Isn't it obvious?' he said. 'Flavius Ablabius is full of schemes. Everyone knows it. He's always plotting to undermine everyone around him. He wants confidential reports on everything we do, so he can use them to his advantage!'

Castus circled the table, taking the tablet and holding it before Sollemnis. The Gaul was sweating heavily, his jaw tight.

'You believe what you wrote here?' Castus asked him in a low voice.

Sollemnis nodded curtly. 'That's my assessment of the situation,' he said. '*Excellency*,' he added.

Castus could not fault his bravery at least. Nor could he forgive it. Dropping the tablet, he seized Sollemnis by the front of his tunic and dragged him close. 'You *dare* to say these things about me?' he hissed. But he knew he was acting from weakness, and from malice. The accusations in the message had struck at him, and he could not let it show. With a snarl of disgust he shoved the man away from him. 'Take him back to his quarters,' he told Egnatius. 'He's to remain here under guard when we leave for Antioch.'

Sollemnis was trembling as the two soldiers led him away.

'So,' Diogenes said, once the prisoner was gone. 'We've uncovered one spy tonight, at least. But whoever wrote *this*,' he said, plucking at the leather scroll, 'still remains concealed!'

The road to Emesa led westwards, and after three days Castus and his party had left the desert fringes far behind them. They travelled now between spreading fields of wheat and barley, ripe for the harvest. After so long in the desolate wilderness, the sight of cultivated land and green hills, the flanks of the mountains on the far horizon, was a balm to the eyes. Traffic on the road had increased too, with carts and gangs of labourers moving out of the towns and cities into the fields. The men of the cavalry escort and Castus's staff rode in good spirits, sensing ahead of them the end of this lengthy tour of the frontiers, and a return to the comforts of Antioch.

Castus himself could not share in their pleasure. He knew these men well, most of them by name, even the slaves who handled the baggage camels. He had fought beside them, shared their meals and their camp fires. But the terrible words that Diogenes had read to him that night in Palmyra still gouged at his soul. How many of these men, he thought, believed him to be weary and confused, and lacking in stamina? How many of them thought he was too old and too tired for his job? Did they talk about him behind his back – laugh about him even?

He tried to push those thoughts from his mind. He had always believed that men should be judged by their actions, not their words. And had he not given all that he possessed over these last months? Still, the taint of failure lingered. He would not be returning to Antioch in strength, conscious that he had fulfilled his mission, but rather with a crippling sense of weakness and regret.

Lycianus had gone, taking his Saracen irregulars back east towards Circesium. Castus would meet him again on the Euphrates at Soura, they had agreed; privately he was glad that the scout commander would not be returning to Antioch with him. Sollemnis was back in Palmyra, confined and under guard. And soon enough Castus would have to confront the man who had ordered Sollemnis to spy on him. Anger filled his chest as he recalled the syrupy platitudes that Flavius Ablabius had spoken when they first met the previous autumn. His insincere pleas of allegiance, his warnings to beware of the other courtiers. At least, Castus thought, he had never been taken in by the man. But what of those others? What of Domitius Dracilianus, and his ally Mucatra? The possibility that they too had placed spies within his officium had already occurred to him. All of them conspiring against one another, all of them playing for power and influence. Above them, the Caesar Constantius. And above Constantius, the emperor himself.

Too easy, Castus thought, to let gloom engulf him. But perhaps Sollemnis had been right? Perhaps the tasks and responsibilities of high command were too arduous for him now. He knew how they chafed at him, and how fiercely he longed for an end to them. He was a simple man, and he was getting old. Perhaps he should just accept his own limitations?

He was still an hour's ride east of Emesa when the spiral of dust appeared on the road ahead. For a long while Castus paid no attention to it. A carriage, travelling fast in the opposite direction: several of them had passed in the last few days, carrying imperial couriers or tax officials, or landowners travelling out to their country villas for the harvest.

But as the carriage approached the leading riders of the column it slowed, and he heard the shouts of the two slaves that galloped alongside. Roused from his bitter thoughts, Castus spurred his horse forward to investigate; Sabinus was quick to follow him.

By the time he had ridden to the head of the column the carriage had halted, the two slaves dismounted beside it, Egnatius leaning from the saddle to speak with the driver. It was a fast two-horse gig, a covered frame on the back screening the passenger, and both driver and hangings were pale with the dust of the road.

As Castus approached, Egnatius straightened up with a grin on his face, beckoning him closer. 'It seems your day has improved, brother!' the tribune said.

Castus reined in his horse a few paces from the carriage, frowning in bemusement. The hangings that screened the rear of the carriage shifted, and a figure peered out. A woman, swathed in a shawl. Then she dropped the shawl from her face, and Castus widened his eyes.

'Marcellina!'

At once he slipped from the saddle, tossed the reins to Sabinus and ran to the side of the carriage. He threw his arms around his wife, drawing her into a fierce embrace, then kissed her deeply.

'Why are you here?' he exclaimed, beginning to laugh as the joy rose through him. Her touch, the feel of her body, had instantly eclipsed the dread and misgivings in his heart. 'Why are you here?' he asked again.

Then he noticed the expression on her face, the tension in her hand as she clasped him. Marcellina looked harried, dark circles beneath her eyes, her brow creased.

'Husband,' she said, and her smile was taut with worry. 'I thank God I found you! I'd thought I would have to ride all the way to Palmyra!'

'Where's Aeliana?' Castus asked, his grin slipping. 'Why are you travelling alone? Where's Pharnax...? *What's happened?*'

She drew him close again, still with that tense smile, and whispered to him, 'I must talk to you! Get into the carriage with me...'

Castus gestured to Egnatius, who ordered his men to dismount and move off the road. Sabinus remained in the saddle, staring, perplexed. Attempting to hide his consternation, Castus scrambled up into the carriage beside his wife and drew the drape across behind him. The axle creaked beneath him, and the carriage bed swayed. In the close confines of the screened rear seat he pulled Marcellina into an embrace once more. For a few heartbeats she was silent, the joy of their reunion stilling her anxiety.

'Tell me,' Castus said, drawing back.

'The emperor is sick,' his wife said in a hurried whisper. 'Very sick, and close to death, they say...'

'Gods!' Castus hissed. 'Where? He should be close to Antioch by now?'

Marcellina shook her head vigorously. 'No, no. He only got as far as Nicomedia. He was first taken ill during Paschal week, nearly two months ago – I saw it! We were told he'd recovered, and when I left Constantinople all was well... But shortly after he set off for the east he fell sick again, and was taken to some thermal baths near Nicomedia. The last message reached Antioch five days ago. The sickness has got worse. Caesar Constantius left the city at once by relay carriage, to go to his father's side. But all this I know from rumour, from palace gossip... The high officials are trying to keep the news secret. They wouldn't even send a messenger to inform you!'

'If the Caesar's gone to Nicomedia, who's in charge?' Castus demanded, but he already knew the answer.

'The Praetorian Prefect, Ablabius. He's issued strict orders that nobody is to talk of the emperor's health. I petitioned him to send word to you, but got no reply. So I had to come myself… I rode as fast as I could…'

'You should have sent Pharnax!' Castus said, gripping her arms as anguish mounted in him.

'How could I remain there in Antioch, knowing nothing?' Marcellina said, and Castus heard the fury and frustration in her voice. 'I had to come myself – Pharnax is guarding Aeliana and the household. But you must return to Antioch at once!'

Castus nodded, dropping his head. He stroked her cheek with his scarred left hand, gratitude for her prompt action mingling with tumbling fears. 'I'll ride,' he said, 'and change horses at the posting stations. Sabinus can come with me, and a few of the cavalry troopers, no more. Can you follow in the carriage?'

'If I must,' Marcellina said. Both of them knew that he could move faster alone now. 'After travelling for two months to reach Antioch I'm getting quite used to life on the road!'

Castus embraced her, kissing her again. Maddening to think of being separated again so soon after this unexpected meeting. But his mind and body were coursing with energy now. With a last squeeze of his wife's hand, he climbed down from the carriage and let the drape fall.

Castus arrived back in the capital of the eastern provinces on the first day of June, exhausted after two long days in the saddle. It had been a frustrating journey, and Castus's impatient fury had mounted with every delay – a lame horse, a wrong turning, roads blocked by wagon traffic, a stubbornly uncooperative post station superintendent... By the time he reached Antioch he felt worn to the bone. He had expected the city to be in turmoil, convulsed by anxiety, but as he rode along the broad central avenue with his weary cavalry troopers behind him there seemed only a strange calm pervading the population.

The same calm filled the palace. It felt unnatural, like the pause in the air before a thunderclap. As if everyone was just waiting for the next piece of news to arrive, or the final confirmation of their fears. Because, despite the efforts of the palace officials to keep everything secret, Castus soon realised that word of the emperor's illness had seeped out into the city. Through the day a crowd grew outside the palace gates, silently waiting. The churches and temples were thronged, sounds of chanted prayers filtering into the streets. A steady stream of devotees entered the unfinished octagonal church outside the palace; Sabinus was one of them, Castus noticed.

It was the following day before Castus managed to track down Flavius Ablabius. The Praetorian Prefect had been either ignoring or deferring his requests for a meeting for many hours. Finally Castus just marched straight into his wing of the palace, shoving aside the guards and the silentiaries at the doors of his chamber. He found the prefect sitting in the riverfront portico, dictating messages to a pair of slave secretaries. Ablabius leaped up with a flustered look, but as Castus stamped to a halt before him the Cretan's face once more eased into a smile.

'Why was I not informed of the emperor's illness?' Castus demanded before the prefect could speak. 'Why has no public announcement been made to the city people or the troops?'

'Magister!' Ablabius said with a wafting gesture. He was wearing a long gown of Persian fashion, with wide embroidered sleeves. 'As you can appreciate, in this difficult time there are so many things that need to be done. I have no more hours in my day than you! And before we have more concrete details it seemed foolish to say anything public.'

'You should have told me. I should have known about it days ago.'

Ablabius nodded gravely, dismissing the slaves with a gesture and then turning to pace along the portico. Castus followed, glowering at him.

'We had no certain idea of your whereabouts,' Ablabius said. 'Even the most trusted messengers can talk, and the last thing we'd want is for news of this unfortunate situation to be carried about the countryside, perhaps to reach the ears of our enemies...'

'I suspect it already has. When I left Antioch back in March I met a Persian envoy travelling to meet the emperor. He should have returned through here by now.'

'He did! Around a month ago. I met him, of course, and he seemed a reasonable man. Vezhan Gushnasp was his name...'

'The emperor fell sick at Pascha too, in Constantinople,' Castus broke in. 'This Persian envoy must have known of that. By now he'll have carried the word of it to Ctesiphon.'

Ablabius appeared momentarily concerned, his face emptying of expression. 'Ah, yes,' he said. 'But we have nothing to fear from the Persians, for now at least. Your preparations for the military campaign have surely been sound enough to deter them.'

'You also placed a man inside my officium to report on my activities,' Castus said, turning on his heel to confront the prefect. 'Why?'

For a heartbeat it looked as if Ablabius would deny it. Then he narrowed his eyes and turned to face Castus. 'I got where I am today,' he said in a colder tone, 'by keeping myself well informed of all that happens around me. Of course I maintain my own private intelligence network! How else would I stay a step ahead of my rivals?'

'But you have no rivals,' Castus said with a frown. 'You're the most powerful man in the east, barring the Caesar Constantius. Or… is the Caesar your rival?'

Colour rose to the Cretan's face, and he leaned closer to Castus. 'There will be many challenges in the days ahead,' he said quietly. 'Those of us in power will have to work together, yes? So we must keep cool heads, and try not to reach hasty conclusions. Otherwise we could fall into error. And errors can be very costly, magister.'

Castus angled his head, staring back at him. The prefect's words had been almost a threat. Almost, but not quite.

'As for myself,' Ablabius said with a sniff, 'I intend to pray ardently for our emperor to be restored to health. I suggest you do the same.'

That evening Castus shared a simple meal with Pharnax in the private chamber of his residence. When it was done and the bodyguard had departed, Aeliana came and stood beside his couch. The girl was bearing up well; after months on the road, a multitude of strange new sights and strange new people, and the confusion of the last few days, she still managed to appear in good spirits. But Castus could see that his daughter was hiding a lot of fearful uncertainty.

'Will Mama be coming back soon?' she asked.

'Of course! Maybe tomorrow or the day after. We'll all be together again soon enough.'

Aeliana nodded, then pursed her lips. 'And is it true that the emperor's sick? That's what the slaves are saying.'

Castus sat upright; he was about to tell her not to listen to the prattling of slaves… But his daughter was old enough and wise enough to hear the truth.

'Yes, he's sick, so they say,' he told her. He embraced her, drawing her up to sit on his knee, and she settled herself against his chest.

'But if he dies,' she asked – he heard the tremble in her voice this time, the tearful catch – 'if he dies, who'll rule the empire? Who'll keep the barbarians away?'

Raising his hand, Castus smoothed the fine brown hair from her face and kissed her brow. 'If he dies, we'll have a new emperor soon enough. And as for keeping away the barbarians – that's my job!'

She peered up at him, wide-eyed; then she saw his crooked smile and nodded, momentarily satisfied. 'I've been praying for the emperor to get better,' she said in a deliberately serious tone. 'Praying to Almighty God, I mean. I was wondering, though… Would it work better if I prayed to your gods as well?'

Castus made a noise deep in his throat. He had argued with Marcellina about this before; she was intent that her daughter should be a Christian, rather than grow confused about her faith. Castus had never pressed his side of the argument too forcefully. 'Pray to whatever you like,' he said. 'As long as you mean it, that's what counts. But sometimes,' he added, gazing down at her, 'all the praying in the world won't help. Everyone dies one day.'

'When they're old?' the girl asked in a querulous voice, and Castus realised that he had said the wrong thing.

'*One day,*' he said with emphasis. 'But don't you worry about death, my darling.' He kissed her again, and drew her more tightly against his chest. Blinking, he was surprised to feel the tears in his eyes. How is it, Castus thought as Aeliana let out a long sigh, that a child can summon feelings that adults are so keen to repress?

A noise broke into his thoughts. He tensed at once, and Aeliana sat up and slid from his embrace. A man had shouted something outside; Castus heard the bang of an opening door, rapid footsteps on the stairs.

He stood up, straightening his tunic. His chest felt tight. Somehow he had been expecting this.

The messenger wore the white uniform of the Corps of Protectores. He stumbled into the room, and took a moment to wipe his face.

'What is it?' Castus demanded.

'Excellency,' the Protector said.

With a note of dulled surprise Castus noticed that the man was weeping.

'Excellency...' he repeated. 'A message has come from Nicomedia. It's the emperor...'

'Speak clearly,' Castus growled.

The messenger straightened his shoulders, took a breath. 'Excellency... The emperor Constantinus Augustus has passed to his eternal reward... He's dead, excellency. Constantine's dead!'

CHAPTER XIV

'Friends,' Ablabius declared gravely. 'Most of you have already heard the dreadful news. I now have full confirmation of all that we feared. On the eleventh day before the kalends of this month, the fiftieth day of Pentecost, at a villa just outside Nicomedia, our Most Sacred and Beloved Augustus, the emperor Constantine, departed his mortal body and ascended to the heavens.'

The prefect paused to cover his eyes; then his hand strayed to the Christian medallion at his neck. 'He died of a lingering infection of the lungs, with recurring fevers. Shortly before the end, he was baptised into the Holy Church of God. He now sits at the side of his father, the Almighty.'

Dropping his hand, Ablabius swept his gaze around the twenty other men gathered by lamplight in the marble-lined council chamber. The doors were firmly closed, silentiaries stationed before them. Only the most senior officials of the court and the army had been permitted to attend. All remained standing except the prefect, who sat on an ornate folding stool before them. The hush in the room felt awesome, almost supernatural.

'Based on the messages we have received so far,' Ablabius went on, 'it seems impossible that the Most Blessed Caesar Constantius could have reached his father before the final hour.

So we do not know what instructions the emperor might, or might not, have given regarding the succession.'

Standing towards the back of the chamber, Castus tightened his jaw. This was what Ablabius was most concerned about, for all his pious words. But several of the men in the room were still digesting the news, and the shocked grief that it had summoned in them. It was a shock, Castus had to admit, even if most had expected it. Some of the younger officials had known only Constantine's rule for their entire adult lives. Some were red-eyed and tearful. One of the eunuchs, the Primicerius of the Sacred Bedchamber, wept openly and silently.

'So what now?' said Dracilianus, the Comes Orientis, with a brisk snap. Of all the assembly, only he and Ablabius appeared totally in control of themselves. Castus shifted his gaze between them. The prefect, seated on his thronelike stool marshalling his display of piety; his rival Dracilianus, tight-lipped and tensed with anticipation. The air between them seemed almost to quiver with the strength of their mutual hatred.

'What now, my dear Dracilianus?' the prefect said with the barest hint of a smile. 'Well, we could assume that the four Caesars – the three sons of the Augustus and their cousin Flavius Julius Dalmatius – will succeed immediately to joint rule. But that might be pre-emptory, don't you think? If Constantine gave no confirmation of his wishes, will these young men, or those who advise them, agree to share power? The younger Constantine is in Gaul, Constans in Italy and Dalmatius on the Danube. They must meet and debate their terms.'

Castus had always known that Ablabius was a man fatally in love with power. Seeing him now, at the moment of his greatest authority, Castus could tell how much the prefect was enjoying himself. Beneath the mask of sorrow, Ablabius was practically sweating with pleasure.

'And what do we do until the Caesars decide?' Dracilianus cut in with a sour smile. 'Declare a republic, perhaps? A temporary one, of course. Perhaps you, Ablabius, could declare yourself our *Dictator*?'

'*Until then*,' Ablabius said, raising his voice suddenly, angrily, so it echoed, 'we are in the lap of the gods! Or God, I should say... The Roman state stands upon a precipice! One false step could mean ruin for us all. And so we must be prudent.'

'Prudent?' echoed one of the ministers.

'Our official line,' Ablabius declared, gathering his hanging sleeves, 'is that Constantine Augustus still rules. While his body is dead his immortal spirit endures, his divine genius – all laws and pronouncements, all coin issues, everything will continue to be done in *his* name.'

A stir ran through the assembly. Dracilianus was smiling quietly to himself.

'Ox shit!' Castus said loudly, taking a step forward.

The muttering voices were instantly silenced as the echo of his words filled the chamber.

'Do you expect my troops to serve in the name of a dead emperor?' Castus went on, his jaw clenched. 'Do you expect them to salute a corpse?'

'Magister!' said the Chief Treasurer, a slack-faced elderly man. 'You speak impiously of the Sacred Augustus!'

'The Sacred Augustus is *dead*,' Castus growled. He stared around the room, fixing each man with a fierce glare. 'All of you know that I've been loyal to Constantine all my life...'

Muttering again, and several of the ministers averted their eyes from him.

'*All my life!*' Castus repeated, almost shouting now. 'But we're facing an imminent war with Persia, a war the emperor himself decreed, and both the army and the people need to know who's in command!'

His words died away into a brief silence.

When Ablabius spoke again his voice was quiet, his tone cutting. 'You speak of loyalty,' he said, 'and yet only ten years ago you were dismissed in disgrace from the emperor's court. Isn't that so? I hardly think this is the time to be stressing such qualities!'

Castus glared at him, feeling the rage seething in his chest. He could hear the slight sniffs of amusement from the gathered ministers. Yes, he thought, he had no friends at the court of Antioch; he had always known that. His position now was weaker than ever. And if Constantius returned, with the full authority of Augustus, he could expect no better. For the first time, he considered the empire falling into the hands of that arrogant and inexperienced nineteen-year-old. The thought was chilling.

'As for the Persians,' the prefect said, 'we need fear nothing from them, not for some time. The recent embassy to Constantinople did much to calm tensions between our empire and theirs. So, friends – let us return to our labours, and await further developments. All in God's own time!'

Marching quickly along the darkened corridor of the palace, anger in his stride, Castus heard a voice calling his name. He turned, fists clenched.

'A moment, if I could,' Dracilianus said. He gestured for Castus to walk with him, further into the shadowed depths of the corridor.

'What do you want with me now?' Castus growled.

Dracilianus laid a hand upon his sleeve. 'We both know, brother, the game that Ablabius is trying to play.'

'Do we?' *And what of your own game?*

'I told you before that he favours Flavius Julius Dalmatius above the other Caesars. But his greatest wish is to set the four of them against each other, prolong their disputes and set himself up as controller of the outcome. The power behind the throne, whoever ends up sitting on it!'

They had reached a gloomy vestibule, far from any listening ears, lit only by a single flickering lamp in a wall niche.

'That's none of my concern,' Castus said, pausing as Dracilianus hung back in the shadows.

'Ah, but it is! You see, there's something the prefect didn't tell you... Before he left Antioch, Caesar Constantius left very explicit instructions that nothing is to happen in his absence. *Nothing!* In particular, there are to be no further military movements. The main force of the imperial field army is still at Nicomedia, with advanced units all along the road as far as Tarsus; they won't move any further without orders. The eastern field army is to remain in camp here at Antioch. Constantius hopes to lead both armies himself against the Persians, of course, once his power is secure.'

'If only the Persians were so obliging!'

'Yes, well,' Dracilianus said, and a curious spasm passed across his features, almost hideous in the lamplight. 'That's not the issue, you see. We may need the army here.'

'Why?'

Glancing quickly back over his shoulder, Dracilianus leaned closer. There was something unnatural in his cold eyes now that Castus did not like at all. 'Think!' he said. 'The Caesars have little love for each other, and the three sons of Constantine detest their cousin Dalmatius. What are the chances they'll agree to share power? And if they do not... well, if it comes to war between them, we may need to pick our side and seize power in the east. Valerius Mucatra commands the eastern field army – a good man, although I know you've had your disagreements – but you're the commander in chief. I need to know I can rely on you, if the time comes.'

Castus felt a swell of sickening dread rising in his throat. He remembered the bloody field after the battle at Milvian Bridge, the even greater carnage after Chrysopolis... He had believed that never again would he see Roman soldiers killing each other.

The thought of another civil war was horrifying. And yet it was all too possible.

'And which side are you on, Dracilianus?'

The other man smiled, then took a step backwards, his face vanishing into the darkness. 'The right side, of course,' he said from the shadows. 'The side of justice. And of the security and power of the Roman Empire!'

The following days passed in a haze of suppressed anxiety. No news came from Nicomedia, none from Constantinople. The crowds still gathered outside the palace gates, worshippers thronged the churches and the temples, but a strange uneasy calm pervaded everything. Ablabius had circulated careful rumours that the emperor had recovered from his illness and once more sat upon the throne. Few believed them, perhaps, but it was enough to prevent any outbursts of popular grief or anger. Through the long hot summer days, under the punishing Syrian sun, Antioch simmered and sweated in a torpor of fearful uncertainty.

Marcellina returned to the city the day after the news of the death, riding in her carriage with Diogenes and Egnatius and the remains of Castus's military staff accompanying her. She had already learned what had happened, or guessed it. In the private chambers of Castus's residence, once the slaves were dismissed and they were alone, she fell into his arms and wept.

But she was not crying for the dead emperor.

'When I think of all you've done!' she said, raising her head and scrubbing the heel of her hand across her cheek. 'All these months of effort and danger... And now it's all for nothing! They're saying you'll be stripped of your command as soon as Constantius returns.'

'Who's saying this?' Castus asked, cradling her head in his hand.

'Egnatius and the other officers. Oh, not with any satisfaction – they're as angry as I am!'

And with good reason, Castus thought. They had shared his struggles for the last three months; if he kept his command he could reward them with honours and promotions. But now they were as friendless as Castus himself.

'There's a few people at the court here who might help me, all the same,' Castus said. 'For their own reasons. Dracilianus for one, maybe.'

He felt Marcellina shudder violently. 'That man!' she said. 'He makes my skin crawl. He has the eyes of a corpse. Every time he looks at me I feel... *violated.*'

'He has that effect on a few people, I think. It's nothing personal. We'll just have to hope for the best.'

Marcellina dropped her head against his chest again, holding him tightly. 'All that you've done,' she mumbled again, 'just to be dismissed, without thanks, without reward. It's criminal!'

'None of us know what the future holds,' Castus said, running his hand down the curve of her spine. She was still dressed in her travelling clothes, and smelled of dust and faint sweat. Her body was tense, and he felt her shudder as she relaxed. Warmth rose through him, calming his mind. He kissed the top of her head.

'Peace, let's hope,' Marcellina said. Then she kissed him on the lips, took his hand, and led him to the bedchamber.

Hours later, Castus lay beside her as she slept. He thought about peace, that most fragile of states. Only late in his life had he come to desire it. But he felt it now. Frowning, he gazed at the ceiling. For the first time since the news came in, he realised that he would miss Constantine. It was an odd thought, and a troubling one. He had known the emperor for over thirty years, half his life. Everything he had achieved had been by Constantine's command. The emperor had built him, as he had rebuilt the empire itself on a new foundation. And in some secret part of his soul, Castus had been looking forward to his moment of reconciliation with the man he had both respected and despised for so long. He wanted to stand before him, face to face, and reach some final understanding. Now that was denied to him. Constantine was dead, but his long shadow still lay over them.

And for all his feelings of newfound warmth for the man's memory, almost affection, Castus could not forget the faces of the dead. Both those he had known, and all those unknown others, the soldiers who had died in their thousands to pave Constantine's path to glory. Truly, he thought, he had seen enough of war and bloodshed.

Turning on his side, he laid his arm across Marcellina's back and drew her close. She mumbled in half-sleep, shifting her body into the curve of his own.

Peace, he thought. Yes, that was all he wanted now.

But he would only be granted a few more days of it.

The courier arrived on a lathered horse, grey with dust, and galloped in through the Beroea Gate on the fourth day after the news of the emperor's death had been received. He came at once to Castus's residence, barely slowing until he entered the courtyard outside and slid from the saddle.

Sabinus found Castus standing by the window in his upper chamber, the message in his hand. The courier, a military despatch rider, stood a few paces away, swaying on his feet with exhaustion.

'Sit,' Castus told the rider, then ordered the slaves to bring him water. 'See his horse is cared for as well.' He turned to the rider again. 'Have you shown this despatch to anybody else?'

'Nobody, excellency. It was addressed to you, so I came here directly.'

'Good.' Castus peered down again at the message, frowning. His mind was very clear, but his body felt heavy and slow.

'Father?' Sabinus said. 'What's happened?'

Castus gestured for his son to follow him into the next room. When they were alone he dropped the message tablet on the couch and turned to Sabinus.

'Word from Romulianus at Nisibis,' he said. 'Our scouts have sighted the Persian army. They're moving north, on the far side of the Tigris, but they have boats and bridging equipment with them. Looks like they're planning to cross the river east of Singara.' He was speaking calmly, but he could feel the tightness in his throat. The kick of his heart.

Sabinus just raised his eyebrows, stunned. 'Anything about their numbers?'

Clenching his back teeth, Castus turned away and gazed out of the window. 'The scouts estimate eighty to one hundred thousand,' he said. 'They have elephants and large numbers of cavalry, and King Shapur himself is leading them.'

Sabinus let out a low whistle. 'They saw him?'

'They saw the royal standard, apparently. None but the Persian king can display it. And this was five days ago.'

'Before we heard of the emperor's death! They must have known…'

'They knew he was sick, yes. Seems that was enough for them. That courier must have flown like Mercury to get here so fast.'

'So they'll strike from the east,' Sabinus said, sitting down on the couch, elbows braced on his knees. 'Through Singara and Nisibis, then Edessa…'

'Yes. They'll know the imperial field army's immobilised at Nicomedia. And most of our forces in the east are either here at Antioch or stationed on the middle Euphrates. And there's nobody to order them to advance.'

'Except you,' Sabinus said, glancing up.

'Except me.'

Castus rubbed his knuckles across his scalp. He ought to send a report to Ablabius. That would be the correct procedure. But

Ablabius was still obeying the Caesar's orders that the army was not to move. Or at least, he claimed to be. Dracilianus wanted the troops to remain at Antioch too, in case of civil war. Castus drew a deep breath. He was Magister Equitum per Orientem; he still held supreme military command in the east, and nobody had yet tried to take it from him. He needed to act fast.

'Summon all senior military officers,' he told Sabinus. 'Send riders out to the field army camps. I want all of them here in the city by the second hour of the night, no delays. We assemble at the Katagogion in the old agora. But tell nobody else – no word to the palace ministers, understood?'

'Understood, dominus!' Sabinus said, getting to his feet and saluting.

The hours passed quickly, the sand glass turning, the great water clock above the palace gate sounding out its metallic chimes. Castus paced his chambers, dictating messages and studying troop rosters. He had already summoned Diogenes, Egnatius and all of his staff who remained in the city. By the time the sun sank below the looming flank of Mons Silpius he had done all he could. It still did not feel enough; at any moment he expected the message from the prefect demanding an explanation, demanding a halt. But none came. His chamber was dyed with the colours of sunset as Castus shrugged on his best tunic and stood while the slaves arrayed him in his arming vest, gilded cuirass and red general's cloak. Then, with his helmet clasped under his arm, he strode out to the waiting carriage that would take him across the city to the old agora.

The Katagogion of Antioch had once been part of the Baths of Severus; later it had served as a rather palatial lodging house. Now it was the praetorium of the Magister Equitum. Castus was supposed to conduct his official business there, although he seldom used it. But it was far enough from the palace, and the oversight of the palace ministers, to be useful to him now.

By the time he arrived the forecourt was already crowded with horses and men, soldiers of the field army who had escorted their commanders to the meeting. They moved aside to let Castus through the throng, raising their hands in wary salute. Most of them remembered him well from their rigorous training over the winter.

Slamming open the main doors, Castus strode into the central hall with his staff officers at his back. He was pleased to see that most of the army commanders had already arrived – he noted their faces, and noted the names of those who had failed to attend in time. Over thirty officers: tribunes and prefects, a few senior centurions and drillmasters, most of them in military dress and some of them in armour. And every officer had his slaves and secretaries, his orderly or optio. The crowd parted before Castus, forming an aisle down the centre of the hall, and he strode between them. Expectation on every face. Fear on more than a few.

Mounting the steps to the dais, Castus turned and faced the assembled officers. Sabinus and three more Protectores flanked him, with his personal standard-bearer holding the draco. Another man held the imperial standard, with the image of Constantine still proudly displayed above his sons. A moment of hush, then the officers raised their hands and the words of the salute rang out.

Castus stood in silence. Once he spoke, he knew, there could be no turning back. In the flickering glow of the lamps, the faded paintings on the walls appeared to loom from shadow.

Quietly he cleared his throat. 'Brothers,' he declared, his voice rolling out over the heads of the assembly and echoing from the vaulted ceiling. 'The Persians are on the march. King Shapur has taken advantage of our uncertain condition, and means to invade our empire from the east. His army is currently on the upper Tigris, in considerable force. They may already have crossed the river into our territory.'

Uncertain condition, he thought. A nice euphemism. Every man before him now knew that the emperor was dead, although such a thing could not be spoken of aloud. But Castus could see the effect of his words. The assembled officers stood straighter, gazing up at him in attentive silence. Down at the front of the crowd, Castus saw the muscular, black-bearded commander Valerius Mucatra, his shaved head gleaming in the lamplight. A knot of his loyal subordinates stood arrayed behind him. If only, Castus thought, he had rid himself of that man while he had the chance... But it was too late now.

'The Dux Mesopotamiae, his excellency Julius Romulianus, is holding his troops at Singara, Nisibis, and the fortresses on the upper Tigris,' Castus continued. 'But he can only be expected to delay the Persian advance for a short time. It's vital that we move to reinforce him as soon as possible, with all the strength we can muster.'

In his mind, numbers were still whirling. For hours he had been turning them over, as if he could increase them by mental effort alone. But he knew that, with the emperor's own field army immobilised, whatever force he could draw together would be insufficient to oppose the Persian advance. There were eighteen thousand men of the eastern field army here at Antioch; another twenty thousand scattered between the garrison fortresses in Mesopotamia and Osrhoene. As many again were gathered at the mustering points on the Euphrates: would the messengers he had dispatched that day reach them fast enough? Would their commanders act with sufficient speed to rouse their troops and march them north to meet him on the road? Castus had also sent a message to Lycianus, ordering him to cross the Euphrates by the boat bridge at Soura and join him at Edessa. He was to bring as many of Hind's Saracen *symmachiarii* with him as possible.

Plans and strategies – but all of them so tenuous, so hurriedly assembled. And so easily they could collapse into ruin.

'You intend to take the entire army east, excellency?' Mucatra asked in a gruff tone.

'All our troops, yes,' Castus replied. 'We muster at first light on the old drill ground. I'll set out myself with a cavalry vanguard once the sun's up. With me will go the Equites Armigeri, the Equites Armeniaci Sagittarii and the Third Equites Stablesiani. Tribune Flavius Egnatius will lead them, as my deputy. We'll ride east by rapid stages to Edessa, changing horses along the way. When we get there, we should meet the detachments from the Euphrates.'

Silence from the assembly. Mucatra just stared, frowning.

'Meanwhile,' Castus said, 'the comes rei militaris Valerius Mucatra will get the leading detachments of the field army on the march that same day: the First and Fourth Italica, the Seventh and Tenth Gemina, Fifth Macedonica and Fourth Martia, together with the two Flavia legions and the rest of the cavalry. The remainder of the army will follow as soon as they can under their own commanders.

'You'll be pushing your men hard! They'll be eating dust for thirty miles a day, between stations. Every man is to carry seven days' rations in his pack. I've ordered ninety thousand *modii* of grain milled in readiness for us at Edessa, together with oil, wine, salted meat and fodder. We assemble and resupply there, on the ides.'

He paused, letting his words register and giving the secretaries time to scribble in their tablets. A few of the officers had gasped as he told them what was required of them. He was not surprised. Months sitting idle at Antioch, and now this. His throat was dry and his head was beginning to ache, but he still felt the surging energy that had propelled him through the day flaming in his blood. How long before that energy burned out?

'One question,' Mucatra said, his harshly accented voice cutting through the stir of whispers.

Castus turned to him, jutting his jaw.

'What if this is a ruse?' Mucatra asked. 'I mean to say, what if the Persians are making a feint attack from the east to draw all our forces in that direction – only then to attack up the Euphrates?'

Castus inhaled deeply, filling his chest, before replying. He had considered that himself. It was possible, he knew. And if it was true, he was throwing the entire eastern empire into peril. But the peril was there, however he acted. And what he needed now was a show of supreme confidence.

'Our scouts in the east have reported that the enemy carries the royal standard at their head. I'm no expert on the Persians, but I believe that means the king himself is leading them.'

'And you're certain of this... belief?' Mucatra said. 'How do you know?'

Castus stared down at him. Then he smiled, and gestured to the hooded figure who stood, unobtrusive, to one side of the room. 'He told me.'

Throwing back his hood, Hormisdas climbed to the lower step of the dais. The young Persian prince had only returned to the city the day before, from his country estate south of Daphne. Castus had been glad to see him; he was even more glad of his presence now.

'His excellency Aurelius Castus is quite correct,' Hormisdas said in a conversational tone that nonetheless carried to the back of the hall. 'The Dirafsh-i-Kaviyan is carried only by the King of Iran-Shahr himself. And King Shapur would not place himself at the head of a diversionary force.'

'So you're taking advice from the Persians now?' Mucatra said in a low growl. 'And they've got good eyes, these scouts, to pick out a single banner in the middle of an army!'

'Oh, the Dirafsh-i-Kaviyan's very distinctive,' Hormisdas replied casually. 'Twelve feet square, bright purple and red, and covered in gold and jewels. You really couldn't miss it!'

The swell of laughter was almost a relief. But Castus could sense the nervous energy gathered in the darkened hall. He felt it himself; every tendon in his body felt drawn tight.

'Brothers!' he cried. 'You've heard my commands. All of us have a long night ahead, and an early start tomorrow. Go – and may we meet again in Edessa a week from now!'

The assembly broke up, most of the officers turning at once and making for the doors. Only when they reached the far end of the hall did the talking begin, a torrent of voices rushing together.

'I wish I were going with you,' Hormisdas said as Castus stepped down from the dais. 'But as it is, I could only march to war against my own people with the express permission of the emperor. Which, in our *uncertain condition* may be difficult to obtain!'

'You're better off here,' Castus told him. 'But staying out of the city might be a good idea. Things could get ugly.'

'Oh, I fully intend to observe the ugliness at close quarters,' Hormisdas said with a shrug. 'I enjoy your violent Roman spectacles, you know. But if you need a safe refuge for your wife and household, my villa beyond Daphne is quite commodious.'

'I'll consider that, thanks,' Castus told him. 'How do you say good luck in Persian?'

'You don't need Persian luck,' Hormisdas said with a cool smile. 'You need Roman luck, my friend. Lots of Roman luck. My people fight hard, and Shapur has Ahura-Mazda on his side!'

'Don't worry. The Roman army isn't in the habit of losing battles.'

*

Leaving the hall, Castus walked into a scene of torchlit commotion. The courtyard was filled with milling figures, officers mounting horses or calling for their slaves, soldiers forming up around their commanders, and a mass of civilian onlookers in the gathering darkness of the agora beyond them. But amidst the crowd stood a large litter, eight bearers waiting beside it, the purple drapes displaying the insignia of the Praetorian Prefect. Castus halted on the steps, seeing Ablabius striding towards him through the throng.

'Have you entirely lost your mind?' the prefect demanded. He was dressed in a light tunic of patterned silk; Castus guessed he had come straight from a disturbed dinner as soon as he heard what was happening. Ablabius had soldiers with him too, palace guardsmen of the Schola Armaturae.

'Far from it,' Castus said. Some of the troops and officers had gathered behind him, others flanked him on the steps. He was surprised to notice Valerius Mucatra among them, backing him.

'The Caesar Constantius left strict orders that the field army was to remain at Antioch!' Ablabius cried. 'Now you intend to take our entire military force on some doomed expedition into Mesopotamia!'

'The enemy are invading Mesopotamia,' Castus said, lowering his brows. 'So I'm going to drive them out. Or do you expect Roman soldiers to cower in their billets while the Persians overrun our frontiers, sack our cities and enslave our people?'

A low growl of agreement came from the officers and men behind him. A few soldiers in the crowd cheered and yelled. Castus noticed the tribune of the Armaturae standing behind Ablabius, looking very unsure of himself.

'And if your ragged force is defeated in the field, what then?' Ablabius shouted, turning as he spoke to address the mob of soldiers. 'You leave the road to Antioch wide open! The capital of the eastern empire itself, defenceless before the barbarians!'

Shouts from the soldiers; some of them raised their fists, and a lump of rotting fruit came arcing out of the darkness to spatter across the paving at Ablabius's feet. The prefect flinched, taking two steps backwards.

'The army is under my command,' Castus said, raising his voice as he gripped the hilt of his sword. 'And I intend to do my duty and lead them against the invaders. If you believe the Persians will turn back, you're wrong. If you believe you can negotiate with them, you're wrong. The enemy is in the field, prefect. Stand aside!'

This time the cheering from around him was an angry roar. Castus hid his smile. He knew that soldiers would always back a military man over a civilian, and they loved to see the haughty ministers of the palace humiliated.

'I shall write to Constantinople at once,' Ablabius called out as he retreated towards his litter, the guardsmen forming up to protect him. 'I shall write to the Caesars!'

'Do that,' Castus said. By the time any reply reached him, the issue would already have been decided on the battlefield.

A few men slapped Castus on the shoulders as he pushed his way between them. He felt very tired suddenly, the ache in his head redoubling; he needed a bath, and he needed to see Marcellina. The smoke of the torches was getting in his eyes.

'And so it begins,' a quiet voice beside him said.

Dracilianus had sidled his way through the crowd, dressed in a plain cloak and hood. The gang of armed palace slaves that surrounded him were similarly inconspicuous. Castus glanced at him, raising one eyebrow.

'I can't say I'm happy that you're taking the army east at such a critical moment,' Dracilianus said. 'But you've manage to greatly discomfort *his eminence*, and that pleases me immensely!'

'Leave me out of your political games,' Castus said from the side of his mouth. 'I've got proper work to do.'

'I won't oppose you in that,' Dracilianus replied. 'You're right: the Persians are the greater threat, for now. But be sure to beat them quickly, won't you? We may need you back here before long!'

CHAPTER XV

First light. Dust billowed in the greyness of morning on the plain outside Antioch, mingling with the smoke of the cooking fires. Trumpet calls sounded in the murk, and the shouts of legion centurions and cavalry *centenarii* as they assembled their men. The troops billeted in the city had marched out to join their comrades from the military camps, and now the entire force was mustering, ready to begin the arduous march eastward. Christian priests attached to some of the units were leading their men in dawn prayers, and the fumes of their incense blended with the surrounding haze.

Castus rode slowly between the scattered formations. His head felt heavy and his limbs ached; only nine hours had passed since the meeting of officers, and he had slept for only three of them at best. Now the short summer night was gone, and he was back in the saddle. He heard cheers and shouts of acclaim from some of the troops as they saw the bold purple draco waving in the dusty air above his retinue. It was not Castus himself they were cheering. Not the old warhorse general who had bullied them into harsh training all through the months of winter and spring. They cheered what he represented: the commander who would lead them to victory, and bring them out alive once the battles were won.

Among the assembling ranks of infantry, Castus spotted

the standard of the Tenth Gemina legion detachment. Beneath it stood Barbatio, the stalwart young ordinarius centurion he had promoted to temporary command the previous autumn. He drew in his reins, and the officer saluted briskly.

'All your men fit to march?' Castus asked.

'Have been for months, dominus!' Barbatio replied, and his broad face split in a grin. Some of his men groaned and laughed.

'I'll see you in Edessa then!' Castus called back, smiling as he nudged his horse forward. As he moved away he was sure he heard the muffled chant, *'Knucklehead! Knucklehead!'* Amazed, he glanced back, but heard only laughter. It had been many years since anyone had called him that.

Moving between the blocks of troops, speaking here and there to an officer he recognised, Castus picked out the standards and the shield emblems, and made a quick assessment of the state of each unit. Better than he could have hoped: the army appeared in good shape; the men mostly looked eager enough. He saw one soldier saluting him as he passed, and recognised him too; the man had been one of those punished by Mucatra the previous autumn, and made to stand in humiliation outside the camp dressed as a prostitute. Now he and those who had stood with him were proud soldiers again, or so it appeared. There had been no more desertions, no more absences. It had been a hard winter, but the effort had paid off.

As he surveyed them all, Castus felt strangely moved. He was about to lead these men into war, all eighteen thousand of them, against a far superior force. Many would die. And all of it was his decision. Their lives were in his hands now. And yet he felt so old, so tired already at the thought of what was to come.

Shaking his head angrily to dispel the thoughts, he returned to join Egnatius and his cavalry vanguard. The tribune had his men assembled, nearly a thousand troopers standing by their horses in formation all along the verge of the road. Each man carried a bundle of fodder and a ration bag on his saddle; they were riding light, no baggage mules or camels. Castus had sent orders to every station along the route of march to have food, fodder and remounts prepared for them. In four days they should reach Edessa; then, Castus knew, they would discover what Shapur and his Persian army were doing.

Cries from the troopers at the head of the column. Castus turned, and saw that the sun had appeared above the eastern horizon, a huge red disc burning through the haze. All across the plain soldiers were turning and raising their arms in salute, crying out blessings to the rising sun. Castus felt a surge of exhilarated pride; there were still plenty in the army who revered the old gods, and custom at least had not been outlawed.

Slipping down from the saddle, he stood with Egnatius and a band of his officers, closed his eyes to the red glare and lifted his arms. '*Sol Invictus*,' he chanted. '*Unconquered Sun. Your light between us and darkness!*' And he added a prayer of his own. '*Preserve us from the fury of the enemy, Lord of Heaven. Bring us victory and a safe homecoming...*'

A line of carriages was approaching along the road from the city. Castus did not expect any of the palace officials to come out and watch the army depart; these were the wives and families of the senior commanders, come to bid them farewell. He moved a few paces away from Egnatius and his men and waited.

Pharnax arrived first, riding up on a pony, his scarred face dark with glowering anger. 'So you're off to fight battles without me again, eh?' the ex-gladiator said, leaning across the saddle horns. 'Leaving me to mind the womenfolk. A man might feel offended!' Then he grinned.

'I need you back here,' Castus told him, stepping closer and seizing the Numidian by the arm. 'There might be trouble in Antioch over the coming month. Watch over Marcellina and Aeliana, and keep them safe.'

'Don't worry, brother,' Pharnax said. 'Nothing gets past me, as well you know!'

But now Castus could see the carriage drawn up on the far side of the road. As he walked towards it, the drapes parted and he saw his wife and daughter inside. Marcellina climbed down and stood waiting. Castus halted, a pace away from her, and she reached out and caressed his cheek, then scratched lightly at the silvery stubble of his beard.

'Well,' she said with a sorrowing smile. 'Everything I feared has happened!'

'Not everything,' Castus told her. 'Not yet. Have some faith.'

Then he gave a low groan and stepped forward, pulling her into his embrace. She kissed his neck, then pressed her face against his chest. 'Come back to me,' she said. 'Come back alive.'

They had argued bitterly the night before. Marcellina had raged in her grief, blaming him, and then blaming herself for allowing him to come to the east in the first place, allowing him to re-enter the world of war. And he had raged back at her, frustrated and guilty, knowing she was right, that she had always been right. But their anger could change nothing. Their reconciliation, when both were too exhausted to fight any more, could not change anything either.

Aeliana was sitting in the carriage, her nursemaid beside her, and Castus went to the girl and hugged her tightly. Then he looked at her face, and smiled as he saw that she was not crying. But she was frightened all the same.

'What will happen now the emperor's dead and you're going away?' she asked. 'Who'll protect us from the barbarians, and the... the others.'

'Which others?' Castus asked, still trying to smile.

'There are men who want to harm us. I keep dreaming about it. I'm sorry.'

'Don't be sorry, darling. You're right to be worried. But

Pharnax is here to keep you safe, you and your mother. And I'll be back soon.'

Her chin trembled, and she curled her fingers around his big scarred hands.

'Listen,' he told her, leaning closer. 'If anyone ever threatens you, or tries to harm you or your mother in any way, I'll come right back and kill them for you!'

Aeliana looked startled for a moment, then she nodded. 'Do you promise? Whoever they are?' she asked.

'Yes, I promise.' Then he gave her another hug and kissed her brow.

There was little more to say. Marcellina would not remain to watch him depart; they embraced again, and then Castus stood with clenched jaw as he watched the carriage taking them back to the city.

'Ready to go, Father,' Sabinus said as he strode back to join his officers.

Castus checked his horse's tack and girth straps, and then heaved himself up into the saddle. Diogenes was riding down the line, wrapped in an old brown cloak.

'This is your last chance, you know,' Castus called to him. 'You don't have to come with us.'

'Oh no, I want to come,' Diogenes replied. 'I have an idea that I bring you luck somehow. Besides, I'd appreciate the opportunity to see the eastern cities again.'

His cloak shifted, and the three-legged dog scrambled free; it jumped from his saddle to roll and stagger upright in the dust, yapping.

'You've still got that awful-looking animal with you?'

'Of course!' Diogenes said. 'I could hardly leave him in Antioch. The other hounds would oppress him, I think. And I consider him a lucky totem, you might say.'

'Suit yourself,' Castus muttered. 'You're becoming strangely superstitious in your old age!'

But then the sound of trumpets shattered the morning, one answering another all across the plain. The troopers of the Equites Armigeri, the Armeniaci Sagittarii and the Stablesiani vaulted into their saddles and spurred their horses onto the road, and the column began to move.

Cheering came from the infantry ranks, lost in the sunshot haze. As he rode forward, into the glare of dawn, Castus heard the thunder of spears battering a rhythm on shield rims, then the familiar massed cries, the call and response of old Roman military tradition, booming across the plain.

'*Are you ready for war?*'

'*READY!*'

Through the furnace heat of the day and the breathless cool of the night they rode eastward. It was the same route that Castus and his men had taken months before, at the end of winter. Many of the smaller towns and villages along the way had heard nothing of the Persian invasion, and the people stood and peered in bemusement as the powerful column of cavalry thundered past them. But in Beroea and Hierapolis the news had already arrived. Panicked civilians were streaming west, back towards Antioch, as if they expected the Persian cataphracts to start charging through their streets at any moment.

After three days they crossed the Euphrates by the bridge of boats at Caeciliana, and two days later, after a fast ride across the flatlands of Osrhoene, the column reached the walled city of Edessa.

And it was at Edessa, in the upper chamber of the governor's residence, that Castus received the first premonition that fate had already destroyed his hastily constructed strategy.

'He did *what*?'

'Marched them east, excellency, towards Nisibis and Singara.' The superintendent of the armoury fabrica was one of the few military officers left in the city. All the rest had gone with their troops, on the orders of the Dux Mesopotamiae, Romulianus.

'He doesn't even have authority over the garrisons in this province!'

'No, excellency, but with our own commander away at Circesium there was nobody here who could countermand the order. I believe Dux Romulianus was intending to assemble a field force at Nisibis...'

Castus let out a loud cry, pressing his hands to his head. This was exactly what he had ordered Romulianus not to do. He should have guessed, he thought, that the ambition and resentment of the Dux Mesopotamiae would lead him to try and seize the initiative, and make a hero of himself.

'So he intends to confront the entire Persian army in the field with his garrison troops alone?'

'A *delaying action*, I think, was mentioned...' the fabrica superintendent said in a nervous tone.

With a shout of fury, Castus slammed his fist on the table and stalked across the room; Romulianus should have been holding a position that Castus could reinforce, not throwing his men away in a vainglorious counter-attack in the desert somewhere. Setting his jaw, exhaling fiercely, he crossed to the window and stared out to the east, and then to the south, willing the appearance of dust clouds along the straight highways, the first sign of marching troops coming to support him.

But the following day brought no word of reinforcements. Lycianus rode in from the south, but he had fewer than a hundred of his own Saracen horsemen with him.

'What about Hind and her symmachiarii?' Castus demanded as the weathered old scout commander made his report.

'Nothing!' Lycianus said with a thin sneer. 'What did you expect? That the tribes would take orders from an inexperienced girl they suspect of murdering their last king? They've scattered to the desert – you won't see them again.'

210

'You blame me for that?' Castus asked quietly, stepping closer.

Lycianus glared back at him, his eyes very blue in his tanned face. 'I told you that you were making a mistake, dominus,' he said coldly. 'But the decision was yours.'

Castus shrugged. Perhaps Lycianus had been right all along. Perhaps all of them were right – Sollemnis, Mucatra, even Ablabius... He was very weary suddenly. But the worst news was yet to come.

It was evening when the horseman arrived from the east. A solitary biarchus of the Equites Mauri Illyricani, he was wounded and his mount half-blown, but he delivered the message from his tribune before slipping from the saddle. Sabinus brought the message to the upper chamber of the residence, and Castus read it without taking a breath. The words were ragged, scratched violently into the wax, but the phrases were correct and clear. He waited, struggling to focus his mind, then summoned Egnatius, Lycianus and Diogenes.

In the shadowed dining chamber of the residence they sat on the facing couches. A slave brought cups of wine and water, while Sabinus read the message.

'*I regret to report...*' Sabinus said, halting as he tried to make out the hastily scribbled script, '... *a disastrous engagement which took place on the morning of the seventh day before the ides of June between the vanguard of the army of the Persian King Shapur... and our own forces under the command of his excellency Romulianus, Dux Mesopotamiae...*'

'By all the gods,' Egnatius said in a harsh whisper. 'It's happened already!'

'*The enemy, in overwhelming numbers,*' Sabinus went on, '*launched a highly disciplined attack on our troops at Zagurae, and in spite of our gallant resistance, the majority of our force... numbering fourteen thousand infantry and cavalry, was either captured or completely... annihilated. The camp, containing all of our provisions, together with the fortress of Singara, was taken. Only a few of its defenders escaped and are now retreating towards Nisibis.'*

'That's it?' Lycianus demanded. 'Nothing more about the current position of the enemy? What of Romulianus – is he alive or dead?'

'Nothing,' Sabinus said, closing the leaves of the tablet. The blood seemed to have drained from his face. Castus knew that he looked the same himself. He felt as if all his strength had deserted him.

'Friends,' he said, trying to keep his voice steady and not betray the plunging dread that filled his mind. 'You all know the situation. You're my military council now. What course of action would you advise?'

From a long while none of them said anything. Egnatius picked up the tablet, peering at it as if he could discern some additional meaning in the words. 'It seems to me,' he said at last, looking up, 'that our only choice is to retreat. Nisibis won't hold out long with only a handful of defenders, nor will Edessa. If we fall back on Mucatra's main force, destroy the boat bridge at Caeciliana and take up a position on the west bank of the Euphrates, we can hold off any Persian attempts to get across.'

Castus nodded. It was one of the options he might have debated with himself. But the notion of retreat did not appeal to him, and he doubted that Mucatra would receive him with any respect after so undeniable a failure. He turned to Lycianus.

'Dominus,' the scout commander said, 'I advise against giving up any ground we currently hold. The Persians cannot be defeated in the field – Romulianus has shown that eloquently… But they'll be moving very slowly, with elephants and a siege train. If we split up between a multitude of strongpoints and launch harassing attacks on their flanks, and on their supply lines, we can make it impossible for Shapur to advance further. Perhaps we can even hold him long enough for the imperial field army to arrive here…'

'Under whose command?' Egnatius broke in. 'That could take months! Besides, only your own men are experienced in raiding and skirmishing like that, and you have fewer than a hundred – it'd be like flies attacking an elephant!'

'Perhaps...' Sabinus broke in. He was frowning, gazing into space; the two senior officers turned to him, waiting for him to speak. 'Perhaps,' he said again, 'Nisibis is all Shapur wants?'

Egnatius immediately made a scoffing sound. Castus raised a hand for silence, then gestured for his son to continue.

'We think he means to invade Syria,' Sabinus went on, 'as we meant to invade his territory, but maybe he doesn't? Nisibis was the most important city mentioned in the treaty the Persians signed decades ago, the one they found so humiliating... Didn't you once call it the *bulwark of the east*, Father? Shapur's won a victory against Romulianus already. If he takes and holds Nisibis, he's won the war, in effect.'

For a long while all the men were silent, pondering the idea. Castus saw Diogenes raise his eyebrows. He gestured for the secretary to speak. 'It's true,' Diogenes said. 'Nisibis would be a great prize for Persia. Shapur could not advance and leave such a strong fortification in his rear either. And he surely needs the supplies kept there, to provision his army. But if he takes it, we'd find it very difficult to drive him back out again.'

Castus rubbed a palm over his jaw. The faces of the men at the table, all of them looking to him for a decision, blurred. *What if...?* he thought. *What if Shapur does not attack Nisibis? What if he bypasses it, or turns south, towards Circesium? What if this really is a feint attack? What if...? What if...?* He scrubbed his scalp, then exhaled.

'Yes,' he said, with a decisive snap in his voice. 'Yes, we go to Nisibis. Shapur needs to take it, and we can't let it fall. Send riders west to Mucatra, telling him to push his troops on as fast as possible. The rest of us ride for Nisibis at dawn tomorrow. And may the gods send us wings!'

CHAPTER XVI

Mile after mile, Castus led the column at a furious pace, men and horses pushed to the limits of endurance. The long straight road took them east, through the hill country and out onto the Mesopotamian plains. They rested briefly at Constantia, a day after leaving Edessa, and again the following evening at Macharta, but after sunset they were back in the saddle and moving once more. The hooves raised a vast plume of dust, pale in the glow of the moon.

Shortly after midnight, Castus noticed the orange haze across the horizon to the south and east, and smelled the scent of burning on the night breeze. His grim mood lifted slightly; they were still ahead of the Persian advance, and Castus knew that neither landowners nor peasants would voluntarily burn their own unharvested crops. Clearly somebody had taken charge at Nisibis, and issued orders to deny the invaders any forage.

Two hours later, he heard the cries of combat from up ahead. The archers of the Armeniaci Sagittarii were riding at the van of the column, and as he spurred his horse forward he met a biarchus of the unit riding back to find him.

'Deserters, magister!' the biarchus reported, reining in his mount. 'Looting the villages, we think. We charged them and they ran, but my boys shot a couple of them down as they fled.'

'Good work,' Castus told him. His throat was dry and harsh with dust. 'But if you see any more, round them up and bring them in if you can.' He needed all the men he could get, and could not be scrupulous about where he found them. He was still hoping that the bulk of Romulianus's shattered force had retreated to Nisibis, rather than fanning out across the countryside to plunder the civilians.

They met the first groups of refugees soon afterwards, desperate bands of peasants and villagers who scattered at the noise of the approaching horsemen, then lined the verges crying out for protection and rescue as the cavalry rode past with their banners streaming. But Castus knew he could afford no delay now. As the eastern sky lightened, the bands of fugitives on the roads grew more frequent, and he could make out other groups straggling across the open country, all of them hurrying towards the sanctuary of Nisibis's walls.

An hour before sunrise, the city itself appeared, dark on the far horizon, and as Castus rode up to the head of the column he saw the towers and the pediments of the temples outlined against the pale glow of dawn. The road led straight to the whitewashed arches of the western gate, but as they rode between the towering masonry tombs that lined the approaches to the city, Castus swung the column away to the right, along the narrower track that followed the line of the wall down to the postern gates of the military camp. He had no idea what the situation in the city might be, and leading a thousand horsemen through the streets could be perilous.

'Egnatius,' he cried as the gates in the outer wall opened before him, 'I need a troop of your Armigeri as escort – I'm going straight to the Strategion. Find barracks and stables for the rest, and send all senior officers to report to me at the sixth hour.'

He paused outside the *principia* of the castrum only long enough to gulp down a flask of water. Then, without dismounting, he led his retinue on through the camp and out the far gate into the main avenue of the city. Turning to the left, they rode up the slope towards the citadel mount. In the morning light, Castus could see the colonnades on either side packed with refugees, huddled with whatever meagre possessions they had managed to bring with them from the villages and outlying towns.

The crowd in the street grew thicker as he rode into the oval agora between the theatre and the Bouleuterion. The sun was up now, illuminating the façade of the Church of the Saviour and the broad steps that climbed to its doors. Both the steps and the open space at their foot were covered with people, city-dwellers and refugees together, all of them gazing up at the lone figure who stood, arms stretched wide, in the sunlight before the gate of the church atrium. Castus recognised the ragged man at once.

'Brothers and sisters in Christ,' the bishop cried, 'I say to you now, do not put your hopes in earthly weaponry, but in the power of prayer, the power of faith!' Iacob appeared as wretched as ever, and his voice was a thin creak, but it carried powerfully across the plaza. 'Fall upon your knees, brethren, and pray to the Lord our God for your salvation! For was it not God who in the testament sent the flaming chariots to the aid of Elisha, when the city of Dothan was beset by the ravening foe?'

Iacob paused, catching sight of Castus and his mounted retinue, the purple draco banner hanging above them. He raised his arm again, pointing with one withered finger. Castus reined in his horse and leaned onto the saddle horns as the congregation turned to peer anxiously at him.

'Put no trust in the agent of evil!' the bishop yelled. 'Put no faith in the worshipper of devils and the companions of persecutors! Turn away from him, brethren... Cast him from your hearts! For he brings only *death* to this city, both of the body and of the soul!'

With a snort of disdain, Castus spurred his horse forward again, cantering through the fringes of the crowd as the bishop's congregation scattered before him. On the far side of the agora he tugged at the reins and rode on up the broad stepped street that climbed the northern slope of the citadel mount. The hooves of the horses clashed on the marble paving, loud in the morning calm.

Reaching the open area before the Strategion, Castus halted and eased himself down from the saddle with a deep groan. His legs felt weak as they took his weight, and he paused, braced against the heaving flank of his horse. Sabinus dismounted beside him, and led a party of troopers to the Strategion portico, where the slaves were already gathering, staring in bemusement.

'Not a journey I hope to make again in a hurry!' Diogenes said, clambering down from the saddle with considerable effort.

Castus frowned. 'Let's hope we both make it again soon enough, in the opposite direction.'

Inside the building, slaves and attendants fussed around him. But Castus needed no guide to lead him to Romulianus. He could hear the strangled gasps and cries of pain as he circled the palm courtyard. The Dux Mesopotamiae was lying on a couch in one of the airier side chambers, the sheets beneath him soaked yellow with sweat and spattered with bloodstains. His chest and belly were bound with linen bandages, and his face was grey and corded with pain. Castus guessed that the wounded man must have been awakened by the noise of his arrival.

'Excellency!' one of the surgeons kneeling beside the couch exclaimed. 'My apologies, but the dux is in no condition to speak to you now!'

'I can see that,' Castus said quietly, gazing down at Romulianus. The wounded man opened his eyes briefly, and a flicker of recognition hardened his gaze. Then another spasm of pain racked his body and he turned his head away, gasping through his teeth.

'They brought him in six days ago, excellency,' the steward said in a low voice. 'He has wounds in his abdomen and his flank, his liver is pierced and infection has set in. The surgeons have done all they could...'

Castus nodded curtly. Anyone could see that Romulianus was dying. He had a day, perhaps two more at best. Looking at him now, Castus could feel little anger for the man. Romulianus had led thousands of Roman soldiers out into the desert to be smashed into the dust at Zagurae. He had done it against orders, and against all sense. But he had paid the highest price for his folly.

'Give him whatever he needs,' he told the steward, turning away. 'And keep him quiet if you can. Where's the governor?'

'The praeses Gidnadius left as soon as news of the battle came in, dominus,' the steward said with an embarrassed sigh. 'He claimed he was going to Amida to raise more troops.'

Castus choked back a bitter laugh. He had expected little of Gidnadius, but such open cowardice was hard to swallow.

The morning was already getting hot, but the dim interior chambers of the Strategion still trapped a little of the night's cool beneath their heavy vaulted ceilings. Now he was at his destination, Castus felt the fatigue of his journey washing through him, his mind blurring as his muscles ached and burned. But he forced himself to climb the steps to the roof terrace, praying that he would see no hostile army arrayed across the southern horizon.

His prayers were answered. The blue distance of the plain shimmered with heat, but the sky was empty of dust trails and he could see no roving horsemen out beyond the scorched brown fields that lined the Mygdonius. Breathing his thanks, Castus stumbled back down the steps and across the smaller courtyard into the chamber he had used during his previous visit. Vallio was already there, cajoling the slaves as they set out the bedding and brought food and drink.

Castus flung his cloak aside and slumped heavily onto the couch, drinking a cup of watered wine as Vallio pulled off his boots. His head was spinning with weariness, and he eased himself down to lie on his back. A moment later, with not another thought, he was asleep.

Snapping awake again, he lay blinking in confusion, still feeling the couch beneath him rolling with the motions of the saddle. He was barely aware of having slept at all, but once the turmoil in his mind had stilled he felt slightly refreshed. Distant trumpet calls came from the direction of the castrum. Sitting up, yawning massively, he called for Vallio.

'What hour is it?'

'Approaching the sixth, dominus,' his orderly said. 'The officers are here and waiting, but I thought it best not to wake you.'

Glancing at Vallio, Castus saw that the man was flagging. While he had slept for three solid hours, he realised with a twinge of guilt, his staff had been hard at work.

'Get some rest,' he told the orderly as he stood up and stretched his arms.

The surviving officers of the Mesopotamian army were waiting in the main audience hall. Castus was shocked to see how few of them there were. A handful of senior centurions and drillmasters, and a bare half-dozen unit commanders. Several bore the scars of battle, and a couple had bandaged limbs. Those that were unwounded stared at the floor, shame-faced.

'Claudius Oribasius,' Castus declared as he seated himself on a folding stool before them. The heavy-featured prefect of Legion I Parthica straightened up, staring at the far wall above Castus's head.

'Excellency!'

'Your commanding officer is on the edge of death,' Castus told him. No surprise there; all of them could hear the anguished cries and gasps of pain through the archway to the palm courtyard. 'Your legion has been driven from the field of battle in disarray, and from what I hear it's been more than decimated. And yet, you stand before me without a wound upon your body. Explain yourself!'

'Excellency,' Oribasius said again, through a gulp. 'Dux Romulianus placed me in command of the camp. I... When I saw the rout developing I ordered a retreat. It seemed better to conserve as much of my own force as possible.'

Castus glared at him, tight-jawed. He could see the flickering expressions of the other officers, and could read them fluently. But the messenger at Edessa had already told him much of what had happened during the battle.

'You fled the field, Oribasius,' he growled. 'And rode clear with your mounted troops, leaving your own men to die trying to defend their fortifications. Is that not so?'

Colour rose to the prefect's face. He opened his mouth, stammered something, then visibly regained control of himself. 'I take full responsibility,' he said in an ashen voice. 'As the senior surviving officer, all blame falls to me, I know.'

'Luckily for you,' Castus told him, 'I have insufficient men left to be vindictive. Let's hope you can redeem yourself pretty soon, eh?'

Oribasius almost gasped with relief.

One by one, the other officers stepped forward and gave their reports. Castus knew them all from his previous visit, and was grieved to see that most of the better men had died during the battle. The only surviving tribune he rated highly was the commander of the numerus of Gothic auxilia. Flavius Gunthia was a big man, his heavy beard shot with grey. The barbarian troops he commanded had mostly been taken captive after the battle of Chrysopolis over a dozen years before, and had been serving out on the eastern frontier ever since. Gunthia had kept them together during the rout, and had fought a running battle with the enemy vanguard as he retreated towards Nisibis.

'I lost near a hundred of my men, magister,' the tribune said with sombre pride. 'But we killed twice as many of the Persian bastards!'

Diogenes had been compiling the numbers of the troops remaining in the city, and those who had escaped the rout at Zagurae. Now he passed the tablet to Castus, who ran his eye over the columns of figures. *Legio I Parthica – 762 / Legio VI Parthica – 343 / Numerus Gothorum – 498 / Ala I Nova Diocletiana – 167...* The further he read, the smaller the numbers became.

His heart ached.

'Together with the mounted troops I brought with me,' he said quietly, 'we have a little over three thousand men. The enemy, at our best current estimate, has... around *thirty times* as many.'

For a moment his eyes glazed, a sense of terrible futility clouding his mind. He drew a long breath, flexing his shoulders. 'Several of you,' he said, 'have failed in your duties as soldiers, and as commanders. But I'm prepared to forget those faults. The coming days will be a trial for us all. I'm relying on you to remember your sacred oaths to the emperor, and to do your duty in full.'

He stood up, gestured towards the imperial shrine at the rear of the hall and then raised his arm. He had no idea whether news of Constantine's death had reached Nisibis yet. Perhaps it was still a rumour, but when the assembled officers straightened to attention, all of them shouted the salute with gusto.

'*... and at every command we will be ready!*'

Only when the last of them had departed did Castus slump back onto his stool, kneading at his brow with his knuckles. A slave brought him wine and he sipped, barely tasting it.

'We need more men,' he muttered to himself. 'We'd never even hold the circuit of the walls as it is.'

'Might it be possible to conscript some of the civilian

population?' Diogenes asked. 'They'd surely be willing to defend their own city.'

Castus nodded. 'We'll have to,' he said. 'But I need to speak to their chief men first…'

'If you'll forgive me, I took the liberty of summoning them here already, while you were asleep,' Diogenes replied.

'You did?' Castus said, raising his eyebrow. When, he wondered, did Diogenes rest? The secretary was older than he was, but despite an increasingly desiccated look Diogenes still appeared remarkably brisk. The three-legged dog lay sprawled at his feet, tongue lolling.

The dignitaries of Nisibis arrived an hour later, just after Castus had finished his midday meal of bread and cheese. Lycianus had sent his Saracens out on patrol, but neither they nor the sentries on the rooftops had yet sighted the enemy. Even so, the crowd of civilians filing into the audience hall had the look of men besieged. Twenty of the principal councilman of the city Boule, together with the chief priests, all of them led by the curator Vorodes and his colleague, Dorotheus the Defensor Civitatis. Only the Christian bishop, Iacob, had failed to attend.

Castus stood before them, his thumbs hooked in his belt. The walls of the chamber were lined with troopers of the Equites Armigeri, all in burnished armour. The assembled civilians were dressed in their finest garments, but they appeared suitably cowed.

'Gentlemen of Nisibis, greetings,' Castus said, and gave them a tight smile. 'As you know, King Shapur of Persia is marching on this city with a formidable army. In only a few days he will have surrounded us entirely, and will commence siege operations. It is vital to the security of the empire that Nisibis does not fall! Therefore, from this moment the city is under military control, and every men, woman and child within it is under my sole authority.'

He paused, scanning the faces before him. Dorotheus the defensor had a sour, guarded look, but most of the rest appeared resigned to their fate. They would already have guessed what was about to happen.

'The enemy will be sending scouts and spies to survey our defences,' Castus went on. 'So I'm ordering the gates sealed, and no one allowed into or out of the city. I'll require your cooperation in keeping order. I'll also need a full inventory of all food supplies, together with a list of the entire population by household and any resident strangers. Deliver the lists to my secretary.' He gestured towards Diogenes.

'We only need hold out for a short while,' he told them, 'before the imperial field army arrives to relieve us. There are already troops marching from Antioch, and from the Euphrates garrisons, and I expect them here very soon.' Castus tried not to drop his gaze as he spoke; he did not expect many of them to believe him. He hardly believed it himself.

'I was glad to see,' he said, 'that the standing crops in the fields have already been burned. Who gave the order to do that?'

He glanced at Vorodes, expecting him to answer, but the curator just shrugged. The other men exchanged glances, but none spoke.

'I gave the order!' came a voice from the back of the hall.

The ranks of councillors parted, and Bishop Iacob paced between. Two of his priests accompanied him, a younger man supporting the bishop by his elbow as he walked.

'Very prompt,' Castus said. 'I thank you.'

'I require no thanks from the likes of you!' Iacob snapped, spittle flecking his chin. 'Nor do my congregation recognise your *authority*! I am the appointed shepherd of the Christian flock of Nisibis. They recognise no other master but God, and the emperor himself.'

Castus tightened his jaw, grinding his back teeth. The old bishop had a look of almost ferocious disdain on his face. The priests accompanying him just looked blankly pious.

'Then, as you've already shown yourself capable of commanding them,' Castus said quietly, 'I suggest you command them to assist in the defence of their city. Shapur, I'm told, has no love for Christians.'

'Shapur is God's scourge!' the bishop declared. 'All happens as God wills it. If the barbarians come to Nisibis, they do so by the will of God. They come to punish this city for its sins, its perversions, its heresies!'

'Blessed Iacob,' the defensor broke in, fingering his holy amulet, 'what punishment could the Almighty wish upon us? The Persians are the devil's people!'

'The devil is all around us now,' the bishop muttered, in a low and threatening voice. 'You know it, Dorotheus! You, who consort with pagans and Jews! You who consort with Manichees and Arians, and spend your afternoons tattling with women!'

'Enough!' Castus yelled, his voice echoing off the high vaulted ceiling. 'Your religious squabbles are unimportant. But I tell you this...' He paced before them, staring each man in the eyes. 'Anyone who refuses his duty in defending the city, or works to undermine the morale and unity of the people, will be punished. *Is that understood?*'

'We understand, strategos,' Vorodes said. The councillors all made hurried noises of agreement.

Iacob just tipped back his head, and appeared to close his eyes. 'I shall seek the intercession of the Almighty in our deliverance,' he said. 'But all will happen as God alone decrees.'

Hours later, Castus stood alone on the flat roof of the Strategion, watching the last colour of sunset bleed from the western sky. Still no sign of the enemy. Below him the barrack lines of the military castrum glimmered with lights. When he looked to his left he could see the regular grid of city streets picked out with similar glowing flickers. Beyond the walls the land was falling into blackness, but within the circuit of the defences were tens of thousands of people, tens of thousands of individual lives packed together. Castus tried to picture them: families gathered in the lamplight around evening meals, refugees bedding down for the night in the public colonnades and the porticos of the temples and bathhouses. All of them fearful, anxious of what the coming storm might bring.

In his mind he heard the questions that he had feared the city councillors would ask. Questions that he could not adequately answer.

What experience do you have of defending a city under siege?

None, he knew. He had once tried to defend a hilltop in Britain. He had watched the assault on the walls of Byzantium. He had seen the preparations for the siege of Massilia many years ago. But beyond the most obvious expedients, he was a novice.

How do you know the city will be relieved?

He did not. Every hour throughout the day he had gazed to the westward, hoping to catch sight of Mucatra's approaching column, or Hind leading her Saracen horde. Pointless even to consider the imperial army at Nicomedia.

And is the emperor really dead...?

No, he could not bear to confirm that rumour; not yet. Squaring his shoulders, Castus tried to ignore the weight of his responsibilities. He held the lives of every single person in the city in the palm of his hand now. Their futures depended solely on his decisions, his wisdom.

He glanced up at the vast blackness of the sky above him, and felt very small, overwhelmed by the immensity of what lay ahead.

Then something caught his eye, away across the plain. A glint of orange light that came and went. He squinted, and the light reappeared. With a slow gasp he noticed another point of light away to the left, and then another beyond it. As he stared, narrowing his eyes, he picked out more of them, like sparks floating along the line of the horizon.

Turning slowly, he scanned the distance to the west, and then the east. Sparks of flame everywhere he looked. He knew what they were now. The Persian outriders had moved up with the night, and they were burning the surrounding villages.

In all directions, Nisibis was ringed by fires.

CHAPTER XVII

'**B**ring it all down,' Castus said, leaning from the ramparts of the Gate of the Sun. 'All of that, along the river – I need it cleared today.'

Beneath him, at the foot of the city's towering eastern walls, the River Mygdonius flowed along a deep bed. Dry earth bluffs rose steeply to either side, and the foundations of the wall stood directly above them. But the narrow sandy banks of the river were crowded with a mass of temporary structures, crude huts and shacks, canvas awnings and palm-roofed shelters. They housed a random population of drifters and peddlers, prostitutes and beggars drawn to the city's riches; they also presented good cover to any attacker approaching the walls from the east.

'I'll send a party of troops to help your municipal slaves with the demolition.'

'I think we can deal with it on our own,' Vorodes said with a sniff. 'I've been arguing for months that we should clear the riverside of vagrants.'

A couple of women were gazing up at them, waving and calling out. They wore thin gaudy garments; prostitutes of the cheaper sort, Castus guessed, who plied their trade among the shacks. There were other women down by the river, kneeling as they scrubbed wet cloth over the flat stones.

'It's up to you to accommodate the people who live down there as well,' Castus told the curator. 'Don't just drive them out into the countryside. The Persians'll find uses for any they don't kill.'

In front of the gates the river was spanned by a five-arched stone bridge. On the far side lay the eastern suburb, enclosed by its own rough semi-circle of wall. The defences of the suburb were puny compared to the walls of the city itself, but Castus had sent Gunthia and his five hundred Gothic troops to defend them. He had considered abandoning the suburb, which mainly held workshops, warehouses and hostelries for the caravan traders, but even a slight defence might hold back the enemy on that side for a while.

Descending the steps from the gatehouse roof, Vorodes following him with Sabinus and his bodyguards, Castus paced along the broad rampart walkway. He had almost completed his circuit of the city walls now, and they looked as formidable as Diogenes had reported, months before. All along the walkway there were soldiers waiting at their posts, legionaries and dismounted cavalry troopers, Arab irregulars and Armenian archers, all saluting smartly as he passed. Every fifty paces or so was an artillery emplacement, the big arrow-throwing ballistae each with stacks of ammunition laid ready. Some of the weapons had names carved into their stocks: *Striker*, *Far-Darter* and *Sudden Death*.

Behind the wall, at further intervals, were massive masonry platforms that supported the single-armed stone-hurling catapults called onagers. The big machines had too fierce a recoil to be mounted on the ramparts; their crews had to shoot blindly, guided by the sentries on the walls, but Castus had watched them being tested earlier that day. The range and accuracy of their plunging missiles was impressive.

Castus paused and stepped over to the battlements, peering out across the countryside beyond the fortifications. A party of

Lycianus's scouts were riding in from the east, but they showed no sign of particular haste. The enemy, for now, were still keeping their distance.

There had been no sign, either, of any reinforcements approaching from the west. The scouts had discovered nothing of either Mucatra or Hind. But Castus was determined not to worry too much about them at the moment. He had slept unusually well the night before, deeply and without dreams, and woken refreshed and filled with a renewed sense of purpose. The city's defences were strong, and while the troops were few in number their morale seemed high. The city's population, for now, had accepted military government without complaint, and in some cases with obvious relief. Things, Castus told himself, could certainly be worse.

He almost had a skip in his step as he descended the steep stairway from the rampart to the street below. But he was careful to keep his expression grave as he marched through the city, across the market district and the central avenue. His bodyguards and staff officers were formed up around him, his standard-bearer and trumpeters marching ahead of him, and the citizens of Nisibis hung back in the doorways and the porticoes and stared at him as he passed. Castus kept his neck stiff, glancing neither to one side nor the other, ignoring the occasional calls and cries. What did they think, these eastern civilians, when they looked at him? Did they see the living personification of Roman military power, or just a big old grey-haired man with a sunburnt face, sweating in his cloak and cuirass?

There was a crowd gathered on the marble paving of the precinct around the Tychaeion. Castus was glad to see that so many had attended the summons promptly. The heralds had gone out at dawn, and the placards were fixed at every street corner in every ward: each household in the city was to contribute one able-bodied man to serve in the militia and help defend the walls.

It had been Diogenes's idea to link militia service with the food dole: a harsh ruling, but a necessary one. Only those who served would be fed at the city's expense.

The crowd parted as Castus and his entourage approached. They were a motley selection: field labourers and city tradesmen; merchants and caravan guards; some who looked like slaves or beggars. Most had improvised weapons, hunting spears or tools, while others were empty-handed, gawping and nervous. Castus noticed more than a few women among them too. In rough lines they filed up to the steps of the great temple, where the city clerks were recording their names in the ledgers.

'Sabinus,' Castus said as he reached the steps, 'I'm giving you responsibility for organising the city militia.'

His son straightened, squaring his shoulders, but he had a dubious look. 'Yes, Father,' he said. 'I mean – *Yes, dominus.*'

'You can draw a dozen or so soldiers to help. You'll have to select the best men to act as unit leaders, weed out the unfit, see that all the rest are armed and given as much training as possible, and divided into *numeri* of around a hundred or so...'

'I know what to do,' Sabinus broke in.

'Good.' Castus gave him a cuff on the shoulder. He had to remind himself sometimes that his son was a grown man, and an experienced military officer. But Sabinus had no direct experience of command; he made a note to appoint one of the more able *campidoctores*, the veteran drillmasters of the legions, to assist him.

Climbing the steps, he found Diogenes sitting beneath the tall statue of the emperor Severus. The secretary was eating an apple, and watching the slow assembly of the militia with open curiosity as his dog lounged beside him.

'The population seem quite happy with the Rule of Mars, so far!' he said with a smile.

'So far,' Castus repeated in an undertone. He stepped into the shade of the statue. 'Mostly they're just frightened of the alternative... But it won't take long before they start complaining. Civilians always do.'

Diogenes nodded, chewing. 'It occurred to me,' he said, 'that we might order all private food stocks surrendered to the public storehouses. If there are shortages, any notions of inequality could easily breed discord.'

'Do it,' Castus said firmly. He was not sure how effective it might be, or how easy to enforce, but he needed to keep the city and its people on a short rein. 'There's something else I need you to do,' he added quietly, stooping beside Diogenes. The dog gave a low whine and slunk away. 'There are too many different factions here, too many strangers from different places... I need to know what's happening in the city. What people are saying...' He broke off, unsure how to phrase the request.

'You need a secret network of informers to spy for you?' Diogenes said briskly. 'And you want me to organise one?'

'Yes... yes, that's it,' Castus said. He was uncomfortable with the idea – spies and informers had always seemed odious to him. But without information he could only rely on blind trust. Sooner or later, he knew, that trust would prove misguided. Most likely there were already those in Nisibis plotting to hand the city over to the enemy.

'I could certainly do that,' Diogenes said. 'It would take money, sadly. Such people as I would need to employ seldom act out of love for their *polis*.'

'That's not a problem,' Castus said with an unexpected sense of relief. 'You can draw coin from the treasury – I'll give you the warrant. But I'd need to know everything, and up to the highest levels...'

'Oh, don't worry about that, dominus,' the secretary said with a glint of pleasure. 'I'm sure the dignitaries of the city have plenty to hide, and as a student of human nature I shall enjoy uncovering it!'

For a professed philosopher and intellectual, Castus thought, his old friend Diogenes had always taken an unusual delight in probing the sordid details of other people's lives. Wealthy people especially. He assumed that it accorded in some way with the man's eccentric political beliefs.

Down in the open space of the temple precinct, the sun was blazing back off the marble paving. As Castus crossed to the far portico, the curator Vorodes fell into step beside him. 'Everyone in the city is eager to help in any way they can,' he told Castus. 'My son Barnaeus will serve in the militia, of course. I'm sure you can find a suitable position for him?'

'Oh, surely I can,' Castus said, distracted. He was shading his eyes as he stared at the rooftops all around him.

'And if you need to commandeer any of the city's buildings, just let me know. Either public or private.'

'I do,' Castus told him. 'I'll need a central command post – a place that gives me a good view over the defences.' The Strategion terrace provided an excellent vantage point, but the view to the north was screened by the other structures on the citadel mount. Now, as he gazed in that direction, Castus made out one building that towered above the surrounding rooftops.

'Well, if you need to requisition a suitable place,' Vorodes said, 'I can give the order for the residents to hand it over to you.'

'No need,' Castus said, and pointed to the tall building. 'I'm taking your house.'

Towards evening, he was standing by the low wall of the curator's rooftop garden when a messenger brought word that Romulianus was dead. Castus just nodded curtly; he could not bring himself to mourn the dead officer, but at least his sufferings were over. It was a callous thought, but sharing his quarters with a dying man had seemed a bad omen. How many of his officers and staff, listening to the anguished cries, must have wondered if they too were fated to meet such an end?

But the city itself looked tranquil in the soft light, now the heat of the day had receded. Far away in the northern quarter, Castus could make out the tall pediment of the temple of Baal Shamin; Vorodes would be there now, leading the evening rituals to his god. And from away to his right Castus could hear the sounds of massed chanting from the Church of the Saviour, where Jacob's Christian congregation had gathered to pray for deliverance from the Persians.

And where were the Persians themselves? Except for the night raids on the outlying villages, there had still been no sign of Shapur's advancing army. Nervous tension tightened Castus's guts; had the Persian king decided to avoid Nisibis, and march west by a different route? Stifling a curse, Castus muttered another quick prayer instead. He thought of Marcellina and Aeliana, waiting for him back in Antioch, and hoped desperately that his actions had not left them defenceless before the enemy advance.

A quiet footstep behind him, and he turned.

'Am I disturbing your tactical deliberations, excellency?'

Aurelia Sohaemia walked from the darkened arch of the dining pavilion, wrapping a shawl around her head and shoulders. There was a hint of warmth in her voice, but her expression was grave. She came and stood beside Castus, looking down at the city.

'It's your house,' Castus said. 'I was just enjoying the peace, to be honest.'

'Ah, yes. Peace.'

From the street below they heard the sound of laughter, a woman singing, the cry of a child.

'Is it true what they say?' Sohaemia asked. 'Is the emperor really dead?'

Castus looked at her. 'Yes,' he said. 'It's true.'

'I thank you for not pretending otherwise. Nobody likes to be treated as a fool.' She drew closer, turning to face him. 'So in whose name will you fight your battles?' she asked.

'In the name of Rome. As I've always done.'

'So it doesn't matter to you who sits on the throne? Your rulers are interchangeable? Their faces alter but their essence remains the same.'

'It's not a matter for discussion,' Castus said with a twitch of annoyance. 'Nisibis is part of the Roman Empire, and so I'll defend it. That's all the certainty I need.'

'It must be nice to live in such a simple world!' she said. But she was smiling, and Castus could only shrug. He remembered all too well the attraction he had felt for this woman at their last meeting. How long ago that seemed now. But the same feelings stirred in him now.

'Do you think,' she said, gesturing towards the city spread below them, 'that all those people down there care for the Roman Empire, or who rules it? Rome is far away. They care about their own homes, their families, their livelihoods. Their city too. Does it matter to them whether Rome rules them, or Shapur?'

'You husband seems eager enough to show his loyalty.'

Sohaemia laughed lightly. 'Yes, doesn't he? Vorodes is very proud of his Roman ancestry. Proud of his status too, and at the moment you're the one who can guarantee it.'

'And what of you? You don't feel the same way?'

She frowned, considering. 'My grandmother was first cousin to Zenobia of Palmyra,' she said, 'and I trace my family back to the royal house of the Nabataeans. With a lineage like that, empires can seem quite transient things.'

Sohaemia let her shawl drop, uncovering her hair, and Castus caught her scent on the warm evening breeze.

'You promised me that your emperor's war would not affect Nisibis,' she said in a low voice. 'And yet now your emperor is dead, and war threatens us all. Even my own son must take up arms.' She moved a step closer to him. 'Try not to kill too many of us in your battles, general.'

'You think I'm some kind of monster?' Castus asked with a grimace.

'No. I think you're a man who cares so deeply for honour and duty that you'd sacrifice yourself for them. All I ask is that you don't drag the rest of us down with you.'

A light cough disturbed them, and Sohaemia stepped back, rearranging her shawl. Lycianus stood in the doorway of the dining pavilion.

'Magister,' he said. 'You need to see this.'

Leaving the curator's house, Castus climbed the slope and crossed the paved square to the Strategion at a jog. He was breathing heavily as he reached the steps and scaled them to the terrace. A group of other officers were already standing there, all of them gazing towards the southern horizon. Castus joined them, shading his eyes with his scarred left hand. He saw only the countryside stretching empty to the horizon, the sky still lit by the last of the sun.

'There,' Lycianus said, pointing.

Castus squinted, and for a moment more he could distinguish nothing. When he raised his eyes he saw the glowing blueness, the pale disc of the moon. But as he dropped his gaze he noticed, all along the horizon, a belt of deeper colour like a stain seeping upwards to pollute the sky. His blood stilled.

'*The mother of dust*,' he breathed.

Lycianus nodded grimly. 'They're here,' he said. 'They'll be making camp for the night. Tomorrow we'll see them.'

Along the line of the terrace wall, men raised their fingers to their lips and then to the heavens, muttering quiet prayers to the protecting gods. Castus just clenched his jaw and stared. At least now he knew that Shapur was marching on Nisibis. And the dust raised by his enormous army was rising to fill the sky and blot out the moon.

CHAPTER XVIII

They heard the drums first, roaring across the plain at dawn in a constant low pulse of sound. The dust had settled in the night, but now it boiled up from the horizon once more in a thick brown pall that seemed to roll steadily towards the city, cloaking the Persian advance.

Castus was back on the terrace of the Strategion. He had been there since first light, sitting beneath an awning with his staff officers. Now, as the sun climbed the eastern sky, the vanguard of the Persian force came into view. Figures of men and horses seemed to form out of the haze, the heads of marching columns, banners hanging above them, their armour blazing.

'They're building a bridge of boats, about a mile downstream,' Egnatius said, shading his eyes from the morning glare.

Castus squinted, wishing his own sight was sharper. He could see that the main enemy force was massing to the south-east of the city, on the higher ground beyond the river. But there were other columns away to the west, cavalry crossing the low marshy ground and moving up to encircle the city from the far side. The noise of the drums came and went, cut through by the high screaming of trumpets.

'Look, there,' Egnatius said, pointing. 'Elephants. Scores of them!'

At first Castus could not make them out in the haze of sunshot dust. Then the haze shifted and he saw the hulking grey shapes: vast beasts moving slowly, carrying fighting towers and canopied howdahs on their backs. He felt a tremor of dread in his gut. He had seen elephants before, many years ago, but never as many of them.

'Do you remember Eumolpius?' Diogenes asked. The old secretary was sitting on a stool in the shade.

'Of course,' Castus said. Eumolpius had been his orderly and armour-bearer; he had died during the naval battle of the Hellespont, more than a dozen years before.

'He always wanted to see an elephant, as I recall,' Diogenes said. 'A shame he never did! Perhaps he would have liked to be here now, eh?'

Castus gave a dry laugh. 'I doubt many men alive have seen an array like this one.'

Except for the rapidly moving light cavalry on the flanks, the main Persian force advanced at a lumbering speed. Shapur was taking his time over the deployment. But that too was intentional, Castus realised. The Persian king was making a show of strength, trying to intimidate them. All around the walls of Nisibis men stood on the ramparts and stared at the massive force assembling before the city. There were plenty of civilians among them, serving in the newly mustered militia; others had climbed up onto the tops of the houses, and the roof of the temple near the Singara Gate. They would take word of the formidable enemy numbers back to their families. Soon all would know that they were surrounded by an unbeatable foe.

'The Dirafsh-i-Kaviyan,' Lycianus said, joining Castus on the terrace and pointing. Sure enough, Castus could make out the Persian royal standard flying above the centre of the main force. Just as Hormisdas had said, it was clearly visible even from this distance, the gold and gemstones glittering in the sunlight. Below it, Castus guessed, would be the king himself, although he could see nothing except massed ranks of cavalry.

'Over to the left of the standard – you see the elephants with the tall towers?' Lycianus asked. 'That must be the royal harem. The Persian kings don't travel anywhere without their women!'

Castus wished he had Hormisdas with him now, to point out the other units of the royal army and give some assessment of their relative worth. But the sun was beginning to hurt his eyes, and his face felt raw and creased from squinting so long. After a while, the vast Persian array seemed to blur into a slow dark tide that filled the plain and the high ground to either side of the city, steadily expanding to encompass it on both flanks.

All morning the deployment continued, the men on the walls of Nisibis remaining at their posts as the sun rose to its zenith and the air became so hot it almost hurt to breathe. Now and again troops of enemy cavalry rode closer to the defences, but none came within range of arrows or artillery. By mid afternoon the dust had settled, and the Persian force was revealed in all its strength. Nisibis was completely surrounded.

'Food, dominus,' Vallio said, appearing at his side. The slaves behind him carried jars of wine and platters of bread and meat. 'You need it.'

Castus acknowledged him with a grunt. He had eaten nothing that day, but the food just tasted like grit in his mouth and he could hardly swallow. The wine, well diluted, eased the tightness of his throat at least.

'Report from the north gate, dominus,' said the Protector Iovinus. 'The sentries say the enemy have thrown a trestle bridge across the river a mile or so upstream, just above the ravine.'

'So they can circle us at will!' Egnatius said grimly.

But now there was a disturbance in the ranks of the enemy force arrayed to the south. Castus saw it, and stood up. The royal standard appeared above the heads of troops, and he could hear the noise of cheering; not like the tumult of a Roman army shouting out their acclamations, but more of a slow gathering chant.

'The king,' Lycianus said.

At first Castus could make out only a solid block of horsemen riding clear of the enemy lines, the standard flying above them. Then, as they got within a few hundred paces of the wall, they turned to the right and spread out. Both vanguard and rearguard were made up of heavy armoured lancers, cataphracts on scale-clad mounts, horses and men glittering with silver and gold, tall plumes and bright silk tassels. Their long lances weaved above them as they rode.

Between the two bodies of cataphracts was another group, men in bright costumes, some in armour. Court officials, Castus guessed, ministers, commanders and bodyguards. And at the heart of the retinue rode another figure, dressed entirely in purple, with a black beard and a bulbous white hat. At this distance, Castus found it hard to make him out, but he knew at once who the rider must be. Shapur, King of Kings and ruler of the Persian Empire.

'I want a closer look,' he said. 'Follow me.'

At the western end of the citadel mount, a cluster of old towers and buttresses stood directly above the city wall. It was a short walk from the Strategion, along an alley and through a gate, then down a narrow stone stairway that opened onto the ramparts. Followed by his officers and standard-bearer, Castus turned to the right at the bottom of the steps and paced northwards towards the Singara Gate. The Persian royal retinue had just doubled the far corner of the city wall and were negotiating the marshy ground to the south-west, still keeping just out of range of the defending artillery.

All along the ramparts, soldiers stood in the embrasures, craning outward to watch the king and his party. Castus paused and glanced back. As Shapur rode along the front line of his besieging troops, they appeared to form tighter ranks in his wake, shields raised in a solid wall. The sound of their cries rolled in great waves across the plain. 'SHA-PUR! SHA-PUR! SHAH-AN-SHAH! PE-ROZ!'

But while the sight of the encircling army had filled the men on the walls with dread, the sight of the enemy king roused them to fury. As Shapur approached, the Roman defenders responded with jeers and cries of their own.

'Bastard!' yelled one grizzled legionary of the Sixth Parthica. 'Go and wash your face in piss!'

'Goat-fucker!' another shouted. 'Bugger off back to your perfume shop!'

Raucous laughter broke the spell of fear. Slowly a ragged chant was building along the wall, countering the roar of the Persians.

'RO-MA VIC-TRIX! RO-MA VIC-TRIX!'

Then, as Castus jogged up the steps to the summit of the gate tower, the chant changed.

'CONSTANTINE! CONSTANTINE!'

A shudder ran down his spine as he heard the dead man's name. *Either they don't know, or they don't care...* But he grinned nonetheless. He had heard that same name chanted on battlefields all across the empire. It meant one thing – *victory*.

'Constantine!' he shouted, hoarse but loud, raising his fist. 'Constantine lives and reigns!'

Cheering erupted around him, then the rattling clamour of blades on shield rims, spear-butts hammering the rampart paving, the stamping of hobnailed boots.

Shapur had paused as he reached the cluster of tower-tombs along the Edessa road, and seemed to be studying the fortifications. If he heard the noise, or noticed Castus's draco banner flying over the gate, he gave no sign of it. He appeared entirely unconcerned by the bellowing of the defenders. Castus saw the king turn to one of his attendants, make a comment or give an order, then turn his horse and ride onward.

Then he noticed the man riding directly behind the king. Immediately he recognised the powerful jet-black stallion, the rich dark blue coat and the distinctive curving moustaches. Impossible to be sure, but the man appeared to be staring back at Castus.

'Zamasp,' he said under his breath, remembering the name. '*I hoped never to see you again…*'

The king moved onwards, leaving the serried ranks of his troops formed up behind him. In the simmering mid-afternoon sun the Persians stood immobile, their banners raised. Shapur and his party had dwindled into the distance, and soon Castus could make out only the dust they left behind them as they turned around the northern walls of the city. The king would make a complete circuit, he guessed. A gesture of ownership over the city and all within in. Anger beat in his chest, but the brief exultant rage had lifted his spirits. The men on the ramparts had subsided into silence once more.

'Reckon he'll do anything more today?' Egnatius asked.

'I doubt it,' Castus said. 'But we'll keep the men at their posts for now. Best get some rest while we can.'

The night was hot and airless, and Castus slept only fitfully, starting awake at the whine of mosquitoes in the darkness of his bedchamber. A bright spear of moonlight came from the slot window, and from somewhere outside he could hear one of the sentries singing a mournful eastern-sounding lament.

It had been a long day, made all the more maddening by the enforced passivity. The Persians had maintained their display of encirclement all through the hours of the afternoon and evening, only returning to their camps around the perimeter of the city at nightfall. Castus knew they would be keeping strong piquets on all the roads and strongpoints, and maintaining patrols through the night, but he doubted they would make any attempt on the walls in darkness. Even so, his every nerve felt strung tight, and he could not still the thumping of his heart.

Whenever he closed his eyes he saw again the distant figure of Zamasp. He guessed the Persian officer must have been rewarded with promotion after his trip to Constantinople. He was clearly one of the king's most senior commanders now: chief of the royal bodyguard, perhaps. He remembered the man's mocking words when last they had met, on the rainy road to Hierapolis.

A high whine close to his ear, and Castus lashed out at the invisible insect. With a groan of frustration he tugged the sweat-dampened blanket over his head, trying to force himself back into sleep. The sentry's song had ended now, replaced by the rasping pulse of crickets.

Then another sound reached him. Distant voices, a shout, and the noise of running footsteps. Castus sat up, throwing aside the blanket. For a few moments he heard nothing, then the sounds came again, more insistent now. Growling low in his throat, he swung himself out of bed and pulled on his tunic.

Outside in the vestibule, Vallio and the two other slaves were stumbling up from their pallets in confusion. Castus strode through the far door into the moonlit inner courtyard. The sound of shouting had grown to a tumult, but still too distant to make out. A figure appeared, running in panic and stopping himself: Metrophanes, the plump numerarius.

'What's happening?' Castus demanded.

'Dominus!' Metrophanes replied. 'It's the Persians! They're... *inside the city*!'

'*Gods!*' Castus felt a surge of almost sickening anguish rise through him. For two heartbeats he just stood, braced in the doorway. How had this happened? How had he failed so soon?

'Vallio!' he shouted. 'Boots and kit – *now*!'

But the orderly was already scrabbling about in the darkened bedchamber, bringing Castus his boots and belt, his sword and armour. Cursing in frustration, Castus pulled them on and stood while Vallio tied the laces. He tugged the padded linen arming vest over his tunic, and was already striding across the courtyard as he threw the sword baldric over his shoulder. Vallio was following him, holding his cuirass and helmet.

'Leave them!' Castus cried. He needed to move fast; armour would only slow him down.

Torchlight met him as he jogged from the front doors of the Strategion. Lycianus was in the square outside with three of his Saracen scouts, all of them mounted. Egnatius was there too, and a groom was saddling Castus's horse.

'The alarm came from the Edessa Gate, dominus,' Lycianus said, his voice grim and clipped. 'We don't know what's happening yet, but some are saying the gates were opened and hundreds of enemy troops have already entered...'

'Treachery!' cried Egnatius. In the flaring torchlight every man's face was distorted into a savage mask.

As soon as he was mounted, Castus led them off. Egnatius had a handful of his troopers behind him; a few more soldiers followed on foot. Castus could hear the screams clearly now, the shouts of panic coming from the streets below. The news was ripping through the city, rousing the sleepers in the porticoes and the sentries at their watchfires.

'We need to avoid the central avenue,' Egnatius called. 'Too many people!'

Castus agreed. The last thing he wanted was to get caught in a mob of panicking civilians. As they rode down from the citadel mount, he turned his horse to the left, taking the narrower street that led behind the Bouleuterion and the Tychaeion precinct, northwards towards the Edessa Gate.

Was hour was it? Glancing up, he saw the moon low in the sky, just above the rooftops. It must be nearing dawn. Then he was in the deep trench of the street, and darkness closed around him. All across the city there was the noise of heavy wooden shutters slamming down, iron bolts rattling as the citizens secured their shops and houses. Fugitives were running from all directions, apparently in complete confusion, crying out in Syriac and Greek and scattering as they heard the noise of the hooves on the cobbles.

'Save us!' a woman cried. 'Save us – the Persians will murder us all!'

As he rode, Castus realised that he was charging towards a scene of combat with no armour, no weapon but a sword. So be it. Better to go down fighting at the first rush if the city was lost. Better not to have to contemplate surrender. Up ahead he could make out soldiers in the street, gathered on the corners with weapons in hand. They let out nervous cheers as he passed, but none seemed to know what was happening.

Reaching the end of the street, Castus galloped into the broad colonnaded avenue that led from the Edessa Gate. He slowed at once. The street to either side of him was filled with milling troops, shields and spears catching the weaving torchlight, the air resounding with shouts and cries. Castus gripped his sword, drawing it partway from his scabbard.

Then, with a sharp jolt that rocked him in the saddle, he realised what he was seeing.

The shouts were not cries of fierce battle, but cheers of jubilation.

Blinking, he stared at the shields around him. Some blue and others yellow, all with a design of radiating black acanthus leaves. The emblems of the Tenth and Seventh Gemina legions.

He threw back his head and cried out with joy and relief.

'Excellency!' somebody was calling from the crowd. 'Magister!'

Egnatius and Lycianus rode up beside him. Egnatius was slack-jawed and grinning in amazement.

A man in a helmet was pushing his way through the throng. Castus recognised the blunt face of Barbatio, the centurion he had appointed to command the Tenth.

'Excellency,' Barbatio said again, saluting. 'Apologies it took us so long to get here. We marched double pace through the night, then broke through their piquets at the charge. Lucky the sentries at the gate recognised our signal!'

'Well done,' Castus said, grinning as he leaned from the saddle and seized the man by the shoulder. 'How many are with you? Where's Mucatra? Is he following?'

Barbatio's face closed, and he gave a tight shrug. 'Just us, dominus,' he said. 'My own detachment, and Mamertinus with his men of the Seventh. We lost a few coming in, and my boys are dead on their feet!'

Straightening up, Castus saw the exhaustion on the faces of the soldiers. Some had dropped to kneel in the road, braced on their shields. Other staggered to the pavements under the colonnades to sit, heads in hands. People were running from all sides now, bringing flasks of water and wine, and the soldiers tipped back their heads and drank like men who had been parched for days.

Slowly the exultation was dying away, replaced by dulled fatigue. Castus sat in the saddle, exhaled quietly and tried not to show his disappointment. For a moment he had almost believed that they were saved.

'The *snake*!' he yelled. 'The filthy Thracian dog!' Enraged, Castus kicked at a stool, and sent it crashing into the corner of the room. The five officers just looked at him, too tired to share his anger.

Valerius Mucatra, it turned out, had ignored Castus's order to advance rapidly in his support. Instead, so Barbatio reported, the army commander had halted his troops at Edessa, shortly after receiving Castus's message, and then turned them around and marched back towards Hierapolis, burning the boat bridge over the Euphrates behind him. He may even have retreated all the way to Antioch by now.

'Fucking coward,' Egnatius muttered, leaning against the wall with his arms folded. In the grey dawn light, all of the men gathered in the meeting chamber of the Strategion appeared haggard, their faces dark and hollow after a sleepless night.

'When we got the order to retreat, we thought it must be a mistake,' said Mamertinus. 'The rider who brought it seemed dubious himself.'

Mamertinus was a Spaniard, and had served nearly thirty years under the standards. He was only a *campidoctor*, a drillmaster, but he had temporary command of the light troops of the Seventh Legion. Both he and Barbatio had been marching at the van of Mucatra's column, a day ahead of the main force. Both had taken the decision to ignore the order, and push their men onwards instead. It had been an incredible feat; Diogenes had commented that even the great Julius Caesar could not have moved so rapidly. But they had only nine hundred men between them; their troops were exhausted, and after fighting their way through the Persian siege lines they would need days to recover their strength.

'I'll have barracks and provisions arranged for you,' Castus told both officers. 'See that your men have all they need, and as much rest as they can get. I'm giving both of you temporary promotions to tribune as well. You'll join my military council.'

'Appreciate it, dominus,' Barbatio said. He appeared too weary to say more.

Mucatra too, Castus guessed, would be getting a promotion soon enough. He did not doubt that the decision to pull back had been prearranged. Dracilianus must have told Mucatra to retreat at the first opportunity. Now, with Castus besieged in Nisibis, Dracilianus could move his own man into supreme command of the army. Sour bile rose in his throat, and he swallowed it down. *One day*, he thought, *one day, if the gods grant I escape this place...*

Clattering footsteps, a cry from the vestibule, and a soldier appeared at the door. He gave a hurried salute. 'Excellency – message from the sentries at the Singara Gate,' he said, gulping the words. 'The Persians want to talk.'

'Talk?' Castus inhaled slowly, raising his eyebrows. Then he nodded curtly. 'Egnatius, Sabinus and Lycianus,' he said, 'come with me. The rest of you return to your commands. Hopefully this won't take long.'

He took his time preparing, splashing his face with cooled water and waiting while Vallio strapped on his polished cuirass and arranged the heavy general's cloak around his shoulders. Then, with his plumed helmet clasped under his arm, he marched from the Strategion and down the slope towards the agora. The sun was just above the eastern ramparts, and it glared in his face. Already he was starting to sweat.

As he walked, he distracted himself with calculations. Barbatio and Mamertinus's reinforcement, were prime soldiers, but Castus's fighting force in the city still numbered less than four thousand. The militia ought to double that amount, but they could only be trusted to hold the walls at best. He was turning the numbers in his mind as he noticed the group of civilian dignitaries waiting for him at the base of the church steps.

'Magister,' said Vorodes, stepping forward. 'We're told that the Persians are requesting negotiation. As representatives of the citizens, we ask that we attend with you.'

'It's customary,' the defensor, Dorotheus, added. 'And in keeping with the dignity of our magistracies.'

Castus peered at them, trying to hide his instinctive sneer. Civilians, he thought, were never welcome at a time of war. Several of the elders of the Boule and the high priests were with them.

'The Persians don't want to negotiate,' he said. 'They want us to surrender, and I'm going to refuse. This is a matter for the army.'

'Nevertheless,' Vorodes said with a quick tight smile, 'as curator of the city and high priest of Baal Shamin I should accompany you.'

'I too will come,' a cracked voice said.

Castus looked up and saw the bishop, Iacob, clambering down the steps with his young assistant at his side. He stifled a groan.

'I must represent the Christian congregation of Nisibis!' the bishop went on.

'Follow if you like,' Castus told them all. 'But stay back, and don't speak. This isn't going to be a polite conference.'

As he walked on past them, he told Egnatius to make sure the city dignitaries were kept at a safe distance. 'Particularly the bishop,' he hissed.

Further down the colonnaded avenue that led south towards the gates, Castus picked up a guard of legionaries as he passed the military castrum. A large mob of civilians were following behind the city officials, and Egnatius ordered his cavalry troopers to block the street fifty paces from the gates themselves and keep back the crowd.

Leaving the dignitaries waiting beneath the gate arches, Castus jogged up the narrow stairway of the flanking tower. The soldiers on the roof stepped back smartly as he emerged, red-faced and heaving breath, and walked to the parapet. At the sight before him, Castus sucked air through his teeth.

The Persians had once more assembled in their encircling ranks, a line of shields four or five deep stretching all around the circuit of the city walls. Behind them, on the flat ground to the south, stood twenty massive war elephants, all with fighting towers. The beasts shifted, raising their trunks. Beyond the elephants, on a low dusty hill crowned with old tombs, King Shapur had set up his standard. Castus could just make out the king, seated on a high throne beneath his banner, ringed by guards and ministers.

And ahead of them all, with fifty mounted archers to back him, was Zamasp.

The Persian commander sat patiently as his magnificent horse pawed the ground. A rider behind him carried a green branch on a pole – where they had found it in that arid and fire-blackened land Castus could not guess.

'They have prisoners too, dominus,' the centurion commanding the gate detachment said. 'Took them at Singara, I'd reckon.'

Sure enough, ahead of the horse archers stood a score of men in unbelted tunics, Roman soldiers, with rope halters around their necks. They were Zamasp's security; if anything happened to him, the men would die.

'I want all your artillery loaded and aimed at the road,' Castus told the centurion. 'Archers on the ramparts, and on the outer wall too. But nobody shoot unless I give the order myself – understand?'

The centurion saluted, and after one last glance Castus dropped back down the steps.

'Open the gates,' he cried, and Egnatius repeated the words. The huge bronze-studded doors jolted as the locking bar was lifted, then groaned slowly open. Castus strode forward, down the paved ramp beneath the gate arches and out into the killing ground between the inner and outer walls. Vorodes and the other councillors followed, looking far more nervous now.

'Close the main gates behind us,' Castus told Egnatius. 'If anyone tries to break through, kill them.'

Across the cleared expanse of scrubby grass between the walls, Castus reached the outer gateway. He glanced up, and saw the archers and slingers already lining the narrow rampart above him. Then he gave the signal, and the outer gates swung open. He walked out into the bright sunlight beyond the walls.

The roadway from the gate ended at the brink of the dry moat, only a few paces from the arch. In times of peace a wooden bridge crossed to the far side, but it had been pulled back inside the gatehouse now. Castus walked forward until he stood at the brink, planting his feet wide and gripping the hilt of his sword. The moat was sheer-sided, twelve feet deep and cut into solid rock, the bed lined with jagged stones. Too wide for a horse to leap, but narrow enough to talk across it. And down here, whatever was said would not be heard by too many of the men on the inner wall or the civilians in the city behind them.

Castus waited in the hot sun while Zamasp approached. The Persian rode slowly, making his horse step high in a prancing and aggressive gait. The branch-carrier and a few of the mounted archers followed him. When he reached the far side of the moat, Zamasp tugged on the reins, and the horse kicked and pawed at the dust. The bridle trappings, and the gold and silver embroidery on the man's coat, glittered in the brilliant light.

'We meet again, Roman!' Zamasp cried.

Castus just inclined his head.

'I bring greetings in the name of Shapur, the Immortal, King of Kings, Lord of Iranians and Non-Iranians, of the race of the gods! My king is merciful. If you surrender this city to him now, he will spare all within it. Even you, old man! Surrender, and submit to the rule of Iran-Shahr, and all shall live in peace.'

Castus said nothing. Sweat was streaming down his back.

'Do not be foolish!' Zamasp cried, raising his voice to address also the crowd of civilian councillors in the gate arch behind Castus. 'Or, if you insist on foolishness, do not sacrifice the lives of every man, woman and child in this city! None can stand against the might of Shapur!'

'Nisibis belongs to Rome,' Castus said. 'Tell your king he can't have it.'

Zamasp grinned, and his horse circled at the brink of the ditch, arching its neck. 'Then Shapur will take it!' he yelled. 'And when he has taken it, he will kill any with arms in their hands. The rest will be marched back to Persia as slaves, never to see their homes again. The walls of Nisibis will be torn down, every house and temple levelled to the ground! The very name of your city will be forgotten by mankind. Nisibis will become... a pasture for sheep!'

Castus's face twitched into a crooked smile. 'Tell your king,' he said, 'that he can break his army against our walls if he dares. Nisibis will be the graveyard of the Persians!'

'Ha, foolishness then,' Zamasp shouted. 'So be it! You will be guests in the House of Falsehood, and made to consume scorpion and frogs!'

He kicked at his horse, dragging on the reins so the animal reared and spun on its back hooves, kicking dust and stones down into the moat. Riding a few steps away, he turned in the saddle and stretched upwards, calling to the men on the wall ramparts. 'Your emperor is dead! Constantine is dead! He has joined his master, the Prince of Lies. And soon, men of Rome, you will dine with him in hell!'

Castus set his jaw, then glanced back with a start as he heard a parched cry from behind him. Iacob had staggered forward from the gate arch, arms spread wide.

'Spawn of the devil!' the bishop yelled after the retreating Persian, spittle flying from his mouth. 'Unnatural offspring of Satan! The Almighty will smite you down! For the Lord our God protects Nisibis!'

Zamasp spurred his horse straight into a flat gallop away down the road. Castus let out a breath, watching him go. But when the Persian commander reached his mounted guard he slowed, snatching a spear from one of his men. With his face set in a mask of fury he turned, his horse kicking, and then galloped back towards the gate once more.

Castus stood still, watching the Persian as he rode closer. Zamasp leaned back in the saddle, raising the spear to throw. Gasps and cries from the men gathered under the arch as they shrank back, but Castus forced himself not to move. The Persian rode right to the far brink of the moat, and only then hauled back on the reins. With a wild cry he hurled the spear.

The weapon arced across the ditch, and Castus set his muscles to avoid flinching as it passed only a handspan from his head. He heard it strike the paving of the road beyond the threshold of the gates as the councillors scattered.

He blinked, and sweat broke and ran down his face.

Beneath the arch, Vorodes and the other councillors had recovered from their fright and emerged from where they had been cowering behind the gates. The spear lay on the paving between them. Iacob stooped and picked it up. Castus could see that the head and the top of the shaft were bright with fresh blood.

'A message!' the bishop said. He was holding the bloodied spear before him like a trophy. 'The Persian devils have declared war upon us!'

PART THREE

CHAPTER XIX

Antioch, June AD *337*

An hour's ride south of the city, the road climbed a spur beneath a hedge of flowering hawthorn, and from the carriage Marcellina saw the valley opening before her. Villa terraces appeared between the groves of tall bay trees and dark cypress, with pillared gazebos and the domed roofs of bathhouses. In the dells beneath the sacred enclosure of the Temple of Apollo, cool waters rushed between banks of ferns. This was the suburb of Daphne, the hot-season retreat of the wealthy of Antioch.

It was a beautiful sight, Marcellina had to admit, and a balm to the eyes after the heat and dust of the city. But it angered her that the elite should be relaxing in these shady arbours while other men marched across arid plains and fought in desperate battles far away.

She could have been living near here herself; Hormisdas had offered the use of his country villa. But Marcellina had preferred to remain in the city, close to the news coming in from the east. If only everyone had been as assiduous, she would not have had to make this journey up into the hills. But Flavius Ablabius, Praetorian Prefect and, in the absence of any higher authority, virtual ruler of the eastern empire, had chosen to move his court to Daphne. And it was Ablabius she needed to see.

The driver turned the carriage into a lane that curved away from the road and passed through the dappled shade of the trees before coming to an end at a gateway with little ornamental towers on either side. Marcellina climbed down from the carriage, feeling the sun's heat on her shoulders. She arranged the shawl around her head, then nodded a greeting to the pair of house slaves who had come to conduct her inside.

Ablabius kept a discreet sort of establishment. There were guards, and plenty of attendants, but they were mostly out of sight. As she followed the slaves along the garden pathway, under a box trellis hung with flowering vines, Marcellina noticed the figures stationed amid the greenery around her. Messengers came and went frequently, she knew, keeping the prefect well informed of all that happened in his domains. She had used that messenger service herself to request this meeting, and Ablabius had taken a leisurely amount of time granting it.

In the cool of the pillared atrium she waited while the house slaves removed her cloak and exchanged her shoes for soft slippers. A steward appeared, holding an ivory staff, and bowed from the neck as he gestured for her to follow him. The interior of the house was lined with marble, filled with the gentle sounds of fountain water and the distant trilling of songbirds. Marcellina followed the steward around the walkways of the central garden court, then to the left through a double arched gazebo into a pillared enclosure. In the centre, open to the sky, was a bathing pool. Sunlit steps entered the water at the nearer end. At the far end, in the shade, the pool ended in a curve of smooth marble.

Marcellina came to an abrupt halt between the pillars, took in the scene and drew a sharp breath, looking away quickly.

Flavius Ablabius was lounging at the shaded end of the pool, arms spread over the marble rim to either side of him. He was naked, his shoulders and chest thick with black hair. Beside the pool was a gold dish of ripe figs.

'Greetings, domina!' he said, and smiled. 'Hope you don't mind the informality. It's really too hot today. Perhaps you'd care to slip off your gown and join me, hmm? The water's refreshingly cool... There are some fish in here somewhere, and they give one the most interesting sensation!' He had a cup of iced white wine beside the dish, and took a sip from it.

'I think I'll stay as I am,' Marcellina said.

She had been introduced to the Praetorian Prefect when she first arrived at Antioch in the spring, but had never spoken with him privately. Seeing him now, she realised that Flavius Ablabius was just a grossly inflated version of a type of man she had met often enough. A man in love with prestige and authority, and eager to demonstrate it by humiliating others. She tried to keep her expression neutral, and not recoil.

'You wished to talk about something?' the prefect asked. His pretence was maddening. There was only one reason for Marcellina to have come here.

'Eminence,' she began, keeping her eyes raised. 'As you know, my husband Aurelius Castus has gone to defend the eastern cities against the Persian invasion. And yet we now hear that the field army has retreated to Hierapolis. You alone have the authority to order them to advance again. I believe you must do so, for the security of the empire.'

'*Must?*' said Ablabius with a frown. He selected a fig from the dish, lifted it daintily and put it in his mouth.

'That is to say...' Marcellina said, her voice faltering. 'I'm asking you...'

'*Asking?*' Ablabius said, chewing.

Marcellina felt the colour rising to her face. Anger tightened her throat, and she forced herself to remain in control of her temper. An impassioned outburst now would accomplish nothing. She swallowed down the bile of her disgust.

'Eminence, I am... begging you.'

'Ah!' the prefect said. He smiled as he took another sip of wine. 'You know,' he went on, 'your husband is a very rash and foolish man. Rushing off into battle like that... The Caesar

Constantius left very firm instructions that the army was not to move except on his orders. You know this?'

'I know this.'

Marcellina also knew that Castus had humiliated the prefect in public before he left Antioch. Her husband had never been the wisest of men, but she wished she had been there to witness it. She wished Castus were here now, to make this smug bureaucrat quail in terror.

'Yes, he really is a very foolish man, your Aurelius Castus,' the prefect said. 'A very *old* man too. Too old for a position of such responsibility. Much older than you, I think.' He raised himself slightly, the water lapping around his hairy chest. 'You're not that old at all, are you?' he enquired, peering at Marcellina. 'What are you, forty-five, I would guess? And you've kept your figure admirably. I admire that in a mature woman. I've known many of the wives of our senior officials in my time...'

'Eminence,' Marcellina broke in, grit in her voice. 'This is a serious matter.'

'And I am a serious man,' Ablabius told her. 'I may be able to reconsider the military situation, but it will take much thought... While I think, perhaps you might try one of these figs? They are *seriously* delicious!'

Marcellina looked at the dish of fruit, which lay on the rim of the pool. The figs were split at the top, their dark skins peeled back to reveal the moist pink flesh within. Ablabius took another, then raised his hand and beckoned her closer. Marcellina felt a sudden chill down her spine. The slaves standing around the margins of the bathing court were not looking at her, and the steward with his ivory staff had withdrawn out of sight.

'Come closer,' the prefect said. 'Why are you frightened? It's only a fig...'

And he's only a man, she told herself. *Only a man... I can walk away from this whenever I want.* But the fear was real now, a cold kick at her breastbone. How accustomed she had become to safety and security in the years since she had married Castus. But now she was alone, and all the fears of her past crowded her mind. The terrors of war and death that she had thought so safely banished. She had to play his game, she knew.

Slowly, barely drawing a breath, she paced around the margin of the pool, following the line of pillars until she stood close to him. Ablabius looked up at her with a glazed smile, and she wanted to kick the gold dish right in his face.

Instead she lowered herself carefully onto her haunches, stretched out her arm and took a fig from the dish. As her fingers closed on the soft fruit, Ablabius moved faster than she could have anticipated, his hand flashing out, spattering water, and seizing her wrist in a tight grip. Marcellina tried to pull away, but his fingers dug into her flesh and she was paralysed.

'Now,' he said, his smile chilling, 'perhaps we could enjoy ourselves a little? You might begin by massaging my back...'

A noise came from the far end of the court, the scrape of hobnailed boots on tile. Ablabius glanced towards the intrusion, his grip slackening, and Marcellina pulled away from him and scrambled clear. As she stood up, her head reeling, she saw three men enter the court through the arches of the gazebo, trailed by the steward. Two were soldiers, in dust-stained travelling cloaks. The third was a square-faced man in a patterned tunic and the red belt of the imperial service.

'What's this?' Ablabius demanded. 'Theodas, what's the meaning of this intrusion?'

The steward raised his hands helplessly. The man in the patterned tunic stood at the far end of the pool, thumbs hooked in his belt. Marcellina felt she recognised him from somewhere, although her mind was still whirling.

'You there!' the prefect shouted to the newcomer. 'You can't just march in here unannounced! Do you know who I am?'

'Flavius Ablabius,' the man declared. 'I come direct from Constantinople with an order from the emperor, Constantius

Augustus. You are hereby dismissed from your post as Praetorian Prefect, with immediate effect.'

Ablabius slid down in the pool, the water lapping his bristly shoulders. He opened his mouth to speak, but could not form the words.

'Furthermore,' the man went on, 'we are ordered to escort you from here to your estates in Bithynia, where you are to remain pending the decision of the emperor as to your future.'

'But...' Ablabius managed to say. 'This isn't possible! I...'

'No more words,' the man snapped. 'We leave at once. Prepare yourself.' At his nod of command, the two soldiers advanced down either side of the pool. Their studded boots grated on the tiles.

Barely conscious of moving, Marcellina slipped out of the court and paced quickly back through the house. The slaves and attendants appeared dumbstruck; none said a word to her as she snatched her shoes and cloak and went outside. Now that the moment had passed, she felt the fear and disgust she had been suppressing rise more keenly. In the front portico she paused, one hand pressed to her brow. A hard shudder ran through her body, and she felt sick.

'Domina,' a voice said. Marcellina turned and saw that the man in the patterned tunic had followed her from the house. 'I apologise for any interruption,' he said. 'But you should leave now, and say nothing of this.'

'Of course,' she replied. Suddenly she remembered his face. 'You know my son-in-law, I think,' she said. 'Laurentius, of the Notaries?'

'I do,' the man said, his expression growing less grave. 'And perhaps I remember you too... Constantinople, back in April?'

'That's right. You're with the Notaries as well.'

'Eucharius, domina,' he said with a slight bow. '*Tribunus Notariorum*.'

'What's happened?' Marcellina asked, dropping her voice.

Eucharius tightened his lips, staring into the sun-drenched greenery of the garden. He looked as though he would refuse to tell her, but then he frowned and shrugged. 'Events,' he said. 'Very *bloody* events.'

'Constantius is definitely the emperor now?' It was hard to believe; Marcellina had seen the young Caesar when she first came to Antioch, and he had seemed a rather petulant child.

'Oh, yes,' the notary said. 'Him and his brothers, most likely, although they still have to meet and decide how that's going to work. But the fourth Caesar, Dalmatius, is dead. Murdered by the palace guards ten days ago, along with his father and his brother, and more than a dozen of their supporters. Ex consuls and prefects among them. They'd only just arrived in the capital for Constantine's funeral.'

'Constantius ordered this?' Marcellina asked, barely above a whisper.

'Officially speaking,' Eucharius said, grimacing, 'it was a spontaneous action by the guards, the Schola Gentilium and others. But unofficially... yes. Our new emperor certainly knows how to take care of business.'

Marcellina felt chilled. After what had happened in the bathing court, this news was doubly horrifying. The world seemed ruled by callous tyrants.

'As for Ablabius,' the notary said, 'he's just too dangerous to keep in office. Constantius must have associated him with Dalmatius's party, even if he doesn't have any direct evidence as yet. But he will, no doubt.'

'And Constantius is returning here? Back to Antioch?'

The notary shook his head briskly. 'No, he needs to meet his brothers first, to negotiate the division of power. And just before I left Constantinople there was news of a Sarmatian invasion across the Danube; the army's already marching for Thracia and Moesia, and the new emperor'll march with them. You won't see him here for a good few months yet, I'd say.'

'But what of the Persians?' Marcellina asked, her thoughts reeling. 'Doesn't the emperor care about the invasion?'

'Nobody knows of it in Constantinople,' Eucharius told her, shrugging. 'Or they didn't when I left. As far as Emperor Constantius knows, the eastern frontier's still tranquil.'

'And so who governs in his place?' she asked him. 'In the east, I mean?'

Eucharius just widened his eyes. 'No idea!' he said. 'There hasn't been time for any other arrangements. So for now I suppose the Comes Orientis holds the senior position here. A man called Dracilianus, I think.'

At the name, Marcellina's hand went to her throat and she glanced away quickly, before the notary could see the distress in her eyes.

'Dracilianus,' she whispered, as her horror turned to dread. 'May God save us all…'

CHAPTER XX

At the sound of the trumpets, tongues of flame burst upwards from the roofs of the warehouses and workshops, and the troops began to stream back towards the bridge. Within moments, the whole of the eastern suburb was wreathed in black smoke, the circuit of walls and the mass of the attacking enemy obscured from view. Many of the retreating soldiers were wounded; others carried wounded comrades on makeshift stretchers. In rough bands of four or five they staggered back across the bridge towards the shelter of the city.

Castus stood on the walkway above the arches of the Gate of the Sun. For the last four days he had watched as Gunthia and his five hundred Gothic auxilia had defended the arc of walls around the suburb on the eastern bank of the river, against everything that Shapur had flung at them. Incredible they had held out so long. But now the casualties among the defenders had grown too great, and rather than reinforcing them further Castus had ordered the suburb evacuated and the surviving men pulled back across the river. They had burnt everything that remained behind them.

'There he is,' Sabinus said, leaning across the wall parapet. The tiny figures spilling from the burning buildings had formed into a close phalanx behind a wall of locked shields at the far end of the bridge. As Castus squinted he could make out Gunthia among them.

'*Come on, come on,*' he was saying under his breath. As the smoke eddied, the men on the wall could see the first Persian infantrymen scrambling across the breaches in the wall and pouring into the open spaces between the buildings.

'Should we order them to run while there's time?' Sabinus asked.

Castus shook his head. 'He knows what he's doing.'

Over the last two days, the engineers had demolished the arches of the bridge. Now only a narrow platform of planks spanned the remaining masonry piers. Trying to cross it at a rush could bring the whole structure down. Instead Gunthia was holding his position, waiting until the last of his injured warriors had escaped to safety before retreating, one step at a time, the perimeter wall of shields shrinking as the men at the rear moved back across the plank bridge.

'Cavalry,' Sabinus said, pointing. 'They must have got the gates open.'

Sure enough, horsemen were advancing though the haze of smoke. Mailed Persian lancers, cataphracts on armoured horses. They came on at the trot, slowing to form up as they saw the knot of Gunthia's men still holding the bridgehead in tight formation.

Castus watched with clenched teeth, sweat rolling down his face. The sun felt like it was directly overhead, the heat brutal. In the smoke and the flames from the burning warehouses the scene appeared to warp and shimmer.

'Ready the artillery,' Castus said.

The walls of Nisibis bowed inwards to either side of the Gate of the Sun, following the curve of the riverbank. The ramparts flanking the gate overlooked the bridge and the approach road at an oblique angle, and Castus had ordered most of the artillery from the eastern wall concentrated there. Even with the bridge gone, he needed to show the Persians that an attempt to repair it and storm the gate would be costly.

From either side he heard the ratcheting click of ballistae being spanned, the artillerymen turning the windlasses that would draw the slides back against the pressure of the torsion drums.

'All ready and loaded, dominus!' the artillery chief cried.

A billow of smoke swept the rampart, making Castus's eyes water. He blinked away the smart, and saw the last of Gunthia's men breaking formation and running back across the bridge. At once, the Persian cavalry surged forward in pursuit.

'Range!' came the shout from the tower.

'Loose,' Castus said.

The signaller raised his flag, and at once the crack-crack-crack of the ballistae sounded all along the ramparts, a massed volley of iron-tipped projectiles hurtling down at the leading Persian riders. Dust sprayed up from the road, hazing the shapes of tumbling men and horses. Already the artillerymen were reloading, sweating as they spun the windlasses.

From directly below him, Castus heard the crash of timbers. Gunthia's men were destroying the plank bridge behind them. On the far bank, the solid formation of cavalry had disintegrated into a chaotic mob. But already more horsemen were riding to reinforce them, some pressing forward towards the ruined bridge. Castus stared, hoping to spot Zamasp among them.

'*Onagers,*' he said.

Another signal, and a heartbeat later he heard the earth-shaking thump of the huge torsion catapults from just behind the wall. Projectiles arced overhead, flickering black against the blazing sky. Most of the onagers flung huge pottery urns, packed with small stones; as the missiles plunged down and struck the ground they burst apart, spraying fragments in all directions. Watching with bared teeth, Castus saw one Persian cataphract struck by a direct hit; horse and rider vanished in a fountain of dust and spattering blood. All along the wall the defenders were cheering, archers shooting at long range at any Persians who strayed close enough.

A warm breeze shifted the curtain of smoke and revealed the enemy falling back from the bridgehead. Bodies of men and horses lay strewn across the road and the open space of the riverbank, where the huts and shelters had once stood.

'You seem to have turned a retreat into a victory,' Lycianus said in a dry voice, joining Castus at the rampart. 'You think they'll try and repair the bridge?'

Castus shook his head. 'Not any time soon.'

Gunthia came up the steps to the gatehouse rampart, saluting. He looked exhausted, his face dirty and his beard crusted with dried blood.

'All back, dominus,' the Gothic leader said. 'Bridge down.'

'You did well,' Castus told him, clasping his shoulder. 'Now get some rest.'

Crossing to the far parapet, he gazed westwards along the line of the colonnaded main avenue, towards the opposite gateway just over half a mile away. While Shapur had been directing most of his attention so far at capturing the suburb, the Persian king had enough men to launch simultaneous attacks at several points on the perimeter.

In the six days since the enemy had first thrown their noose around the city, there had been assaults from the south and the north. Castus knew that the Persians were probing for weak spots, and was determined that they would find none. He had ordered a system of flags, to communicate along the lines of the main avenues between the gateways, and from the walls in between. If the Persians attacked anywhere, he would know about it soon enough. No signal showed above the western gate, and none was relayed from the four-sided arch at the centre of the city. But the pressure of constant vigilance was wearing at his nerves and sapping his strength.

Down through the stifling gloom of the gatehouse interior, Castus crossed the street and walked towards the main city baths, half a block to the north. At the beginning of the siege, he had requisitioned the baths to serve as the central hospital. The huge chambers were cool enough, and well ventilated, but as he stepped through the entrance portals he tried not to choke at the cloying stench of blood and mortifying flesh. Flies swarmed in the shadows and whirled in the shafts of light falling from the high windows.

'Strategos,' said a stooping bearded man, wiping blood from his hands with a cloth. 'You continue to send us new guests!'

Castus shrugged. 'Don't blame me.'

The man was named Nicagoras; he was a Cappadocian Greek, and reputedly the best surgeon in the city. He had volunteered his services several days before. Now his fine white tunic was daubed with stains, some brown and some bright red.

Following the surgeon through into the main hall, Castus scanned the lines of straw mattresses on the polished marble floor. Men lay bloodied and bandaged, some immobile, others thrashing in agony. Their cries echoed from the marble-clad walls. The slaves were still dressing the wounds of the Gothic warriors newly arrived from the evacuated suburb. A pair of slave women were kneeling beside one of them, trying to hold him down, both of them weeping openly. In the middle of the room, another slave was mopping up a lake of blood. Castus stared at it, his eyes glazed, entranced by the washes of bright red across the veined grey marble. Exhaustion clouded his mind.

'Strategos?' the surgeon said again. Castus snapped upright, focusing his thoughts. A fly buzzed in front of his face, and he swatted it away.

'I was saying that we need more clean linen for bandages, and more wine. Fresh straw for bedding too – these Goths in particular seem to bleed a prodigious amount! I suppose it must be true that the peoples of the north have more blood in their bodies, which is why they're so fierce and intemperate. The few Arabs I've seen in here so far are almost desiccated by comparison...'

'You'll have what you need,' Castus said, bemused by the surgeon's detachment from the gory scenes around him. The man reminded him in some ways of Diogenes. He turned to one of the staff secretaries following him, who made a note on his tablet.

Leaving the hospital, Castus exhaled heavily, then breathed in the warm dusty air. The mob of wounded soldiers gathered in the shade of the portico raised their hands in salute as he passed. But he could see the way that the civilians in the doorways along the street looked at him, the mingled fear and suspicion in their eyes. Six days of siege, he thought, and already they've had enough. How much longer until the people of the city turned against him?

'So, tell me some good news.'

'Nobody's plotting to murder you yet,' Diogenes said. 'At least, not as far as I've been able to discover.'

Castus stared out to the west over the line of the walls. They were standing amid the remains of the curator's roof garden, in the scant shade of a palm-leaf awning. The urns of ornamental shrubbery had long since been removed. 'Good to know,' he said. 'And what else have you found out?'

'How much do you want?' Diogenes asked with a dry smile. He had let his beard and hair grow, and had taken to wearing his ragged old philosopher's cloak again. With the crippled dog hopping everywhere after him, he appeared an eccentric figure. But in a city like Nisibis, he blended in quite well.

'Disturbances in the bread queues,' he said. 'Rumours the bakers are going to refuse to work without payment in coin. Rumours that the Jews are planning to poison the cisterns.

Rumours that the enemy are infiltrating murderers into the city, disguised as Bactrians...'

'Any truth to it?'

'Not that I can determine,' Diogenes said, then sucked his teeth. 'But one never knows. The close confines of a besieged city seem to breed and incubate such stories in remarkable profusion. And there have been effects: yesterday a mob attacked a group of Armenian merchants in the market district, accusing them of being Persian spies. Another mob, Christians this time, tried to burn a Jewish synagogue for the same reason.'

Amazing, Castus thought, that he had failed to notice any of this. For days now he had imagined that he held the city firmly in his grip. But so much was happening that he had missed altogether. 'What about the council,' he asked, 'and the other prominent citizens?'

'There was a secret meeting last night,' Diogenes said, 'at the house of the defensor, Dorotheus. Several senior members of the Boule attended. They were apparently discussing whether to approach you and demand that you negotiate with Shapur.'

'Were they indeed?' Castus exclaimed with a snort of laughter.

'I have a list of their names, if you want it.'

'Is Vorodes on the list?'

'No, he's not. Although I've been unable so far to determine his relations with them... I'll keep working on it.'

Castus had never enquired where Diogenes came upon his information. Such things, he suspected, were best left in the shadows. But he made a note to order doubled sentries on the ramparts throughout the night; if anyone in the city wanted to communicate with the Persians, they would have to cross the wall somehow. There was no way out through the gates now.

'I've been learning Persian as well,' Diogenes said. 'One of the Sogdian residents is teaching me. Fascinating language. All things considered, I thought it might come in useful.'

'Let's hope it doesn't come in *too* useful, eh?' Castus said, and turned his attention back to the walls.

Two days had passed since the evacuation of the eastern suburb, and the enemy were now directing their assaults upon the western perimeter. Only on that side of the city was the ground beyond the walls level enough to bring up heavy siege engines. But the defences were strongest there as well: first the wide rock-cut dry moat, and the outer wall behind it. Inside that wall was the open strip of land, the killing ground, before the much higher and thicker inner wall rose above it with its towers and battlements. And on every tower and every rampart walkway there were ballistae, archers and slingers waiting to rain death upon the attackers.

But even now, as Castus stared out from the roof garden, he could see the siege works creeping closer. First, the Persians had encircled the city entirely with a trench and palisade wall. Then, three hundred paces north of the Edessa Gate, they had begun to build a causeway across the dry moat, packing it with rubble and debris torn from the demolished monumental tombs. A fog of brown dust almost obscured their work, but Castus could make out the dark shapes of the mantlets, massive sloping hide screens, pushed forward on rollers, that sheltered their archers and engineers. Far out on the parched plain he could see the hulking shapes of elephants, dragging great sleds of rubble towards the moat. And amid the dust men swarmed and seethed, thousands of them labouring in the heat. When they died under the missile storm of the defenders, their bodies were flung down into the moat among the heaped debris, to raise the causeway with their own flesh and bones.

This, Castus had realised, was how the Persians conducted sieges. They seldom used artillery – Egnatius had told him that they distrusted torsion engines – and instead relied on brute force and overwhelming numbers. They ground cities down with the pickaxe and the spade, the ladder and the ram. Then the rush at the walls, heedless of casualties.

Watching the steady and relentless Persian approach, he was filled with a sense of utter hopelessness. Surely nothing could stand against such a force. Nisibis might hold out another few weeks, even a few months, but in the end the pressure would be too great. The city would break open, and all within would die.

Perhaps, he thought, that was their fate. Perhaps that in itself would be a kind of victory: if they could destroy enough of Shapur's force here, he would not have the strength to push his advance further west. Nisibis would be the rock that blocked his path, even if the city itself was destroyed in the process...

But then he remembered what Sohaemia had said to him, in this same place days before. *Don't drag the rest of us down with you...* Castus had seen little of the curator's wife in recent days; with the house full of soldiers and military staff, she had chosen to move elsewhere. He was glad of that; even the memory of her words undermined his resolve. He needed no such distractions now.

Turning his gaze, he stared across the rooftops of the city. Total stillness under the noon sun. The streets were empty, deep cracks of shadow between the buildings. There was nobody on the flat rooftops or in the temple precincts. It seemed as if some sudden plague had wiped out the entire population, or an enchantment had lulled them to sleep. He could see figures along the rampart walks, most of them sheltering from the sun under rough awnings. Now and again the arm of a catapult would jolt up from behind the wall, flinging its missile out into the fog of dust. But, compared to the ceaseless activity of the enemy, Nisibis seemed almost entirely passive. A victim, he thought, powerless against impending fate.

A shudder ran through him, and he made a warding sign against bad omens. He wiped the sweat from his brow. From somewhere in the streets below him he could hear a child calling out for its mother. A barking dog. Slowly the sounds of the city, the sounds of humanity, drifted back to fill the noon silence.

No, he thought. *We're not dead yet.*

CHAPTER XXI

'What in the name of God is *that*?' Sabinus cried as he joined Castus at the rampart.

From the tower roof of the Edessa Gate, they gazed out westwards across the outer wall and the moat towards the Persian siege works. In the middle distance, ahead of the surrounding palisade and just outside the extreme range of the defending artillery, a vast construction was rising in the dawn sunlight.

'The doom of Nisibis,' muttered Oribasius, commander of the First Parthica.

Castus hissed at him, and the prefect looked abashed. But all the officers gathered on the tower shared Oribasius's unease. Castus himself had spent the night in one of the chambers of the gatehouse, and had slept badly. All through the hours of darkness he had been disturbed by noise from the enemy lines, shouts and trumpet blasts, and the noise of hammering and clanging metal that had filled his sleeping mind with troubled dreams of his father's forge. He had woken before sunrise, weary to his bones, and called a meeting of his officers on the tower top. Now all were gathered, and the results of the Persians' night of labour were clear for all to see.

It had taken the enemy only three more days to complete their ramp across the moat, three hundred paces north of the gate. Three days of grinding struggle for the men on the ramparts as they hurled down everything they had at the attackers, and all of it in vain. The ramp formed a broad road that sloped up from the plain to the outer wall. Already the Persians had sent their engineers against the base of the wall, parties of men hacking at the bricks and stones with pickaxes and crowbars, while the defenders above them dropped rocks and burning incendiaries down onto them. Their casualties had been enormous, but they had not been daunted. And now they were preparing for the final crushing assault.

They must have built their siege tower in sections, Castus guessed, and then raised it and assembled it under cover of darkness. It was a monstrous structure, over sixty feet high, with sloping sides rising from a broad wheeled base to a fortified archery platform at the top. At present, in the first light of day, only the framework was standing, a scaffolding of huge timbers and planks lashed and bolted together. But, as Castus watched, the Persians were hoisting plates of metal to armour the lower half of the tower, and hanging rawhide over the upper sections.

'The men have already given it a name,' Egnatius said with a wry smirk. 'They're calling it *Shapur's Bastard*!'

Castus snorted a laugh. 'Looks evil enough,' he said, and spat over the ramparts.

He could see that the lowest section of the tower formed an open gallery; hundreds of men were labouring in its shade, lifting a massive wooden beam into place and suspending it from thick cables. The beam was tipped with iron: a battering ram. Once the tower was moved forward across the causeway that bridged the moat, the swinging ram would quickly bring down the weakened section of the outer wall. Then the Persians would have to level the broken foundations and heave the tower across into the open space between the walls. Only then could they lower the two broad drawbridges that already hung from one of the tower's upper storeys. And once that happened, Castus thought, the city would be theirs: nothing would be able to stem the tide of men surging across the bridges and onto the inner ramparts.

'How quickly could they move it close enough, do you think?' Sabinus asked.

Castus sucked his cheeks, considering. 'It'll take them most of the day to bring it up to the outer wall,' he said. 'They'll probably aim to hit us when the sun's in our eyes. We'll need to pound them with everything we've got before then.'

He knew that the greatest challenge for the Persians would lie in forcing their huge tower in over the ruins of the outer wall. For all that time it would be exposed to the defending artillery, archers and slingers. That, he thought, would be their one good chance to destroy the beast, and bring *Shapur's Bastard* to its knees. He turned to face the sun, kissed his fingers and raised them to the light. A quick muttered prayer. Several of the officers around him did the same.

'Egnatius,' he said. 'I'm giving you and Mamertinus command of the southern defences, either side of the Singara Gate. Barbatio – you take the north. Gunthia's already holding the Gate of the Sun. The enemy'll probably send feint attacks against all sides while we're distracted by the tower. Lycianus will remain in the central market with two hundred mounted men, as a reserve. I'll take command here, with Sabinus and Oribasius as my deputies. May the gods watch over us all.'

The officers around him straightened, raising their hands in salute. There was nothing more they needed to say. Castus watched them as they departed, with a dull tug of anguish in his gut. He trusted all of these men – even Oribasius, who was eager to make up for his failings in the earlier battle. He had drawn them all here, and now he was sending them into a fight that could bring death for them all. Their obvious faith in his command was a bitter comfort.

As the sun rose higher and the shadow thrown by the western wall contracted, Castus stared at the line of mantlets at the far end of the Persian causeway. The big hide-covered screens covered the enemy archers, but could easily be rolled aside when the siege tower was moved closer. Already the big onager catapults behind the wall were in motion, the throwing arms jerking upwards with a shuddering crash, the slings whipping heavy boulders up in arcing flight over the fortifications and down against the mantlets. Castus had ordered the battery of catapults along the wall here reinforced; there were six of the machines that could feasibly hit the tower as it approached, all of them capable of throwing the heaviest missiles. Could the armour plates and hides covering the tower protect it against repeated direct hits? Soon enough he would find out.

Drums rolled, and high-pitched trumpets wailed out on the plain. The Persians were moving now, bringing up columns of assault troops and archers, thousands strong. There were elephants too, Castus saw as the sun rose higher. Four of the huge animals were positioned on either side of the tower, with great cables lashed around them to drag it forward. The tower had six storeys above the ram housing, all with slits for archery; he guessed that the Persians would only send men up there once the tower was a lot nearer the outer wall.

As he descended the steps from the gatehouse and emerged onto the wall walk, Castus noticed a strange huddle of figures gathered close to the next tower. Baffled, he quickened his pace, his small group of staff officers and bodyguards following him. Many of the figures were civilians, he noticed, members of the city militia, with a few soldiers among them, and most were kneeling on the walkway. A high cracked voice rose above the noise from the Persian siege lines, intoning solemn words.

'What's this?' Castus demanded as he approached. 'What's happening here?'

The kneeling people were entirely blocking the walkway; across their bent backs, Castus caught sight of the shabbily dressed group at the heart of the congregation. Christian priests, he realised. And the bishop, Iacob, was leading their prayers.

'Amen!' the kneeling men cried in unison. Castus was just about to push his way between them when a voice stopped him.

'Excellency, please.' It was the grave-looking young priest who so often accompanied the bishop. Presbyter Ephraim, Castus recalled. 'This is the day of the Lord,' Ephraim said in a hushed and hurried voice.

Castus took another step forward, and the young priest laid a hand on his chest.

'If you forbid our flock to come to the House of God,' he said, 'then the House must come to them!'

Castus gazed at the priest, fighting the temptation to swat him aside for his effrontery. The Christians' holy day was better known as the Day of the Sun; he had not realised that it had come again so soon. Eleven days, he calculated, since Shapur had first appeared before the walls of Nisibis. And, true enough, he had ordered that none of the militia or the Christians among the troops were to leave their posts to attend the church.

'Please,' Ephraim said again. 'The most blessed Iacob is conducting the ceremony of the Eucharist. Allow us this, and we will depart.'

Stifling his outrage, Castus stared at the bishop and his attendants. The kneeling men were shuffling forwards, heads bowed, then taking sips from a cup of wine as Iacob muttered over them.

'Father,' Sabinus said. 'It would be best to let them proceed. I... I gave the bishop permission myself.'

'You did?'

Sabinus did not flinch from Castus's fierce expression. 'The ritual might help inspire the militia at least,' he said.

Now Iacob had finished distributing the wine, he straightened and spread his arms, addressing the whole group of congregants. 'Remember, brethren, that though we live in this world of the flesh, our weapons are not those of this world! Fight rather with the weapons of the spirit, of prayer and the power of faith! For the word of God is a mighty sword, and in his name we will trample the serpents and the scorpions that beset us!'

As he spoke, he caught sight of Castus glowering at him from the walkway. Many of the kneeling men turned, then scrambled to their feet and shuffled aside. Iacob moved between them, Ephraim and the other attending priests rushing to aid him.

'The evil ones have raised a strong tower against Nisibis,' the bishop cried as he approached Castus, pointing at the Persian siege engine. 'But the Lord will strike it down, as he struck down the tower that the Babylonians raised against heaven! We put our trust in the power of God alone to deliver us…'

'That might take a while,' Castus broke in. 'I'd rather put my trust in the power of Roman artillery.'

Iacob grinned sourly back at him. 'As the farmer winnows wheat, so God winnows cities,' he said. 'Your impiety may destroy us yet.'

Castus stepped aside for the old priest and his attendants to pass. He watched as they clambered slowly down the steps from the ramparts. They would return to the walls south of the Edessa Gate, he guessed, and make a circuit of the defences. Behind them, the troops and militiamen were already returning to their positions.

'He respects you, you know,' Sabinus said.

'Who? The bishop?' Castus laughed. It seemed incredible. 'You've talked to him then?'

'A little,' Sabinus replied, glancing away. 'We supposedly share the same faith, after all, so I thought it might be… beneficial. He's a fanatic, certainly, but many in the city revere him. You shouldn't regard him as your enemy.'

'He acts as if I'm *his*,' Castus said. Being lectured by his son did not appeal to him. Nor did the notion of the bishop's respect.

Allowing Christian rituals on an embattled rampart was bad enough, without having to indulge any finer feelings.

'You know, it might be better,' Sabinus suggested, 'if you took a position a little further back from the defences. You could see everything quite well from the roof of the curator's house, maybe…'

Castus turned sharply. None of the other officers were close enough to overhear them. 'Trying to tell me what to do?' he snapped.

'Trying to keep you safe, Father,' Sabinus replied at once. 'We can't afford to lose you! Who would take your place if you were injured or killed up here?'

Castus scrubbed at his brow. A dark pressure loomed in his mind. 'I'm sorry,' he said, wincing. 'I slept badly. I shouldn't have spoken so harshly. But I have to stay here – I have to remain close to the action. It's only here I can do any good.'

Sabinus shrugged, frowning. 'Forgive me,' he said. 'But I promised Marcellina I would try and keep you out of the worst danger.'

'You did? When?'

'Before we left Antioch. Although we've been corresponding for some time. Since before she came out here to the east – I should have told you, but she wanted to keep it between us. I've never told her anything you wouldn't want her to know,' he said hurriedly, 'but I've tried to reassure her…'

Stunned, Castus stared at his son. He had known nothing of this. With slow comprehension he remembered the suspicions he had held about Sabinus, about the messages he was sending so scrupulously. All the while, his son had been writing to Marcellina. He grinned in amazed happiness, clapping Sabinus on the shoulders.

'You're not angry?' his son said, frowning more deeply.

'No, no I'm not. But listen.' He drew Sabinus closer, slipping an arm around his shoulders. 'I've made a lot of promises to

Marcellina too. And I've broken every one of them. Not intentionally, you understand. Sometimes we're not masters of our own fate. Right now, we just have to do what we can, as well as we can. I'll not hang back from the fight. But I'm grateful to you.'

Sabinus nodded, his frown easing.

A shout came from along the rampart – 'They're moving!' – and at once both men stepped to the parapet, staring out between the merlons over the western plain.

Dust billowed from the Persian lines, and as Castus watched he saw the top of the great siege tower shudder and the whole structure begin, almost imperceptibly, to edge forward. Down below it the elephants were heaving at the towing cables, men moving up on either side to roll the mantlets ahead of them. The columns of troops behind the tower were forming too, as the trumpets cried and the drums thundered.

Castus glanced to the left, and picked out a figure on a black horse. Zamasp, directing the assault. Further back, a high mound was surrounded by flags and covered with a white awning. Shapur would be there, enthroned amid his guards to watch the assault as it drove forward towards the walls. There were more elephants too, bearing draped canopies; the women of the royal harem would also observe the attack. Castus tasted the sourness in his mouth, and spat.

'Archers!' somebody cried from along the rampart. 'Cover yourselves!'

From the line of mantlets at the far end of the causeway, Castus saw a volley of arrows launched upwards towards the walls. He dropped at once, Sabinus kneeling beside him, two soldiers covering them both with their shields. Two heartbeats later the black storm of iron-tipped shafts struck home, clinking on the rampart, arcing down onto the walkways, hitting anyone who remained standing. Screams from along the wall; a militiaman toppled backwards off the rampart with an arrow through his shoulder. A legionary yelled in agony, a shaft pinning his thigh. Castus straightened up, raising his head above the parapet only to see a second massed volley arcing upwards.

'Down, keep down!' Sabinus hissed. A pair of arrows banged into the shield above his head.

The Persians were shooting in constant relays, hundreds of archers sheltering behind the mantlets loosing arrows blindly at the wall. And all along the inner and outer ramparts the defenders were returning shots, archers and slingers pelting missiles out into the dust cloud, ballistae shooting and then reloading as fast as the crews could work. But none could raise their heads against the incoming storm, none could aim or check where their missiles fell. All the while the rain of arrows kept coming, spent shafts rattling across the rampart walks, every shield and every covering bristling with them. Every few moments there was a cry of pain as one of the arrows found its mark in human flesh.

And all the while the great siege tower was edging closer.

'Range!' came the shout from the wall.

'Loose!'

The crew stepped back from the catapult as the artillery chief hauled on the cable, tripping the release. With a mighty heave the throwing arm swung upwards, lifting the sling and its forty-pound stone missile. The sling whirled, the missile flew free and the arm slammed into the padded support with a crash that raised dust from the masonry platform.

Castus gazed upwards, tracking the stone as it curved into the noon sky. The glare blinded him, and he blinked; when he looked again the missile was gone. The sun was directly overhead now, the heat punishing, and with the siege tower in range all of the big onager catapults were directing their shot in its direction. But with the archery storm unrelenting, it was hard to judge the aim of the artillery with any accuracy. Still the arrows were taking their toll; every now and again one would drop almost vertically from the sky. The space behind the wall was covered in bodies, the dead laid out in their scores, the injured suffering in the heat.

'Dominus!' a soldier cried, running up the steps to join Castus. 'Message from Tribune Egnatius – the ladder attack against the south wall near the Singara Gate's been thrown back.'

The attack had been a feint, as Castus had expected. No news from the other sections of the defences.

Further away, two more onagers loosed almost simultaneously, the hard double crack sending a tremor through the ground. It was impossible to imagine that the enemy tower would stand up to such a battering, but it had already shrugged off several direct hits. The flexible covering of padded hides that clad its upper reaches, and the iron plates covering its base, had proven invulnerable so far.

'Two more strikes,' Oribasius said with a worried frown. 'Didn't even mark the thing. And soon it'll be too close to the wall for the catapults to hit it...'

Castus nodded grimly. In only a few hours the huge siege tower had moved forward to the far end of the causeway. It loomed over the fortifications now, the archers stationed on the top platform and in the upper storeys shooting down directly at the ramparts of the outer wall. The elephants had been unshackled and led away – two had been injured by catapult stones – and instead the tower appeared to be grinding forward by its own momentum.

'There are men beneath it,' Oribasius said, 'pushing against the axles and the chassis. Slower than hauling, but they're moving the thing sure enough. It looks like most of them are Roman prisoners.'

Castus heard the pained catch in his voice. If the Persians were using captured Roman soldiers to move their tower, then the prisoners must have been taken at Singara. Men of Oribasius's own legion.

A brief flicker of shadow crossed the walkway as another missile arced overhead. A breathless hush as it flew, then a burst of sudden cheering.

'Yes!' Oribasius cried, leaping up, oblivious to the arrow storm.

The stone had smashed into the topmost storey of the tower, bursting through the protective covering of hides. Castus heard the crack of timbers, and saw the whole structure shake with the impact, the iron plates rattling and clanging. Wails and groans went up from the besiegers as the tower ground to a halt. Then, after a pause, it lurched forward once more.

'Again!' Oribasius cried, punching the bricks of the rampart. 'We're hitting them now! *Again!*' An arrow struck the wall beside him, its tip raising sparks, and he jerked his head down.

Castus heard a second thud from the artillery behind the wall. A blazing projectile passed overhead, a wicker basket stuffed with pitch, tow and naphtha and set alight. Keeping a shield raised above him, Castus glanced over the parapet to track it as it flew. The flaming missile plunged towards the tower, hitting it just below the breach where the stone had struck. Spats of flame showered down the rawhide covering.

But already he could see half-naked men swarming around the topmost storey of the tower, rigging a temporary cover of wicker and hides to cover the gap. Water was pouring down the structure too; there must be siphons inside, Castus realised, to pump the water up to the top. The fires were quenched, the damage repaired, and still the tower groaned forward.

Slaves shuffled along the rampart walkway, moving at a crouch as they dragged baskets of arrows and slingshot. Others carried sacks of bread and amphorae of wine and water, distributing the food to the defenders. Past noon now, and the sun was dropping to the west, glaring in the eyes of the men on the walls.

All along the rampart the ballistae snapped, sending iron darts tipped with burning tow to pelt the advancing tower. Some of the missiles struck, jabbing into the hides or bouncing off the metal plating. But the streams of water soon extinguished the flames. The whole tower bristled with arrows, but none had penetrated the coverings. Castus felt a plunging sense of impending failure. *Shapur's Bastard* appeared unstoppable, and impervious to all attack.

Now the great structure was halfway across the causeway that spanned the moat, and Castus could hear the creaking of the timbers, the wail of ropes, and the cries and groans of the men beneath it as they heaved. The crack of whips too; the Persians were driving their prisoners with the lash. When he narrowed his eyes against the glare, Castus could see the trail of bodies that the tower left in its wake. He dropped his gaze, and saw the tangle of dead and injured men on the ramparts of the outer wall, lying amid the litter of arrow shafts. How many had already lost their lives? How many would die in pain of their wounds?

Another stone whirled across the wall: once more the hush, then the burst of exultation. This time the missile had crashed through the platform at the top of the tower, pummelling the Persian archers that sheltered within it. Smashed bodies cascaded downwards with the debris. But the tower only paused before moving forward again.

'Ladders!' a voice shouted from the outer rampart. 'They're bringing up ladders!'

With a sharp curse, Castus glanced down at the causeway and saw columns of men streaming along either side of the tower, carrying long scaling ladders between them. Whips cracked, and the tower vibrated as the men beneath it redoubled their efforts. On the outer ramparts, the surviving Roman defenders were gathering to repel the assault, as the arrows continued to spit from the sky.

'We've got to pull them back,' Castus said, crouching beside Oribasius. 'There's not enough men left down there to drive off a ladder attack, and we need them to reinforce the inner wall.'

Oribasius nodded, white-faced. He looked quite sick. But he yelled the order, and a moment later the trumpets sounded. Raising his head, Castus saw the men rushing down the steps from the outer ramparts and spilling back across the open space between the walls, most of them running southward towards the Edessa Gate.

With the outer wall undefended, the Persian attackers swarmed across it, each ladder sending a tide of men over the ramparts. But the arrow storm had slackened now, and with a vast roar the troops up on the higher rampart of the inner wall leaped to the battlements and began pelting missiles down at the attackers. Armenian archers gathered handfuls of enemy arrows from the ground and began shooting them back in rapid succession. Militiamen heaved chunks of rubble over the brink as the slingers craned across the parapet to whirl their shot down at the horde below.

Trapped in the killing ground between the walls, the Persians were dying in their scores. Castus could see them clearly now: bearded men in conical caps and headscarves, tribal warriors from the eastern fringes of the Sassanid empire, sent by their ruler into the first wave of the assault. Torrents of boiling water and sprays of blistering hot oil spewed from the ramparts, the defenders screaming abuse as the men below them fell back, or tried to shelter at the base of the inner wall.

But the siege tower had reached the top of the causeway now, heaved right up against the base of the outer wall. At the first blow of the ram a great cheer rose from the besieging horde; answered by a groan from the defenders. A second blow came, and then a third. The noise was a percussion through the earth, a punch that stirred the dust from the rampart walks and seemed almost to shake the bricks in their mortar.

Castus felt the noise in his chest. He could hear the rhythmic cries of the men working the ram, the heavy creak of the cables as it swung. With every blow, the outer wall appeared to shiver. Undermined from the far side, it could not stand for long. How many hours had passed? Already the sun was low, the sky to the west beginning to glow like beaten gold.

With a grinding crack, a huge fissure ran up the inner face of the wall. The rhythm of the ram did not slacken. Most of the attacking troops had been driven from the space between the walls now, and the defenders on the high rampart could only stare, aghast, as the mighty siege engine pummelled at their outer fortifications. Another crashing blow, and the wall appeared to ripple and smoke. Another, and dust exploded from the cracks. Then a sudden roar, and in a vast plume of gritty brown debris the wall collapsed inward.

The attackers came surging through the breach at once, yelling in the choking fog. Many of them carried portable hide screens, and they erected them in an arc around the gap in the wall. There were labourers with them too, men stripped to their loincloths carrying pickaxes, hammers and crowbars, and before the dust had cleared they were attacking the mound of debris, levering out the foundation stones of the wall and smashing wildly at the lumps of fallen brickwork and mortared rubble.

Archers had packed every storey of the tower; more of them gathered around its base, protected by the screens, and the storm of arrows doubled its fury. Men were dying all along the rampart. Persians were dying too, down among the rubble heaps and around the broken foundations of the outer wall. In the lowering light the scene had a hazy nightmarish quality.

Castus crouched beneath the parapet, sucking water from a flask. He rinsed his mouth and spat. Behind him he could hear the artillery crews frantically repositioning their catapults, heaving them off the masonry platforms and dragging them backwards, trying to get enough distance for a short-trajectory arcing shot over the wall that might hit the tower. A blazing pitch-coated basket tumbled from the rampart, scattering fire over the Persians labouring in the rubble below.

'Can they widen the breach enough to force the tower through?' Sabinus asked, dropping to crouch beside Castus. He had a cut across his brow; dried blood had crusted on his cheek.

'Eventually they will,' Castus told him. 'They've got enough men down there to flatten the whole city, given time. But soon it'll be dark...'

The siege tower stood only fifty feet from the inner wall, and already there were torches moving in the deep shadow beneath it. Arrows and slingshot filled the air between the tower and the battlements. The noise of the labourers was a constant percussive ringing of hammers and picks breaking rubble, and they were working in a maddened frenzy. But the tower was immobile, standing before the breach that it had made, unable to advance.

'Could we...?' Sabinus asked.

Castus could almost hear his thought. 'Perhaps,' he said. He chewed at his cheek, considering. The risk was great, but the danger of allowing the tower to advance further was greater. Only a dozen more paces, and it would be close enough to drop a boarding bridge across onto the ramparts. He had to do something; he had spent the entire day in a state of enforced passivity, and his nerves were at breaking point.

'Pass the order to Oribasius,' he said. 'He's to ready a hundred of his best men – we can't spare any more. You know what to tell him.'

Sabinus saluted and ran for the steps.

A roar from outside the walls, and Castus hauled himself up, ducking quickly to avoid an arrow. Unbelievably, the tower was in motion again. Its massive wheels turned slowly, grinding the rubble beneath them as it heaved across the mound of flattened debris. Castus noticed that the Persians had dismounted the ram, and evacuated the upper storeys to lighten the tower. Still it groaned and shuddered, the sound of the whips cracking from the darkness beneath it. The labourers were breaking down the wall foundations directly ahead of it, even as it crept forward.

Hardly daring to breathe, Castus pressed himself against the side of a merlon and watched. Did the Persians really intend to attack the walls by night? They must know the tower was vulnerable, so close to the inner rampart. Perhaps, he thought, perhaps the gods might favour them yet.

A loud creak sounded from the tower, and the noise of grinding debris as the structure shuddered to a halt.

'They've grounded it!' Castus cried, hammering his fist on the wall beside him. In the half-darkness he could see men seething around the base of the tower, overseers yelling to the labourers to free the obstruction. But it would take time – many hours – before the tower was mobile again. And Castus intended to use those hours well.

'Dominus,' Oribasius said, joining him at the rampart. 'My men are ready. They have what they need. I request permission to lead them myself.'

Castus knew that the prefect had waited a long time for this opportunity. But could he be trusted to fulfil his duty, after failing so badly at Zagurae?

'Father,' Sabinus said quietly, kneeling beside him, 'I want to go as well. I don't ask for command, just a chance to take the fight to the enemy.'

'No,' Castus said. 'You remain here.'

Sabinus opened his mouth to protest, and Castus grabbed him by the shoulder. 'Remain here!' he repeated. 'That's an order.'

He understood Sabinus's desire; his first thought had been to lead the night attack himself. If he had been twenty years, or even a decade, younger he would have considered it. And the thought of having a more trustworthy and capable man as leader was a strong temptation. Was he only refusing because Sabinus was his son?

'Go now,' he told Oribasius, before his doubts could take hold. 'Ready your men at the postern below the Edessa Gate. I'll send word when it's time. And may the gods guide you.'

CHAPTER XXII

Sentry fires glowed along the rampart. With any luck, Castus thought as he looked down from the tower of the Edessa Gate, they would dazzle the eyes of the Persians watching the wall. The firelight illuminated the upper reaches of the grounded siege tower, which rose out of the gulf of darkness below the wall, looking impossibly close. The shaggy hides that clothed it, and the spiny bristle of arrows that covered its upper section, gave the thing a truly monstrous appearance. Lamplight gleamed around its base, showing through gaps in the protective screens; men were working down there, hammering and digging to level the ground ahead of it, ready for a final assault at dawn. And beyond the walls, the darkened plain flickered with the night fires of the Persian horde.

Castus wondered what King Shapur was doing now. Was he asleep, or did he remain wakeful, alert and anxious, through the long passages of the night? As he paced the walkway, he thought too of Marcellina, far away in distant Antioch. Did she even know where he was?

A quick shudder ran through him, although the night was warm. On the ramparts the defenders were raising a steady stir of sound: some of them singing, others sharpening weapons or talking. Nothing that would seem unnatural, perhaps – but it might help to cover any noises from the darkness below.

Running footsteps, and Iovinus appeared at the head of the steps. The Protector saluted quickly as he caught sight of Castus.

'Give the word,' Castus told him quietly.

The man dropped out of sight. No turning back now.

With his senses primed, he listened carefully for the creak of the ironbound postern door in the gate arch beneath him. Loud, drunken-sounding singing came from the rampart walkway, covering all other sound. His shoulders were tight with nervous tension, and he paced to the parapet and back again, suppressing the urge to glance down into the darkness; he did not want to attract the attention of any sharp-eyed Persian observer.

Long moments passed. The night seemed to vibrate with sound, but there was only silence in the deep gulf of darkness between the walls. Oribasius would be taking his men out through the postern quickly and quietly, forming them up in the cover of the projecting tower just to the north. From there it would a three hundred yard dash to the Persian breach and the base of the siege tower. Oribasius's party were all legionaries, men of the First Parthica; they would have their faces blackened, their shields covered and their weapons and equipment muffled. One in every five men would be carrying a smoking firepot, another a heavy basket of pitch-soaked tow, naphtha and turpentine. A supremely combustible mixture, and very hard to extinguish.

His nerves prickled, and he sensed rather than heard the mass of men assembling below the wall. He could almost detect the acrid smell of the incendiaries. How many Persians guarded the tower? There was only space in the breach for a few score, but more would be inside the tower itself and potentially many more on the causeway outside the walls. Oribasius's troops would have to burst through the cordon of screens, capture the breach and hold it for long enough to set fire to the tower. Cursing to himself, Castus realised that he should have sent more men. He should have appointed a better officer to lead them. He should have...

A scream from the darkness, then the clash of iron and the dull thunder of collapsing hide screens. Taking two steps to the parapet, Castus stared down into the black gulf between the walls, desperately trying to make out what was happening. But he could see nothing; under the waning half-moon the twin lines of ramparts and the upper section of the tower were lit by a pale radiance, but the space below them was lost in shadow. Sparks danced, and the flickering light caught the flash of blades. Castus could hear the braying of the Persian trumpets, the yells of the officers mustering their troops to defend the breach. Men were fighting down there. Men were dying, and Castus could only stand braced against the parapet, watching with gritted teeth.

'Iovinus,' he called, and the Protector appeared from the stairhead. 'Send Sabinus to me.'

'Sabinus?' the man replied, baffled. 'But, dominus, he's...' He gestured towards the darkened battle at the foot of the siege tower.

'*What?*'

'I thought you knew... He went out with Oribasius and the attack party.'

'Gods!' Castus snarled, hurling himself away from the parapet. He was two paces from the stairs when Iovinus blocked his way.

'Dominus, you can't go out there! Your place is here... I'm sorry!'

For a heartbeat Castus wanted to strike the man, heave him aside, run down the steps and out into the darkness. But Iovinus was right, and he knew it. With a wild cry of anguish Castus gripped his head in both hands. How could Sabinus have disobeyed him? How could his son have thrown himself into such a desperate attack?

Staggering back across the tower rampart to the parapet, he recognised his hypocrisy. He would send other men's sons out to die, but not his own. The realisation did nothing to ease the pain in his heart. *Merciful gods, protecting gods… watch over him. Bring him back safely…*

Fire burst in the darkness, blooming out from the base of the tower. The flames illuminated an infernal scene, throwing vast dancing shadows across the city walls. Figures whirled in the fiery glow, blades rising and falling, spears clashing. Castus saw shields raised in the firelight, then saw them battered down. The noise of the fighting was a constant muffled roar, cut through with screams of rage and pain. The men on the ramparts were cheering, yelling encouragement to their comrades fighting below them. The flames lit the upraised faces starkly, and Castus could feel the wave of heat even from his position on the gate tower.

'I'm going down,' he told Iovinus. 'Come with me – I need to wait just inside the postern.'

He jogged down the cramped stairway in hot darkness, then strode out into the stone-flagged passageway just inside the gate arches where the narrow tunnel from the postern opened. Men were already stumbling back in, many of them wounded. The first few wore only loincloths, whip-scars on their backs. Some of the Roman prisoners the enemy had been using to push the ram, Castus realised. Soldiers followed them, their blackened faces streaked with runnels of sweat. Their shouts echoed in the confined space.

'Centurion,' Castus cried, seizing a passing man. 'Where are the two officers? Did they return with you?'

'The prefect's dead, dominus,' the centurion said, expressionless. 'I saw him fall when we first attacked their perimeter. Two men went to help him, but the bastards had already done for him.'

'And the other officer? Flavius Sabinus?'

The centurion shrugged, too stunned to reply, and Castus let him go. Quite possibly few of the men in the party would have recognised his son anyway.

He stayed in the gate passage as the remains of Oribasius's command straggled back. They were not followed; the Persians were too busy trying to quench the flames around their tower. With every figure that came staggering in through the postern Castus's hopes flared, and then died.

'Forty-six men returned, dominus,' Iovinus reported. 'Nearly thirty liberated prisoners. Sixty-five men dead or missing.'

Dead or missing. The words punched into Castus's soul. No, he could not allow himself to believe it.

'Shall we pull back the guards and close the postern, dominus? Quite a few hostiles gathering out there...'

'Yes,' Castus heard himself say. 'Yes, close it now.' Deadness in his heart, stilling the wild panic of his blood. *If my son is lost I cannot live... I cannot go on...*

Shouts from the tunnel, animating the men waiting in the passage. A last band of fugitives were piling back in through the postern, just before it was closed. Iovinus was counting them in, others rushing forward with flasks of water and wine as the new arrivals dumped their weapons and shields on the flagstones.

The last two came staggering from the mouth of the tunnel, carrying a third man between them. Castus could hardly bring himself to look at the injured figure. Only when the two had laid the body on the ground and stepped back did he take a pace towards them. He cried out at once and dropped to his knees.

Sabinus's face was a mask of blood. The front of his tunic was blackened, and he had burns on his neck and up his left arm. But he was alive, his chest moving as he breathed.

'Water!' Castus yelled, his hoarse voice echoing under the gate arches. 'And call for the surgeon! Bring Nicagoras from the hospital!'

Iovinus was beside him, drawing him to his feet as the medical orderlies gathered around Sabinus with their salves and bandages. 'Dominus, there's nothing you can do here,' the Protector said. 'Come back up to the rampart – you should see what they've done.'

Moments later, Castus hauled himself from the stairhead and out onto the rampart of the gate tower. The air was fogged with smoke, and acrid with the smell of burning, and the sky above the walls was lit a garish orange.

The great siege tower was a pillar of flame. The fires that Sabinus and his men had lit in the base of the structure had roared upwards, consuming the dry timber and the rawhide cladding. As Castus stood at the parapet and watched he saw burning figures leaping from the topmost storeys, where they had climbed to escape the blaze.

A vast creak and a crackle of bursting wood, and the tower sagged. Sheets of fire curled upwards into the sky, showering sparks across the wall ramparts. Heedless of the few arrows that still spat from the darkness, Castus climbed up onto the parapet and stood braced between the merlons. The blaze illuminated him, and he felt the heat washing over his body. His lips tightened into a savage grin, and he drew his sword and raised it above his head as he watched *Shapur's Bastard* dying in flames.

'Truly war is a grisly business,' the curator said, holding a cloth to his mouth as he gazed out from the rampart in the greyness of dawn.

'Good thing too,' Castus told him.

Vorodes gave him a puzzled glance.

'If it wasn't so grisly, all sorts of fools would want to get involved.'

The curator laughed oddly, unsure if he was joking. His son was with him, sixteen-year-old Barnaeus; the youth gazed at Castus with an expression of mute wonder.

Castus certainly did not feel like joking. The blackened wreckage of the siege tower was still pouring smoke, and the walls were wreathed with the fumes of the fire. The sky above them was smeared a dirty grey. When he peered across the parapet, Castus could see the dead bodies heaped over the smashed rubble, some of them partly burnt. The ground was a mire of broken rubble, charred timbers, blood and ash. He had already sent out a party to locate and retrieve the bodies of the slain Romans. They had found Oribasius among them too, his body covered with wounds. All of them on the front; the prefect had redeemed himself with a true soldier's death.

It had been a small victory, and a costly one, but it had humbled the pride of the Persian king. Beyond the broken wall and the smoking wreckage, the mantlets had been dragged back towards the enemy siege lines. As if, Castus thought, the burning of the tower had demoralised the attackers into a hasty retreat. Shapur's pavilion was gone too, and a distant wailing came from the Persian encampments as they mourned their dead. Perhaps they would make another attempt at the breach, but not for some time. Once the last fires died down, Castus thought, he would send men to repair the wall with rubble and charred beams.

He closed his eyes, and exhaustion massed in his skull. With a quick shudder, he forced himself to wakefulness. He needed to return to the Strategion; he had ordered Sabinus to be taken there, and he had to check on his son before he could allow himself to rest. The sun appeared behind him, sudden and dazzling above the eastern walls, and the scene of destruction was lit with golden light, the swirling smoke turned into a glowing blue haze.

'I didn't just come to inspect the damage, I'm afraid,' Vorodes said, shrugging his shoulders. 'I have... a request, I suppose. An invitation, if you like.'

'An invitation from who?'

'The elders of the city, and the defensor, and others. They wish to meet with you, at noon today in the Bouleuterion, if you have the time.'

Castus felt he would never have the time for such things. But he remembered what Diogenes had told him a few days before. If there were men in the city hatching plots against him, he wanted the chance to confront them face to face.

'I'll be there,' he said, then yawned massively, and strode away down the rampart walk.

Sabinus had been taken to one of the inner chambers of the Strategion; not the room where Romulianus had died nearly two weeks before, but a smaller one close to Castus's own bedchamber. Nicagoras, the Greek doctor, was still there when Castus arrived.

'The wounds upon his body are mostly superficial,' Nicagoras said. 'I've spread a poultice on his burns, and dressed the other injuries as best I can. But his eye, I'm afraid, is ruined. A shame, such a handsome young man...'

Castus pulled up a stool to the couch where his son lay. Sabinus's face was washed of blood, but his head was wrapped in a thick linen bandage that covered his left eye. He stirred as Castus sat down, and his other eye flickered open.

'Father,' he said, his voice weak and hoarse. 'I disobeyed you.'

'Why?' Castus managed to say. The word almost choked him.

Sabinus tried to laugh, and his chest heaved as he winced in pain. 'Pride,' he said. 'All my life I wanted to... prove myself to you. Show that I could act for myself. But you held me back...'

'I thought you were the one who was supposed to be protecting me!'

'Did we succeed at least? Is the tower gone...?'

'You did well. Rescued some prisoners too. We're safe for a few days more, I reckon.'

Sabinus smiled, and his eye closed. Castus could see that he was in great pain, but was trying not to let it show. In silence, he wrestled with his thoughts, trying to find the right words. But he had never been good at expressing his feelings. Clearing his throat, he laid a palm briefly on his son's shoulder and then stood up.

'Check on him whenever you can,' he told Nicagoras as he moved for the door. 'See he has everything he needs.'

'And what of your own needs, excellency?' the doctor replied. He peered at Castus's glowering face. 'You appear very red in the features, if I may say so. For a man of your age, this exertion is most dangerous. It would be unfortunate if our commander in chief were to fall to some ailment…! Might I examine you, and determine your state of health at some point?'

'Another time,' Castus said, and left the chamber.

All over the city, he thought, there were men suffering and dying in agony. But he only cared about one of them. He felt his heart hardening inside his chest.

The Bouleuterion of Nisibis stood on the oval agora just below the citadel mount, opposite the theatre and the main church. Castus had been in there once or twice to speak with Vorodes, but never on an official visit. Now he strode through the bronze-plated doors, Iovinus and a party of Armigeri troopers behind him, and found the elders of the council assembled in the hall in dignified state to receive him. Sixty men, sitting on the semi-circle of banked seats. All rose as he entered.

'Domini,' Castus addressed them in a gruff shout. 'I only have moments to spare. Our enemies do not wait upon our convenience.'

It was the magistrate, Dorotheus, who remained standing as the others took their seats once more. 'Excellency,' he announced. 'We thank you for accepting our invitation. May I say, on behalf of us all, how much we rejoice in your defence of our city!'

A chorus of congratulatory mumbles rose from the assembly. Castus knew that none of the men here had stood upon the ramparts the day before. Most were too old, of course, but the younger ones had found substitutes. The chamber reeked of perfume, barely covering the tang of stale sweat – with water rationed in the city, even the wealthy had been going without daily baths. But as they sat fanning themselves, the councillors looked only mildly inconvenienced by twelve days of siege. *Civilians*, Castus thought, with an instinctive sneer of contempt. He was tired, after only a few hours' sleep, and in no mood to listen to pleasantries.

'Shapur has learned that Nisibis will be no easy prize,' Dorotheus went on hurriedly, reading his mood. 'He surely knows that taking the city will cost him dearly, both in men and in time. It occurs to many of us, therefore...' He paused to glance left and right at the other men of the assembly. '... that this might be a propitious time to approach the Persian king and make an offer of negotiation.'

Castus had been expecting something of this sort, although nothing quite as bold. 'To what end?' he said.

'To... to the end of, well... of ending the siege!' Dorotheus stammered awkwardly. 'Of preventing further needless loss of life and destruction of property! The honour of the defenders has been satisfied, and now we can treat with Shapur as equals.'

'As I understand it,' Castus said, 'Shapur regards no man as his equal.' He glanced at Vorodes, who sat alone at one side of the hall. The curator did not meet his eye.

'So you're determined to continue this war?' another councillor asked, speaking Greek with a very thick Syriac accent. 'Even when so many must die?'

'Would you rather be slaves?' Castus's voice grated in his throat. Anger swelled through his fatigue, and he could barely articulate what he needed to say.

'We know,' Dorotheus said, dropping his pretence of civility, 'that the emperor Constantine is dead. His son Constantius is surely too concerned with affairs of the succession to lead a relief army to break the siege. But if we negotiate with King Shapur ourselves, he might agree to spare the city, perhaps after the payment of a certain sum of money. What better option do we have? How much longer can we hold out against such odds?'

Castus could only glare at him. Words massed in his head, angry, bitter words. With only one of those words he could condemn this man Dorotheus to instant death. He could sense Iovinus standing ready behind him, the six soldiers – selected especially for their size and brutal appearance – were ready to follow his orders without question. For a moment he considered it.

A burst of fierce laughter came from the back of the hall, and all turned. Bishop Iacob had struggled upright, and stood pointing at Dorotheus, his face twisted in mirth. 'The flock has seen the wolves!' he cried. 'Ha! Behold how terrified they are! Are you so quick to yield to the evil one, Dorotheus? Does the silver quail in the smelter's furnace? Does the earth quail before the plough? The Lord scourges all his adopted children!'

'Bishop, please,' Dorotheus replied, spreading his open palms. 'We do not yield. We merely seek peace...'

'Peace!' the bishop spat. 'What does Shapur know of peace? Does the lamb beg mercy of the ravening wolf? You bend your head to the Persian and he will smite it off! The destruction of his great tower has wounded his pride, and now he is angry. He will not rest until our city is laid low, our churches destroyed, our people slain or led in chains... Walk out of this city if you dare, but do not expect mercy, and do not expect anyone else to follow you!'

Silence followed the bishop's words as Iacob subsided, wheezing slightly, into his seat.

'The priest's right, for once,' Castus said, hooking his thumbs in his belt. The support had been so unexpected that he wanted to laugh with relief. 'There will be no negotiation with the enemy.'

At once a storm of muttering broke out, cut through with hissing whispers. Castus motioned to Iovinus, and the Protector barked an order. All six troopers behind him took a step forward, slamming the butts of their spears on the marble floor in unison. The councillors fell silent again. Castus noticed Vorodes closing his eyes with an expression of resignation.

'The matter is settled,' Castus declared, then swept the chamber with a fierce glance, turned on his heel, and marched towards the doors.

'You underestimate them at your peril,' Sohaemia said. 'Remember these are proud men, accustomed to power. You take away their power, treat them as children, make them appear ridiculous, and they will hate you for it.'

'Their feelings are none of my concern,' Castus replied.

From the denuded roof garden of the curator's house he could see the breach in the outer wall, the ruin of the Persian siege tower a twisted black skeleton in the evening light.

'All the same,' the curator's wife said. 'They are like water, always trying to find the easiest path. You block them one way, and they will find another.'

Castus turned to her, quizzical. 'Sounds like you're giving me a warning,' he said with a half-smile.

He had not seen Sohaemia for many days. She had slipped into the house unobtrusively – he could hardly ban her from her own home – and come to find him on the roof terrace with a casual air, as if she were just taking in the view. He knew her visit was deliberate.

But she made no answer to his statement. 'I was sorry to hear about your son,' she said instead. 'His injuries are not too grave?'

'Thanks to the gods, no.'

'They say he was a hero. Without him, the tower would never have been destroyed. He insisted on freeing many of the prisoners too. You must be very proud.'

'Always,' Castus said quietly.

'My son Barnaeus wishes to fight. Vorodes is trying to stop him. But if this war continues, perhaps all of us will experience it directly.'

'There's no other way,' Castus said firmly. 'You understand that? Shapur will never rest until Nisibis is destroyed. But if we hold out long enough… He lacks supplies to feed his vast army for a long time – already he's stripped the country bare for miles around. This siege will end, one way or another.'

Sohaemia closed her eyes, and Castus saw her mutter a prayer. He wondered again how much control she exerted over her husband, and how much in turn Vorodes held over the other grandees of the city. He could only hope that she did not share the delusions of Dorotheus and the others who counselled surrender.

'Bishop Iacob has announced that he will fast until the city is delivered from evil, as he puts it,' she said. 'He's gone to the church, and says he'll remain there, praying and fasting. Fasting and praying… Many of the ignorant, you know, are already saying that it was he who defeated the Persian attack – he cursed their tower and made it burst into flames! Now they flock to his church… Do you think his methods will prove better than yours?'

Castus snorted a laugh. 'No. But at least he'll be out of my way.'

Sighing, Sohaemia pulled her shawl around her and turned to go. For a moment she looked at Castus, and he saw something like pity in her eyes.

'You are a very inflexible man,' she said. 'But the best iron bends with the strain. And if it does not – it breaks.'

CHAPTER XXIII

Castus leaned out over the parapet of the eastern rampart, staring down at the river.

'You see what I mean?' Gunthia asked, his thick Gothic accent giving his words an accusatory bite.

'It doesn't look natural, agreed,' Castus said. 'It's not usual for this season?'

'No, dominus,' said the centurion of the Sixth Parthica, who stood with them on the rampart. 'I've been stationed here in Nisibis for eight years, and I've never seen the river like this. It falls towards the end of summer, after the last meltwater from the mountains slackens and before the rains, but never so fast. It's been dropping steadily for two days now.'

Castus made a sound in his throat. The River Mygdonius, usually a wide expanse of swift-flowing grey-brown water, had contracted to a slow trickling stream. To either side, the riverbed showed as an expanse of mud, still wet and dark at the centre but drying rapidly to a cracked yellow crust. The sight was uncanny, ominous. As if the river was somehow flowing backwards. A few hundred paces upstream, the masonry piers of the demolished bridge in front of the Gate of the Sun stuck up like broken teeth in a withered jaw.

'So they've dammed the flow,' Castus said quietly, pulling his head back from between the merlons of the rampart.

'They must have done it just up there to the north, where their siege lines cross the ravine,' Gunthia said.

Castus nodded, sucking his teeth. Were the Persians trying to cut off the water supply to the city? Surely they would know that Nisibis was supplied by a spring inside the walls, and had deep rock-cut cisterns.

'You think they'll try and attack the gate across the dry riverbed?' the Gothic tribune asked.

'Maybe.'

Castus scanned the ruins of the abandoned suburb on the far side of the river. He saw the burnt shells of the buildings shimmering in the waves of heat, and the decaying fly-blown remains of men and horses slain in the fighting over two weeks before still lying out in the open; bleached bones, shreds of blackened flesh and scraps of armour, picked over by the carrion birds. There was no enemy in sight; since the burning of the Persian tower, the besiegers had retreated to their camps behind the palisades that ringed the city. There had been no further attacks, although several times the people of Nisibis had heard drums beating and the wailing of horns, and the men on the walls had seen the dust clouds as the Persian army paraded or manoeuvred.

Over twenty days the siege had lasted now, and in the midsummer heat Nisibis was suffering. The sense of entrapment, and the prospect of imminent assault, had worn at the nerves of the defenders and stoked the discord among the city factions. Only the day before, there had been rioting in the market district, and Castus had ordered Egnatius and Lycianus to clear the streets with their mounted troopers. No doubt, he knew, the trouble had been partly the work of enemy agitators.

The militia still mustered for their duty on the ramparts, but with every passing day their numbers thinned, men creeping away to conceal themselves rather than stand the long watches in the punishing heat, or spend the night gazing anxiously out into the blackness, expecting at any moment a sudden assault.

And with every passing day the crowd around the steps of Iacob's great church above the agora grew greater. Woman and children and old men huddled on the steps, many kneeling and praying, others calling out to the bishop in piteous voices to save their city from destruction. All knew that Shapur was planning something, and the drying of the river suggested that it would come from the east this time.

'Quite a drop from the wall foundations to the riverbed,' Castus said, almost to himself, as he peered down from the wall. 'They'd have trouble bringing siege engines across... Even ladders would be difficult.'

Frowning, he scratched the mosquito bites on his neck. Even with the river running dry, the deep bed presented an obstacle to attackers. But here, on the eastern side, Nisibis had only one line of defence. He leaned out again, further this time, studying the base of the walls.

'You think they might try tunnelling?' Gunthia asked, leaning from the next embrasure.

Castus made a noise in his throat, non-committal, then pulled himself back from the parapet and turned to face the city. Vallio passed him a flask, and he swigged from it – the water was warm, sulphurous-tasting – and wetted his scarf to wipe his face.

'Keep watching them,' he told Gunthia. 'Whatever they're planning, we'll find out soon enough.'

By the first light of the following day the men on the eastern wall could see the rows of heavy mantlets that the enemy had moved forward under cover of darkness, and by sunrise the Persian engineers were already labouring in the cover of the big hide-covered screens, building a line of fortified mounds along the far bank of the dry riverbed.

'Archery platforms,' said Barbatio as Castus joined him. The stolid young commander of the Tenth Gemina had brought all his men and half of the Seventh to reinforce the eastern defences. Already the archers and the ballista crews on the ramparts were lofting arrows and bolts across the river, aiming at any Persian who showed themselves from behind the covering screens.

Castus sucked his cheek, squinting into the low sun. 'What would you do,' he asked, 'if you were Shapur?'

'Me, dominus?' Barbatio said, and shrugged. 'He's got the numbers, and he don't much care about losses... Mass assault across the riverbed, maybe? Archers on the mounds to keep our heads down, then bring up ladders and storm the wall?'

Nodding slowly, Castus peered into the far distance, beyond the screens and the mounds to the circuit of Persian palisades and the camps beyond them. Sure enough, he could make out the huge royal banner gleaming in the morning sun. What was Shapur really thinking? And was there any way to counter his planned attack?

By midday, it was clear that the Persians intended something more than a simple assault on the walls. The line of fortified mounds now stretched all along the far bank of the Mygdonius, each manned by archers, and under their covering volleys the enemy were pushing their hide-covered screens forward across the dried riverbed. Behind the screens came long wheeled sheds, linking together to form galleries that protected the men within from the missiles of the defenders. As the galleries crossed the cracked mud, the men on the ramparts began heaving down huge rocks and blazing baskets of pitch at them. Wood shattered, men screamed, but still the enemy advanced, pushing steadily forward until they reached the dry bluffs below the city walls. Then the engineers moved in, hacking at the bluffs with pickaxes and mattocks.

Castus watched it all with a sense of horrified amazement. Nothing the defenders could throw at the enemy seemed to daunt them. The Persian engineers worked surrounded by their own slain, under a relentless barrage from the ramparts above them. Stripped to their loincloths, their limbs dark with mud and filth, they swung their picks and hammers with a wild ceaseless fury. The noise of iron scraping rock and gouging earth rose above the shouts of the defenders and the screams of the dying.

Leaning from an embrasure, Castus watched as the men on the rampart levered a massive rock out over the brink and let it plunge; the missile spun in the air, and then crashed down against the head of one of the galleries: dust and fragments of broken stone flew, blood spattered, and then the screaming began again. But almost at once a fresh surge of men were dragging the mauled bodies of the dead and injured aside and throwing themselves into their work.

'They really do mean to tunnel under the walls, then,' Gunthia said.

'I wouldn't be so sure,' Castus replied. He was up on the north tower of the Gate of the Sun, where he had established his command position. Iovinus and Vallio accompanied him, both with shields ready to block any incoming arrows. The storm of missiles had become so constant now that it was easy to disregard them, just as Castus had learned to disregard the flies and mosquitoes that filled the air.

'The wall foundations are dug deep,' he said. 'And if they got far enough to tunnel beneath them, we'd easily see where they were going to break through on our side, and we'd be waiting for them to appear.'

'So what then?' the Gothic tribune asked, his brow creased.

Castus could only shrug. Black smoke billowed from the riverbed, where one of the burning projectiles had set a gallery alight. The flames were doused quickly, but the smoke remained, hazing the scene of ongoing destruction.

There was a new moon that night, nothing but a bright sliver in the sky, and Castus sent Gunthia and a hundred of his men on a scouting expedition out through the Singara Gate and up the western side of the ravine. They returned within the hour; Gunthia reported that he had located the dam that the enemy had built to block the river, but it was too heavily guarded to approach. 'Too big to break either,' Gunthia said. 'Like a fortress wall, heavy timber packed with wet clay. They've built it up on either side of the ravine as well.'

No chance of destroying the dam then; Castus had hoped that it might be possible. By sunrise the following morning he was back on the gate tower, tired after a sleepless night. Diogenes joined him, and as they breakfasted on bread, cheese and olive oil they heard trumpets braying from the Persian camp. The excavation work that had continued through the hours of darkness showed no signs of slackening.

'They're not tunnelling, anyway,' Barbatio said, saluting wearily as he emerged from the stairhead. He crouched beside Castus and then gestured downwards, towards the base of the wall. 'It looks like they're quarrying out caves or hollows, just up to the foundations. Most of them are to the north there, past where the wall of the eastern suburb meets the far bank of the river. More of them a couple of hundred paces south... It's strange. Why not just dig in one place?'

The same question had been haunting Castus all through the night. Shapur's engineers were directing their energies at a multitude of points all along the north-eastern quadrant of the wall defences. They were taking terrible casualties in the process too. Why waste so many men for so little gain?

'Maybe they're just probing for the weakest part of the foundations?' Iovinus suggested. 'Then when they've found it, they'll bring up a ram or something...'

'They'd need a massive ram to break down that wall, even with the undermining,' Barbatio said. 'We destroyed their last one – I doubt they'd find another one more powerful still!'

Castus paused as he chewed. He felt a strange slow stillness creeping over him. Gulping heavily, he reached for the flask of vinegar wine beside him. His hand was shaking as he lifted it to drink. Cold realisation flowed through his blood, and he felt his scalp tighten.

'They've already got their ram,' he said quietly. 'And it's getting more powerful with every passing hour.'

The crowd gathered on the church steps resembled a tide of black rags in the midday sun. They scattered as Castus rode up with his escort behind him, shrinking back to either side as he reined in his horse and leaped from the saddle. Setting his jaw, seizing the hilt of his sword, Castus marched up the steps as a path opened before him. The sun glared back off the exposed marble, and he felt the tight ache gathering in his skull.

Reaching the top, he stepped into the merciful cool of the church atrium. Several priests had already appeared at the doorway, gazing at him with worried expressions. With two troopers of his escort behind him, Castus pushed past the priests and entered the basilica. His studded boots grated on the mosaic floor, and he was blind in the deeply scented darkness.

'What is this?' one of the senior priests cried, a fat man with a pale face, rushing from the gloom with hands raised. 'You cannot enter the House of the Lord in battle array!'

Castus blinked heavily, pausing only long enough to make out the dimensions of the hall before striding forward again. The priest made a tentative effort at blocking his way, then fell back. At the far end of the chamber, before the apse where the high altar stood, what looked like a bundle of old clothes lay strewn on the floor. As Castus approached he made out the figure of a man: Iacob, lying full length and face down, his arms stretched out to either side of him.

'Dominus, please,' said the young presbyter, Ephraim, appearing from the shadows. 'The Blessed Iacob is praying... He has been praying day and night for our salvation – do not disturb him, I beg you!'

'He'll be disturbed soon enough, and not by me,' Castus growled.

Now his eyes had adjusted, he could see that the great basilica was packed with people: many wore far better clothing than the ragged congregation on the steps outside. All glared at him in stark terror and open hostility.

At the sound of the raised voices, the bishop had stirred from his prone position. Ephraim and another priest rushed forward at once, helping the old bishop to turn and sit upright, then struggle to his feet. Castus peered at them, unimpressed. It hardly seemed possible, but Iacob looked even older and more infirm than ever before. Had he really been starving himself all this time?

'Listen to me, all of you,' Castus declared, raising his voice so everyone in the basilica could hear him well. 'The Persians intend to break down our eastern wall. They've dammed the river, and undermined the foundations by quarrying. Very soon, they'll breach their dam and release the river water like a flood. The pressure will be enough to wash out the foundations, and the walls will come down.'

Gasps from the packed multitude in the darkness.

'Is that even possible?' the fat senior priest asked, his voice quavering.

'It might be...' Ephraim said. 'Many years ago, in the days of the Persecutor Diocletian, the river flooded at Edessa and brought down the walls! The same thing had happened before, during the reign of Severus...'

'And doubtless Shapur knows all about that,' Castus said grimly.

He turned to face Iacob again. The bishop was standing

upright, supported by the two priests. His jaw hung open, and his eyes appeared unfocused.

'We need to build another wall,' Castus told him. 'Inside the first one. We need to do it fast, so when the outer wall comes down we'll still have a defensive line. That means demolishing houses to give us rubble for building materials. It also means we need manpower. *People.* Even women and children. Anyone who can pick up a brick or lift a beam. We need thousands of them, and I can't pull too many men off the ramparts. So – I need your help, bishop.'

Iacob raised his head, and his mouth tightened into a smile. Castus inhaled slowly, fighting down his angry discomfort. He would not have come to Iacob like this unless he had no other choice. Already panic had gripped the streets of Nisibis. Most of the inhabitants of the north-eastern quadrant had abandoned their homes and fled to other parts of the city. Many of those that remained would fight to stop their houses and temples being torn down on Castus's orders. He needed a civic leader, somebody with the power to command the people. Vorodes could never do it, and Dorotheus was unwilling. Castus had not forgotten the burning fields as he approached Nisibis. Only the bishop had the authority to direct what needed to be done.

Iacob just stared, still with his slow, tired smile. Then he threw back his head and barked a laugh. 'Man of blood!' he said, his voice thin and hard. 'Devil-worshipper! You ask for my help? I am fighting evil with the power of prayer – the power of Almighty God! The name of the Lord is a mighty fortress, and the righteous shall run to it and be saved!'

A chorus of mutters came from the darkness: '*Amen, amen...*'

Castus clenched his fists, tightened his jaw. He wanted to shout, to grab this scrawny old man by his filthy garments and shake him until he relented. 'When the Persians break in here, the name of your god will be erased from Nisibis! Didn't you say as much yourself, when you spoke to the councillors? You can hide in your dark church and pray as much as you like – it won't save you!'

But Iacob had subsided, his legs folding beneath him as the two priests eased him back to sit slumped on the floor before the altar. '*A day of wrath is that day...*' the bishop muttered, chewing at the words. '*A day of destruction and desolation...! Trumpet and battle cry, against the fortified cities... against the high towers...*'

Spitting a curse, Castus turned on his heel and stormed back towards the church doors. He had heard enough, and would not abase himself further before the bishop's arrogance. Perhaps the fasting had addled the man's mind; perhaps he had always been mad. But he could do nothing to save this city now.

'Dominus,' said the presbyter, Ephraim, hurrying after him. 'Please, allow me to speak to the bishop. His mind is so fixed upon the glory of God, he has almost passed beyond the world of the flesh... But perhaps I can intercede in some way.'

'Make him see sense, you mean?' Castus snarled. 'Good luck with that!'

The sunlight outside the church doors was almost overpowering, the heat like a heavy weight falling across his shoulders. Castus stood in the archway as sweat burst on his brow, then he wiped his face and stamped down the steps, the crowd falling away before him.

'Runner just came from the south gate, dominus,' said the *centenarius* of his escort as Castus reached the bottom of the steps. 'The enemy are moving – strong detachments of infantry and cavalry redeploying eastwards across the river.'

Castus nodded curtly. Shapur was massing the greater strength of his entire force to the east of the city, ready for the assault when the walls fell. He swung himself up into the saddle. How many more hours remained? He gave the signal to move, then tugged on the reins, kicking his horse forward into a canter as he crossed the agora once more.

★

'Everything east of this line,' Castus ordered, 'we need it all destroyed. We'll run our fortification up this street for four blocks, then angle around to the right to meet the wall.'

The two centurions with him saluted, then ran to give the orders to their men.

'And we'll need the wounded evacuated from the baths,' Castus went on, turning to another group of officers. 'All the people from these blocks as well – use any force necessary.'

Already the work had begun, and the streets north of the old bathhouse just inside the Gate of the Sun were a scene of chaos. The soldiers brought down from the ramparts laboured with enthusiasm, legionaries and Gothic warriors stripped to their tunics in the airless heat, glad of the chance to escape the withering archery volleys and turn their energies to fierce destruction. Men shouted, women screamed, and the noise of falling masonry was a crashing assault on the ears.

This area was the old part of the city, and most of the buildings were of mud brick. A few more substantial structures stood among them, with stone walls and pillared porches; Castus watched as a gang of soldiers hauled down one portico with ropes. The pillars toppled, sending a hot wave of gritty dust billowing down the street. Already the air was filled with a brown fog, and every breath Castus took rasped.

'Water, dominus,' Vallio said, appearing beside him with a slopping skin bag. Castus took it and drank, then poured the sulphurous liquid over his head. A brief gasp of relief, then the heat dried his scalp once more. 'Thanks,' he said.

Vorodes strode from the dust cloud, with his son at his heels. Young Barnaeus was wearing an infantryman's helmet that appeared too big for him, and carried a sword slung over his shoulder.

'How long, do you think?' the curator asked, scratching at his chin. His beard had grown ragged and wiry over recent days, and he no longer appeared as smoothly composed.

'Could be hours,' Castus told him. 'Maybe they'll wait until tomorrow morning. Not long enough, either way.'

'May the gods give us strength,' Vorodes said with a nervous smile.

With the curator and his son following him, Castus made his way along the street, stepping around the heaps of debris, keeping an eye out for tumbling masonry. One whole block of buildings between the wall and the line of the new fortification was coming down; amid the wreckage Castus could see figures struggling and fighting, terrified citizens trying to gather their belongings, soldiers trying to herd them away. Looters too, he did not doubt. He had already given Barbatio orders to execute without mercy anyone caught stealing from the abandoned buildings, but the city was filled with the poor, the desperate and the daring.

But while demolishing walls and porticos was easy enough, it would take many more men than Castus had available to rebuild the rubble into a new defensive fortification. Two hundred paces north of the bath portico, a runner found him with a message from Gunthia.

'General!' the man reported, breathing hard. 'The enemy are pulling their engineers back from the river!'

Castus cursed beneath his breath, then strode quickly towards the steps that climbed to the battlements. He was barely aware of the curator and his son following him.

Gunthia met him at the head of the steps. 'Just started moving,' he said. 'And look out there...'

He pointed away across the river. In the dusty light the whole plain on the far side of the Mygdonius, both inside and outside the walls of the suburb, was thronged with men and horses. Banners stirred the air, and Castus could make out the distant sound of horns and shouted commands drifting in across the noise of the demolitions behind him.

'Elephants too,' Gunthia said. Castus spotted them a moment later, a double line of the massive beasts drawn up among the ranks of the army, each with an armoured fighting tower on its back. And beyond the elephants, on a raised mound, stood the Persian royal standard and the glittering block of the bodyguard troops. Shapur himself had come to watch his water ram bring down the walls.

'Pull as many men back off the ramparts as you can,' Castus told Gunthia. 'I just want observers up here, nobody else. And have the men fed too – they'll need their strength soon enough.'

Gunthia nodded tautly, and Castus saw the flicker of a smile pass across the Gothic leader's face. He knew the feeling: after all this time waiting and holding the walls, the real fighting was about to begin. It was a raw sensation, a fire in the blood.

Leaning from the embrasure, Castus gazed down at the dry bed of the river, and the sight shocked him. Directly below, the cracked mud was almost obscured by a tangled mess of shattered wood and half-burnt hides, bodies sprawled in cloying lakes and runnels of gore, all of it hazed with flies. A powerful reek of death rose from the base of the wall.

Castus was surprised to notice that the sun was already low behind him, the eastern sky a deep blue above the dust clouds. The distant margins of the plain were almost drowned in evening twilight. As he peered once more at the assembling Persian army he made out a mounted group riding along the far bank of the river, pausing at times to study the condition of the wall and the riverbank. Castus recognised Zamasp riding at the head of the party; the Persian officer halted right opposite where he stood on the ramparts. Only a few hundred paces separated them. A long bowshot could have plucked the Persian from the saddle. A ballista might even do it – Castus was about to give the order when he saw Zamasp raise his arm and kick his horse into motion again.

Marching along the rampart towards his command post above the Gate of the Sun, Castus heard a shout from behind him, then another. He turned and saw the men on the walls gesturing wildly towards the river valley to the north. Stepping to the battlements, he glanced downwards from an embrasure, and his breath caught. A thickly corded stream of brown water was racing along the centre of the river's dry bed, washing away the half-burnt remains of the Persian siege works and the heaped bodies of the slain.

A sound reached him. A rushing hiss, like flames in dry thatch, but coupled with a low grinding noise that seemed to rise from the earth itself. Leaning outward, Castus looked to his left up the bed of the river. A moment later, he saw a wall of brown water, churning and boiling as it came, surging around the bend of the river below the walls. It rose taller than the height of two men, and rolled within it all the detritus of the collapsed Persian dam and the rock and earth it had scoured from the riverbanks.

Castus could only stare as the water rushed onward, faster than a galloping horse, the noise so loud that it drowned out the yells of the men on the wall. In only a few heartbeats the head of the surge had passed beneath him, the enormous volume of water and mud and timber crashing around the masonry piers of the broken bridge, foaming upwards in dirty brown spouts and sprays.

'Dominus, get back!' he heard somebody shouting. 'Get off the wall!'

The flood tide was nearly forty feet below the level of the ramparts, but the spray was falling over the walkway as a dark rain. Castus could hear the water heaving at the base of the walls, rushing into the cuts and crevasses excavated by the Persian engineers and bursting open the bluffs of the riverbank below the foundations. The level of the river was still rising, the dark swirling mass of water bearing all before it.

Screams from his left, and Castus pushed himself back from the embrasure. Men were spilling from the ramparts and down the steps off the walls. Too late; as Castus stared he saw one of the towers sway, the regular lines of brickwork appearing to shudder and ripple. Further along the wall, an enormous crack split the rampart walk. The tower collapsed into the seething water, raising a torrent of spray, and as it fell Castus saw the whole section of wall beyond it give way suddenly and topple outwards. Three men still remained on the wall, trying to manhandle a ballista from its mounting as the solid rampart beneath them dissolved into tumbling rubble.

Castus took a step backwards, then another. Then the paving beneath his feet dropped and tilted, and for a long sickening moment he sensed the wall beneath him teetering on the brink of collapse. A jolt, and he lost his footing and fell sprawling.

With a slow grinding motion that he felt through his entire body, the mass of brick and mortared rubble beneath him began to give way.

CHAPTER XXIV

'Dominus!'

Castus rolled, scrabbling on the tilting slabs, and managed to get his knees beneath him. He felt hands grasping him and dragging him forward, and stumbled upright. Barnaeus was to one side of him, Gunthia to the other; ahead of them a gaping fissure was opening in the rampart, and the far side appeared to be lifting upwards. Running and stumbling, the three men reached the fissure and threw themselves across it. Solid masonry beneath them; a few more staggering strides, and they were dropping down the partially collapsed steps.

Dust and grit filled his mouth, and Castus spat furiously. Tremors were still running through his body, and he was light-headed and reeling. Vorodes appeared, hugging his son to his chest, but Castus strode onwards, past the ruins of the demolished buildings. Only then did he halt, turn and look back at the wall.

The section of rampart where he had been standing only moments before had dropped, but had not fully collapsed. The wall had slumped downwards onto its foundations, great cracks opening in the brickwork to either side, but the rubble core had held solid. Castus gave a cry of relief; only a few feet more and the whole thing would have toppled beneath him. The air was still full of swirling gritty dust, figures staggering and running in confusion.

'What's happened?' Castus yelled, his own voice ringing in his ears. 'Report, quickly!'

Runners came in from either side. The tower just to the north had collapsed, although the wall behind it still remained standing. But to the south, and a hundred paces further beyond the tower, the flood had brought down whole sections of the defences and breached the wall in two places.

'The southern breach is narrow,' a centurion of the Sixth Parthica reported. 'But the northern one's wide enough to march a formation of infantry through it!'

Staring into the gathering gloom as the dust cleared, Castus could make out the shape of the northern breach from where he was standing. The wall was entirely demolished, as if a mighty hammer blow had smashed it. To either side the broken ramparts jutted up, dark and jagged against the evening sky.

'All commanders to me,' he called, the words rasping in his throat. Gunthia was already with him; Barbatio and a handful of junior officers gathered quickly. Castus stared back at the secondary line of defence, still only a wavering mound of rubble, barely knee-high in places. In the panic and confusion all discipline and unit cohesion appeared lost.

'I need a hundred men to hold the southern breach,' he ordered. 'Twice that number to the northern one. Gather as many of your best troops as you can find. Get ballistae up onto the remaining stretches of wall, and archers as well – keep them clear of the weaker sections if you can, but they need to watch what the enemy are doing.'

'You think they'll come soon?' Gunthia asked.

'They'll need to wait until the waters drop further. My guess is we have until dawn, but they may try and cross before that. The rest of your men need to keep building that second wall – push them to it. No sleep tonight, brothers!'

As the officers saluted and ran to muster their troops, Castus felt a last quick tremor of suppressed fear rise from his chest. Then he gritted his teeth, stuck out his jaw, and strode towards the northern breach.

Clambering across the fallen rubble, he pushed his way between the crowds of men already surging into the gap in the wall. As he reached the brink of the collapsed section, he climbed up onto a large square-cut stone that projected from the foundations and surveyed the damage. The collapse of the wall had gouged out a section of the bluffs above the riverbank, but the debris had filled the hole as it fell. Now a solid ramp of rubble and earth sloped from the broken foundations down into the muddy flowing water of the river. Rough-hewn timbers stuck up in places, carried downstream from the Persian dam.

In the fading light the water swirled and eddied around the mass of fallen rubble. The flood was ebbing fast, but the river still flowed outside its usual limits, lapping the far shore a hundred paces away. And beyond it, drawn up across the plain in the last glow of sunset, the Persian army waited. As Castus stared, they raised their banners and let out a vast rolling cry.

'PER-OZ! SHA-PUR! PER-OZ! SHA-PUR!'

'Watch yourself, general,' a soldier said, stepping up smartly beside Castus and raising his shield. Only then did Castus notice the arrows arcing in out of the twilight. The Persian archers on the mounds across the river had begun shooting at the men gathering in the breach. A choked cry, and one of the legionaries staggered and toppled forward onto the rubble, an arrow jutting from his neck.

Jumping down from his perch on the broken wall, Castus heard the shields butting together, sealing the breach. It was a rough array, but a solid one, the front-rank men kneeling with shields grounded before them, the second and third ranks raising their own shields above them in a testudo formation. Barbatio and Gunthia were both there, giving orders to the centurions and the junior officers. They were pushing their best men forward to the front ranks, the veterans and campidoctores of the legions, all in full mail and scale armour.

Looking at the shields, Castus saw that the soldiers were all from different units. The yellow and dark blue shields with the radiate acanthus emblem of the Seventh and Tenth Gemina legions stood beside the red and white shields of Gunthia's Gothic warriors; the sunburst blazon of the Armigeri troopers beside the golden caduceus of the Sixth Parthica. Castus watched them in the low light, and felt a thrill of pride running through him. These were true soldiers, men of the type he had known and fought beside all his life. If they could not hold the breach, nobody could.

'Keep them solid,' he told Barbatio, as he moved back through the ranks. 'If anything comes over that river, throw them back. I'll get observers onto the walls to give you good warning if the enemy start to move. And send runners to bring food and water too – it's going to be a long night!'

Back across the rubble, stumbling in the gathering gloom, Castus found Vallio waiting with his shield and a flask of watered wine. There were fires burning at the edge of the demolished stretch of buildings, and flaming torches mounted on the line of buildings just behind the new rampart. The soldiers were working hard, forming lines to pass chunks of rubble and lengths of timber back to their comrades, but there were so few of them. Too few, Castus could see at once. At least now the breaches had opened he could tighten the new perimeter, shortening the line to where it was needed. A number of civilians were working with the soldiers already, but they would need many more hands if the new defence line was going to stand against a concerted attack. He felt his earlier flush of enthusiasm die inside him.

'Father!' a voice said, and Sabinus came striding from the darkness. He had a bandage around his head, covering one eye, and another strip of linen binding his left arm to his chest.

'Why are you here?' Castus snapped. 'I ordered you to remain at the Strategion!'

'I'm honouring my promise to my stepmother,' Sabinus said gravely, and then grinned. 'Somebody's got to keep you out of trouble!' Castus winced as he saw the burns and scars covering one side of his son's face crease. 'Besides,' Sabinus went on, 'I've been on my feet for days now, and there's nothing I can do up at the citadel.'

'Very well,' Castus said grudgingly. 'Stick close to me though, and don't try anything heroic!'

Up on the wall rampart, a party of men were working with a makeshift block and tackle, lifting one of the big ballistae up into position. Castus could see the flicker of arrows passing above them; every now and again a shaft dropped behind the wall, and he heard the sharp clink of metal striking stone.

Vorodes appeared, with his son Barnaeus close behind him. The boy was still wearing his helmet, and gazing at the scenes around him as he gripped the hilt of his sword.

'I have to thank your son, curator,' Castus said. 'He dragged me off the wall very promptly earlier!'

'I told him to keep back,' Vorodes replied stiffly. 'You'd have done the same, I'm sure. But... I'm happy to see you survived.'

Castus noted the bitterness in the curator's voice. The collapse of the wall seemed to have shaken the man's confidence considerably.

'You'd best try and round up as many people as you can to help with the construction,' he said, nodding towards the new rubble rampart.

The curator was looking at it with a pained grimace, his top lip curled back from his teeth. 'You really think that'll stop them, when they come?' he asked, almost swallowing the words.

'It might,' Castus said. 'If we can build it high enough.' He slapped Vorodes on the shoulder. 'We've all got work to do before dawn.'

*

The night was dark, the young moon shedding only a faint light, and the air felt warm and thick with humidity. Insects hazed the fires and the torches set along the line of the new fortification. Steadily the barricade of rubble and timbers grew higher, but still the work was progressing too slowly.

Shortly after midnight, Castus scaled the surviving flight of steps to the top of the wall and picked his way along the rampart, feeling certain that the masonry beneath him would begin to shift at any moment. Right at the brink of the wide northern breach, a ballista had been erected inside a rough embrasure of piled bricks and sacks of sand. *Sudden Death*, the machine was called; there was another like it on the far side of the breach, and others stationed on rubble mounds just inside the line of the wall. Castus crouched beside the artillery crew, sighting along the bolt-groove of the ballista. The aim was good, angled down at the ramp of debris below the breach.

'Should be able to pick them off nice from up here, dominus,' the chief *ballistarius* said with a gap-toothed grin.

Castus grunted his agreement, then straightened and peered out across the cracked lintel of the embrasure. The dark water reflected a ghostly gleam of moonlight, but the plain beyond was lost in darkness. In the far distance, the sentry fires of the Persian encampments flickered along the horizon.

'Something's moving out there,' one of the soldiers said in a hushed tone.

Edging over to join him, Castus followed his pointing finger. He squinted, but could make out nothing in the gloom.

'There, again!' the soldier said urgently. Others had joined them now, all staring out into the blackness.

'Your eyes are better than mine...' Castus said. But even as he spoke he caught the stir of movement near the edge of the water. He gestured for silence. All he could hear at first was the low mumble of voices from the soldiers in the breach below him. Then other sounds: a scrape of timber, the bright clink of metal.

Light burst suddenly from the mounds on the far riverbank, and Castus covered his eyes. When he looked again he saw fire blazing in the darkness; the flames seemed to dart upwards, rising as fluttering sparks into the night.

'Burning arrows! Guard yourselves!' the solder beside him shouted.

Castus flinched, but kept his eyes above the level of the parapet. The volley of flaming arrows filled the river with a dancing reflected flicker of orange. Then they fell, arcing down into the open breach in the wall. Castus heard men crying out, the clatter of shields, a scream of pain. But his gaze was still fixed on the far riverbank.

In the brief rushing glow of the fire arrows, he had seen the mass of men gathered along the water's edge, and the burdens they carried.

'Get a message down to Barbatio and the men in the breach,' Castus yelled, grabbing one of the soldiers beside him. 'Tell them the enemy are coming across on rafts!'

The ballista crew were already loading their machine, spinning the handles of the big windlass that drew back the slide. A second volley of burning arrows came spitting upwards from the darkness. Castus snatched another look over the parapet, and saw the enemy launching their rafts into the water. The vessels were built of bundled reeds lashed together, and the attackers were packed onto them, kneeling upright as they began to paddle. It would only take moments for them to cross.

'Aim carefully,' Castus told the chief artilleryman. 'Don't loose a shot until you get a clear target.'

'Don't worry about us, dominus,' the ballistarius said. He patted the stock of his weapon. 'We don't miss!'

A snap from the far side of the breach as the other ballista loosed, then a louder crack as *Sudden Death* hurled a bolt out into the blackness. Screams from the river, and the ballista crew howled in triumph.

Another flight of burning arrows arced from the night; one struck the parapet near Castus's head and spun away, trailing smoke. Dropping to his knees, Castus edged forward until he could look down over the brink of the broken wall into the breach below. He saw a mass of locked shields beneath him, some of them stuck with smouldering arrows. But the front ranks were solid, a wall of armoured men bristling with levelled spears.

From the river came the crashing noise of paddles in water and the high-pitched yells of the Persian attackers. Already the first of the rafts had grounded at the base of the rubble slope below the breach. As Castus watched, mastering his trepidation as he leaned over the brink, he saw men swarming from the raft and wading up onto the ramp of debris. In the half-darkness he saw raised spears and shouting faces; the attackers wore loose baggy tunics, breeches and round caps, and carried small square shields, hooked axes and spears. They looked like the same tribesmen that Shapur had sent to storm the outer wall during the tower attack. He pulled his head in as an arrow whistled close by him.

'Sakastanis,' the artilleryman said as he cranked back his ballista. 'Fucking barbarians!'

Stifling a curse, Castus scrambled to his feet and ran, head lowered, back to the steps. As he dropped down to street level he met Sabinus coming in the other direction.

'Where are you going?' his son demanded.

Castus just gestured towards the breach, but Sabinus blocked him with a hand to his chest. 'That isn't your place!' he said. 'You need to keep back from the fighting!'

Castus growled, deep in his chest, then swatted his son's hand aside. 'Either come with me or get out of my way,' he said.

Sabinus took a step back, startled, and Castus saw the anger creasing his brow. He grabbed his son by the nape of his neck and squeezed, managing a crooked smile. 'Sorry,' he said. 'But if you want to protect me, stay close!'

They ran together over the broken ground, pushing in through the rear ranks of the wedge of troops holding the breach. Some of the arrows were still burning – the tips were wrapped in rags, soaked with naphtha, Castus guessed – but the Persians were shooting further volleys out of the darkness. The sound of them striking the shields was a constant percussive thudding.

'Get those flames doused,' he shouted. 'The enemy are using them as a mark to aim at!'

'General!' Barbatio said, saluting quickly as he recognised Castus in the darkness. 'Any idea how many of them there are?'

'Too many,' Castus replied, low in his throat. His body was coursing with trapped energy, and his face ran with sweat. He longed to draw his sword, push forward to the front ranks and take a position in the fighting line. But Sabinus had been right – that was not his place now.

Instead he climbed up onto a chunk of the broken wall, a vantage point. From there he could see over the heads of the soldiers in the breach, but although he could hear the sounds of the Persian attackers scaling the rubble towards the Roman shield wall, he could see nothing of them.

'Third rank,' Barbatio yelled. 'Ready darts...! Loose!'

At the command, the men in the centre of the formation hurled a volley of lethal iron-spiked darts over the heads of the men in front of them.

'Fourth rank – ready darts!'

The Armenian archers behind the infantry lines were already shooting, lofting their arrows over the breach to hit the advancing attackers. Slingers whirled and flung their shot; it was impossible to aim, but Castus could hear the screams from out in the darkness. The Sakastani warriors must be packed so closely together that it was almost impossible to miss. A moment later, he heard the familiar clash of hand-to-hand combat. The

Roman lines wavered, then surged forward again, and the night was filled with the roaring pulse of battle.

Iovinus stepped up beside Castus, lifting a shield to cover him. Just as he did so, an arrow darted from the blackness and struck him in the shoulder. The Protector let out a tight gasp, then dropped without another sound. At once Sabinus grabbed the shield with his good hand and raised it. Vallio was down on his knees beside the fallen man.

A shuddering crash from behind them, and something whirled through the air overhead. Water burst up from the river and sprayed back over the men in the breach. A catapult stone, Castus realised; one of the crews must have repositioned their big onager to hurl missiles straight through the gap in the wall and into the river. He grinned fiercely; the men in the Roman ranks were cheering.

But the noise of fighting was gathering in intensity now, and Castus saw bodies carried back from the front line, other men moving up to replace them. The Sakastanis were raising wild high war cries, and the Romans fought back in grim silence. None of them had shifted a single pace since the attack began.

Then, abruptly, it was over. Castus had not heard a trumpet or a shouted order, but he saw the ripple pass through the troops as their enemy fell back. Another catapult stone coursed overhead, raising a spout of water from the river.

'Drove them back, dominus!' Gunthia said, appearing from between the rear ranks. 'We're shooting them down as they flee, but I reckon half of them are drowned already!'

Castus gave a tight nod. Iovinus was sitting up as one of the surgeons tried to draw the arrow from his shoulder. Assuring himself that the man would live, Castus strode forward into the breach. The ground beneath his feet was uneven with rubble and crackled with broken arrows. Bodies too, those who could not be dragged back from the fighting line. The men parted to let him through, and he stood behind the forward row of shields and gazed down at the scene of slaughter.

The dead lay in a thick mound all across the breach. More of them were sprawled over the rubble that sloped down into the water, and more again in the shallows around the grounded and broken rafts. In the faint moonlight the blood spilt over the stones looked black. Some of the bodies still moved; some whined in agony or cried out in their own language. For several long heartbeats the men in the breach could only gulp breath and stare.

'ROMA VICTRIX!' somebody yelled. At once the same cry burst from a score of throats, then a hundred more. Spears banged against shield rims in a deafening volley of noise, echoing between the broken walls and across the dark waters.

The sky was lightening above the Persian encampment, and already the dust was stirring across the plain. In the dawn greyness Castus looked at the faces of the men around him and saw the fatigue on every one. Only a few hours had passed since the vicious battle in the darkness; none had slept, and the day promised further bloodshed.

Climbing wearily to the rampart once more, Castus surveyed the enemy lines, trying to guess their movements. His head felt fogged and his eyes were blurred. Scrubbing at his face with the heel of his hand, he tried to shake himself into alertness, but he felt old. Far too old to be doing this.

'You held them. Well done,' Lycianus said, pacing along the rampart to join Castus. The scout commander had remained with his reserve cavalry force in the market district throughout the night, and appeared comparatively well rested.

'They haven't begun yet,' Castus said, gesturing towards the far margins of the plain. As he watched, the first gleam of sun broke the eastern sky, illuminating the Persian banners and the glitter of armour and weaponry. Stepping back from the parapet, Castus closed his eyes and raised his hands in salute. *Sol Invictus, the Unconquered Sun.* He breathed a quick prayer, almost instinctively.

'River's low,' Lycianus said, peering over the parapet.

Castus could only agree. The level of the water had fallen rapidly in the night. He guessed that the Persians had built another dam to cut off the flow upstream, or diverted the river altogether. He could not fault their engineering, at least. Now the bed was almost fully exposed, only a few pools remaining between the rubble heaps. But the mud was thick down there too, all the sediment brought down by the flood filling the riverbed. It would be many hours yet before the enemy could hope to cross on foot.

'Would you ever consider surrender?' Lycianus asked with an odd tilt to his voice.

Castus glanced at him quickly. The scout commander was squinting in the sun, his weathered features drawn tight. 'Would you?' he replied.

Lycianus just shrugged, then shook his head. 'That inner wall's not getting built half quickly enough,' he said.

Castus could not deny it. The men working on the new fortifications had raised a chest-high wall of packed rubble in the night, but it would still be a long time before it was strong or high enough to make a difference. In the slow tired greyness of dawn the defences seemed less sturdy than ever. With a long sigh, Castus followed Lycianus down off the wall.

The streets of the city were still filled with cool twilight. Bodies were sprawled across the open ground inside the wall, some of them wounded or dead, others men who had dropped, exhausted, to sleep while they had a chance. Castus saw Nicagoras the surgeon with a party of city slaves moving between them, administering whatever help he could. How long would it be before the enemy launched their next assault? Already the

dawn sun would be drying the mud in the riverbed. After the
night's triumph, there was a feeling of impending defeat in the
air. Castus could almost taste it.

'Do you hear that?' Lycianus asked abruptly.

Castus turned to him, frowning. He could hear nothing at
first, only the groans and whispers of the injured disturbing the
dawn stillness. But then he heard it too. All of them did: the men
still labouring at the defences, the wounded and the exhausted,
Nicagoras and his slaves. All of them heard, and straightened
up, listening.

From the streets behind them came the sound of chanting.

No, Castus realised, not chanting – it was singing. Many
people, all singing together, and getting closer. He drew back
his shoulders, staring at the mouth of the nearest street. He did
not know the song; it was nothing like the raucous tunes that
soldiers sang. But he had heard singing like that often enough,
back in Antioch.

Then the first of the figures appeared from the mouth of the
street. A man in a loose white tunic led them. Ephraim, the
young presbyter from Iacob's church. And behind him, walking
in a swelling column, came a mass of other civilians, both men
and women, all of them singing a Christian hymn.

'Your bishop sent you?' Castus asked as the presbyter
approached him.

'The Blessed Iacob has commanded all the faithful to come,'
Ephraim replied, his grave face breaking into a smile. 'And in the
name of God, we will help defend God's city!'

And Castus clapped his hands onto the young priest's
shoulders and grinned back at him. Now, he thought, perhaps,
they had a chance.

CHAPTER XXV

'So how did you convince him, in the end?'

Ephraim composed his features into a pious expression. 'It was not I who changed the bishop's mind,' he said, and gave a self-deprecatory shrug. 'How could I? In the fervour of his prayers, during the early hours, the Blessed Iacob was granted a vision of the Archangel, who pointed to a verse in the Book of Ezekiel: *Your prophets, O Israel, are jackals in the desert! You have not gone into the breaches, or built the wall that it might stand in battle on the Day of the Lord...!* And so the Blessed Iacob instructed us to clothe ourselves in the armour of God and take a stand against the devil's schemes, to...'

'I understand,' Castus said, cutting him off.

Hours had passed since the arrival of the presbyter and his congregation, and this was the first opportunity he'd had to speak to the young priest man to man. But clearly he would get little sense out of him. The realisation that had seeped into the old bishop's starved and prayer-dazed mind might have come from some god or divine vision, Castus supposed. More likely it had come from the suggestions of the younger priests. He would never know.

Whatever had caused the change, it had certainly worked. All along the line of the new fortifications there were people labouring hard in the hot morning sun. Dust-covered men and women, even children, were pulling down the remaining buildings inside the wall, scraping up the debris, passing bricks and masonry hand to hand, and stacking the rubble onto the growing breastwork. Now that the engineers had checked the surviving stretches of wall and pronounced them stable, Castus had been able to tighten his line of defence around the two large breaches. The new walls would be rough, but they would stand six feet tall and six feet thick, solid masonry with a fighting parapet. But he hardly dared to imagine how they might stand up to a full-scale Persian attack.

He was surprised to see Dorotheus among the labourers. The magistrate gave him the briefest nod of acknowledgement; as a Christian himself, he had apparently decided that the bishop's command could not be ignored. But there was no sign of Vorodes. Only the curator's son remained, working hard in his father's place.

A thin screen of soldiers still held the two breaches; the rest of the defenders were sprawled amid the rubble mounds, sleeping, or trying to sleep. Castus joined Barbatio and together they clambered onto the low spur of broken wall and stared out over the riverbed and the plain beyond.

'At least the bastards have stopped shooting arrows at us,' the legion commander said, wiping the sweat from his brow. 'Saving their shafts, I reckon.'

Castus made a noise of agreement. He was looking down at the riverbed and the drying crust of cracked earth that covered the broad expanse of mud. The sun was hot on his head. Sol, he thought; his own patron deity was aiding the enemy now. The sentries had already reported Persian scouts probing the riverbed further upstream, just beyond archery range.

Where are they? he said under his breath. The army that had mustered the day before had disappeared almost completely, back to their camps and entrenchments. Did Shapur and Zamasp intend to wait all day before sending in their troops? Nervous tension jumped in his gut, and he felt a cool flush across his brow. *This could all be a ruse... They could be massing to attack another part of the wall...* Castus had already pulled most of his best soldiers from the other sections of the city ramparts to hold the breaches. But no, he thought – the Persians would not pass up the chance to attack. The assault would come here, and it would come soon.

Back at the rubble wall, he met Diogenes wandering along the line of the fortification. The old man looked dazed and reddened by the sun, but his hands were blistered and his tunic dirty; clearly he too had been helping with the construction.

'I'm amazed,' Diogenes said with a cracked smile. 'You have half the world under your orders, brother. Men and women, soldiers and civilians... It appears the efforts of the Christians have shamed the other citizens into action too. I've seen temple priests and slaves, merchants and caravan guards, Sogdians and Armenians, even Jews, all working together. For the first time in my life I see a vision of genuine collective labour – a shame that it takes the threat of imminent annihilation to bring it about!'

'So it's always been,' Castus said. Despite his habitual disdain for civilians, he had seen them roused to action once before, at Massilia, and knew they could be brave if it came to it. And with the breaches yawning wide, few could be under any illusions of safety or security now.

A small boy ran past, carrying a single brick. Castus watched as the child passed his load to a woman, who handed it up to the men on the new fortification.

'But are you sure you shouldn't rest, brother?' Diogenes asked, leaning closer. 'May I summon the doctor, Nicagoras, to examine you? You're looking much worn, much burnt by the sun, if I may say so.'

'You may not,' Castus snapped, hiding his discomfort – Diogenes looked quite bad himself. Could Castus possibly look worse? They were both old men, pushed to their limits. He could only pray silently for a few more hours, a few more days, of strength and endurance.

Time passed rapidly, the sun blazing overhead and then slipping below the rooftops to the west. It was the end of the tenth hour, the day's heat beginning to drop into the cool of evening, when a runner came from the ramparts.

'Dominus, they're mustering.'

Castus followed him at a steady stride; there were plenty of people watching, and he did not want to cause a panic by running. Labouring up the broken steps, he crossed the rampart and peered out towards the Persian lines. The first rolling noise of drums came from across the plain, the first wail of trumpets.

The enemy flowed out of their camps and gathered on the plain like men assembling for a parade. Out of the evening haze came blocks of cavalry in glittering armour, elephants with tall towers filled with archers, squadrons of light horsemen wheeling and gathering on the flanks. And before them all, a vast spreading host of infantry filled the dusty plain. How many Persians, Castus wondered, had they slaughtered already? Thousands. But tens of thousands remained. And now, before night fell, all of them would be storming the breaches in the walls.

'Send word to all the unit commanders,' Castus said to the staff tribune behind him. 'We can expect a full-scale attack in an hour or less. Signal to other sections of the defences too. And have Lycianus send us as many dismounted archers as he can spare from the reserves. Keep the rest of the people busy at the construction work.'

The tribune departed, and Castus turned his attention back to the enemy. As he narrowed his eyes to distinguish the details in the haze, he could make out the dark shapes carried by the front-rank infantry. Fascines, he realised: great bundles of reeds and sticks, like the ones they had used to build their rafts the night before. Now the Persians would use them to lay a path across the field of thick mud below the breaches.

Trumpets sounded, and the mass of enemy troops began to move forward. Along the rampart the ballistae were clicking as the crews winched back the slides. Down below him, Castus could hear his officers mustering their troops and assembling them in phalanx formation in the breaches. Many of the people labouring at the inner wall had ceased their labours as they heard the sound of the Persian drums and horns; stunned, they stood slack-mouthed and open-handed, transfixed by fear. Already the overseers were pushing them back to work. The wall was finished in most places, but there were still large gaps where some groups had not worked as hard or as fast as the others. It would be several hours yet until the defences were complete. If the enemy broke through before then, all would be lost.

With as much calm as he could muster, Castus descended the steps and located his group of staff officers. Sabinus was with them, and Castus called him aside while his orderly dressed him in his linen arming vest and cuirass. 'Keep a watch over the inner wall,' he said. 'As soon as you judge it's ready enough, give a signal. But not until you're sure.'

'Where are you going to be?' Sabinus asked. He had stripped the linen bindings from his arm, and was wearing a scale corselet and helmet; his bandaged eye and the glazed pink scars of his burned face showed beneath the rim.

'At the breach,' Castus told him. His son looked appalled, but Castus clapped a hand on his shoulder before he could speak. 'That's where I need to be,' he said quietly. 'You have your orders – now go, and we'll meet again soon.'

'May God grant it,' Sabinus said, and pulled his father into a tight embrace.

Barbatio already had his men assembled in the breach, and the rear ranks opened as Castus moved between them. He climbed up onto the same spur of wall he had used as a vantage the night before, then turned to address them all.

'You know me,' he called, then paused and coughed. A few of the men gave wry laughs, and coughed back at him.

'You know me,' Castus said again, finding his old voice, the parade-ground roar he had known in his younger years. 'You know I trust all of you to stand your ground like soldiers. I saw you do it last night. Now you have to do it again! The bastards out there,' he shouted, 'want to come in here. Are you going to let them?'

'No!' a few men cried back. 'Never!'

'Only a few more hours, brothers,' Castus called to them. 'Then we fall back to the inner wall. Wait till you hear the trumpet. Until you hear it, stand fast! It's going to be hot, and it's going to be bloody. But remember you're soldiers. Legionaries or cavalry, Goths or Armenians, it makes no difference. We are Romans! *We do not yield!*' he shouted, raising his fist.

The answer was sudden, two hundred men yelling in unison, spears beating against shields. 'RO-MA VICTRIX! RO-MA VICTRIX!'

And from across the plain came the cheering of the Persian host as they began to advance, the noise of drums and trumpets meshing to a wild pulsating din. The first arrows came slanting across from the mounds on the far side of the river, rattling off the broken rubble.

'Shields! Form testudo!'

Castus jumped down from the wall, pulled on his helmet and took a place between the fourth rank and the reserves. He fumbled slightly as he tied his helmet laces; his hands were shaking. Barbatio joined him, nodding a quick greeting. Then the shields rose around them, screening them from the incoming missiles.

Peering between the heads and backs of the men in front of him, the shields overhead, Castus tried to glimpse what was happening on the far riverbank. At first he saw nothing; then a tide of men advanced out of the dust, many toting the big fascine bundles and flinging them down into the riverbed. The arrow storm was growing thicker, a steady hail of shafts slamming down into the locked covering of shields. Head lowered, back bent, Castus listened to the battering of arrowheads punching into wood and rawhide. The air beneath the shields was dense with sweat and dust, and the sun broke through in blinding shards. A man dropped, his blood spattering the soldiers to either side of him, and the formation shifted.

Screaming battle cries came from beyond the wall. Castus could see only the dense press of armoured bodies all around him, but he knew that the first wave of the attackers would be crossing the muddy riverbed and throwing themselves at the corpse-strewn rubble below the breach. Already they would be scrambling upwards, climbing the ramp of debris. Arrows were still falling, arcing down at a steep trajectory, but the Armenians and slingers at the rear of the Roman phalanx were returning the volleys. Above the roof of shields the dusty air was filled with flickering death.

Castus held fast to the mailed shoulder of the man in front of him, gripping his sword hilt with his other hand. Jolts of panicked dread pulsed through him, and bursts of exhilaration, and all he could hear was the muffled thunder of his own blood.

Then, with a sudden rush, the attacking horde struck at the wall of shields that closed the breach. The formation shuddered, then heaved. Every man threw his shoulder into the hollow of his shield, pressing forward against the ranks in front. As the shields lifted from above him, Castus got a brief flash of sun and a gust of fresh air. Then the dust rose like smoke between the press of bodies, and a murky brown twilight consumed everything.

Through the screaming of the attackers came the clash and grate of iron, the thud of spears and axes against shield boards, the hack of blades cutting flesh. Castus kept his head down, sensing the battle rather than seeing it; he felt every shove and surge, every blow through his whole body. Choking dust masked his vision, and the air reeked of fresh blood and sweat. A spear arced down, and he dodged it, then broke the shaft beneath his boot. A surge from the rear and he stumbled forward, his feet catching on the uneven ground. The man ahead of him jolted and then reeled back, his face a ruin of blood where a slingshot had struck him. Castus caught his body as it fell; the men behind him seized the fallen man, then he stepped forward into the vacant place.

All along the front line the fighting was close and savage. Castus caught glimpses of it between the men ahead of him. The Persians were hurling themselves at the shields in a wild frenzy, hacking with their axes and slamming with clubs and mauls, others behind them stabbing out with spears at every gap in the line. In the second rank, a tall soldier in scale armour and a gilded helmet, a centurion of the Tenth Legion, was striking over the heads of his comrades, yelling with every blow, a steady chant of fury as he fought. '*Decima! Gemina! Decima*, you bastards!'

Another soldier fell, just in front of Castus. Clambering over the injured man, Castus moved forward again. Now he could see the attackers clearly. Wiry bearded men in conical fur caps, howling as they fought. The men in the front two ranks were cutting them down with grim methodical vigour, a steady and relentless butchery, but still they came. Fresh waves of attackers swarmed up the ramp of rubble from the trampled morass of the riverbed. Spattered with mud, they clambered over the heaped corpses of their own dead and threw themselves into the fight.

But now the assault was losing momentum. The Roman lines tightened once more, pushing forward over the trampled bodies. Back in the third rank, Castus saw the last few attackers falling back, some of them dragging their wounded comrades with them. For a few brief moments it seemed to be over. The men in the rear passed forward flasks of water; Castus took one, splashed his face and mouth, then passed it on.

Then, as he looked forward again, he saw that the first attack had only been a foretaste of violence. The real assault was about to begin.

Marching up from the riverbed, across the mire of mud, blood, bodies and trampled fascines, came a solid phalanx of armoured men. Dismounted cataphracts in full-length scale cuirasses, mailed sleeves and gauntlets, tall plumed helmets. They wore mail hoods that covered their faces, with staring eyeholes just below the helmet rim. Some carried heavy maces or straight-bladed swords; others wielded long lances in both hands. As the remnants of the first attack wave parted before them, the cataphracts climbed the ramp of debris and corpses and advanced. They came on in silence, implacable, invincible in their heavy armour. The Roman lines rippled before them.

'On my command,' yelled the centurion of the Tenth, 'two steps forward!'

A heartbeat of hesitation, then the troops around him tightened ranks, shields clashing together. The centurion shouted, and the formation surged. They caught the advancing Persians just as they reached the top of the slope, the impetus of their brief counter-charge slamming the attackers back. Castus saw several of the armoured men fall at once, others stumbling. He grinned with fierce satisfaction; the centurion had earned himself a gold torque, if he only lived through the fight.

But already the cataphracts were recovering, pushing forward again. Maces and swords hammered at the shields; lances jabbed down across them. Some of the Persians just rammed themselves against the Roman line, trying to break through it by strength alone. The weight of men and metal appeared unstoppable. Castus braced himself, grinding his boots in the dust, but he could feel the formation edging backwards. Men were falling in the front ranks, the crush too great to drag them clear.

Over the shields the long lances reared and struck, angling down to stab at heads and shoulders. And all the while the hammering blows of the swords and maces beat at the shield wall, a constant deafening assault. Castus saw the Romans trying to strike back, their weapons glancing off the Persian armour. Impervious, the cataphracts pushed forward, more like armoured automatons than men. The centurion of the Tenth fell, a Persian mace beating in the side of his helmet. Slowly the Roman ranks were fraying; the enemy were over the foundations of the broken wall now, and the line of shields bowed before them. Soon, Castus knew, it would surely break.

Barbatio was shouting commands from behind him. Men turned, reaching, and Castus saw that they were passing new weapons forward from the rear. Mattocks and pickaxes: entrenching tools, taken from the workers on the inner wall. With a savage smile, he remembered the battle at Taurinum, years ago. They had used just such improvised weapons against the enemy clibanarii then. Now the troops in the second line had thrown down their spears and shields, the front rank tightening in a defensive cordon as the men behind them hewed over their heads at the armoured attackers. Iron clashed, the heavy tools breaking through the mail and scale of the cataphracts. With a slow steady grinding of metal and flesh, the tide began to turn.

Something dropped through the dusty air, and Castus heard screams from beyond the fighting lines. He risked an upward glance and saw men on the broken ends of the ramparts on either side of the breach hurling down rocks, the ballistae shooting their bolts at a sharp angle into the closely packed enemy phalanx. The men at the rear of the Roman formation were beginning to cheer, hoarse and ragged yells, as they pressed forward once more. Castus saw one of the cataphracts stagger and fall, a man in the third line darting his spear forward between other men's legs to stab the fallen Persian through the eyehole of his helmet.

Another surge, the lines straightening, and Castus was shoved forward into the second rank. He managed to drag his sword free of its scabbard, levelling it to strike wherever he saw an opening. But the defenders' brutal battering was driving the Persians back now; more and more of the cataphracts were struck down or stumbling. Stones were still dropping from the walls, smashing at their flanks. Castus almost tripped over a fallen body at his feet. A mailed figure appeared before him, and he stabbed out wildly with his long spatha. The blade clashed against the Persian's shoulder, grating over the armour scales, and the cataphract flinched away from him. A moment later, a swinging pickaxe split the man's helmet and mashed his skull.

The curtain of dust parted, and Castus saw open space in front of the shield wall. Men hunched, shuffled, readied their weapons. Was it over? Impossible to tell whether they had won or not – but the lines still held.

Then, through the gasp and heave of breath, came a strange trumpeting sound. Castus wiped his face with his free hand, staring forward over the rims of the shields. The sound came again, closer this time. And as the dust fell and the air cleared, he saw the huge shapes lumbering down the far riverbank and moving towards the breached wall.

'Elephants!' somebody cried. 'They're sending elephants!'

Horror flowed through the Roman ranks like a racing tide. Now all could see the advancing threat: a trio of huge beasts, armoured with hides, their hooked tusks tipped with bronze, and each with an iron-plated fighting tower on its back. The retreating cataphracts were forming up along the near edge of the muddy riverbed, opening lanes to let the elephants through.

'Merciful gods, we'll never stand against that,' a soldier gasped.

Castus sensed the panic gathering around him, threatening to break into a wild rout. Fear kicked in his chest, and despite the overpowering heat he felt his blood turning icy in his body.

'They're only animals!' he heard himself shouting. He shoved his way forward into the front rank. 'We can drive them back! Archers, and anyone with javelins – aim for the eyes, aim for the drivers!'

The lead elephant was crossing the riverbed now, planting its huge feet with slow care into the swamp of rutted mud. Castus could see the driver perched above its neck, armoured like a cataphract, goading it onwards. The light appeared grainy, although the dust had settled, and with a shock Castus realised that the sun was gone, and the day was dropping rapidly into night. They must have fought for over an hour already. How much longer could they stand?

Swinging its tusks, the elephant raised its trunk and let out another trumpeting roar: almost mournful in the dying light, but again it sent a ripple of fear through the Roman lines. *Come on*, Castus thought, wanting to glance backwards. *Come on – finish the inner wall – give the signal to retreat…*

A low stir of sound was rising from the Persians gathered at the side of the river. A hum and hiss of voices, muffled by the mail hoods of the cataphracts. The elephant paused, took another step forward, paused again. It was in the centre of the riverbed now, its feet sinking into the mud with every stride.

Breathless, Castus watched the animal advance. The other two elephants were moving forward to follow the first, the towers on their backs swaying. Behind them Castus could see more beasts drawn up in the fading light, a score of them at least. Horsemen cantered around them, waving banners.

When he glanced down again he saw that the lead elephant had come to a halt. It raised one leg from the mud, then set it down again. The driver was flogging at its head, trying to urge it forward, but the animal would not move.

A yell from the Roman lines, gathering to a fierce cheer. There were arrows flying now, javelins and slingshot. None hit the elephant, but it stood in midstream, tossing its head, stumbling as it tried to shift backwards.

Castus heard a shout from above him, and raised his head. A snapping sound, and he caught the brief flicker of a ballista bolt. The crew of *Sudden Death* let out a cry of triumph, and when Castus glanced back at the river he saw the elephant driver sagging to one side. Another snap from the ballista on the far side of the breach; the elephant groaned, heaving back onto its haunches in the deep mud. As it turned, Castus saw the black stub of a bolt jutting from behind its ear.

The animal raised its trunk to the sky, its huge mouth yawning open. With a long loud moan and a shudder, its rear legs folded and it collapsed backwards into the mud of the riverbed, the tower crashing from its back. The Roman lines erupted in a wild roar of victory.

On the far bank of the river, the other two elephants had come to a halt. Men were rushing forwards with fresh bales of reeds, more fascines to pack the mud and strengthen the crossing. At the base of the rubble ramp, the mass of Persian foot soldiers were forming up again, gathering for a renewed assault.

Castus felt a hand on his shoulder, and turned sharply. Barbatio was right behind him, his face caked with matted dust and sweat.

'The signal!' the tribune hissed. 'The wall's complete!'

'Fall back from the rear,' Castus ordered. 'From the *rear* – and stay in formation!'

Snatching a glance forward, he saw the Persians already beginning their advance towards the breach. If the men holding it retreated too quickly, they would be cut down before they could reach safety. Castus could hear Barbatio shouting his orders, the centurions repeating them. He felt the ranks around him shudder. *Discipline*, he thought. Only Roman discipline could save them now.

'Hold,' he growled to the men around him. 'Hold fast – *do not run* – hold the line steady!'

He could sense the ranks behind him opening up, the men at the rear spilling away to either side. A shout went up from the mass of Persians at the base of the ramp; someone had noticed what was happening. With a savage cheer the horde of men began to surge forward, scrambling over the mounds of the dead.

Castus stood with teeth clenched, hand tight on the grip of his sword. The shields were still firm around him, but they were only two ranks deep. Dust stirred behind him. Only a single rank remained.

A heartbeat, then another. The attackers were almost upon them. He drew a breath, then roared the command.

'Go!'

CHAPTER XXVI

The shield wall broke, every man turning and running for the shelter of the inner rampart. Castus ran with them, his lungs heaving. Flames bloomed in the darkness, firing the clouds of dust with orange light, and the air tasted of smoke. The first wave of attackers would be delayed only momentarily by the heap of corpses along the line of broken wall foundations; Castus could almost feel them behind him as he ran. With every stride he expected the punch of a speartip against his spine. The ground was rutted and uneven; he stumbled, disorientated. His boot skidded out from beneath him and he fell forward, the sword slipping from his hand.

'Father! Get up – get up and run!'

Sabinus caught him by the shoulder, hauling him to his feet. Castus threw himself forward as he ran. Then the inner wall was in front of him, rearing out of the smoky darkness, higher than his head. The men on the parapet had let down a ladder; Castus saw soldiers scrambling upwards, but he jumped and seized a projecting timber, dragging himself up. Sabinus grabbed him from below, lifting him, and a multitude of hands pulled him in across the parapet. Sabinus was the last man on the ladder, and two men dragged it up after him.

Dazed and gasping, Castus subsided onto the fighting step behind the parapet. Vallio was there, pouring water over his face, and Castus grabbed the flask and sucked from it. The water was hot and tasted of dirt, but he gulped it down.

Already he could hear the noise of fighting. Vallio was trying to get him to remain seated, but he pushed the orderly away and crawled upwards until he could look out over the parapet.

He had ordered two shorter ramparts constructed on either side of the breach, connected to the surviving sections of wall. Together they formed a rough box, two hundred paces wide and half as deep. And as the Persian attackers swarmed through the breach, they found themselves advancing into a killing ground.

Fires burned amid the rubble heaps, illuminating the invading men. The parapet of the three-sided fortification was packed with defenders, soldiers and civilians together; as they saw the attackers stumbling into the firelight they raised a vast bellow of defiance. Arrows and javelins whipped from the parapets, slingshot, even flung stones. Castus saw the leading ranks of the Persian wave cropped down at once under the hail of missiles. Up on the battlements of the outer wall, archers and ballista crews had turned to aim down into the killing ground, picking off the attackers as their advance faltered and died.

Another wave came through the breach. Armoured men, dismounted cataphracts, their armour gleaming in the light of the fires. This time they got further, almost up to the inner line of defences. Stones fell on them in volleys, and the ballistae shot, cranked back, and shot again. With no way of scaling the inner walls, the cataphracts were trapped; one by one they died, or fell back in retreat. Castus saw the last one of them, tall plumes nodding from his helmet, his scale cuirass bristling with arrows. He strode forward, mace raised. Then a ballista bolt, shot from the rampart at close range, struck him in the chest and punched through his armour. He swayed, then toppled over into one of the fires.

The brief hush was filled with the cries of the wounded and dying. Then cheers burst from the defenders on the parapets, and the first swells of a Christian hymn.

Castus was grinning as he sank down to sit with his back to the piled stones.

He woke to a cool grey light, and the sourness of straw bedding. For a few moments he lay in blissful calm, then the aches ran through his body, jolting him into wakefulness. He sat up, cursing.

'How long have I been asleep?'

'A good few hours,' Diogenes said. They were in the portico of the old baths near the Gate of the Sun. Castus was glad that he had managed to struggle out of his armour before he dropped onto the mattress.

'You needed it,' Diogenes went on. 'But don't worry – Vallio here would have woken you if anything happened!'

The orderly was slumped against the wall, head back, snoring quietly.

'What about you?' Castus grunted, rubbing his face. 'You never sleep?'

'As a matter of fact, I've been training myself to do without it,' Diogenes said. He was sitting on the ground, his legs crossed beneath him. 'A simple technique. Relaxation of the body, while retaining full consciousness. I learned it from one of the gymnosophists in the market district. I could teach you, perhaps, although this probably isn't the time...'

'It certainly isn't,' Castus muttered, clambering to his feet. He found a flask of water nearby, drank, and then washed his face and scalp. Slightly refreshed, he stamped his feet to get the blood back into his legs before striding from the portico.

The sun was not yet up, and the morning twilight was smoky and dim. Fires were still smouldering in the killing ground, and along the ramparts people were slumped in fatigued torpor, some of them sleeping while others stared, grey-faced, over the rough parapet. Castus climbed up onto the fighting step and gazed out towards the breach.

The bodies of the enemy slain were still lying where they had fallen the evening before, bristling with arrows, flies circling around them. Castus saw the dead piled thickly around the breach, a vast mound of them along the line of the previous day's fighting. The bodies of the Roman soldiers had already been removed, he noticed. High on the city wall the sentries were clearly visible against the pale sky. A staff tribune approached and made his report; they had lost over a hundred men in the battle, most of them trained soldiers. Gunthia had held off a minor attack on the southern breach before sunset, but there had been no further assaults in the night.

Now that he could see the defenders better, Castus was amazed by their variety. Most of those who had laboured on building the wall had stayed to defend it; soldiers and civilians held the rampart side by side, women and even children among them. Pacing slowly along the line of the wall, stepping over sleeping figures, Castus saw Aurelia Sohaemia standing with a knot of defenders. He did not recognise her at first; she had a scarf tied around her head, partially covering her face, and she was holding a spear.

'You were with us last night?' he asked her.

'For a time, yes,' she replied in a bitter tone. 'It seems none of us can avoid your war now.'

'I don't see your husband.'

'My husband's nerves are not good. He has never been an active man. Now he has gone to the temple of Baal Shamin, to offer prayers to the god.'

'But you're made of stronger stuff, I suppose.'

She gave him a tired smile. There were dark patches beneath her eyes. 'What choice do I have?' she said, gripping the spear tightly in her hands. 'I am here, and my son too. Do not ask too much of us, strategos.'

Castus could only nod, then walk onwards. Every few paces he peered out across the killing ground, towards the breached wall and the glow of the eastern sky. Another attack would come that day, and none could doubt it.

'Excellency,' a voice said, and he turned. Ephraim was waiting on the step of the rampart, his long white tunic grubby with dust and smuts. Castus inclined his head in greeting.

'I have just come from the church,' the presbyter said, solemn as always. 'The Blessed Iacob continues to raise his prayers to the Almighty. As you know, he has vowed not to leave the sacred precinct, but he has given me permission... that is, I must ask your permission...' He paused, apparently uncertain how to proceed.

'What do you want?' Castus demanded. He guessed the priest desired some kind of public worship or ritual, but he had little time for religious niceties now.

'The Blessed Iacob has entrusted me with a holy imprecation against the devil-worshipping Persian foe!' Ephraim declared. 'I am to pronounce it from the walls, but I need your permission to ascend to the battlements.'

'A holy *what*?' Castus said, frowning heavily.

'A curse, he means,' another voice said. It was Dorotheus, the magistrate. 'The bishop wishes to send a curse against the enemy, and the presbyter Ephraim is to deliver it for him.'

'He is?' Castus said, baffled. He had no idea such things were possible. Nor did he know if they were effective, although he remembered the stories of Iacob's curses. A tremor of unease ran through him, and he tightened his shoulders. 'Can't hurt, I suppose,' he muttered. 'Hurt us, I mean. Well – off you go!'

Perhaps, he thought as the presbyter stalked away towards the steps, the strange ritual might strengthen the flagging morale of the Christian defenders. He was curious too, despite himself. Dorotheus had a small group of other civilians with him, and together they watched as the presbyter climbed to the ramparts of the city wall and stood silhouetted against the dawn sky.

Ephraim raised his arms and threw back his head. For a long time he remained like that, as if he were daring some Persian archer to take a shot at him. Then he began to cry out, a long stream of words that carried over the walls and drifted eerily through the stillness. It was in Syriac, of course, and Castus understood none of it.

'What's he saying?' he asked Dorotheus. He was still nervous – magic always had that effect on him.

'The Blessed Ephraim,' Dorotheus said, 'is calling down God's wrath upon the impious Persians. He says... as the impious ones turned the river against the walls of Nisibis, so God will turn all nature against them... The sun will burn them and the dust choke them... Even the smallest creatures of the air will plague them and strike at them... Now he calls upon the angels to witness his words...'

Castus cleared his throat, frowning deeply. The sun and dust were affecting both sides, and while a plague of flies and mosquitoes would certainly be irritating, it could surely be endured. He shrugged, wishing that the priest had perhaps cursed King Shapur to a sudden death, or sent some virulent disease against the enemy.

But, when Ephraim descended the wall once more, Castus noticed how many of the civilian defenders were staring at him with rapt attention, many raising their hands towards him, as if in prayer or salute. While the presbyter may have done little, he had lifted their spirits at least.

'So,' he said to Dorotheus, 'while we wait for your god to do his work, let's look to our defences.'

★

The assault came less than an hour later, as the first rays of the rising sun glared through the breach in the outer wall. Just after the sentry's cry, the roar of the attackers broke the morning's quiet. All along the inner ramparts, the defenders tensed, crouched at the parapets. Ballista crews cranked back their machines, the soldiers readied their javelins, and the civilians gripped their spears and clubs and muttered last quick prayers to a multitude of gods.

Archers came first, rushing in through the breach with big wicker shields held before them. They stormed forward in a solid mass, sheltering from the hail of the defenders' missiles as they advanced, shooting from behind the shields. Stones dropped from the wall ramparts, and the onagers lobbed blazing baskets of pitch across the defending lines to fill the breach with fire.

Castus stood on the fighting step at the centre of the line, dressed in his cuirass and helmet, his standard-bearer at his side holding the purple draco banner. Around him were a picked band of infantry veterans, armoured legionaries who pelted the advancing Persians with darts and javelins. The first wave of the attack slowed and then halted, the archers crouching behind their grounded shields, surrounded by their own slain. But they were only the advance party, the skirmishing line. Already the dust was rising, billowing in through the breach in sunshot clouds, and the ground seemed to shake under the tread of giants.

Out of the glowing dust came the elephants, three of them walking abreast, with another three behind them. The enemy, Castus realised, must have used the hours of darkness to pack more fascines into the river mud and strengthen the crossing sufficiently to take the weight of the great fighting beasts. And the sight of them was spreading panic through the defenders.

High in the swaying towers on the elephants' backs, archers and javelin men were shooting arrows and casting missiles. And all around them, flowing through the breach on either side of the elephants, came a mass of Persian foot soldiers carrying ladders.

'Aim for the towers!' Castus heard an officer shouting to the nearest ballista crew. 'No – aim for the drivers!' somebody else cried.

The defenders on the ramparts were quailing, crouching behind the parapets as if the sight of the elephants alone could cause destruction. The first three animals were already into the killing ground and advancing on the inner wall, stepping slow and heavy, swinging their tusks. Their legs were caked in mud, and the dust seethed around them as they moved.

Ballistae snapped all along the wall. Castus saw one tower struck, a Persian spearman topple. A cheer from his left: another elephant had been hit in the leg by a ballista bolt, and had halted. Raising its trunk, it let out an anguished trumpeting cry. Further to the left, the defenders on the inner rampart had mustered with long spears and pikes and were trying to drive an elephant back from their section of the defences. The animal roared, smashing at the spears with its trunk and tusks, as the men riding in the tower picked off the defenders with their bows.

And now the ladders were swinging up against the parapets, the first attacking infantry beginning to scale the rungs. It was a short climb, but the parapets above were packed with defenders, missiles raining down. Castus saw a woman stand up on the wall, wild-haired and screaming, raising a stone in both hands; she let it drop and the ladder below her smashed, the climbers tumbling. He could only stare; the scene before him had a dizzying quality, like a fevered dream of dust and smoke and noise.

Screams from his right; one of the elephants had lowered its head and charged at the wall, butting against the parapet and almost breaking through it. The defenders had scattered in panic, but already some of them were scrambling back, spears and mattocks in hand. As the huge beast heaved forward, they began stabbing and hacking at it. Several had flaming brands, and at the sight of the weaving fires the elephant reared back, bellowing.

Smoke laced the sky, and another of the burning pitch baskets, flung by a catapult, crashed down into the tower on an elephant's back. The crew leaped clear, plunging to the ground wreathed in flame. The elephant that had been pushed back from the wall turned suddenly, trunk raised, and charged to one side, Persian ladder parties scattering before it. Not fast enough; the animal stormed straight through them. Castus saw two men crushed beneath the thundering feet, another caught by a swinging bronze-tipped tusk and almost torn in two.

The narrow expanse of ground between the city wall and the inner defences was a surging mass of men and animals. All around, on the ramparts, a mob of people screaming and flailing. *Like a beast show in the amphitheatre*, Castus thought. An arrow jarred off the wall and flicked up against his shoulder, and he barely felt it.

The ladders had been thrown down, and the Persian attackers were mostly huddled against the base of the walls, more terrified of the maddened elephants than of the defenders above them. Two more of the animals had turned to charge wildly through the ranks of their own side. The drivers lolled on their necks, dead but still held upright, and the tower on the back of one of the crazed animals had caught fire and was blazing fiercely. As Castus watched, the elephant threw itself down and rolled over, crushing the burning wreckage.

But another of the beasts was still slamming at the wall, and the parapet had almost collapsed before it. The four men in the tower on the animal's back were pelting arrows down at the defenders, one of them leaning out with a lance to stab at anyone trying to get close.

A pair of figures appeared on the parapet, soldiers stripped to their tunics, swords in hand. Silently they leaped down into the milling dust; Castus saw them dash beneath the elephant's belly and begin hacking at the thick leather girth strap that secured the tower. The elephant took a stride backwards, knocking one of the soldiers down and crushing him. Another figure leaped from the wall; with a shock, Castus noticed that it was Barnaeus, the curator's son.

Now the Persians had seen what was happening. The second soldier dropped, a spear striking him in the back. Barnaeus alone remained, the youth standing upright beneath the elephant, legs braced, sawing with both hands at the girth strap. The tower gave a sudden lurch, the weakened strap parting beneath it, then slid and toppled from the elephant's back. A mighty yell went up from the defenders.

'Get him!' Castus roared, but his voice was lost in the noise. He felt half strangled, the blood surging in his neck. In his mind, it was Sabinus he was seeing. 'Somebody get down there and rescue the boy!'

The elephant, freed of the tower's weight, had swayed backwards and lurched away to one side. The wreckage of the tower, still secured by chains and ropes, dragged after it. One of the Persians who had fallen from the top was hauled along too, trapped in the wreck, but there was no sign of the curator's son.

Helpless, Castus could only watch as the elephant stumbled back from the wall, bellowing in anguish. A couple of men jumped down from the parapet, and Castus saw them struggling in the dust. But the cheers along the wall had redoubled; three of the elephants were down, dead or immobilised, and the other three had somehow found their way back to the breach and were pushing back out through it, away from the tormenting darts and the fires. In the bowl of smoke and dust the enemy were falling back, abandoning their ladders and retreating behind their wicker shields.

'He's dead,' somebody said. Castus blinked at the man; it was Nicagoras, the Greek doctor. 'Barnaeus is dead. They found his body. There was nothing I could do.'

'Tell his mother,' Castus managed to say. Then his throat clenched, and he shut his eyes tight against the sting of tears.

Try not to kill too many of us in your battles, general.

There were further attacks, all through the day. Again and again the Persians rushed the breach, screaming men with faces blanched by fear as they saw the death that awaited them. Arrows showered, the artillery along the ramparts shot and shot again, and the waves of attackers fell like wheat before the sickle. By late afternoon the killing ground within the circuit of walls was choked with the bodies of the slain, dead men lying so thick that they covered the rutted dust like bloodied sea wrack left by the tide. Among them, the vast carcasses of the dead elephants rose like islands.

The Persians sent two more of the great beasts into the breach at noon, but the animals would not advance far. Castus saw one of them halt beside another fallen elephant, and brush its trunk along the flank of the dead animal. Then it let out a long mournful groan and began to back away. He felt sorry for the creature; despite their fearsome appearance, the elephants had more care for their own survival than the men that fought beside them. They remained only long enough for the archers and ballistae to pick off the drivers that goaded them, then they retreated.

Finally, as the sun began to set, a glitter of metal showed in the corpse-piled gap of the breach. Men in armour – a solid wedge of them advancing on foot, climbed in over the foundations of the old wall and the mound of the slain. Shield-bearers went before them, holding a cordon just inside the killing ground. The low sun lit the armoured men, turning their mail and scale to rippling gold.

Castus could see the banner at the centre of the wedge. Then, beneath it, he picked out the figure of the commander himself.

Zamasp stood tall, flanked by his bodyguards, all of them encased in gleaming metal. But they did not advance; instead they held their position in the breach, their faces masked by silvered iron and bronze.

All along the ramparts the defenders readied themselves for a renewed assault. The sea of fallen bodies between the walls rippled and heaved, the wounded and dying groaning and crying out for mercy, and the flies swarmed.

Castus moved to the parapet, standing directly beneath his own draco standard. He knew that Zamasp could surely see him. Chin raised, jaw jutting, he stared back at the Persian commander across the killing ground.

Zamasp turned his head to one side, then to the other. He raised his hand, a mace gripped in his fist. He let the mace fall, then turned and strode back through the breach. The formation of men that had accompanied him retreated too, keeping formation, facing to the front. The glitter of their armour faded into the twilight.

'Nisibis!' one of the cavalry troopers beside Castus cried, raising his spear. 'Bulwark of the east!'

The cheer burst along the wall, a thousand voices raised in triumph as the defenders saw the last Persians retreating.

Castus was swaying on his feet, still staring at the milling dust where the Persian commander had stood to survey the carnage. All around him now was the jubilation of the defenders: men were hugging women, soldiers and civilians raising their arms as they cheered. He tried to force a smile, but the muscles of his face felt frozen. Redness in his eyes, a dead weight in his soul. He turned away from the rampart, away from the vast slaughter.

Behind the wall there were more people, cheering and shouting, some of them chanting in praise to their gods. But amid the celebration Castus heard one voice, keening in grief. He saw the knot of figures: the woman and those who surrounded her, supporting her.

'He died a hero, kyria!' a man was saying. 'He died to protect us!'

Then the figures parted, and Castus saw Sohaemia gazing up at him, her face glazed with tears. As she caught sight of him her eyes widened, and she let out a long gasping cry.

'Curse you!' she yelled, raising a finger to point at him. 'You brought this war here! You killed my son! Curse you!'

Dumbstruck, Castus raised his hand, as if he could ward off her rage and pain. Her words struck into his heart. A moment later, those that surrounded Sohaemia had bundled her away.

Castus stood, rooted by dread. He felt old, haggard, and the air was suddenly too thick to breathe. 'Where's Sabinus?' he managed to croak. 'Where's my son? Where's Sabinus?'

'I saw him, dominus,' one of the staff officers said. 'A few hours ago, during the last attack. I saw him fighting...'

'*Where is he?*' Castus roared. He took a step, and felt his eyes blurring.

'Brother,' Egnatius said, taking by the arm. 'You need to sit down...'

Castus lifted his arm to shove the man away, and pain burst through him. He gasped, teeth clenched, his heart crushed in his chest.

Then his legs went from under him and he fell to the gritty stones. Voices around him, shouting. He tried to draw a breath, and could not.

Blackness closed over him, and he felt himself plunging down through deep water.

PART FOUR

CHAPTER XXVII

Antioch, August AD *337*

From the topmost tier of the theatre, the area set aside for the wives of senior officials, Marcellina gazed down through the balustrade at a seething mass of humanity. The curving ranks of seats that dropped vertiginously below her to the orchestra pit were packed with people, most of them dressed in gaudy colours. The piping notes of a water organ competed with the rushing roar of mingled voices. Leaning forward on the marble bench, Marcellina tried to still the nervous tension in her body.

Today was the twentieth birthday of Constantius Augustus, and the city of Antioch was consumed with festivities. The citizens might have seen little of their new emperor – many of them were unsure whether he was their new emperor at all; Constantius himself had still not returned to the east, and few knew where he might be – but to a casual observer their customary appetite for games and shows appeared undiminished even in these troubled times.

Or so things seemed, Marcellina thought to herself. Behind the façade of apparent levity and celebration, the city was in a ferment. The abrupt removal from office of Flavius Ablabius towards the end of June, and the unusual promotion of Domitius Dracilianus to the post of Praetorian Prefect, the chief magistracy of the eastern provinces, had left a dangerous uncertainty at the heart of power. News that a vast Persian horde was laying siege to Nisibis, and that the Roman field army of the east, rather than opposing them, had been withdrawn to their old camp outside Antioch, had sent shocks through the already volatile population. They had little fellow feeling for the citizens of distant Mesopotamia, but if Nisibis fell only the Euphrates would stand between the Persians and their own province, their own city. The Sassanid kings had sacked Antioch before; they could easily do so again. And Dracilianus and his military commanders appeared paralysed before that threat. In the parching midsummer heat, Antioch felt like dry tinder waiting for a flame.

But, even so, today the city appeared in festive mood. There had been chariot races in the circus earlier, and now some of the crowds that had attended the races had thronged to the great theatre below the slopes of Mount Silpius for the evening performance. Red awnings projecting above the seats cut the low glare of the sun, but lamps were already glowing in the great ornamental façade of pillars, pediments and statues that rose above the stage.

Every few moments, Marcellina glanced towards the canopied podium to one side of the seating area: the imperial tribunal, where the emperor or presiding magistrate would sit. The podium was ringed by guards – the archers and clubmen who served as the city watch, and a group of Scholae from the palace – but the chair beneath the canopy remained unoccupied. Would Dracilianus show his face?

A figure caught Marcellina's eye, a drably dressed man moving between the seats of the slaves and *humiliores* directly below her. For a heartbeat the man looked up, and seemed to wink. He appeared entirely anonymous, but she recognised him at once. Then he was gone.

The man had come to her house two nights previously, slipping in past the sentries at the door, dressed as a slave. For many weeks now, ever since the sudden fall of Prefect Ablabius, Marcellina, her daughter and their household had been kept under guard, discouraged if not overtly forbidden to leave the palace quarter. She had not spoken to Dracilianus in person – he refused to meet with her – but he had communicated that the measures were for her own protection. Marcellina was not fooled. Her repeated requests for an audience with the new Acting Praetorian Prefect had been turned down. Why was he keeping her and Aeliana as virtual prisoners? No doubt, she thought, it was connected with Castus's military command. She knew that he was surely at Nisibis, under Persian siege, and prayed daily for his deliverance. But no news came, the guards remained at her door, and in the long hot days of summer she had felt herself driven close to madness.

'His name's Europas, domina,' Pharnax had told her, the evening before the anonymous-looking man came to the house. 'Or that's what he calls himself, anyway. But he's an actor, so who can say... That's all we need to know about him.'

Marcellina had grown up in the countryside of northern Britain, and aside from a few years spent at Treveris she had lived most of her life in a rural environment. The society of cities was alien to her, and she understood little of how they worked. But Pharnax had explained it to her; cities, the scarred ex-gladiator had told her, had their own sort of government, alongside the officials and the magistrates. A secret government, of the people. The chariot-racing factions and the actors' guilds ran things on the streets of Antioch; they controlled the allegiances of the city's masses.

And this man who called himself Europas was one of them. He was a man, so Pharnax believed, who could make things happen.

Scanning the crowd in the theatre, Marcellina tried to pick him out again, but he had vanished into the throng. The first of the performances was already beginning, a selection of popular pantomime excerpts, and the crowd stilled and quietened. Marcellina could not spare any attention for the masked dancer's gesturings, the music or the keening voices of the chorus. Where was Dracilianus? *He had to be here.* Everything depended on his presence.

'Your husband's at Nisibis, so they say, kyria,' the man who called himself Europas had said, casting back his hood in the dim lamplight of the upper chamber. 'Not much we can do to help him.'

'You know what I want,' Marcellina said, hiding her anxiety. Pharnax leaned in the doorway, chewing a toothpick. If the gladiator had not vouched for this man himself, Marcellina would never have trusted him.

'I remember your husband,' Europas went on in a smooth voice. An actor's voice. 'He didn't make many friends when he was in Antioch over the winter. But people liked it when he stood up to Ablabius. And now he's an enemy to Dracilianus too, you say? Interesting man!'

Dracilianus, Marcellina knew, had not made himself popular either. But why he appeared to have turned against Castus she did not know. Valerius Mucatra, the commander of the field army, now went everywhere with the new prefect; had Dracilianus just wanted to clear a position for his own man? No, there had to be more to it than that. But the most pressing thing was to force them both to take action. Explanations could wait.

'I can't offer you much, as you know,' she told Europas. 'If you can do what Pharnax claims you can… I can pay you a certain sum.'

Europas made a gracious gesture. 'Most generous,' he said. 'But it doesn't work that way. We do something for you – and, in time, you do something for us.'

'I can't do anything for you if I'm dead,' she whispered. Aeliana was in her sleeping chamber, out of earshot, but she wanted to be careful.

'Staying alive's *your* job, kyria,' the actor said with a glinting smile.

They had discussed nothing more that evening, and Marcellina still had little idea of what would happen. It would be here, though, at the theatre. Europas's domain. How many others knew of what was planned? How far had the secret networks of the city carried their schemes? Biting her bottom lip, Marcellina concentrated on watching, and waiting.

The first performance had come to an end, and through the spattering of applause came a blast of trumpets. Figures had appeared beneath the canopy of the tribunal: with a shiver of nervous relief, Marcellina recognised Dracilianus among them. A tribune of the Scholae stood behind him, with the squat, bearded figure of Valerius Mucatra, dressed in his full military regalia, at his side. As Dracilianus seated himself, a herald mounted the opposite podium.

'All rise!' the herald cried. 'All rise for his eminence, the most distinguished Domitius Dracilianus, Praetorian Prefect of the East!'

Marcellina got quickly to her feet, pulling the silk shawl tighter around her head and shoulders. The richly patterned fabric had come from Nisibis; a gift, Castus had told her, from the councillors of that city. She wore it now for good luck, and to send a message: surely none could mistake its origin. Most of the other ladies on the higher seats were standing too, but with a shock Marcellina noticed that the greater mass of the crowd below had remained seated. Here and there men were on their feet, but they resembled stray stalks in a field of harvest stubble.

'*Noble Dracilianus,*' the herald declared, stretching out his arms towards the podium, '*lover of your country! Defender of the city! You dignify us with your presence!*'

He turned to the crowd, raising his arms to signal the acclamation. Marcellina breathed the words silently, her mouth dry. The women to either side repeated the praises in a mumble. But from the stalls below came only a few voices; instead, a strange sound was rising from the multitude on the lower seats. A whisper at first, rising to an eerie low chirring, like the distant sound of swarming bees. Marcellina stared down into the crowd, wide-eyed.

'*Noble Dracilianus,*' the herald went on, a catch in his voice, '*may you rule over our provinces with wisdom…!*'

But now the strange noise, the humming buzzing clamour, was rising to drown out the herald's words. Dracilianus was looking baffled. Beside him, Mucatra stared with clenched fury into the crowd.

'Where is our emperor?' a voice cried, seeming to come from nowhere but carrying across the auditorium. 'Bring us our emperor!'

'Who defends the cities?' another voice called out. 'Who repels the Persians? Why do our troops refuse to fight?'

Glancing to either side of her, Marcellina could not make out who had spoken. Actors, she had heard, were trained to throw their voices; some could make words appear from the very air.

'Dracilianus is a false governor!' a higher voice yelled. 'To the river with Dracilianus!'

But now the steady buzzing of the crowd had gained a pulse. Feet stamping in the stalls, hands clapping. The slap of leather against stone. Marcellina saw a few missiles flying from the upper tiers. Shoes, she realised, they were throwing shoes… Many of the people below her were passing baskets between them, each filled with worn old sandals and boots.

'Silence!' Mucatra bellowed into the wall of noise. One of the flung shoes landed on the podium beside him, and he kicked it angrily away.

The calls from the crowd had built to a steady chant now. '*WHO DEFENDS THE CITIES? WHO DEFENDS THE CITIES…?*'

'Dracilianus to the river!' somebody yelled.

'Dracilianus to the lions!' another cried.

And now a sudden wave of motion flowed through the packed stands. Leaning forward over the balustrade, Marcellina watched in amazed horror. The guards that had ringed the tribunal were wading into the crowd, striking out with their iron-tipped staves, trying to isolate and capture whoever was leading the chant. People screamed, scrambling upward over the ranked seating. The orchestra pit was in turmoil as the dignitaries from the lower tiers made a rush for the exits.

Dracilianus was gone, and the tribunal was empty.

'Domina!' a voice said, and Marcellina turned from the riotous scene below her. Pharnax stood in the rose-tinted shadows. 'Domina, best leave now,' Pharnax urged, his scarred face looking demonic in the ruddy glow. 'I've got a litter outside – Aeliana's there, with some of the household slaves.'

'Yes, yes,' Marcellina said hurriedly. Many of the other women were also making their escape, packing the upper colonnade and the stairway, stifling their shrieks. From the stalls, Marcellina could hear roars of combat, the thud of staves striking bodies, the screams of the injured.

Her mind was racing. She had imagined many times in the last two days what sort of disturbance Europas and his confederates might cause, but she had never anticipated this level of violence, or this sudden a conflagration. As she followed Pharnax down the booming funnel of the stairway, the burly gladiator forging a path ahead of her, she fought to control her terror. *What have I done? What have I caused to happen?*

She had assumed that it would be an easy matter to escape the city with Aeliana, once Dracilianus and his guards were distracted. A boat was waiting at the river dock below the palace island, and it would take them down the Orontes to Hormisdas's estates south of Daphne. They would be safe there at least.

But as she rode in the litter along the colonnaded street towards the river, Marcellina saw that things would not be so simple. The riot that had ignited at the theatre had already flowed out into the city, racing like a wind-driven blaze, faster than a man could run. How had it happened? At every street corner there were gangs of men chanting slogans, abusing Dracilianus and the army commanders. She heard the crash of shutters breaking, of amphorae smashed on the cobbles. Holding Aeliana beside her in a tight embrace, she kept the drapes of the litter closed. Pharnax was striding alongside.

Bodies shoved against the side of the litter as it passed a crowded intersection. Suddenly the drape was snatched aside, and a man leered in. Unshaven, gap-toothed, his breath stinking of wine, he grinned at Marcellina and her daughter. 'Hello, ladies! Looking for some *fun*?'

Marcellina hugged her daughter closer, drawing the dagger she kept beneath the litter cushion. But before she could move, Pharnax had punched the man on the side of the head and knocked him down, then casually stamped on his face. The drapes fell closed, and they moved on.

By the time they had crossed the bridge and reached the river dock, night was falling. The bearers set the litter down on the quayside, and as she climbed out Marcellina saw the boat tied up only a few paces away. But figures were gathering from the shadows; light flared as one of them uncovered a lantern.

'In the name of Constantius Augustus,' a man cried, 'remain where you are!'

Pharnax had already pulled a short sword from beneath his cloak. Aeliana was still inside the litter, and Marcellina shrank back against it, gesturing for her daughter to stay seated. The men around them were from the city watch, she realised, with an officer of the Scholae leading them.

'No need for trouble,' Pharnax said, moving to stand between the officer and Marcellina. He held his sword low, in a fighting grip. 'The ladies are leaving the city – things are getting too hot here...'

'Take them,' the officer said, and the guards closed in.

Aeliana screamed, throwing herself from the litter and clasping Marcellina's legs. Pharnax had dodged forward to intercept one of the guards, feinting with his sword. The officer shouted another command, and bows thrummed from the darkness.

Pharnax jolted upright, the sword falling from his hand. He turned slowly to Marcellina, and with a cry of horror she saw the three arrows jutting from his chest. The scarred old gladiator's face creased in pain, and he tried to speak. Then another arrow struck him in the neck, and he dropped without a sound.

A pair of lamps burned on tall stands, illuminating the polished marble floor, but the high ceiling of the chamber was lost in darkness. Marcellina sat upright on a stool, Aeliana standing beside her. The girl had not made a sound since they were captured at the river dock. She appeared to be holding her breath.

'Tell me,' Dracilianus said, 'why I should not have you thrown in a cell? Tell me why I should not have my *quaestionarii* scourge the flesh from your back? Yours, and your daughter's too?'

'Why would you do such a thing?' Marcellina managed to say. She was struggling to maintain an appearance of calm, but the blood was pulsing fast in her head.

'Why?' the prefect said with cool severity. 'You don't think that conspiring to provoke a riot in the city of Antioch is a grave offence? A treasonous offence? Think of the damage to property, the injuries, the possible loss of life. Not to mention the insult to my own office, and to the dignity of the emperor I serve!'

Marcellina could smell smoke, trapped in the clothes of the guards and military officers who stood around them in the gloom. There were fires still burning in the city. Dracilianus himself appeared unruffled, as usual. In the low light his eyes looked like smooth grey pebbles, pressed into the waxy mask of his face. He smelled only of rosewater.

'I did not provoke anything,' she forced herself to say. 'How could I?'

'Don't weary us with your excuses,' Dracilianus said. 'My investigators quickly determined who was responsible for this outrage. Indeed, they already knew you were plotting something. We might not catch the instigators... the *principal actors*, we might say... but we've caught the director. The patron. *You.*'

'I've been asking to speak with you for weeks,' Marcellina said, forcing a tight smile. 'Now, at least, I have your attention, don't I?'

Dracilianus flinched slightly, as if her audacity had disarmed him. 'Cleverness does not suit a lady of your years and status,' he said quietly. 'Although,' he went on with more assurance, 'I'm not sure exactly what your *status* might be...'

'My husband,' Marcellina declared, her voice ringing off the marbled walls, 'is Magister Equitum per Orientem – his rank equals yours!'

'Your husband,' Dracilianus replied, his expression hardening, 'is a traitorous worm. At present he's probably rotting in a stinking grave pit outside the walls of Nisibis!'

Marcellina felt the chill of renewed fear. 'Aurelius Castus is no traitor,' she said quietly, 'and you know it. He's always been loyal to the emperor – always!'

'Oh, so we believed,' Dracilianus said, shaking his head. He began to pace, back and forth before his captives. 'I confess I was rather taken in myself by his simple-soldier act, his *knuckleheaded* demeanour...! But now we know different.'

He fanned his arm towards the officers and guards surrounding him. 'Since we disposed of that oaf Ablabius, new evidence has come to light. Treasonous correspondence, between Ablabius and Aurelius Castus, proving that they conspired to raise a mutiny of the troops against the rightful Caesar Constantius and place Flavius Julius Dalmatius upon the throne.'

'This is madness!' Marcellina cried. She had flinched back on the stool at the prefect's words, hugging Aeliana to her side.

'But what should we expect?' Dracilianus went on. 'It was always a mistake, I think, to promote such base men to high office. Ablabius, born in the scum of a Cretan brothel. And Aurelius Castus, the son of a nobody, a common soldier... To think that he once dared to marry a lady of the Roman aristocracy! A daughter of the Domitii... How my family loathed him. He killed her too, or drove her to her death with his brutal ways. He murdered another cousin of mine too, in cold blood. We could never forgive him for that. By all the gods, I've prayed long and hard for the chance to cleanse our family name of that particular taint.'

'So that's what this is about?' Marcellina said, cold horror flowing through her body. 'You hate him because he insulted your *family*?'

'Why not?' Dracilianus said. 'As good a reason to hate a man as any. Besides his treachery, of course!'

He was smiling, but his eyes were still expressionless, dead in his face. No, Marcellina thought, that was not the reason. However this man may have hated her husband, there was something more behind his actions. *What threat did Castus pose to him?*

'It was you, wasn't it?' she said with icy realisation. 'You sent those men to attack Castus in his own quarters, back in the autumn...'

'That matter was investigated thoroughly,' the prefect said with a slight shrug. 'I see no reason to dwell on it now.'

Marcellina flinched in shocked disgust. He had as good as admitted it... There was no limit to the hatred she felt for this man.

'Incidentally,' Dracilianus went on, 'it may interest you to know that I've ordered Valerius Mucatra to march the field army east to Edessa, to counter any further Persian incursions. Now the succession is assured we have no more need for troops in Antioch. The detachments currently stationed at Soura on the Euphrates will join him on the march. Although I assure you this has nothing to do with today's disgraceful episode – I'd planned it several days ago.'

Liar, Marcellina thought. Her fear and horror were turning to anger now.

'As for you,' Dracilianus continued, 'I'm afraid your options are both bleak, and limited. The property of a condemned traitor is seized by the state, as you know. All of it. So unless you wish yourself and your daughter to live in the public porticoes with the other vagrants, I suggest you look to your future. You're still quite presentable, and not too old – I believe Valerius Mucatra wants a wife. Perhaps you could make yourself charming to him, when he returns from seeing off the Persians?'

Marcellina gasped, feeling the colour rush to her face. But before she could answer the insult, Aeliana had pulled away from her side. Glaring, the girl confronted Dracilianus.

'My father will kill you!' she cried. 'He'll come back here and kill you – he promised he would!'

'Be silent!' Marcellina hissed, grabbing her daughter's arm.

But Dracilianus had taken a step closer, stooping to peer at the girl. He reached out and seized her by the chin. 'What's that, little chicky? Your father said he would murder an officer of the state? What a bloodthirsty traitor he must be!'

'Get your hands off her!' Marcellina screamed, pulling Aeliana from him. Her daughter was breathing fast, sucking back tears, all the terrified panic she had been suppressing since Pharnax was killed rising up in her.

Dracilianus stepped away, shrugging as he smiled. 'A dangerous pair, eh?' he said to the officers behind him. A couple of them laughed. 'I think we must hold them securely until the emperor returns and determines their fate. Till then, let them remain within their house, under close guard.'

Through the numbing fog of her fear, Marcellina heard the words and realised their implication. *Hostages*, she thought. *We are to be hostages.*

She knew what that meant: for all his bluster, Dracilianus was still not in total control of the situation. He still did not know how the dice would fall.

And somewhere, just possibly, Castus still lived.

CHAPTER XXVIII

Birds were wheeling around the citadel mount, fast and black against the pale glow of the sky. He tipped his head, watching them as they flew.

'Untroubled creatures,' the doctor said, following his gaze.

Nicagoras had appeared silently on the roof terrace of the Strategion, where Castus had taken to sitting during the brief cool of the evening.

'Perhaps we could learn from them?' the doctor went on. 'They appear to act in such instinctive harmony, without strife or coercion!'

'The bigger birds still attack the smaller ones,' Castus said.

'Hmm. I suppose that is nature's way... But I always find it amazing that they have such energy, with such small hearts inside their bodies!'

Castus grimaced. He did not want to think about hearts. Especially not his own.

'You have suffered a paroxysm,' Nicagoras had told him, when Castus had first emerged from the unconsciousness and delirium that had gripped him for days. 'Excessive physical and mental strain, coupled with overheating of the blood, caused the vessels within your body to swell and become clogged, thus stopping the motion of your heart.'

'Will it happen again?' Castus had asked him, still dazed and aching as he lay on the mattress in his darkened chamber.

'Oh, certainly,' the doctor had replied, smiling. 'As I suspect it has happened before, no...? You've survived this time, the gods alone know how, but if you continue to exert yourself the next paroxysm will certainly come, and you will die.'

'And if it doesn't?'

'If it doesn't... I expect you may live a good few years yet. Ten, I would estimate. You have a very dense body, and a great deal of blood – I assume you have some barbarian ancestry. But currently you must rest, continue the course of medication, and avoid undue stress.'

And so it had been for nearly a month now. For the first half of that time Castus had remained in his chamber, sleepy with the drugs the doctor fed to him. He had dreamed often, feverishly; he thought that Marcellina came to him, and he reached out for her, shouting loud enough to summon the slaves from the vestibule. He dreamed of his first wife, Sabina, as well, and woke troubled and sweating heavily. But the fever passed, and steadily his strength had returned.

His son brought him news from the city twice a day. There had been further attacks, while Castus lay incapacitated. A ladder assault against the Singara Gate, thrown back with minor losses. Mamertinus had died there. Also a night attack against the western wall, where the Persian ram had breached the defences. But for the last two weeks the enemy had remained in their siege camps, and no further attacks had come. The river flowed along the eastern wall below the repaired breaches, a swamp of half-dry pools and marshy rivulets, choked with debris and decomposing corpses.

And in the city, the slow grinding discomfort of blockade. The food rations were down to a cup of grain and one of oil a day, and water was rationed likewise. Thin sulphurous gruel was the only meal available for most. But at least there had been no further talk of surrender.

The shock of Castus's own collapse had been almost entirely eclipsed by another tragedy. Bishop Iacob, spiritual defender of Nisibis, had finally died on that very same day, shortly after the last Persian attack on the breaches had been thrown back. He had expired, Castus heard, with a loud cry to God, still praying before the altar of his church. The old man had consumed nothing but sips of water for over a month. Ephraim had conducted the funeral service, and the death had been greeted with passionate mourning by Christians and non-Christians alike. But Iacob had given his life for the city, as everyone agreed. To fail now, to even *think* of surrendering now, would be an insult to his memory.

'I see you've been consuming meat,' Nicagoras said gravely, lowering his eyebrows as he glanced at the remains of Castus's evening meal.

'Only a little, and don't ask me what it is. Horse, probably.'

'You should not. Red meat in particular heats the blood, you know!'

Castus just shrugged, then sat patiently while the doctor checked his pulse, his tongue and the colour of his eyes, before leaving him in peace.

Alone again, Castus picked up the sword that lay on the low table beside him, and swung it for a while to loosen his muscles. He had spent far too much time in idleness while he was recovering; now he felt rested, and he needed exercise. But soon his eye was drawn to the plain south of the city. The air was filled with fluttering, swooping shapes. Vultures, Castus realised, feasting on the Persian slain. He shuddered. The enemy did not bury or burn their dead, but exposed them in great enclosures. Soon, he thought, the enclosures of the dead would be larger than the encampments of the living...

'Father,' Sabinus said, approaching from the stairs. 'You look well!'

'Better each day,' Castus told him, setting down the sword. 'I almost feel like riding a horse again. If there are any which haven't been eaten.'

'I have Robbers,' Sabinus said, setting the rolled gameboard and the bag of playing pieces on the table, 'and some quite good wine. Which is in short supply!'

They sat down together to play, and the slaves brought lamps as the evening darkened into night. Castus was getting better at latrunculi too – although he wondered if Sabinus was letting him win.

'You know,' he said, sipping wine. 'After the battle, when I... when I fell. I was sure that I'd lost you. The same as when you went out to attack the Persian tower.'

'That was what caused the paroxysm?' Sabinus asked, frowning.

'Maybe. That and the curator's wife, perhaps. The death of her boy. If you'd been killed...'

'Don't speak of it, Father,' Sabinus said hurriedly, and moved one of his pieces into a winning entrapment.

The sound of trumpets woke him, and he snapped into sudden awareness, reaching for his sword. As the darkness pulsed around him, he thought he had dreamed the sound, or some last ebb of fever had summoned it. Then he heard the distant blast again, and the carrying cries of men.

Up from the bed, head reeling, he struggled into his tunic. Lamplight flared in the vestibule, and Vallio stumbled in, rubbing his eyes.

'What is it?' Castus demanded. 'What's happening?'

Vallio did not know, but by the time Castus was dressed and pacing out into the courtyard the messenger had arrived.

'The Persians,' the man said, gulping breath. 'The Persians have broken in through the eastern postern! They're in the streets!'

'You're sure?' Castus said, as Vallio strapped the linen arming vest over his tunic.

The messenger was nodding. 'I saw them myself, dominus – they've seized the wall ramparts.'

Castus cursed, still struggling to digest the news. The white linen vest was almost glowing in the darkness, an easy target for an arrow, and he pulled a darker tunic on over the top, then tightened his belts and flung the sword baldric across his shoulder.

'Where are you going?' Sabinus cried, emerging from the lower chamber. He too was dressed for battle.

'You expect me to sit here and wait for the Persians?' Castus growled. 'I'm going down there – *now*!'

He could feel the blood thundering in his body as he swung himself up into the saddle in the Strategion courtyard. Sabinus mounted a horse beside him, and four men of the guard followed them as they rode down the slope towards the agora.

Now the sounds of fighting were clear and distinct on the night air, carrying across the city from the eastern walls. Kicking his horse into a canter, Castus passed the flank of the theatre, the arches rising ghostly pale in the moonlight, and plunged into the grid of narrower streets that led eastwards through the Severan district of the city. Soldiers were rushing in the same direction, and parties of militia too; organisation had improved greatly in the many days since the last scare. As Castus rode, his mind awoke to the danger: how could the city have been taken by surprise, after holding out so long? How had the Persians got inside the defences? Fury rose within him, but his body was freighted with dread.

By the time they got within three blocks of the eastern wall, they could see the shapes of men fighting on the rampart. 'Centurion, what's happening?' Castus yelled, dragging back on the reins as he caught sight of a crested helmet in the darkness.

He could hear ballistae snapping, shooting along the walkways from the shelter of the interval towers.

'Dominus,' the centurion called back, saluting quickly, his face lost in the shadows beneath his helmet rim. 'Some bastard opened the postern and let them in! But we've driven them back and secured the gate – a band of them got up onto the ramparts, and our boys from the First Parthica are clearing them off. There's another lot in the courtyard at the end of this alley, but we've got them surrounded, and there are archers on the roofs.'

Castus glanced up, and saw figures running across the narrow plank bridge that spanned the street. He slid down from the saddle. 'Come on,' he told Sabinus.

There was a flight of steps at the corner of the street, leading to the flat roof of the building. Sabinus got there first, and held his father back. 'I'll lead the way,' he said firmly, then drew his sword and ran up the steps.

Castus followed, his limbs already aching. As he reached the roof he paused and glanced towards the wall; the rampart was clear of Persians now. All across the rooftops there were people, civilians roused from sleep, and militiamen and archers rushing towards the courtyard where the remaining enemy soldiers were trapped. Sabinus had crossed the plank bridge; Castus went after him, trying not to glance down at the dark gulf of the street below.

The buildings on the far side were packed close together, their flat roofs forming an undulating terrain, separated only by low walls. With Sabinus going ahead of him Castus picked his way carefully, clambering from one roof to the next. As he reached the brink of a higher building he stopped and peered over the edge.

Below him was a small courtyard, an irregular dusty space, but it was packed with men. Castus saw conical Persian helmets, the glint of spears in the moonlight. And on the roofs all around were archers, Lycianus's men and the Armenians, pelting shafts down into the confined mass of enemy soldiers. Militiamen had joined them, flinging spears and stones; the Persians were screaming as they died.

'Hold back!' Castus yelled. 'Who speaks Persian? Call on them to surrender!'

But there was no stopping the slaughter. For another few heartbeats the archers continued to shoot, then a wild roar rose from the trapped men in the courtyard, and a knot of them surged towards the mouth of an alley. Castus stepped up onto the wall and saw their charge pass directly below him; then the alley was sealed by a wall of Roman shields. A thunder of voices, echoing between high walls, a clash of iron on wood, iron biting flesh, stamping feet in the darkness. Then it was over.

They dropped back down the steps, and moments later Egnatius found them. Sweat was tiding down his face as he tore off his helmet. 'All secure, dominus!' he reported.

'How did they get in?' Castus demanded. His body was still a riot of aggressive energy. 'Who opened the postern?'

He found out soon enough. One of the soldiers from the gate garrison had survived the attack, a Syrian trooper of the Ala Nova Diocletiana; he was brought before Castus under guard, trembling in the flare of the torches.

'It was one of the civilian magistrates, dominus,' the soldier said. 'He told us we were to open the gate – a messenger was coming in, from the relief force, he said…'

'Relief force?' Castus growled to himself. He shook his head. 'Since when do you take orders from civilians, soldier?'

'He said the order came from you, dominus!'

'Who was it?'

'Not him,' the soldier replied. Castus turned, and saw that Dorotheus had joined them, still dressed in his light sleeping tunic. 'The other one – the curator.'

Clenching his fists, Castus let the tide of anger flow through him. He inhaled slowly, trying to remain calm. 'Half-rations,' he ordered, pointing at the soldier, 'and put him on burial duty. He's lucky he's not dead himself.'

Egnatius muttered something under his breath. Clearly many of the other troops had wanted a harsher punishment. They had lost many comrades in the attack.

'And bring me Vorodes,' Castus told them. 'Alive or dead, I don't care.'

Light was in the sky by the time he arrived at the curator's house. He had already been told the news, and his anger had faded to a dull weary nausea, a sense of pained fatigue. As he climbed the steps from the deep well of the central courtyard, a foul smell met him. The men were gathered in the upper chamber, Dorotheus and Egnatius among them.

'Sorry about the stink, dominus,' a soldier said. 'He emptied his bowels as he died. Must've been the poison he took.'

Septimius Vorodes, Curator Civitatis of Nisibis, lay sprawled on the floor of the chamber, spattered with filth and blood. He had died neither cleanly nor painlessly. His face was still contorted, but it looked more like an expression of shame than of agony. Castus guessed that the curator had taken the poison shortly after returning home, only an hour or so after he had ordered the guards to open the postern.

'His wife's upstairs, on the terrace,' the soldier said. 'Shall we bring her down here?'

'No,' Castus said quickly. Sohaemia would already have witnessed her husband's ignoble end. No need for her to see it again. Pushing past the soldiers on the landing at the head of the steps, Castus climbed towards the top floor. He was remembering the first time he had come this way, during his first visit to Nisibis. The elegant dinner party that Vorodes had hosted in his rooftop chamber. Entering that same room from the steps, Castus saw no signs of elegance. The mosaic floor was dusty from the tread of boots, weapons were piled on the couches, and empty jugs and amphorae stood around the walls. He walked out through the wide arch onto the roof terrace, into the glow of morning.

'You've seen him?' Sohaemia asked. She was dressed for mourning, in a gown and shawl of coarse black cloth, and stood with her back to Castus, looking out over the city.

'Yes. Why did he do it?'

'Why did he betray the city to the Persians, you mean? Despair. I've felt little but despair myself, since Barnaeus died.'

'I'm sorry,' Castus said. It was all he could find to tell her.

'My husband believed that if he let the Persians into the city they might agree to spare at least some of our people. Nisibis might not be destroyed utterly.'

'Nisibis isn't going to be destroyed,' Castus said quietly, the words rough in his throat.

'Oh yes, you're so sure of that,' Sohaemia replied, turning to face him. She dropped her shawl, and he saw that she had cut off her long dark hair. Only a short ragged crop remained. Many women in the city had done it, he had heard; the hair was used to repair the torsion bundles of the catapults. But in Sohaemia's case it appeared almost vengeful. Her face was drawn, harrowed by grief.

'I would like to speak with you, general,' she said with great dignity. 'Alone, if I could.'

Castus gestured, and Egnatius and the others who had followed him up the stairs drew back into the dining pavilion.

'I'm sorry too,' Sohaemia said quietly, taking a few steps closer. 'I should not have blamed you for my son's death. He died, as I hear, most nobly. His father should have been proud, but instead...' She shuddered quickly, closing her eyes. 'Can you comprehend a loss like that?'

'I've often tried to,' Castus told her. The dawn breeze was warm, but he felt coldness running through him.

'And now you promise that the city will not fall,' she said in a mild and almost lilting voice. 'But I've heard your promises before. Why should I believe you now?'

'What choice do you have?'

'Oh, I have a choice, general,' Sohaemia said. She took another step towards him, then stretched out an arm and brushed his cheek. Her fingers rasped through the grey stubble of his beard. 'And I should have chosen a long time ago.'

Leaning closer, she turned her head, as if to kiss him. Castus stood motionless, wanting to flinch away from her but unable to move. For a heartbeat he felt a strange warm compassion rising through his body.

Then Sohaemia drove the knife into him.

He noticed the sudden movement of her arm, and twisted by instinct before he felt the hard jab of the steel against his kidney. With a startled yell he shoved her away, staggering backwards. Glancing down in shock, half expecting to see his own blood pouring from the wound, he saw instead the ripped tunic, the gashed linen and the tufted padding beneath. His arming vest had turned the blade before it punctured his flesh.

Egnatius was in the doorway of the dining chamber, his sword drawn. Letting the knife fall from her hand, Sohaemia took three long paces backwards. She laughed, cold and mirthless in her despair. 'Too late,' she said. 'I was too late...'

Then she turned, took another step up onto the low wall surrounding the terrace, and let herself fall forwards.

'Stop her!' Castus managed to yell as he lurched into motion. Egnatius and the others in the doorway had not moved. A brief silent flicker of black cloth in the breeze, and Sohaemia was gone.

At the brink of the roof Castus stared downwards, and saw her body twisted on the cobbles of the stepped alleyway, fifty feet below. A scrap of blackness in the shadow. Cold remorse poured through him, delayed shock, and a sickening sense of guilt. An old woman appeared at the doorway of the house opposite, and shrieked.

Descending the stairs from the roof, Castus found the men in the chamber where Vorodes lay talking together excitedly. They all turned to him, wide-eyed, as he reached the lowest step. Nicagoras had joined them, and Sabinus. Castus peered back at them, still shaken. His gut was beginning to ache from the blow of Sohaemia's knife, and he probed with his fingers at the gash in his linen vest. He wanted very much to sit down.

'Tell him,' Sabinus said to the doctor. 'Tell him what you've learned!'

'Excellency, I've examined the Persian prisoners we took during the night attack,' Nicagoras said, his words stumbling. 'They're weak – very weak, and several of them are fevered... They all have welts covering their bodies...' He flicked his fingers up and down his arms, across his chest and neck. 'Insect bites, very inflamed. The prisoners report, excellency, that the Persian encampments are plagued by mosquitoes, vast clouds of them. They've bred from the pools of standing water left after the hydraulic operations, and the multitude of bodies left exposed – now they're tormenting man and beast. And fever is spreading through the enemy army. Shapur has lost thousands of men already, with more dying every day!'

Castus was struggling to digest what the doctor was saying. But he could see the men in the room breaking into grins.

'You know what this means, Father?' Sabinus cried. He turned to Dorotheus.

The magistrate was standing in the middle of the room, clasping his Christian amulet. With an exhilarated cry he rolled his eyes to the ceiling. '*Even the smallest creatures of the air will plague them and strike at them...*' he said, his voice quavering with joy. 'The bishop's curse upon the Persians – it's come true! We're saved! Nisibis is saved... Praise to Almighty God!'

*

Seven days later, in the full heat of noon, Castus stood on the steps above the Singara Gate with his officers around him. Along the rampart walks there were soldiers and militiamen, all of them gazing out across the shimmering plain that surrounded the city. The high sun blazed down on them, and in the distance the colours of land and sky flowed like running water.

'Over two months,' Egnatius said in a parched voice. 'And now it ends.'

Castus said nothing. He narrowed his eyes into the glare. Silence from the ramparts. Only the faint rustle of the draco banner stirring in the hot breeze.

Through the rolling clouds of dust, the Persian army was mustering. The glimmer of armour and the bright colours of the flags bled together in the haze. Distant sounds of trumpets and drums, the far cries of men, but all of it fading steadily. Castus was looking for the royal standard, hoping for a last glimpse of that famed banner. But there was no sign of it. Perhaps, he thought, Shapur had already departed.

And, after sixty-three days of siege, the Persian army was departing with him.

Blackness was spreading like a smudge along the line of the enemy entrenchments. As the men on the wall watched, it formed into rising smoke trails. Then the flames appeared, bright explosions in the dusty fog. The enemy were burning their palisades, Castus realised, and the mass of huts and shelters that had formed their camp.

The fires rose, sheets of flame dancing in the heat, all around the city. Beyond the flames, beyond the choking dust and the smoke, the vast fever-stricken army of Iran-Shahr was melting away into the emptiness to the south.

'You did it,' a dry voice said.

Castus turned, and saw Dorotheus standing on the steps. Ephraim was beside him, the young priest now dressed in the filthy cloak and tunic of his dead bishop, Iacob.

'You held the city,' said Dorotheus. 'I did not think it possible... but I was wrong.'

'Save your words, magistrate,' Castus said. 'You'll need to address your people soon. Those that survive. Set them to work, or we'll be facing famine and fever too, just like the Persians.'

The magistrate nodded. For a while longer the men on the wall stood in silence, watching the Persian withdrawal and the ripple of flames from the burning siege lines.

'Excellency,' Egnatius said. Castus glanced back, and saw the tribune pointing to the rampart walkway below them. Soldiers were gathering, men of all the different units, and city people too. All of them staring up at him. Several raised their arms in salute.

Standing at the head of the steps, the sun glaring all around him, Castus lifted a hand in acknowledgement.

'Victor!' a soldier yelled.

And at once the cry was taken up by all the men around him. Their shouts rose from the walls, spreading along the ramparts in both directions in a wave of noise.

'*Victor! Victor! Defender of Nisibis!*'

CHAPTER XXIX

Ashes and bones. Charred timber, flies and blackened dust.
Little else remained of the Persian encampments. Ten
days after Shapur's retreat from Nisibis, and the air around the
city still stank of death. The plague of mosquitoes seemed to
have vanished with the Persian departure, but the atmosphere
of pestilence remained. Riding out from the Edessa Gate,
Castus felt his horse shudder and flinch beneath him. He
shortened the reins, and pulled a scarf over his mouth as he
passed through the wasteland of destruction. Five hundred
paces, and he moved beyond the last of the ruined tower-
tombs and saw open country ahead of him. The road stretched
away to the shimmering horizon. And from the point where
road and horizon met rolled the vast low dust cloud of an
advancing army.

For days all Castus had wanted to do was ride west, away from
the parched and battered city and the troops he commanded,
back towards Antioch, towards his wife and daughter and
the peace he had once known. But the west was an uncertain
place to him now; what had happened in Antioch since he had
left, months before? Whenever he looked towards the setting
sun he felt a great yearning in his soul, but a sense of warning
too. So he sent out his messengers, attended to his command,
and waited.

Already word had come back from the outside world. Scouts had returned from the south, reporting that Shapur had withdrawn beyond Singara. But from the north and east had come news of a smaller Persian force, under the command of the king's cousin, Prince Narses, sent to devastate the upper Tigris valley and the Armenian borderland. Amida and Bezabde had held out against him, and now Narses too was pulling back southward along the river. But from the west had come no news at all – until now.

Waiting beside the road with his bodyguard and standard-bearer, Castus watched the vanguard of the marching column appear out of the billowing dust. He picked out their banners: Legion I Illyricorum, XVI Flavia Firma, III Gallica and Cyrenaica, IV Scythica and Martia... these were the men that had been based at Soura on the Euphrates, in readiness for Constantine's grand offensive against Persia. A campaign that would never happen. Galloping out ahead of them, with his mounted guard behind him, came their commander.

'You took your time,' Castus said with a crooked smile as the man made his salute. Flavius Quintianus was one of Castus's own appointees, a hard-faced veteran soldier with a long career in command.

'Apologies, excellency,' the officer said stiffly. 'We got the order to march north from Soura nearly three weeks ago. I was instructed to wait at Edessa for Valerius Mucatra to arrive with the field army from Antioch, but when I heard that the enemy had lifted the siege, I reckoned you'd need supplies and reinforcement...'

'You did well,' Castus said, and leaned from the saddle to clap him on the shoulder. A billow of dust rose. Clearly Quintianus had made his own assessment of the situation, and decided to ignore his orders. No doubt, Castus thought, those orders had come direct from the palace at Antioch.

He glanced at the columns of carts, piled with sacks of grain and amphorae of wine and oil, that were rolling steadily along the road towards him between the lines of marching men. With infantry and cavalry combined, there were nearly ten thousand soldiers in Quintianus's command. Yes, he had done very well. But Castus could tell that the officer had more to tell him yet, and wanted to wait until they were in a private place to do so.

'Camp your force to the north of the city,' he said, 'upstream and well away from the old Persian lines. When you're ready, find me in the city Strategion. You can make your full report then.'

The slaves were lighting the lamps by the time Quintianus was announced. Castus ordered the chamber cleared and the doors sealed. Only then did he listen to the news from the west. As Quintianus spoke, Castus's jaw tightened and he drew in a long slow breath.

'So Constantius is Augustus now?' he asked. 'It's confirmed?'

'Not exactly,' the officer replied. 'The young emperor's still on the Danube somewhere, either fighting the Sarmatians or meeting his brothers. But since Ablabius was removed and Dracilianus took control, that's been the official word from Antioch.'

Castus had already noticed that the legion detachments carried the portrait of young Constantius on their standards, where the image of his father had once been displayed. But there was more to come.

'What else?'

Quintianus shifted nervously. 'Excellency,' he said. 'We also hear that Valerius Mucatra's been promoted to Magister Equitum in your place... There's a story that you've been accused of treason against the new emperor. Dracilianus has ordered that you should be seized and brought to Antioch under guard...'

'What?' Castus said, stunned.

Quintianus could not meet his eye. 'And he's holding your wife and family under arrest in the city too. If you don't surrender, they'll answer for your actions.'

Turning his back on the officer, Castus stared blindly at the far wall. His heart was in his throat, thunder in his head. For a few long heartbeats he fought to control himself. All the apprehension he had felt over the last ten days had gained sudden and terrible focus. He felt his face reddening with furious despair.

'The troops believe this?' he gasped. 'That I'm...?'

'No, no they don't,' Quintianus said quickly. 'That is... they don't know what to think. Everything's so confused now. But they can see that you've held the city here – you turned back the Persians...'

The idea that the soldiers might doubt him, might think him disloyal, was far more painful to Castus than the news of Dracilianus's condemnation. And what if this new force from the west carried a contagion, a seed of mistrust that could spread through his entire command? Perhaps even Quintianus... No, he could not allow himself to believe that. Marcellina and Aeliana were captives, their lives held as forfeit for his own. It was intolerable, after all that he had done.

With Quintianus dismissed, Castus summoned Sabinus and Diogenes to join him. Once they arrived he again ordered the doors closed behind them. He could allow nothing of what was spoken to escape the room – not yet.

'But this is madness!' Sabinus declared when Castus had told them what he had learned. 'Father,' he said, leaping to his feet, 'let me ride for Antioch at once – or to find the emperor! I can explain everything to him...'

'No,' Castus said firmly. 'If you go back west you'll be seized too, and Dracilianus'll have another hostage. We don't know what the new emperor believes, or even where he is.'

'Then what?' Sabinus exclaimed. 'We just sit here and wait for Mucatra to arrive with the field army? He has eighteen thousand men with him!'

Diogenes was plucking idly at the frayed hem of his cloak. He peered into the dark corner of the room for a moment before speaking. 'It seems to me, brother,' he said, 'that a certain freedom of movement remains to us. You have an army – if a small one – and the opportunity to use it. Not against Mucatra, that would be madness... But there is still another enemy in the field, is there not?'

Castus had already been turning over the options in his mind while he waited for the other men to arrive. The messengers from the north had told him that Prince Narses was retreating down the eastern bank of the Tigris. His army was small, perhaps smaller than the combined force that Castus now commanded. Trap it, defeat it, and Castus might hope to erase the ignominious defeat of Romulianus at Zagurae, and destroy any chance of a second Persian invasion that year. And in the process, he would demonstrate his loyalty to the emperor. Could Mucatra and Dracilianus argue with that?

But even as he considered the idea, a darker thought rose to shadow his mind.

If he himself were killed in the fighting, Marcellina and his daughter, and all of his household, his friends and followers, would be saved.

Victory, then; or a glorious death. Those were his only options.

'We're soldiers,' he said quietly. 'We do what we must. Summon the officers at dawn.'

The road from Nisibis to the Tigris River ran for sixty miles, dead straight across the flat plains of eastern Mesopotamia. It would be a hard march. Only a day before the kalends of September, and in the broiling late summer heat the ground was parched and dry, the air simmering. Every breath burned. There were settlements along the road, at Sisara and Sapha, but Castus knew the wells there would be almost dry as well. He would march his men in the cool of morning and evening, and by night if necessary. But still it would not be easy, and he needed to push them hard if he wanted to reach the river in time to intercept Narses and bring him to battle.

But as the army mustered on the level ground, a mile east of the city just outside the old Persian siege lines, Castus felt a firm sense of purpose firing his blood. Alongside the troops Quintianus had brought with him, Castus had drawn another two thousand picked men from the surviving defenders of Nisibis, placing them under the command of Egnatius and Lycianus, Gunthia and Barbatio. They made a fine sight as they assembled on the plain; there were even a dozen ballistae taken from the city walls, mounted on light carts. But Castus knew that he was short of cavalry – barely a thousand horsemen accompanied his army.

He was with the vanguard troops, discussing the order of march with Barbatio, when a rider galloped up to him. The man flung a salute as he dragged his horse to a halt. 'Excellency!' he cried. 'Message from Quintianus – scouts have sighted a force to the west of us!'

Castus felt his mouth dry at once. He peered back along the stationary column of men, into the bright haze on the western horizon. Then, with a signal to Sabinus and his staff, he pulled his horse around and kicked it into a gallop.

'Cavalry,' Lycianus said, once Castus had located him and Quintianus. The scout commander was shading his eyes, squinting into the glare. 'See the high dust cloud there, fading to the south? Quite a few thousand of them, and they're coming this way.'

Sitting heavily in the saddle, Castus stared until he could make out the cloud. Surely Mucatra could not have caught up with them so fast? But if this was his cavalry vanguard, then the rest of his force could not be far behind. With a sharp ache, Castus sensed his last desperate hope slipping from his grasp.

'Strange sort of formation,' Quintianus said, his teeth bared as he watched the horizon. 'Don't seem to be in column at all. Could they be Persians, d'you think?'

'Let's find out,' Castus growled. He signalled for Sabinus and his mounted bodyguard to form up around him, then nudged his horse forward again.

Steadily the dust on the horizon thickened, and Castus began to make out the leading riders. They were advancing across the plain in a ragged mass rather than a regular military array. He rode further, sweat slicking his brow.

'Do you see what I see?' Sabinus said, leaning forward in his saddle.

Castus nodded, and began to smile.

Now he could hear the high yells of the advancing horde, the wild barbarian cries. There were camels with them, forging through the dust with one and sometimes two men mounted high upon them. In the wavering heat the figures of animals and riders appeared to warp and stretch.

Reining to a halt, Castus sat and waited for them to approach. The advancing horde had split into two long curving horns, ponies and fast camels racing forward on either flank, surrounding him and his escort. Dust rose around them in a swirling ochre fog.

And out of the fog, mounted on a tall white camel, came Hind.

The Queen of the Tanukhids wore a white linen scarf wrapped around her head, but drew it from her face as she approached. She had a padded linen vest over her tunic, a bow and a lance on her saddle, and carried a cavalry mace in one hand like a sceptre. Heavy gold medallions hung at her neck. To either side of her, mounted warriors sat with lances ready.

Castus's horse backed and shied at the sight and scent of the camels. Shortening his reins, Castus brought the animal under control.

'I expected you months ago, phylarch,' he called.

Hind threw her head back contemptuously. 'Three moons,' she cried, her harsh voice carrying through the dust, 'and we have no word from Antioch, none from your emperor. Where are the insignia of command you promised?'

'Don't ask me,' Castus told her, then gestured towards the walls of Nisibis. 'I've been here. Holding off the King of Persia!'

'This we know,' the queen replied. 'Already my people have fought with the Persian insects, driving them southward as they retreated. But what is our treaty with Rome? Where is your emperor now?'

'That I cannot say,' Castus told her. 'But I have an army, and I intend to march east to the Tigris. Are we allies, or not?'

He knew that Hind and her Saracens must have been waiting for many days to see how the siege of Nisibis developed, before committing themselves. They were scavengers, outriders of war. But as he gazed around at the wild desert horsemen that surrounded him, he remembered what Egnatius had once said. *The finest light cavalry on earth.* Hind must have several thousand of them with her, ragged and ferocious, tireless in the heat. Castus felt a tight itch in his right hand, and rubbed his scalp.

'Allies?' Hind said, staring down from her camel. 'With Rome, no.' Then her face split into a grin, her teeth gleaming very white. 'But with you, Aurelios Kastos – yes. We will go to kill Persians with you!'

And Castus grinned back at her as the Saracens began to whoop and raise their lances to the burning sky.

Now, he thought. *Now we are ready for battle.*

*

They were at Sapha, two days east, when the scouts brought word of another force approaching them from the wilderness. The flyblown little settlement on the road had been sacked by Shapur's men months before, the garrison of the fort butchered and the well fouled with the dead. Castus's men were camped a short way further on, in a grove of pistachio trees and some scrubby fields where they could dig for water. All of them were weary, and as the evening darkened quickly into night many had already flung themselves down to sleep.

The scouts found Castus in his command tent and made their report. 'They're still a day or two south, dominus,' the exarch leading them told him, 'but moving fast. Persians, we're sure of it. A powerful force, mostly cavalry. They had light horsemen ahead of them, and we lost a couple of our boys before we got clear.'

'Surely there aren't any Persians still on this side of the Tigris?' Egnatius said.

'Seems we were wrong about that,' Castus said quietly. He stared at the haze of tiny insects swarming around the lamp flames. His army was a day's march west of the river; the scouts had confirmed that the bridge was still standing, but they would need to move fast if they were to reach it before Narses. Frowning heavily, he contemplated the news. Could Shapur have left a force at Singara? How would such a force have known that he was marching eastwards?

Only an hour later, he had his confirmation of the initial report. A group of Hind's Saracens, riding far to the south on a foraging mission, had sighted the advancing Persians before nightfall. They had brought a prisoner back with them too, a Syrian from Singara, who had been forced to lead the enemy across the desert.

'They have six thousand horse, dominus,' the man said,

kneeling on the matting before Castus's stool. 'Heavy cataphracts and archers. Their plan is to cut off the road behind you, then swing east and pin you against the river.'

Castus sat with clenched teeth, his fists braced on his knees. He had guessed as much. The cavalry advancing from the south would trap him, and then Narses' army would move down from the north along the far bank of the river and crush him. A classic pincer. But how was it possible? In order to coordinate their advance, the two Persian armies must have known of his plans days ago, before he had even left Nisibis.

'We have to retreat,' Egnatius declared. 'Otherwise they'll surround us on all sides. Fall back to Nisibis, fast as the men can march...'

'It's too far,' Castus said. 'If their cavalry catch us in open country, strung out along the road, they'll cut us to bits.'

How had they known? The thought pressed at his skull.

Lycianus appeared to have read his mind. 'The Saracens,' he said quietly. 'Hind's people.' He shot a quick glance towards the two desert tribesmen lingering at the tent door. Neither could understand Latin. 'They must have sent word to the Persians. She's changed sides, dominus, it's clear as day...'

'I don't believe that,' Castus said, low in his throat. Even as he spoke, he was not sure. But if the Tanukhids had gone over to the enemy, all was lost already.

'She's *betrayed us*!' Lycianus said with angry emphasis.

'No.' Castus stood up. 'It doesn't matter how the enemy discovered our plans. We have to find a way out.'

He was thinking fast, struggling to formulate a strategy. All that divided the converging Persian armies was the river, and the single bridge. Reach that, and they had a chance to outmanoeuvre their enemy.

'We can't retreat,' he said, 'so we advance, and quickly. Rouse the troops – all of them. We march by night. I want to be on the banks of the Tigris by sun-up.'

The messengers were already running into the darkness as Castus heard the Syrian prisoner speak once more. He turned back to the man.

'Say that again?'

'Their leader, dominus,' the man said. 'The Persian leader, the *spahbed* – he has vowed to kill you, I heard him say it. His name is Zamasp.'

CHAPTER XXX

The waters of the Tigris were a pale and tranquil blue in the early light. To the east rose the stark brown mountains of Corduene; hills closed the northern horizon, while the open plain stretched away into the haze to the west. On a scrub-covered hillock above the river, Castus stood and watched his army filing slowly across the high-arched stone bridge. Thousands of men were bunched together on the western bank, waiting to cross. On the eastern side, below his vantage point, the units were forming quickly and marching away southward in a ragged column, already a mile or more long. Castus stared at them, fuming with anxious frustration at the delay. If the Persians attacked now, from either direction, the result would be catastrophic.

'Such a sight,' Diogenes said, 'makes one realise just how numerous an army of this size can be. I'm reminded of Herodotus's account of the ancient Kings of Persia calculating the numbers of their troops. They herded them in sections into a certain sized pen, and then counted how many times the pen had been filled!'

'Fascinating,' Castus muttered grimly. At least, he thought, his secretary had consented to resume an approximation of civilised costume. Then he stared back at the crossing once more. Men and horses funnelled across the narrow bridge in a ceaseless line, goaded by the yells of their officers. In the further distance, on both banks of the river, Hind's Saracen horsemen and camel riders swarmed.

Castus glanced to the north, and then towards the western horizon. No clouds of dust betrayed the approach of a hostile force. But still he could not feel secure until his entire army was across the river and marching south, out from between the closing jaws of the enemy entrapment.

'You won't make them move any faster by glaring at them, brother,' Diogenes said quietly.

Castus tightened his lips. Diogenes was right, of course. With a shrug of annoyance he turned his back on the bridge and paced across the scrubby hillock to the awning that sheltered his staff and senior officers. Riders had just come in, leaping from their horses and making their reports.

'Dominus,' Egnatius said, saluting as Castus stepped into the shade of the awning. 'The scouts have sighted Narses, but his main force is still half a day to the north of us. It looks like Zamasp's cavalry have yet to pass Sapha.'

'Good,' Castus said. He had ordered the men in the ranks to rest and eat at first light, before they commenced the river crossing. All being well, they could get over the bridge and march another few miles yet before the first Persian skirmishers caught up with them. He breathed deeply, willing the anxiety that tensed his body to lift.

Hind had arrived shortly before him, her attendants setting out a stool for her to sit on, and her bodyguards gathering close around her. The Roman officers kept a wary distance from the group; Castus noticed Lycianus in particular barely concealing his unease.

'Brothers,' Castus announced. 'Allies,' with a nod towards Hind and her party. 'With the blessing of the gods, we've evaded the Persian trap. All of you have done well, but we can't rest yet. Now we set the terms of engagement.'

He glanced around at the faces of the men. They were tired, but resolute. Every one of them waiting on his orders. Hind regarded him with lowered eyelids, smiling slightly.

'It's my intention,' Castus went on, 'to march south down the Tigris and find a position where we can turn and confront the Persians. Zamasp will cross the river behind us and link up with Narses – we'll have to fight their combined force, so we'll be outnumbered. But there's nothing new about that!'

A stir of wry laughter. Many of those present had served on the walls of Nisibis. Castus picked up a cup of wine and sipped.

'I aim to find a position,' he went on, 'where the enemy won't be able to outflank us, and there won't be any hostile force behind us either. I want scouts out ahead of our column for ten miles, surveying the terrain and reporting back here.'

Again he paused. His throat was dry; wine would help with that, but the heat was beginning to make his head ache. He had spoken in Latin, and Diogenes was already repeating his words in Greek, for Hind's benefit. But she broke in before the secretary had finished.

'My people know of a place,' she told Castus.

The officers turned to her, frowning.

'South of here, one hundred stades, maybe more,' she went on. 'Hills come down to the river. And there is a stream, a wadi, dry at this season. It cuts through the hills to meet the river. We call it Nahr As'ara. High land behind, a village, and good water from the ground.'

Castus nodded slowly. It sounded right. He tried not to catch Lycianus's eye. 'Then we march for this... *Narasara*,' he said. 'If it's as good as you say, we wait for the Persians to follow us there. And may the gods watch over us!'

The position was indeed as good as Hind had claimed. As good, Castus thought, as he might have hoped to find. From the north, following the road across rolling open country, the watercourse appeared only as an undulation in the landscape, with rising ground behind it. But from the far side, the situation looked quite different.

Riding along the crest of the stony ridge to the west of his lines, Castus looked down at the twisting course of the dry stream. It was scored deep, with steep banks of crumbling earth to either side. In places along the sinuous gulley there were pools of grey-green water still remaining, screened by vegetation, but most of the stream bed was dry and stony, with patches of thorny scrub bushes in the hollows.

Behind him, on the south side of the ridge, a village straggled down through parched green fields and orchards to meet the road. The Corduenians who had lived there had fled at the army's first approach the evening before, but the two wells provided good water for the troops, and Castus had established his command post in the largest of the mud-brick houses. The rest of the country was open, and arid under the September sun. Thin grass covered the slopes, dried to the colour of bleached bone. Deserted by its population, the land appeared to be sleeping. Soon enough, Castus thought, it would be awakened by the thunder of war.

He had drawn up his infantry a bowshot south of the watercourse. Eight thousand legionary troops formed two close-order lines, each four ranks deep. Quintianus held the command there, in the centre. Behind them, fifty paces back, Barbatio commanded a thousand-man reserve, to plug any gaps in the line. To the left, on the lower slopes of the ridge, the understrength detachments of the Parthica legions were posted to guard the western approaches. The Tigris was two miles away, but the ground descended in that direction into steep ravines and broken country, impassable to all but light troops. To the right, Egnatius had the entire regular cavalry force assembled in one body on the eastern flank. Lycianus had his light horsemen stationed in groups to either side, while Hind's Saracens occupied the high ground beyond.

Gazing down at the assembled army, Castus felt a warm swell of pride rising through him. But the flutter of anxiety remained, the occasional stabs of fear. His plan of battle was simple enough, but there were always things that could go wrong. 'Do not advance beyond the watercourse,' he had told his commander. 'That's our line of defence – hold it but don't cross it.'

And now, as he raised his eyes to the north, he could survey the gathering horde of the Persian army on the opposite slopes. All day they had been assembling, building their camp on a plateau a mile distant. Now, in the late afternoon sun, their squadrons darkened the land as far as the horizon. The familiar noise of horns and drums stirred the air.

'You think they'll attack today?' Sabinus asked, reining his horse to a halt beside Castus.

'Not today,' Castus said. 'They can see we're not going anywhere, and they'll want to rest their men and horses. But we'll hold our positions until sundown.'

Surely by now every man in the ranks must know what they needed to do. Castus had ordered them to find the range with bows and darts, javelins and slingshot. But every time he closed his eyes he saw the ranks crushed under the Persian onslaught, the line disintegrating under the relentless hail of arrows, men cut down by the charging cataphracts as the choking dust billowed around them. Fantasies of defeat and destruction, over and over again. He suppressed a fierce shudder.

'I'm hungry,' he said to Sabinus, forcing himself to smile. 'Might have time for a quick meal before sundown, eh?'

After dark, he sat on the roof of the little mud-brick house with Sabinus, Diogenes and a couple of staff officers. The rest of his senior commanders were away with their troops in their entrenched camp, and Castus was glad of the relative quiet and easy company. He found he had grown fearful of looking the other men in the eye, unsure of what he might find there.

'*The night before the battle...*' Sabinus said, rather ponderously, as he refilled the cups with thin vinegar wine. 'I feel I should... write a poem, or something.'

Castus noticed the nervous catch in his voice. His son had fought well at Nisibis, but he had never experienced a field battle, never witnessed the powerful mounted charge of the Persian cataphracts.

'The less you feel, the better,' he said. 'Try not to think too much either.'

Sabinus peered at him in the darkness. 'I'll try.'

But emptying the mind was far easier said than done. Once, in his younger years, Castus might have managed it. Not now. Thoughts pressed in on him, and the night seethed with images. His wife and daughter, held prisoner in Antioch. The dying Constantine, rigid with fear as he felt life and power slipping from his hands. Bishop Iacob laughing like a maniac before his altar. The fury of the battle to come.

From out in the darkness came the wild chanting of the Saracens. Singing their praises to the moon, Castus guessed. He wondered again about their loyalties, remembering Lycianus's warnings. Too late to do anything about that now. *Trust in the gods. Trust in yourself.*

The night passed quietly, and in the coppery light of the rising sun the troops assembled once more in their battle lines. Castus rode down from the village to the scream of the trumpets and the massed yells of the centurions as they marshalled their men. The sky was already a deep pulsating blue, and every man was sweating.

Riding up onto the slope to the left of the infantry line, Castus drew his horse to a halt and swung himself down from the saddle.

He had woken that morning feeling unaccountably refreshed, almost light-headed. Years seemed to have fallen from him in the night, and he felt his mind and body illuminated by a warm certainty. Something told him that it was a dangerous sort of mood, but he enjoyed it nonetheless. As he looked down along the ranks of troops he was filled with a sense of elation. *Victory*, he thought. *Or a glorious death*. Those were his only options. He raised his hands towards the sun and spoke the words of the prayer to Sol Invictus.

The Persians too seemed filled with new purpose. As the sun's rays lit the rolling plain Castus saw their banners arrayed, their troops drawn up in formation. Far off, on a low rise near their camp, he could make out a brighter cluster of flags. Prince Narses, he guessed, surveying the battle lines just as he himself was doing.

Turning his horse, he rode down from the ridge and along the rear of the infantry lines, followed by Sabinus and his staff officers. Lycianus joined them on the way. He paused briefly at intervals, speaking to each of the senior officers. All understood their task; all were prepared for what lay ahead. Arriving at the eastern flank of the array, he saw Hind and a band of her Tanukhid Saracens moving down from their camp. They raised a guttural wailing chant as they stabbed the air with their lances, the repeated phrases bitter and scalding.

'What are they singing?' Castus asked Lycianus.

'The battle hymn of the Tanukh,' the scout commander replied. '*Upon them, upon them, O Mighty Al-Uzza! Let our spears drink at their hearts! Let our swords drink at their hearts...!*'

'Aurelios Kastos!' Hind cried, sitting tall in the saddle of her camel. 'We go to make war upon the Persian insects! May the Mother of Dust overwhelm them, may she obliterate them!'

'*Ha! Ha!*' her warriors screamed.

Castus raised his hand in salute, and the Saracen horde threshed up the dust as they galloped out onto the far right flank.

And now the cries of defiance were rising from the packed ranks of the Roman infantry. A roar of voices, then a resounding clash of spears against shields, shattering the calm of the morning. From the Persian lines on the far slope came an answering cheer, building to a steady chant.

'*MARD-O-MARD! MARD-O-MARD!*'

'Anyone know what that means?' Castus called to the officers around him.

But several of them were pointing, out towards the open ground that lay between the armies, beyond the dry watercourse. Castus stared, and made out a figure on a black horse riding down from the Persian lines. A herald rode behind him, dressed in a bright lilac tunic, and as they approached the man raised himself in the saddle and yelled towards the Roman ranks.

'It's a challenge,' Diogenes said, riding up beside Castus. 'The spahbed Zamasp desires to fight the champion of Rome, man to man.'

Castus smiled tightly, then spurred his horse forward. Sabinus cried out, and seized his bridle. 'Father, don't go! Let me fight him instead – I beg you!'

'Think I'm an idiot, boy?' Castus growled.

He shook Sabinus away from him, then smiled again and advanced. Just for a moment, he admitted to himself, the idea had seemed attractive. What better way to settle this? But Zamasp would have beaten him, he was certain of that. The Persian commander was younger, a better horseman, and probably a better swordsman too. It would, Castus told himself, have been a fine way to die. But not yet.

The infantry opened a lane before him, and he rode through their ranks and out onto the gentle slope that descended to the watercourse. Slowly he walked his horse forward, until he stood opposite the Persian. Zamasp was dressed in glittering gilded scale armour, blue plumes on his shoulders, his harness decked with silk tassels. In one hand he held a lance, in the other a mace.

He had removed his masked helmet, and Castus could clearly make out his hooked black moustaches and his burning black-rimmed eyes.

'Zamasp!' he cried, raising himself in the saddle. 'You want a duel? Then have one! *These*,' he said, gesturing back at the serried ranks of the Roman infantry, 'are my champions! *Every single one of them*. Come across and fight them if you dare!'

A vast cheer went up from the Roman lines. Zamasp's powerful black horse shied and circled. The Persian commander made no reply; he just raised his mace, and brought it swinging down. Then he turned and galloped back to rejoin his army.

Pulling on the reins, Castus began to ride along the front of the infantry lines. The mood of elation that had gripped him earlier had returned; he felt illuminated by it. The air around him glimmered in waves. He remembered the battle at Oxsa, nearly forty years before; he had stood in the ranks as an infantryman then. How young he been, and how very long ago...

'Brothers!' he cried, drawing his horse to a halt before the centre of the line. 'Fellow soldiers! You see before you the bastard sons of Persia. They came to our lands hoping to sack our cities, ravage our fortresses and drag our people into slavery. But they have failed... The cities and fortresses have repelled them; the people have driven them away. Now they have to crawl back to their king and tell him of their failures!'

A slow chant was gathering from the rear ranks.

'But,' Castus went on, his voice rasping as he shouted, 'unless we destroy them today, they'll return. So it's up to us to show them what happens to those who attack us! Give their king a lesson, brothers, that he'll not forget. Remember – you are soldiers of Rome! You are the sons of Mars, and they... *are the sons of slaves*!'

The chant burst into massed cheers, and the thunder of shields. As he rode on before the lines, Castus felt the dust in his eyes, the tears streaking his cheeks as he grinned. Already he felt that he had won.

But the drums were booming from the opposing slopes, and the vast Persian array was beginning to roll forward. Castus snatched a glance back and saw the banners stirring the air, the big wicker shields of the enemy infantry tightening into an advancing wall. Light troops – archers and slingers – were already racing ahead of the vanguard.

'Here we go,' Egnatius said as Castus returned to his officers. He stretched out his hand and Castus clasped it firmly; then Egnatius rode off to the right to rejoin his cavalry.

A glance up towards the sun. Two fingers raised in salute. 'Protecting gods,' Castus whispered. 'Be with us now.'

Flowing forward in a running charge, archers shooting as they came, the Persian skirmishers poured down the far slope and into the dry stream bed. Many of them took shelter there, using the gulley as cover while they pelted the Roman lines. Castus saw the air flickering with arrows and slingshot; a thunderous clatter rolled along the legionary formation as the men in the front four ranks locked their shields into a defensive carapace. Their own light infantry, the *lanciarii*, were dashing forward now, hurling javelins and darts at the Persians packing the stream bed and sheltering in the thorn thickets.

Castus craned his head, trying to make out what was happening ahead of the battle line. More Persians were advancing into the dry gulley of the watercourse, clambering over the bodies of their own slain. But Castus's eye was drawn further northward, towards the glittering array of heavy cavalry, the Aswaran cataphracts, waiting in formation less than half a mile distant. The air was still clear, the sun bright, and he felt his vision becoming unnaturally sharp. The Persian riders were encased in armour, men and horses alike sheathed in mail and scale. Their lances wavered in the heat. They, Castus knew, would drive the main enemy attack.

The Roman artillery crews gathered around their ballistae were watching the Persian cavalry too; there was a steady ratcheting click as they spanned their weapons. But still the cataphracts remained motionless, threatening.

'Excellency!' a rider cried, galloping up from the left. 'Enemy troops are crossing the ravine to the west. They're already climbing the lower slopes of the ridge, and the Parthica detachments aren't holding them!'

Castus spat from the saddle. 'Ride to Tribune Gunthia,' he ordered. The Numerus Gothorum was stationed on the far left of the infantry line. 'Tell him to swing his men and lead them up onto the ridge, rally the Parthica detachments and hold the high ground. He has to throw back that flank attack, at any cost!'

The rider saluted, spun his horse and galloped away.

'Move the Third Cyrenaica up to fill the gap on the left,' Castus said to the nearest staff officer. Then he turned his attention back to the front line.

Sounds of fierce combat from the distant right, moving closer. Tanukhid Saracens on light horses were sweeping down the line of the dried watercourse, hunting the archers out of the thickets and driving the Persian skirmishers before them. Castus saw one Saracen ride clear of the gulley, yelling in triumph as he brandished a severed head in his fist. Then the man went down in a torrent of dust. But the Persian archers were scrambling back out of the stream bed in disarray. As the arrow storm slackened and died, the Roman infantry roared from behind their shields.

A messenger came from Gunthia; the Gothic warriors had thrown back the flank attack to the west, and held the ridge. Castus smiled tightly, jutting his jaw. So far, he thought, they were keeping the tactical advantage. Vallio rode up on a pony and handed him a flask of watered wine. As he raised the flask, Castus heard the wail of the Persian horns.

The solid wall of cataphract cavalry was beginning to move.

They came on at a walk at first, the riders in close formation, knee to knee, rank upon rank; there must be five or six thousand of them, Castus thought. The flower of the Persian army, every one of them mounted on a powerful horse, trained for battle. He realised he was holding his breath, and forced himself to exhale in a shuddering gasp. Beside him, Sabinus was tensed in the saddle, transfixed by the oncoming horsemen.

Only a few hundred paces separated them from the Romans now. The dry watercourse, which had seemed so formidable an obstacle, now looked as feeble as a line scratched in the sand.

Another trumpet blast, and the cataphracts began to trot. They seemed to throw a wave of heat and glare before them, like the blast from the door of an iron furnace. Dust jumped and seethed beneath the massed hooves. Castus could see the infantry lines rippling, every man hunching tighter behind his shield. The centurions screamed at them to hold their positions.

Then, with a low metallic roar, the huge formation of cavalry broke into a canter, and then into a flat charge. The distance closed with frightening speed. A snapping noise from behind the Roman lines as the ballistae launched their first volley; Castus saw the bolts arc across the infantry ranks and plunge down into the charging wave of cataphracts. Horses stumbled and fell, opening gaps in the array, but the lines closed at once. The ballista crews were already spanning their weapons; they would barely have time for a second volley.

Now the first ranks of the horsemen began to slow as they reached the far embankment of the watercourse. Some of the riders tried to jump it, and fell at once. The rest leaned far back in their saddles, hauling on the reins as they guided their horses down the crumbling bank of dry earth and across the gulley. More riders poured over the brink behind them. Dust boiled upwards, rolling in a thick brown pall across the infantry lines.

The first of the cataphracts came scrambling up from the watercourse and onto the level ground, already urging their horses forward again. Their formation was broken, and the momentum of their advance had died with it. Yet still they came, a torrent of men and horses struggling from the fog of dust, weighted down by their armour but already gaining in strength and numbers.

'Now?' Sabinus hissed.

'Wait,' Castus told him, hard and level.

Dust cloaked the gulley, hiding the mass of horsemen on the far bank. Those who had managed to cross were forming up again; a few moments more and they would be ready to throw their assault directly against the Roman lines.

Castus took a deep breath, then turned to the trumpeter beside him. Another heartbeat's delay, then he gave the order, loud and clear.

'Sound the charge – everyone forward... *Now!*'

CHAPTER XXXI

With a roar that drowned out the noise of the horns, the entire Roman line surged into motion. Keeping their shields up, every man holding the close array, they advanced at a crashing jog towards the milling horde of Persian riders along the nearer bank of the watercourse.

Fifty paces, and the front ranks paused to hurl javelins and darts. Successive ranks coming up behind them added their own missiles to the storm; the Persians were falling, horses rearing. Then the ranks closed up, and with another mighty yell the legions charged forward at the run.

Castus felt his horse trembling beneath him. He seized the reins in his fists, his jaw clamped tight. Then he kicked his heels and moved forward into the wake of the advance, into the scorching dust.

The Persian riders had expected to face a stationary wall of men, a wall that would buckle and break before the shock of their charge. Instead, as they scrambled up out of the wadi, weighed down by their armour, their formation in disarray, they found themselves facing a sudden and disciplined counter-charge, a phalanx of shields and levelled spears and screaming men, racing at them out of the dust. Panicked horses shied and reared, the riders trying desperately to control their mounts as the Roman charge bore down on them and the darts and ballista bolts struck at them from above. In a crunch of flesh and metal, the two sides collided.

Streaming forward from the rear ranks came men armed with studded clubs, pickaxes, entrenching mattocks; they hurled themselves into the packed melee of horsemen, smashing riders from their saddles.

Through the haze, Castus could see maddened horses veering and kicking, lances thrashing. The Roman charge had taken them almost as far as the watercourse, driving the Persians before it; the Aswaran were no longer a disciplined formation of advancing cavalry; they were a mass of individual horsemen, struggling in the dust as the infantry lines rammed against them.

But carrying such a weight of metal, even a stationary horseman was dangerous. Castus could see knots of Persian cataphracts pushing back against the Roman line, trying to force their horses into the shield wall, through the thickets of spears. They angled their long lances down over the front ranks, stabbing wildly into the heart of the legionary formation, until they were brought down under a hail of darts and clubbing blows. Seen from the rear, the Roman phalanx looked painfully thin, the ranks pressed tight together behind their shields; a single breach, and the whole formation could rip apart. Castus glanced back and saw Barbatio waiting with his veteran legionary reserves. He hoped they could move quickly enough, if they were needed.

The dust eddied, and Castus made out the mass of Persian riders still on the far side of the watercourse. Some had halted; others were trying to force their way forward into the fight. The ballistae were still shooting, the crews adjusting their aim to drop their bolts onto the cavalry on the far bank. Impossible to see what was happening in the dry gulley, but Castus could guess. A seething horde of men and horses, pressed together in confusion. An inferno of dust and sweat and metal, shot through with arrows and ballista bolts.

Ahead of him the lines bowed suddenly, a solid wedge of

Persian horsemen driving forward out of the chaos. Another surge from the rear, a din of hammering weapons, screaming men, the high whinnying of maddened horses. Castus could almost taste the blood in the dust-thickened air. Then the lines straightened. A steady chant was rising from the legion ranks, a slow tramping shout. Like men on a drill field, they were pushing their way forward again.

'We're beating them!' Sabinus yelled. 'The Persians won't stand!'

'Not yet,' Castus warned him. 'Not yet.'

He twisted in the saddle, glancing around until he spotted one of the few staff officers who remained with him. 'Find Quintianus,' he shouted. 'Tell him to make sure none of his men advance beyond the gulley! Hold them back – and be ready to sound the recall!'

As the officer galloped into the fog, another rider came up from the right, sweating heavily. 'Dominus! Message from Flavius Egnatius – Persian cavalry have broken through on the right flank – we can't hold them!'

'*Gods!*' Castus yelled, hauling at the reins. His horse jinked around to the right, blowing angrily, then Castus kicked it forward into a canter. He could already hear the trumpet calls from Barbatio's reserves, but as he rode along the rear of the infantry line he could see the whole right flank dissolving into a wheeling cavalry melee. Sabinus was galloping up behind him, leading the mounted bodyguard troopers.

No sign of Egnatius. But Castus could see horsemen spilling back out of the fight, Roman cavalry fleeing in disarray, hurling aside spears and shields. With a snarl of rage he swung his horse to block one of the fugitives. The man was carrying the standard of the Third Stablesiani. Seizing the bridle of the man's horse, Castus dragged him closer.

'Where the fuck are you going?' he screamed. 'Get back there and rally your men! *Rally them!*'

The man gibbered something, then managed to turn his horse and ride back the way he had come, brandishing his standard like a lance.

Now Castus could make out the attackers: Lakhmid Saracens, light horsemen armed with bows and javelins. They must have galloped around in a wide arc and hit Egnatius's force on the flank. Riding in circles, they were spearing and shooting down the Roman cavalrymen, whooping as they killed. One of them cantered past Castus, his mouth open in savage laughter. Castus leaned from the saddle and punched the man in the face, knocking him back over his horse's rump. Then he drew his sword as his escort formed up around him.

'Egnatius!' he shouted. He could see the tribune now, fighting at the head of a wedge of his Armigeri troopers. The high bleating of cavalry trumpets sounded through the din. Castus walked his horse forward, feeling the animal shudder and flinch beneath him. Arrows whipped through the air. The men of his escort were formed into a tight wedge of their own, closing on Egnatius's troops, but in the swirling ochre fog it was impossible to judge how many others surrounded them.

A deeper horn blast from the rear; Castus twisted around and made out the standards of the Gemina legions, part of Barbatio's infantry reserve. They must have swung to the right, he realised, to protect the flank from the Lakhmid attack. Advancing steadily, they were herding the Arab horsemen before them.

'Dominus!' Egnatius cried, cantering over to join Castus. 'We're holding them, but I don't know if we can get clear...'

Now the tide of battle had shifted once again; even through the clouds of dust Castus could see it. There were more riders coming in from the right, galloping fast into the pack of Lakhmids. He saw archers on striding camels, shooting from the saddle. Howling half-naked men, dark-skinned and long-haired, wielding their spears with savage fury. Tanukhids, he realised – the ancient foes of Lakhm.

'*Tha'rr! Tha'rr!*' the Saracens cried. Both sides were raising the same shout, carving into each other with vengeful energy. Hard to distinguish those that fought for Rome from those that fought for Persia.

'Sound the retreat,' Castus yelled to Egnatius. 'Fall back behind the infantry!'

Barbatio's men opened ranks to let them through, continuing their advance as the Tanukhids drove the Lakhmids back in confusion. Then the dust rose once more, cloaking the melee in its pall.

Castus rode westwards, along the rear of the battle line. Frenzy consumed him, and his heart was kicking in his chest. Sweat slicked his head and body. Something was happening up ahead, but he could make out nothing but the shapes of men and horses threshing in wild disorder. A man was running towards him on foot, a staff tribune with blood smeared across his face.

'They've broken through!' the tribune cried. 'Right of the centre, between the Fourth and Sixteenth Legions. The troops pushed forward too far, into the gulley, and the Persians rallied and broke the line!'

Castus reared back in the saddle, pulling on the reins as furious anguish coursed through his body. *Exactly what he had feared most.* Now the scene opened before him. The infantry line was entirely breached, the shield wall collapsed, and the Aswaran cataphracts were powering their way through the gap, like a herd of angry bulls stampeding at a broken fence. Castus saw men cut down or smashed aside by the charging horsemen, and trampled beneath the hooves. Bands of soldiers from the rear ranks were trying to form squares or defensive knots, huddled behind their shields; but all they could do was fend off the attackers. Barbatio's reserves were far away to the right, holding the flank. Gunthia's men were nearly a mile distant to the left. In moments, the cataphracts would have burst through the lines entirely, into the open space behind them, where only the artillery and baggage carts stood. Then they would swing to the right and strike at the unprotected rear of the Roman formation.

Reeling, Castus felt as if he had been punched in the gut. He had dragged on the reins instinctively, and his horse shied and kicked, half panicked by the noise and violent motion.

At the very moment of victory, he thought, the battle was lost.

Trumpets screamed from behind him, and suddenly riders were galloping past on either side. Egnatius was leading them; he had rallied a mixed force of cavalry from half a dozen broken units, all of them charging towards the Persian onrush.

'Rome and Victory!' the tribune cried as he rode. 'Rome and Victory – *attack*!'

The Roman horses were not armoured, and only a few of the riders wore mail or scale. Individually they could not hope to confront the heavy cataphracts. But together, three or four horsemen working in unison, they might bring one of the Persians down. It was a desperate hope, but the best they had.

'Forward!' Castus yelled, spurring his horse. Sabinus was beside him, and the handful of escort troopers formed around them.

Ahead, the dust rose and thickened into a vast swirling rampart, rolling across the battlefield. Teeth bared, eyes half-closed, Castus dipped his head and plunged on into it. At once the sun was eclipsed, and he rode through a rushing brown twilight filled with shadowy figures of men and horses. Someone was shouting: 'Form on me! Form a line on me!'

Then all Castus could hear was the muffled thunder of his own blood and breath, the rapid pounding of his heart. The sweat on his face crusted instantly, and his mouth filled with dirt. He saw one of the cataphract riders appear ahead of him, angling his lance at a charging Roman horseman; before he could react, the Roman was down. Another horse was coming in from the right, decked in scale armour. Castus swerved, but the man in the saddle was dead, his arms swinging loose. The horse galloped past him, and Castus caught a glimpse of the mesh-covered eyes, the huge bared teeth. Then it was gone.

Sounds of ringing steel through the murk, screams of men. But it all sounded so distant. Like being underwater, Castus thought. Somewhere ahead of him there were men fighting, three Roman horsemen tackling one of the cataphracts. The armoured horse circled and kicked, the rider lashing out with his mace.

Sunlight burst from above as the cloud thinned briefly, and with a shock Castus saw a Persian directly ahead of him. A black horse decked in scale and silken tassels, the rider in full armour and masked helmet, blue plumes on his shoulders. The mask turned, and in the black eyeholes Castus almost thought he could see the glint of recognition. His blood slowed, then the heat of rage burst through him.

'Zamasp!' he yelled into the whirling dust, and kicked his horse forward.

Another rider cut in from the left, galloping hard and then dragging back on the reins. His horse veered, and Castus saw that it was Sabinus. His son had a sword in his hand, raised to strike at the Persian. For one frozen moment, the two of them appeared perfectly matched. A vision of glory.

Then Zamasp drove his horse forward again, smashing into Sabinus's lighter mount. The Persian whirled his mace, and brought it swinging down. Castus cried out as Sabinus tried to parry the blow. He saw the sword in his son's hand break, Sabinus rolling backwards and plunging from the saddle.

Castus's horse stumbled beneath him. Pitching forward, he grabbed for the saddle horns. Too slow: his sweating palm slipped on the leather, and he felt himself sliding as the horse went down on its knees. *Move, move!* He kicked one leg out, trying to throw himself clear as the animal fell. The stony ground raced up towards him, and he managed to wrench his body around. Then he crashed down on his back with a solid punch that left him stunned.

Silence. Even his heart was stilled. When he opened his eyes he saw bright blue sky far ahead, through the wavering funnel of dust. He inhaled slowly, feeling the ache of his ribs as his chest filled. But his cuirass and helmet had protected him from the worst of the impact. He flexed his arms, moved his legs: no bones broken, as far as he could tell. His sword was gone, the wrist-cord snapped, and he could hear his horse scrambling upright and cantering away from him.

Just lie here, a voice seemed to say. *Just lie here and wait for death.*

Shadows passed across him. Hooves clattered near his head, and a galloping horse leaped over him.

Where was Zamasp? Where was Sabinus?

Sabinus. With a roar of effort, Castus lifted his head and upper body and rolled onto one side. Pain rushed through him. Scrabbling in the stony dust, he managed to get his knees under him and lever himself up. His helmet felt twisted on his head, the nasal bar digging into his cheek. Cursing, furious, he wrenched the laces loose, pulled off the helmet and threw it aside.

On his feet, legs braced, he stared around him. For a few long heartbeats he could see only dead and dying men sprawled on the ground, fallen horses kicking their legs, a slew of discarded weapons and shields. The battle seemed to have passed on, and left him alone. Distant figures galloped around him, shrouded by dust.

Then the dust cleared, and he saw Sabinus struggling to his feet, the stub of a broken sword still clasped in his hand, Zamasp turning his horse to charge down on the fallen man. The Persian had his mace raised, and the scale skirts flapped and clashed around the legs of his mount.

'Zamasp!' Castus screamed again. He lurched forward into a staggering run, spreading his arms, his empty hands. 'Zamasp, you piss-drinking bastard! Here I am – come and kill me!'

The Persian twisted in the saddle, and his horse shied and turned. The silver mask looked back at Castus. The metal was formed in an uncanny likeness of his face: the beard and the heavy hooked moustaches. It almost appeared to be smiling. The black eyeholes glared.

'No!' Sabinus was shouting. 'Father – no!'

But Zamasp was already spurring his powerful horse forward again, directing its charge towards Castus. And Castus was still running. He stooped, stumbling, and snatched a fallen cavalry spear from the ground. The oncoming horse and rider appeared larger than life, a huge statue of iron and gilded bronze driven into unnatural motion. For a brief instant, Castus had the unnerving sense that he had lived this moment before. This was death, he thought, bearing down on him... But if he died, then his son would die too. The battle would be lost.

Then all thought was gone.

Castus levelled the spear like a javelin. He took a last few running paces, then aimed the weapon directly at Zamasp's armoured chest.

Before he could throw, Sabinus rushed in from the left and hurled the stub of his broken sword. The weapon spun once in the air, then struck the head of the charging horse. The animal screamed, flinging up its muzzle, and just as Castus brought his arm forward he saw a chink of blackness open between the armour of its neck and head. He lunged, hurling the spear, and the shaft quivered as it flew.

Zamasp reared back in the saddle as the iron head of the spear plunged straight through the gap in the horse armour, sinking deep into the animal's throat. Castus threw himself to one side, and as he scrambled back upright he saw the charging horse collapsing forward in a spray of dust. The Persian commander had let his mace fall, flinging his arms out wildly, but as the saddle dropped beneath him he was hurled forward, the bindings that lashed him to the animal's back tearing loose.

The armoured body appeared to vault in the air, over the neck of the falling horse. Castus pushed himself onward again, staggering. Zamasp was sprawled on his back, but already he was trying to stand.

With a slew of grit Castus slid to the ground beside the fallen Persian. He had no weapon, only his fists, the bulk of his body and his desperate fury. Throwing himself across the armoured body, he pinned the Persian down and grappled him, seizing his wrist with his left hand as the man aimed a punch at his head. Zamasp twisted violently, trying to roll Castus off him, trying to kick his legs and lever himself upright. But he was constrained by his armour, the stiff links of scale and mail, the crush of metal. Sucking in fast ragged breaths, Castus straddled the fallen man's chest, pressing down on him with all his weight. The silver mask stared up at him, impassive, but Castus could see the Persian's eyes inside the black sockets, hear the hissing from the mouth slot.

Zamasp thrashed his arms, his helmeted head jerking from side to side. He was fiercely strong; at any moment he would throw Castus off him. Swinging his fist, Castus punched at the side of the Persian's helmet; he barely felt the skin of his knuckles split. He flung out his right arm, and his fingers closed around something on the ground. A rock, half the size of a man's head. Seizing it, he lifted the rock and swung it up, then smashed it down onto the helmet crest.

A clang of metal, and Zamasp jolted and writhed. He was trying to get his arm free of Castus's grip. Again Castus struck with the rock, beating it down onto the silver mask. He released Zamasp's wrist and reared upright, lifting the rock with both hands above his head. Then, with all his strength, he slammed it down again.

A muffled cry from behind the mask, and Castus felt a jolt run through the Persian's body. Again he raised the rock, with a furious gasp between his clenched teeth. Again he slammed it down, beating a dent into the polished silver of the mask. He had a sudden memory of his father's forge; himself, as a child, beating hot metal on the anvil. He raised the rock a third time, and then a fourth, hammering it down in a steady relentless frenzy, until he saw the blood bursting from the mask's eyeholes and the rents in the metal, and Zamasp lay still.

Castus let the gore-spattered rock fall from his grip and rolled sideways off the armoured body to sprawl in the dust. Sabinus took his arms, dragging him a short way clear and then kneeling beside him. He lifted him, bracing his head against one knee, and Castus could hear his son crying out for a water-carrier. His throat rasped, and he tasted blood as he tried to grin.

Other men were around them now, one of them carrying Castus's draco standard on its tall pole, and a couple of troopers of his escort, guarding him with their shields. Castus gripped Sabinus tightly, too weak and dazed even to try to stand. Somebody handed him a flask, and he gulped back watered wine.

He was still lying like that when Egnatius found him. The cavalry tribune dropped to one knee beside him and pulled off his helmet. 'Excellency!' he cried. 'Should we signal the general advance?'

'Advance?' Castus asked, dazed. It hurt even to speak.

'We drove the Persians back, excellency,' Egnatius explained hurriedly. 'We closed the gap in the line... The Saracens have hooked around on the right flank and taken their camp. The enemy are in full retreat! Should we make the signal?'

'Yes, yes,' Castus said, wide-eyed in bewilderment. He was dragging himself up, Sabinus supporting his shoulders. Together they struggled to their feet.

Away on the far horizon, beyond the dust and the massed lines of troops, smoke was rising. Trails of it, curling up into the hot blue sky from the direction of Prince Narses' encampment. Leaning on his son's shoulder, Castus heard the trumpets wailing, the cheers of the infantry as the lines tightened and began to move. All across the far slopes he could see horses and riders, fleeing the battle in confusion.

The men around him were laughing, embracing each other in the joy of victory. Summoning the last ebb of his strength, Castus forced himself to stand upright, chin raised.

'*Now*,' Sabinus said. '*Now* we've won.'

'*Roma Victrix! Roma Victrix!*' the men of his escort were shouting, punching the air in exultation. Castus could only grit his teeth, as the tears coursed through the dust on his face. *Yes*, he thought. *Yes, this is truly victory.* Though he could barely believe it.

For hours the slaughter continued. The advancing infantry crushed any remaining knots of defiant Persians, while the cavalry swooped across the slopes cutting down the fugitives and herding thousands of prisoners before them. Most of the surviving cataphracts had fled west, into the ravines that dropped to the banks of the Tigris; many drowned in the river, dragged down by the weight of their armour.

But the battle had been truly won by Hind and her Tanukhid Saracens; after driving off the Lakhmids on the right flank they had formed up and ridden in a wide arc across the high ground to the east, falling on the lightly defended Persian camp in a screaming wave of destruction. Narses' bodyguard had died fighting to a man, and the prince himself had been killed while he was trying to escape. Then the wild plundering had begun.

The remains of the camp were still burning now, a mass of embers on the hillside as the day fell into evening. Castus stared at them from the roof of the mud-brick house where he had spent the previous night. He sipped wine, and tried not to think too much about the violence the Saracens had wreaked on the Persian slaves and camp followers. Such things were part of war, and he had known them all his life. But there was nothing honourable or glorious about it. All victories bore their tide of wanton bloodshed.

Of the plunder taken from the enemy camp he had seen little. Hind had sent him the princely diadem and pearl-encrusted slippers taken from the body of the dead Narses, and a wooden chest inlaid with silver that her warriors had found in the Persian leader's headquarters. It was filled with documents, rolled parchment and vellum scrolls, tightly packed. The Saracens had no use for such things, but they knew that Romans were strangely keen on them.

Now the chest stood open beside Diogenes, who sat on the low parapet of the rooftop with his legs crossed beneath him, picking through the contents.

'Anything of worth?' Castus asked him.

Diogenes frowned, holding one of the unrolled parchments close to his face and peering at it in the low evening light. He dropped it and took another.

'They're mostly written in court Persian,' he said, 'and I find the Pahlavi script rather hard to decipher. But as far as I can make out a lot of the documents are in verse. Apparently our Prince Narses was a poet. Although not, from the looks of things, a very good one.'

Castus grunted. 'He should have spent more time learning to fight!'

'Hm,' Diogenes said. 'I'll see what I can discover from them. But I suspect our friend Hormisdas might be a better judge. We could give them to him, if we return to Antioch...'

If, Castus thought. A sour turbulence rose inside him. For so many days he had refused to think about what would happen next. He had concerned himself only with the battle ahead, bending his mind towards it utterly, erasing all other considerations. But now the battle was won, and he was still alive. Marcellina and Aeliana were still prisoners in Antioch, and Mucatra was still out to the west somewhere with his army, blocking his road home.

He might have beaten the Persians, but he was still a condemned traitor.

A cry from the street below him, and Castus gazed down from the rooftop to see Hind and a party of her Saracen horsemen cantering back through the village. She slowed as she saw him up on the rooftop, and raised her hands high, grinning.

'Aurelios Kastos!' she yelled. The men behind her let out whooping cries, brandishing their spears. Standing beside the low wall, Castus saluted them as they passed.

He envied them, he realised. For Hind and her people, there were no borders and no laws, beyond friendship and revenge. Their gods demanded nothing of them, and they owed nothing to any earthly ruler. There was only the open desert, the open sky. For them, victory was a pure thing, to be relished in freedom, without doubt or dismay.

But for him, the future held only confrontation.

CHAPTER XXXII

O n the open plain to the east of Nisibis, two armies faced
each other. A thousand strides of parched ground lay
between their camps; at the midpoint, two parties of horsemen
approached and drew to a halt. Both of them carried trailing
draco standards, limp in the motionless air. Far off to either side,
the soldiers at their fortifications watched the meeting, and tried
to guess what was passing between those distant figures, hazy in
the afternoon heat and inaudible above the constant death rattle
of the cicadas.

'*Respect,*' Castus spat. 'He dares to use that fucking word?'

'Respect and *dignity,*' the officer facing him said. He was a
handsome strong-jawed man, and his burnished cuirass gleamed
in the sun. 'As I say, you'll be treated with the respect and dignity
due to your former position – *if* you lay down your arms, give
up your command and surrender yourself to his excellency
Valerius Mucatra.'

'And where is he, this Mucatra?' Castus growled. 'If he respects
me so much, why doesn't he come out here and talk to me? The
Thracian bastard's hiding in his tent, I expect, too ashamed to
show his face!'

The officer was trying to appear dignified himself, but he
had a sour pinched expression, as if he had tasted something
unpleasant. Castus knew him; he was one of the men that he

had dismissed from military command the previous summer. Perhaps, he thought, this very officer had been one of those who had sent men to try and murder him in his chambers. Now Mucatra had reinstated the man, and sent him out here to deliver his messages.

'Surrender yourself,' the officer went on, ignoring Castus's comment, 'and you will be conducted back to Antioch, to face trial before the proper authorities.'

'On what charge?'

The officer widened his eyes just slightly, his nostrils flaring. Clearly he had not expected to have to explain further. 'On... on a charge of treason against the emperor!' he stammered. 'There is evidence against you – written evidence.'

'Fabricated evidence!' Egnatius called from away to Castus's right. Sabinus sat calmly in the saddle on the opposite side, with Iovinus and the standard-bearer

'You have until dawn tomorrow,' the officer snapped, then pulled his reins to turn his horse, signalling his escort to follow him.

'Or what?' Castus said.

But the man gave no answer as he turned and rode away towards the lines of his army.

'They're serious, do you think?' Egnatius asked.

'We have to assume they are,' Castus told him.

His anger was fading to a grim sense of despair. He barely heard the trumpets as he passed back through his own lines, or noticed the salutes of his officers. He rode with his head straight and his jaw set, only dismounting when he reached his command enclosure. Pacing through the circuit of guards, he entered his tent. His hands felt unsteady, and Vallio had to help him unpin his cloak and unbuckle the straps of his cuirass. Freed of their weight, he sank down onto a stool and braced his elbows against his knees. There was food on the table, cold meat and fruit, but he did not feel at all hungry. There was wine too, and he poured himself a cup and drained it in three long swallows. Perhaps, he thought, things would make more sense if he got drunk?

Already he had delayed as long as could. Seven days had passed since the battle, and he had marched his troops back westwards in easy stages, pausing at intervals to send out scouts and gain information. But now Mucatra had intercepted him, and he could evade this decision no longer.

Twelve thousand Roman soldiers were under his command, allowing for casualties; there were Hind's three thousand Saracens too, camped in the groves and abandoned villages to the south. How far would they back him now? Castus had led them to victory, and they had been in good spirits during the march back west. But he knew what victorious soldiers wanted: cheering crowds and acclaim, rewards and trophies. A safe return to their homes and their families. After war must come the blessings of peace. Instead, he had led them into a new confrontation, this time with their own comrades.

No, he thought, *that must never happen*. He had seen enough bloodshed during the civil wars. Enough of Romans killing other Romans. Even if Mucatra sent troops into his camp to seize him, Castus would never order his own men to resist. No soldier would die fighting in his name.

And if he tried to fight, if he even tried to flee, word would get back to Antioch, and Marcellina and his daughter would pay the price for his actions.

With an anguished groan he stood up, gripping his head with both hands. It was impossible. He could trust no one now; a handful of his officers perhaps, but there would be few in the camp who did not know of the allegations against him. The rumours of treason they had heard weeks before, confirmed now. Even the guards that protected his own quarters could not be trusted. There was no way out.

He was still standing, tortured by raging indecision, when Vallio came in from the outer chamber and lit the lamp on the table. Castus had not even noticed that it was getting dark. Almost the ides of September, and the nights were beginning to lengthen. With dull surprise, Castus realised that it was nearly a year to the day since his audience with the emperor, in the palace at Constantinople, when he had first heard of his mission in the east. It seemed a lifetime ago. And how little he had suspected then of what would happen... More than anything he wished he could return to the life he had known before that day. To Marcellina and Aeliana, the villa on the coast of Dalmatia. The simple pleasures of peace.

Surrender, then. That was his only option now. And perhaps indeed Mucatra would treat him with respect and dignity? Perhaps when he returned to Antioch he would be allowed to see his wife and daughter one last time, if only to say goodbye. And perhaps – the fantasy took hold – if he could bear the ignominy of a trial then he could make his case plainly, convince the judges of his innocence...? Perhaps he would be free to return home, even to a life of exile...

He snorted a quick laugh. How easily he grasped at the most slender of hopes! If he were condemned as a traitor he would die, his property would be seized, and his family cast out with nothing. Was it worth the risk, even so? He felt his mind fogging, his thoughts slowing.

'Dominus,' Vallio said, lifting the flap of the tent once more. 'Diogenes to see you.'

'Show him in,' Castus said in a firm voice. He cleared his throat, took possession of himself. As Diogenes entered he sat down again and picked up his cup. 'Come to advise me?' he asked. 'Or just to help me drink myself to sleep?'

'I'm not entirely sure,' Diogenes said. He wore a querulous frown. 'I may bring good news, or bad.'

'Oh?' Castus said. He poured Diogenes a cup of wine, then took a slice of meat from the dish on the table. It tasted of nothing, but eating was a distraction at least.

'You remember those Persian documents the Saracens found in Narses' camp?' Diogenes asked. 'To pass the time earlier I made an attempt at deciphering some of them. Most, as we thought, are fairly worthless... But some appear to be official communications between Narses and the court of King Shapur.'

'Yes?' Castus was chewing steadily, trying to slow the sudden kick of his heart.

'It was hard to make out at first, but I noticed several times a particular name mentioned, not a Persian name but a Roman one. It took me a while to determine what it was, but now I'm sure. The documents mention *Dracilianus*.'

Castus swallowed heavily. His hand trembled as he picked up his cup.

'It seems,' Diogenes went on, 'that Dracilianus had several clandestine meetings with the Persian envoy, Vezhan Gushnasp, when he passed through Antioch in the spring, and also last year. Dracilianus was apparently paid a certain sum, in gold, in return for giving the Persians information on our military and political situation.'

'*Gods!*' Castus said, wide-eyed. 'That message we found, the one Hind gave us – it came from him?'

'Perhaps so. I believe these contacts date from the period before the death of Constantine, and the subsequent fall of Ablabius and Dracilianus's rise to power. Presumably he was trying to enhance his own position at the time, and needed money. Now, of course, it would be highly embarrassing for him if such contacts became known...'

'More than a little,' Castus said quietly. 'He must've feared that I'd discover what he'd been doing – maybe it was him who sent those men to kill me back in the autumn after all? And that's why he's concocted this treason charge against me, at the first opportunity...! *Ha!*' he cried, smacking his fist into his palm. '*He's* the real traitor!'

'Yes, but I'm afraid that's not all,' Diogenes said, and his worried tone quelled Castus's jubilation at once. 'These letters also mention another man, whom they refer to as the commander of the Roman military forces. I thought at first they meant you, of course, but several of the documents date to before our arrival in the east. So the man in question must be...'

'Valerius Mucatra,' Castus said in a leaden voice. Despair plunged through him. Just for a moment, he had believed that he was saved. But if Mucatra himself was part of the conspiracy, then surrendering to him would be fatal. Castus would never be allowed to reach Antioch alive. And what had seemed a glimpse of hope was just the revelation of a greater peril.

'If we could get these documents back to Antioch,' Diogenes said in a musing tone, 'give them to Hormisdas, perhaps – he could present them to Emperor Constantius when he arrives in the east, and explain their full meaning. Your name would be cleared, brother!'

'No time,' Castus said. He pressed his fist against his mouth, trying to think clearly. But it was useless: even if they circulated this news among Mucatra's own officers and men, raised a mutiny against him, word of it would reach Dracilianus soon enough. Marcellina and Aeliana would die.

He stood up and placed a palm on Diogenes's shoulder. 'Thank you,' he said. 'Keep working on the documents, as fast as you can. Perhaps we'll gain something else from them yet.'

Diogenes nodded mutely, with a look of understanding.

Once he had left the tent Castus sat in silence, then went through to the outer chamber and pushed aside the flap. The camp was in darkness, and strangely subdued. No singing from the tent lines and watchfires, no cries from the sentries at the perimeter. Even the men standing guard around the command enclosure appeared unnaturally still, and none glanced back at him. The moon hung low in the sky.

Castus suppressed a shudder, feeling the chill of a dark intuition. He paced back into the main chamber of the tent, took up his sword and drew it from the scabbard. Sitting on a stool, he ran a whetstone along the edges of the blade. The tempered steel gleamed in the lamplight, and the stone made a keen rasp.

'Dominus?'

Castus glanced up – it was Vallio again, at the tent door.

'The praepositus Lycianus, dominus – he wishes to speak with you, alone.'

Castus laid the sword on the table beside him. He remained seated as Lycianus entered. The grizzled scout commander was wearing a cloak with the hood drawn up; he took it off and threw it onto one of the couches, then seated himself facing Castus.

'General,' he said, his voice low and hard. 'There are strange rumours flying about. I wondered if you might tell me what you intend to do?'

'Did you?' Castus replied quietly. He angled his head, gazing at Lycianus, and shrugged in resignation. The man was only a decade younger than him, and he had imagined that there was trust between them at least. *Do we have to do this?*

'I expected somebody,' he said. 'Didn't think it would be you.'

Lycianus had surrendered his sword to Vallio, but he still wore a Saracen dagger in a belt sheath. Castus could see the man's eyes flicking towards the weapon on the table.

'I'm not sure what you mean,' Lycianus said, but the words came out awkwardly. The tension in his body was obvious. Realisation dawned on Castus; he should have guessed sooner, but now it made sense.

'Diogenes just came to see me,' he said. 'About those letters we found in the Persian camp. But you knew that – you must have seen him leaving the tent. That's why you're here, correct?'

Lycianus tightened his jaw, saying nothing.

'You know, I should have paid more attention when you were telling us that story about your captivity among the Lakhmids,' Castus said with a crooked smile. 'Your friendship with their fugitive prince – Imru something, wasn't it? Hind tried to warn me, I think. She told me that you loved one of Imru's sons in particular. Nothing wrong with that, I suppose. But I'd assumed it was one of the sons who died. It wasn't though, was it? It was the eldest, the one who went back east and allied himself with the Persians.'

'A long time ago, general.'

'But old allegiances are hard to break. Especially when there's love involved, eh? An old man's love for a barbarian youth… How long have you been working for them now?'

Lycianus exhaled, slow and quiet. His right hand was clasping his thigh; the slightest movement, and he could grasp the hilt of his knife. 'When you spend a long time out in the deep desert,' he said, 'your ideas about loyalty change. Empires, frontiers – they're nothing but empty dust. Kings and leaders don't matter. Only men are important. The bonds between men. Love, and trust.'

'I remember,' Castus said, 'when I first arrived in Antioch. Dracilianus was away in Edessa at the time – I thought that was strange, but I didn't ask why. He was meeting you there, wasn't he? You were his contact with the Persian agents.'

'The Lakhmid agents,' Lycianus said. 'Yes.'

'And that ambush in the desert, after we left Nisibis? That was you as well?'

'No,' the scout commander said firmly. 'I told them of your plans, but I never expected them to attack like that. It was… ill conceived. And nothing personal, I have to say. As a matter of fact I've always liked you. You seem an honourable man, a soldier. Like me.'

'But you never tried to let the Persians into Nisibis during the siege – why?'

Lycianus could only shrug. 'I've seen cities fall to besieging armies before,' he said. 'It's bloody, and indiscriminate. I wanted to avoid that if I could.'

'And yet when we marched east you sent messages to Zamasp and Narses, telling them where we were going. You allowed them to set a trap for us.'

'Such is war,' Lycianus said. 'You know that as well as anybody.' His eyes were hard as flint now, his hand easing steadily towards the knife.

'So now you've come to kill me yourself,' Castus said, narrowing his eyes. 'You could call it self-protection, I suppose.' He lifted his hands only slightly, his palms empty, then stood up. 'Well,' he said. 'Let's do this.'

The other man had tensed as Castus moved. Now he raised himself slowly from his seat and stood facing him. Castus keep his hands down by his sides, and held the other man's gaze; he could tell that Lycianus was still watching the sword on the table from the corner of his eye.

Castus twitched a quick smile. Neither of them moved.

A slight breeze rippled the leather wall of the tent, and the lamp flame flickered. Lycianus darted his hand towards the knife. Castus knew that he was expecting him to go for the sword; instead he stepped in, fast and close. With his left hand he seized Lycianus's wrist, trapping it against his hip. He had already memorised the position of the sword on the table. Reaching blindly behind him he spun the blade towards him, grasped the hilt, and swept it upwards in a single fluid movement.

Lycianus tried to pull back, but Castus already had the long sword levelled, drawn back in his hand. He stabbed, and felt the honed tip drive between Lycianus's ribs. Dragging the man close, he pushed the blade in deep.

With a single tight gasp, Lycianus fell forward against him, his knees buckling.

'I wouldn't have told anyone, you know,' Castus said. 'You could have just walked away.'

Then he shoved the blade forward, angling it to pierce the other man's heart. A gulping sound from Lycianus's throat, a spill of blood between his lips, then he slumped and toppled backwards onto the matting floor.

Castus flicked the blood from his sword, then wiped the blade. Summoned by the sudden noise, Vallio threw back the tent flap – he stifled a cry of horror as he saw the body sprawled before him.

'Quiet!' Castus said, laying the sword back on the table. 'Help me. We need to move the body into the rear chamber. Nobody must know of this.'

Together they dragged the corpse through into the curtained sleeping area at the rear of the tent. As Castus washed his hands he could hear a strange disturbance from outside. Shouting voices, wild cries in the night.

'See what's happening out there,' he told Vallio.

Now the initial danger had passed, he was sweating, trembling with nervous energy. The shouts from outside were getting louder, closer. The glow of torchlight showed from beneath the tent flap.

Castus swallowed heavily, fighting to compose himself. Mucatra's men, he guessed, had entered the camp. Either that, or his troops were rising in mutiny against him. Calm, he had to be calm. He had to face the end like a soldier. He sheathed his sword and threw the baldric over his shoulder; then he put on his cloak and pinned it to fall across his chest, hiding the bloodstains. Already he was gaining control of himself. Standing in the lamplight, he drew his head up and squared his shoulders.

The tent flap was flung aside, and Egnatius stepped into the chamber. A look on his face of wild panic, or perhaps exhilaration.

'General!' the tribune cried. 'Come outside… It's the troops…'
He looked as though he wanted to scream, or burst into tears.
'They're… They're *acclaiming you emperor*!'

Hot torchlight outside the tent, and a sea of faces. Cheers burst
from the crowd of men as Castus emerged. Arms rose in salute.
There were officers among them – Barbatio and Gunthia, and
Iovinus the Protector. The rest were men of Castus's escort,
mingling with legionaries and Gothic warriors, cavalry troopers
and archers, a great surging mob surrounding his tent. Some of
them had already dropped to one knee before him.

Castus stood up straight, his chin pressed down against
his throat, gazing at the scene in astonished horror. 'What is
this madness?' he managed to say, but the words came out as
a croak.

The madness had begun, Egnatius had told him before they
left the tent, among Hind's Saracens. The desert horsemen had
come riding up to the camp as evening fell, shouting in bad
Greek that Castus was the greatest general of Rome, the true
successor to Constantine, and he should be emperor of the east.
In the rumour-ridden uncertainty of the camp the word had
spread all too quickly, passed between the tent parties and the
cavalry lines. The first shouts of acclamation had come less than
an hour ago, and already there was pandemonium.

'What is this *madness*?' Castus said again, raising his head to
yell at the ring of men who surrounded him in the torchlight.
Voices shouted back, crying out his name.

With a roar of fury Castus paced forward again. He saw
Barbatio dropping to kneel, and seized the officer by the arms,
dragging him to his feet. 'What are you doing?' he yelled. 'What
are you *doing*? Stop this now! Have you lost your mind?'

'General,' Barbatio cried, his face dark with passionate
excitement. 'Lead us and we'll back you! Half of the men at

least – both the Gemina detachments, the Parthica legions, and the Goths... they're yours!'

'Castus Caesar! Castus Augustus!'

Castus gazed around himself, wild with ferocious dread. Yes, he thought – all of them were here. The men who had cheered his name from the walls of Nisibis. The men who had marched east under his command, who had saluted him after the victory at Narasara... Suddenly his voice was gone, and he felt weak at the knees. He wanted to cover his face with his hands, to weep, to run...

Sabinus pushed his way through the throng, a look of astonished confusion on his face. But even he seemed caught up in the madness now. 'Father!' he cried. 'We can't stop this! They're tearing the images of Constantius from the standards!'

And Castus knew at once that all was lost.

Marcellina and Aeliana will die.

'Silence!' he bellowed, raising his arms. Some of the men at the back started chanting his name – they thought he was returning their salute, accepting their acclamation. Two of them carried a shield, and were yelling for Castus to stand upon it and be raised between them. Three more had a sort of purple cape, made from scraps of their own military standards.

Horror, absolute and paralysing.

My wife and child will die.

'Get back!' he bellowed. He drew his sword and brandished it at the ring of men. 'Get back, or I'll kill you *my fucking self*!'

Egnatius was beside him; he too had his sword drawn. 'Listen to the general!' he was shouting. 'The general refuses the purple! Obey his commands!'

There were sounds of fighting in the distance now, angry shouts and yells from away across the tent lines. Not everyone, it seemed, was so willing to change allegiance. And if more swords were bared, Castus knew, men would die.

'Barbatio, Gunthia!' he yelled at the two officers. 'Get your men in order. Get them back to their lines – do it *now*!'

Barbatio stared at him, wide-eyed, his face falling. Many of the soldiers were still chanting wildly, but the centurions and junior officers among them had caught the night's shifting mood and were trying to drive their men back towards their quarters. Scuffles in the dust, a shout of rage or pain. The torches wavered and began to fall away.

Castus stood with clenched jaw, watching the crowd disperse. His face was flushed, filled with blood, but his eyes were wet with tears. Just for a moment, he thought – just for a last dying moment he had been tempted. But it could not happen. He turned, and marched back into the tent.

In the inner chamber he doubled over, braced on his knees. Then he threw his head back and barked with laughter. His shoulders were quaking, and his muscles ached. Emperor, he thought. How could he ever have expected that?

Sabinus and Vallio were waiting at the door, watching him anxiously. Castus turned to them, exhaling. He wiped his face.

'I want all the senior officers assembled,' he ordered. 'As soon as they've settled their men, summon them here.'

Sabinus nodded and went outside. Castus drank back two cups of wine, and waited until the heaving of his chest had subsided. Then Vallio helped him change into his best tunic, the one that bore the silver and gold woven insignia of the Magister Equitum. He put on his white cloak, and secured it at his shoulder with the heavy gold brooch that bore the name of Constantine. Vallio passed him his helmet – still a little scratched and dented after it had been retrieved from the battlefield, but the orderly had hammered and polished out the worst of the damage. Castus clasped it under his arm, tightened his belts and pulled his cloak straight. Then Vallio raised the flap, and he strode through into the outer chamber once more.

All of them were there, waiting for him in the light of the lamps. Egnatius, Gunthia and Barbatio. Quintianus, Sabinus and Diogenes. The other unit commanders and the few remaining Protectores and staff tribunes. Even the plump accountant Metrophanes. Castus stood before them in his full uniform, jaw firm and brow lowered. He threw back his cloak and gripped the hilt of his sword.

'Brothers,' he declared in a voice of command. 'All of you know what must happen now. Once a man's been acclaimed emperor by his troops, there's no way back.'

Turning his head slowly, he scanned their faces. Sorrow and disbelief on some, resignation on others. Vallio was sniffing back tears. Quintianus just looked ashamed.

'All of you,' Castus said, 'are soldiers of Rome. It's been an honour to command you. But I will not have your names and reputations tainted by tonight's madness. It was a mistake, and it must be forgotten. No soldier in this army will suffer for it.'

Barbatio opened his mouth to speak, but Castus silenced him with a glance. He felt very calm now, very much in control. No questions remained. Only cold certainty.

'I know what I have to do,' he said. 'And I require nothing more from you. When it's done...' His voice faltered, and he swallowed thickly. 'When I'm dead, you must let everyone in the camp know it. Take my body... show it to the soldiers. Let Mucatra see it too. And tomorrow, at first light, you will go and present yourself to him, with oaths to Constantius Augustus. Tell him you did the deed yourselves, if you must. But honour my name in private, and tell my wife and family I died well. That's all I ask.'

'Brother,' Egnatius said quietly. 'You don't have to... You could slip away, the sentries would let you go...'

'No!' Castus said firmly. 'My duty is clear, and so is yours. This is my last order to you – if you have any regard for me, you'll follow it without question. Understood?'

A pause, and then Barbatio drew himself up stiffly, raising his hand in salute. 'We will do what we are ordered...'

'... *and at every command we will be ready*,' the others said in unison.

Castus went to Egnatius and clasped him in an embrace, kissing him. Then he embraced each of the other men in turn. One by one they stepped back, eyes downcast. Then Castus gave them a last salute, and dismissed them all.

'A moment with my son,' he said gruffly. 'In private, please.'

When the tent was emptied he took Sabinus by the hand, then pulled him close and hugged him. His son was speechless, struggling to breathe. For six slow heartbeats they stood, clasped together. Then Castus whispered the words in his ear, and released him. He turned his back, and did not see Sabinus leave.

Alone, he stood in the centre of the chamber, staring at the lamp flame. A sudden memory came to him: the old deposed emperor Maximian, sitting in his room in the palace at Massilia. Castus had been with him just before he died, and had found his hanging body afterwards. He shrugged, laughing to himself. The poles of this tent would hardly bear his weight.

No, he thought. He had seen death many times. He knew how it was done. The tip of a sword between the ribs, just over the heart. Then a lunge forward, the pommel driving against the floor, the blade piercing the body...

Now that the moment had arrived he felt strangely composed, almost relieved. Darkness clouded his mind, but then it was gone.

He took off his cloak, drew his sword from its scabbard and felt the weight of it in his hand.

Then he walked through into the curtained rear chamber and did what needed to be done.

PART FIVE

CHAPTER XXXIII

Antioch, September AD 337

Marcellina knelt on the marble floor. Leaning forward, she took a burning taper and lit the small clay lamp that stood on the step of the alcove. There were many other lamps placed around it – several of them by Marcellina herself on previous visits – with tallow candles, votive images and little heaps of ash. She took a pinch of incense and sprinkled it over the flame. As the scented smoke curled upwards she clambered to her feet. Her ash-coloured tunic hung loose around her as she raised her arms, palms outstretched, and tipped back her head.

Silently she mouthed the words of the prayer. When she opened her eyes she saw the images painted on the walls of the alcove, lit by the wavering lamp flames. The Redeeming Christ, surrounded by an adoring crowd stretching their arms towards him. The miracle of the loaves and the fishes.

Her daughter stood beside her, dressed in the same ashen mourning clothes. Aeliana had assumed the same praying posture too, although her lips did not move, and she gazed at the paintings in the alcove with wide and wondering eyes. Marcellina lowered her arms, touched her fingers to her lips and raised them towards the image of Christ. Her daughter did the same.

'Mama,' Aeliana said in a whisper. 'If Papa didn't believe in God or Christ, how can Jesus help his soul get into Paradise?'

Marcellina embraced the girl, stroking her hair. 'It doesn't matter,' she said. 'Your father believed in other gods, it's true... And maybe one day we can pray to them as well. But they can't help him in the afterlife. So for now it's important that we... do the correct thing.'

And be seen to do the correct thing, she thought. She had been trying to hide herself from public view as much as possible, but she knew she was still being watched. At least now Dracilianus had removed the guards from her house, and she and Aeliana were free to go where they chose in the city. But their position was uncertain; Castus had died as an accused traitor, and only the emperor himself could rule on what would become of his family. News had come from Rome that the Senate had approved Constantius's acclamation; now he and his two brothers, the sons of Constantine, would rule the empire between them as joint Augusti. But the new emperor was not expected to return to Antioch for another two weeks at least.

The little Church of Saint Simeon was one of the smallest, and oldest, in the city, standing just across the bridge from the palace island. Few came here, when it was so close to the huge, if unfinished, Golden Church that stood beside the palace itself. But Marcellina had come here several times over this last week, since the official courier had reached Antioch with news of her husband's death.

The horror of that day would never leave her. Only the briefest and coldest of messages, from Dracilianus of all people, had informed her that Aurelius Castus had been killed by his own officers, his body dishonoured, and she was now a widow. Marcellina had felt those words striking through her, harrowing her heart. She had flung herself on the floor, ripped her clothing, and sobbed until she felt her throat would tear open. Were it not for Aeliana, she would have sought death herself, that day or in those following. Gladly she would have drowned herself in the river, or hurled herself from a high window. But her daughter needed her, now more than ever.

Two days later, Sabinus and Diogenes had arrived from the east, slipping into the city by night and telling her what had really happened on the plain east of Nisibis. By that time she was too hollowed out by suffering to react. She had not told Aeliana; better for now if the girl believed only that her father had died fighting the Persians.

Together they walked back through the scented darkness of the church. Gold glowed from the shadows, and the painted figures on the wall appeared almost like real people, hanging in strange suspension.

'Mama,' Aeliana said, taking her mother's hand. She had spoken little since she heard the news. Even now she appeared pale and unwell. 'Mama, I wasn't praying for father's soul to go to Paradise.'

'But... why not?'

'Because I was praying for God to send him back here to us.'

Marcellina looked away quickly, choking back a sob. She tightened her throat, then laid her hand on her daughter's head as they walked towards the spill of bright sunlight from the open doors.

Blinking, Marcellina emerged into the daylight. She paused to hand a few coins to the beggars gathered in the shade of the portico, then saw Hormisdas waiting a few paces away, leaning against a pillar. Aside from his beard and the pearl he wore in his ear, the Persian prince could have been a prosperous Syrian merchant. Two of his hulking Armenian bodyguards waited with him.

'Domina,' Hormisdas said with a respectful bow. 'Matters, I think, are about to reach a critical stage.'

Marcellina pulled the grey shawl tighter around her head and shoulders. She noticed Diogenes standing in the sunlight, beside the two litters that waited with their teams of bearers. With his ragged clothes, his bald head and face dark brown from the sun, and the scrawny crippled dog that lounged at his side, he resembled one of the beggars by the church door. But then, Marcellina thought, she hardly looked better herself. The events of the summer had turned her hair almost entirely grey, and her face was sallow and lined with anguish. She looked like an old woman now, dressed in her mourning drab.

Diogenes was tugging at his tufty beard as she and Hormisdas went to join him.

'You spoke to the man?' Marcellina asked him, holding the hem of her shawl to hide her mouth. Was she still being watched now? Did it matter?

'I did,' Diogenes said, smiling. 'A very interesting person indeed. He agreed to do what we suggested. By now all the racing factions and the city collegia will know, the actors' guilds too. Most of the city, I expect.'

'May I suggest, domina,' Hormisdas said with a casual gesture, 'that the little girl ought not to witness what happens next? It won't be pretty for young eyes.'

Marcellina agreed. She crouched beside Aeliana, taking her hands. 'You must go with Diogenes, my darling,' she said. 'He'll take you in his litter, back to the house by a longer route. I'll see you back there very soon, understand?'

Aeliana glanced warily at the ragged old man beside her. She did not know Diogenes well, but she knew he had been a friend of her father's. She nodded quickly, and Marcellina kissed her on the brow.

Seated in Hormisdas's litter, the curtains drawn and the bodyguards pacing on either side, Marcellina felt herself borne back across the Orontes bridge to the island. They were moving along the broad colonnaded way that led to the palace now.

'I hear that our old friend Ablabius has reached the end of his days,' Hormisdas said. He was smiling slightly, and seemed to be enjoying himself, though his eyes were hard. 'He was summoned from his estates to Constantinople to meet the Augustus Constantius. The meeting never happened. Ablabius was greeted on the steps of his house by a pair of Scholae guardsmen. They dragged him into the street and cut off his head, before a jeering crowd, so they say.'

Marcellina tensed, feeling cold inside.

'And also news comes from the east. That odious man Mucatra is dead too, it seems. Murdered by his own officers in the praetorium at Edessa. They must already have heard the rumours about him. He took quite a while to die, I hear.'

Exhaling slowly, Marcellina rubbed the rough cloth of her shawl between finger and thumb. She pictured the litter as a tiny boat, washed along on a tide of blood. So much killing – when would it end? *Not yet*, she thought. *Not just yet.*

'Look,' Hormisdas told her, flicking aside the curtain of the litter and pointing. Marcellina leaned forward, staring out through the crowd that filled the street. Many of the people were gathered around one of the pillars at the corner of the colonnade, reading a notice pasted there.

'Those appeared all over the city, in the early hours,' Hormisdas told her. 'Your man has done his work well!'

Marcellina knew what the notice said, and all the others like it. Passages translated from the Persian documents that Sabinus and Diogenes had brought back from Nisibis. Hormisdas had confirmed that they were genuine, and that they proved the guilt of Domitius Dracilianus. He had suggested that they wait for Constantius to arrive, but that would take too long. Dracilianus was sure to find out before then, and he would either flee or concoct some plausible explanation, some counter-charge.

Better to do it this way, she told herself, although she could feel the fluttering of panic in her stomach, the fear in her heart. *Justice is its own reward*; that was what the actor Europas had told her when she last spoke to him. With her husband's death, she owed the man nothing, it seemed. Justice, yes – but still she was half-sick with terror and remorse.

Already she could feel the hot breath of riot stirring in the street. The crowds were thickening as the litter moved towards the palace, and she heard shouts and chants, the voice of the swelling mob.

'I think we could descend here,' Hormisdas said, tapping the litter roof. 'Any further and we could get caught up in the proceedings!'

They climbed out, and the Armenians shoved a path through the crowd. Hormisdas led Marcellina through a wide doorway and up some steps, which brought them out onto a raised portico overlooking the street. This was one of his own houses, she supposed – the prince had several in Antioch.

Looking down from the portico, she saw the colonnaded avenue stretching to her right, and the gates of the palace at the far end. A short distance away was the central crossroads of the island. A tetrapylon monument stood in the centre, where the avenues met, a four-sided arch set with pillars, with a bronze statue of three elephants pulling a chariot standing on the pediment. A figure in the crowd around the monument caught her eye, and for a moment she saw Europas looking up at her. He raised his hand; then he was gone.

'Aha,' said Hormisdas. 'Now the action begins!'

He sounded, Marcellina thought, like an idle spectator at some public event. Following his gesture, squinting in the bright sunlight, she saw that the great doors of the palace had been swung wide. A column of horsemen issued forth, mounted guards of the Schola Armaturae, led by a tribune in a plumed helmet. They were forming a cordon along the street that led to the Tetrapylon of the Elephants, Marcellina noticed. Already the jeers of the crowd were growing louder, the mass of people seeming to converge from all directions, gathering with frightening speed.

'He has a boat by the river dock, I think,' Hormisdas said, sitting casually on the rail of the balustrade. 'But he's a fool – he should have had himself lowered from the river frontage of the palace, or just walled himself up in there somewhere and waited for help.'

It was fitting, Marcellina thought, that Dracilianus's arrogance and hubris should be his downfall. For all her hatred of the man, some part of her was praying for his safety in that thronging mob. But another part, bitter and vengeful, was praying for the very worst.

And the worst was happening. The purple-decked litter bearing the insignia of the Praetorian Prefect had emerged from the palace gateway, surrounded by guards and court eunuchs. The cordon of mounted men was struggling to hold back the tide of angry people, but missiles were already flying, bricks and stones and chunks of wood, rotting fruit, old shoes. The litter-bearers staggered under the barrage, and the purple drapes swung wildly. A solid wave of noise rose from the crowd, a steady hiss cut through with screams of abuse.

By the time the litter had reached the tetrapylon and started to turn towards the docks, the press of people in the street had grown enormous. The cavalry troopers were trying to drive them back with their lances and the hooves of their horses, the foot guards trying to forge a path for the litter, but the procession was slowing to a halt.

Marcellina noticed the Scholae tribune gazing up towards her and Hormisdas. With a jolt of surprise she saw the Persian signal to the officer with a wave. The next moment, the cordon of mounted guards parted, and the crowd flooded between them.

She could barely breathe. Clutching the hem of her shawl to her neck, she watched, transfixed, as the mob surged around the litter, driving away the bearers and the eunuchs. She saw the purple drapes ripped aside, the figure of a man dragged from within. Some of the people in the crowd had clubs and sticks; some carried knives and butcher's cleavers.

It all happened so quickly. The yells of the crowd turned to a deafening roar, then a maddened scream. Marcellina wanted to look away, to hide her eyes, but she could not. She told herself that she loathed Dracilianus; he had threatened her, threatened her daughter with torture. He had hounded her husband to the very end. For all his wealth and his cultured urbanity, he was a rabid animal and he deserved to die.

But to die like this, she thought. It was horrible.

She saw the body tossed by the crowd, Dracilianus still struggling, still screaming as the clubs rained down and the knives began to stab and rip. There were women among the throng, Marcellina noticed, even small children. Blood sprayed, spattering the pillars of the tetrapylon monument, and the crowd let out a cheer.

A few rapid heartbeats later, she saw the mangled body carried along by the mob. They were streaming towards the bridge over the river, carrying their bloody trophy along with them, and they passed directly below the portico where Marcellina stood watching. She glanced down and saw torn white flesh, gashed and bloody. The crowd had stripped the prefect naked, and now they were dragging him between them. As the seething throng passed below her, she leaned out across the balustrade and glimpsed Dracilianus's mangled face staring up at her. He almost seemed alive, and she thought she saw his lips move, as if he were crying out to her for help, or for forgiveness.

Then the crowd rushed onwards, towards the bridge and the flowing waters of the Orontes, and Dracilianus was gone.

CHAPTER XXXIV

The dead man awoke before dawn. Throwing off his shroud, he climbed from the tomb to greet the rising sun. Outside the cave mouth, he sat on the cool stone and waited patiently for the first chink of glowing light above the eastern horizon, away across the drab Mesopotamian plain. He felt the slowness in his bones. There was no hurry now.

The sun appeared, a hot coal balanced on the black rim of the world, and he hauled himself to his feet and raised his arms, crying out the salute to his god. *Sol Invictus, Ruler of Heaven, Lord of Daybreak...*

Nearly a month had passed since he had witnessed his own end. He had stood in the darkness and seen his own headless corpse dragged through the camp, still dressed in its finery. Some of the soldiers had wept; others had taken the opportunity to stamp on the body, and spit upon it. Only an hour or two previously they had been acclaiming him emperor. He saw the severed head too, mounted on a spear, bobbing above the milling crowd. Almost unrecognisable now, so bloodied and battered, caked in dust. But he had often noticed that severed heads are hard to tell apart.

As the morning grew warmer, he breakfasted on a nugget of stale bread and the last dribble of olive oil, washed down with warm water. His tomb was once a natural cave, high in the escarpment ten miles north of the city of Nisibis. At some ancient time it had been carved deeper and used as a burial place, but the sepulchre had long ago vanished. More recently, so he had heard, a Christian hermit had made his home there, until he was driven away by brigands. Now the people in the little village down the valley brought him food and drink, leaving them a short distance from the cave mouth. Perhaps, he thought, they believed he was a new hermit, and would work miracles for them? They would be disappointed, if so.

He looked like a hermit, he supposed, with his beard grown tangled and grey, his hair matted, his tunic stained as brown as dust. It was October now and the nights were growing cold, but he dared not light a fire. Instead he lay in his cave at night, wrapped in a blanket shroud, and thought about the living and the dead. He thought about his wife and his daughter, and prayed that he would see them again. He thought of his son, who had been with him at the end. About others too, faces from his past.

Often at night he dreamed of Constantine. The dead emperor visited him in his tomb, and sat beside him. At first Constantine had tried to explain himself, and all that he had been forced to do. But lately the emperor's ghost had fallen silent, and just sat with his head hanging in sorrow and shame.

Often too he relived that last desperate night in the camp beyond Nisibis. The body in the rear chamber of his tent had already begun to stiffen, and it had been a struggle to drag the clothes from it. Lycianus was a slightly smaller man, but after losing so much weight in the last few months, he found that the scout commander's clothes fitted him well enough. Dressing the corpse in his own uniform was more difficult. Sabinus had joined him, stepping silently through from the outer chamber, and together they had wrestled the tunic and breeches onto the corpse, the belts and cloak, the golden brooch. He had even cut away the smallest finger of Lycianus's left hand, to match his own wound. It was hard grisly work in the half-darkness. And when it was done, they had hacked the head from the body and concealed it in rags. Sabinus would ensure that it went missing, after enough people had seen it carried on its spear.

His son had told Egnatius alone about the ruse; the tribune had joined them, and together with Sabinus had dragged the body from the tent. Several of the other officers must have suspected the deception, but they said nothing about it. He had waited in the shadows of the rear chamber, a hood pulled over his face, until the tumult had moved away from his tent; then he had followed. For a few moments he had lingered, just to catch a glimpse of what was happening. It was enough. The sight had chilled his soul, and he'd felt dread scrabbling in his throat.

Sabinus, again, had led him from the camp that same night, and conducted him to the city of Nisibis. It had been Ephraim, the young presbyter, who had concealed him within the gloomy hall of the great church on the citadel mount. Ironic, after he had derided the Christians so much, that they sheltered him now. And, once a few days had passed, it was Ephraim's church slaves that had led him up here to the old cave tomb on the escarpment, and arranged for the villagers to supply him with all he needed.

He had been lucky. So lucky it made his head reel and panic kick in his chest when he thought about it for too long. But he forced himself to sit calmly, staring at the sunlight and cloud shadow that moved across the great dusty plain below him, until the feelings passed.

He had been watching the distant rider for an hour, the solitary figure growing distinct from the wavering heat of noon. The rider wore a wide-brimmed straw hat, and was climbing the trail up the rocky valley slowly, his horse picking its way with care, two mules and a second horse behind him. The sound of the hooves was unnaturally loud in the silence.

He remained seated until the rider had reached the head of the trail. Then he stood. The man on the horse sat upright in the saddle, surprised, then pushed the hat back from his face. His weathered features bunched into a grin.

'Brother!' he said. 'You've turned the colour of dust! I didn't see you until you stood up – like you'd risen from the ground!'

Then he slid nimbly from his horse and strode to the cave mouth. The two men embraced.

'Aurelius Castus,' Diogenes said, gripping his friend by the shoulders. 'You are the Christian Lazarus, risen from the grave!'

Castus grinned back at him, then broke into a laugh. Hearing his own name after so long was glorious. Like returning to life once more. 'I'd offer you wine and oysters, but I'm short of supplies,' he said. His own voice sounded strange in his ears, the words lumpy in his mouth. Weeks had passed since he had spoken to another living person.

'Well, you're lucky I have a little left,' Diogenes said. He went back to one of the mules and pulled a skin from the saddlebag, throwing it to Castus. Castus caught it, pulled out the bung with his teeth, and swigged back wine.

'Gods, that's good...'

Diogenes sat down with a sigh, crossing his legs, and fanned himself with his hat. His three-legged dog curled itself in the dust beside him. Flies whirled around them both. 'I can't see that you're prospering out here in the wilderness,' he said.

Castus took another swig of wine, then passed the skin back. 'You've been in Antioch?' he asked with abrupt urgency. 'You saw Marcellina?'

'Oh yes,' Diogenes said. And then he told Castus everything that had happened.

Castus listened, his mouth slack, his eyebrows bunched. When Diogenes had finished speaking he rocked back on his haunches and let out a cracked laugh. 'And Mucatra too, you say? I congratulate you on your tactical thinking, brother!'

'It wasn't me, so much. Hormisdas was behind most of what happened in the city, and your wife. She has unforeseen organisational talents, you know. And by now Constantius will have returned to take up the throne in Antioch. I didn't stay long enough to see him arrive in triumph. There's a new prefect though, one Septimius Acindynus. He's already issued a proclamation in the emperor's name, thanking the loyal citizens of Antioch for ridding the city of traitors and conspirators. Can you imagine it?'

'What else could Constantius do, I suppose? He couldn't execute everyone.'

'I wouldn't want to guess,' Diogenes said, frowning. 'I have grave doubts about that one. Your new emperor, I fear, is not a gentle soul.'

'My emperor?' Castus asked. 'Not yours?'

Diogenes smiled, pulling his hat back on. 'No,' he said. 'No, I shall not be accompanying you back west, I fear. I will be taking a different road!'

'You said once that you wouldn't make that journey again.'

'I won't. There's a caravan assembling at Nisibis, and I'll be travelling east with them. I know some of the merchants – Sogdians mostly, with a few from further east. I intend to travel towards the rising sun, and seek out the wisdom of distant lands. The west is dead to me now – and what better way to spend my final years?'

'You're going to Persia?' Castus asked, amazed.

'Through Persia, yes, while the roads are still open. But if divine providence allows it I'll travel further still, to the lands of the Yaudheyas and the Guptas. As far as the road takes me, in the mortal span I have left. One day I hope to sit upon the banks of the Ganga, brother, and learn the philosophies of the gymnosophists!'

He fell silent, peering away towards the eastern horizon with a look of such intense yearning and anticipation that Castus could only smile in response.

'We won't meet again then?' he asked, after a while.

'Not in this world,' Diogenes replied.

They parted the following morning, at a fork in the road that led south to Nisibis and west towards Edessa. Diogenes had given Castus a horse and one of the two mules; in the baggage was a change of clean clothes, provisions for the journey and a heavy purse of coin. A sword too, a simple cavalryman's spatha which Castus hoped he would not need.

'You remember what I told you?' Diogenes said as they dismounted. 'The place you're to meet?'

'I remember.'

For a few long moments they looked at each other, and then Castus pulled him into a firm embrace. 'Be careful out there, brother,' he said. 'You'll be meeting some very strange people where you're going.'

Diogenes grinned. 'I can't wait!' Then he scrambled back into the saddle. The dog yapped and bounded along beside him as he moved off.

Castus watched him ride away. Diogenes turned once and waved back at him, then his trotting figure dwindled into the haze of the distance until it was obscured by the dust of the road. For a while Castus remained standing there, whispering a silent prayer to the protecting gods. Then he swung himself back into the saddle and turned his horse towards the west.

For twelve days he rode, skirting the larger cities and avoiding the places where he might be recognised, sleeping at village inns or beside the road, wrapped in his cloak. From Edessa he took the old road to the Euphrates, crossing the river by ferry east of Samosata. He bathed there, and had his hair and beard trimmed in the city market. Then he moved on, through Commagene and the hill country of eastern Cilicia. Finally, a day ahead of schedule, he arrived at his destination.

It was an old shrine, set back from the road in a grove of trees, two miles from the town of Tarsus. Diogenes had known of the place, from the time he had spent living in that area years before. He had told Castus the date he was to be there too: nine days before the kalends of November.

Castus found the place easily enough, the building half-ruined, the doors long gone and only a dusty cell remaining. No way of telling which god might once have been revered here. But he tied up his horse and mule in the grove, and spent the night in the cell with a saddlebag for a pillow. The next morning was fresh, dew on the grass beneath the trees and the feel of autumn in the air. He rose, splashed his face with water, and was standing on the broken steps before the shrine by sunrise.

He waited an hour, and another. Then, far off in the distance, he saw the carriage approaching on the long straight road between the lines of trees, coming from the direction of the town. A man rode beside it, wrapped in a military cloak. Castus felt his mind whirling with nervous hope and dread. It had been so long.

Aeliana saw him first, jumping down from the carriage as soon as it halted on the road and running through the dappled morning sunlight beneath the trees. Castus descended the steps and met her, kneeling as the girl launched herself forward into his arms.

'I prayed!' Aeliana cried as he hugged her. 'Papa, I prayed to all the gods for you to come back – and you did! It's like a miracle!'

Castus grinned. 'I suppose it is.' He knew that the girl had been told nothing of his survival until recently. It was better that way – if she had been questioned, she might have revealed the deception. But everything seemed forgiven now.

He stood up again, keeping his daughter clasped to his side as Marcellina approached. Her mourning clothes were gone, but she was still plainly dressed, wearing no jewels or fine fabrics. She was smiling, her face glowing as she stood and stared at him, her hands clasped over her breast. Never, Castus thought, had she looked so gorgeous.

'Come here,' he growled, taking three paces towards his wife and throwing his arms around her. He could feel her tears on his neck, but she was laughing with relief and joy.

Sabinus arrived next, after tethering his horse. Beneath his cloak he wore the uniform of the Protectores, and the gold torque at his neck had a medallion portrait of Constantius Augustus. Castus embraced him too, pounding him on the back. He wanted to dance, to scream, to wave his arms to the sky and thank the gods.

'There's a boat at the river dock in Tarsus,' Marcellina said, pressing her hand against Castus's chest. 'It'll carry us across to Cyprus, and from there we can take ship for Athens. We'll travel slowly north through Greece, and we can be back at the villa by the ides of November.'

Castus was still grinning. His face was beginning to hurt. 'And who am I going to be?' he asked her.

'My bodyguard, for now,' Marcellina said with a sly smile. 'A former soldier, of course. But once we reach Athens you can return to being my husband again.'

'Athens,' Castus groaned, and kissed her deeply.

Sabinus came back down the steps of the shrine, and Castus clasped him by the shoulder. 'You're returning to Antioch then?'

'Yes,' his son said. 'I've been promised a promotion to tribune...' His tanned and scarred features, and the patch over his eye, gave him a severe look, beyond his years. His voice gained an abrupt urgency. 'Father, let me petition the emperor on your behalf. Now everything's in the open, we could explain what happened. Even if I don't tell them that you still live – your name could be fully cleared, all your honours and titles restored! We've already presented Constantius with the Persian diadem and the standards we took at Narasara... They speak of you as a hero in Antioch!'

'No,' Castus said firmly, tightening his grip on Sabinus's shoulder. 'My name's still my own, and I need no titles. I'm going back home, and I want nothing more from any emperor. Let the world think I'm dead and gone. I'm sorry, Sabinus – you'll have to live with the deception. But that's how it must be. And you've proved yourself well enough – my reputation won't help or hinder you now.'

'Very well,' Sabinus said after a pause, dropping his gaze. Then he looked his father in the eye again and smiled. 'I'll visit you,' he said. 'When I have enough leave. I can tell you all that's happened, out there in the world.'

'You do that,' Castus told him, and pride caught at his voice. Then he embraced his son once more.

Sabinus walked with Aeliana down to the carriage, and Castus stood with Marcellina before the old shrine.

'How long do we have, do you think?' she asked, taking his arm. 'Sabinus told me what happened to you during the siege. Are you fully recovered now?'

'I have another ten years of life, at least. A doctor told me!'

'Since when have you listened to doctors?'

Castus shrugged, grinning. Ten more years: he could ask for nothing more. And that would be the greatest of his victories.

The world would go on. The turmoils of empire would continue. Constantius would march his armies across the parched plains of Syria and Mesopotamia. Cities would fall to siege, or defend themselves heroically, and men would fight and die in the smiting sun and the dust. And the courtiers and bureaucrats, the tribunes and the generals would plot and conspire, one against another. Castus cared no more. All he wanted was to return to his home, his villa by the sea in a forgotten corner of Dalmatia.

Perhaps one day the empire itself would collapse into ruin, and all the monuments of Rome would be abandoned, like the little roadside shrine in the grove of trees, with nobody even to recall the names of the gods and the emperors that had once been revered there. All their glory, all of their triumphs, would be nothing but empty dust.

Marcellina reached up and ran her fingers through the scrub of his beard. Then she clasped his face between her palms and kissed him.

'Do you truly mean what you said?' she asked. 'You won't miss the army? You want nothing more of wars and battles?'

'I meant it with all my heart,' Castus said. 'I have all I need right here with me now.'

AUTHOR'S NOTE

The Middle East has long been the arena of competing empires and ideologies. The site of ancient Nisibis lies on the border of Syria and Turkey; a few half-buried pillars are all that remains of the old city, marooned in no man's land between the barbed-wire fences and minefields. Current events provide a sobering reminder that the conflicts of the ancient world have their distant echoes today.

The war between Rome and Persia that began with Constantine's death in AD 337 was to continue for a quarter-century, but compelling victories were denied to both sides. The imperial concord between Constantius II and his two brothers, sealed in blood, lasted only a few years; in AD 340 the elder brother was defeated and killed in a brief and bitter civil war with the younger, who in turn was murdered by agents of a usurper ten years later. After crushing the rebellion in the west, Constantius ruled as senior Augustus for another decade, until he in turn was challenged by his half-nephew Julian. Before he had a chance to confront this new threat, he died, consigning the empire to Julian's hands.

Determined to force a conclusion to the simmering conflict with Persia, Julian (called 'the Apostate' by Christians for his attempts to revive traditional religion) led an army into the east in AD 363. The campaign ended in disaster: Julian was mortally wounded in a battle near the Tigris, and his successor, eager to extricate himself from an impossible situation, agreed a truce with the Persians that involved the handover of the contested city of Nisibis and a swathe of frontier territory. To contemporaries, it was one of the greatest humiliations suffered by Rome in all her history, although it was soon overshadowed by further woes.

The chronology of the earlier stages of the Persian war is difficult to reconstruct; there may have been clashes in Armenia prior to 337. But the siege of Nisibis that immediately followed Constantine's death seems to have been the official commencement of hostilities. There were two further sieges, in 346 and 350, and in each case the Persians were repelled. Most descriptions mention Shapur's hydraulic works in connection with the third siege, but the Byzantine churchman Theodoret and several other writers clearly state that the Persians dammed the waters of the river and then released them 'like a battering ram' against the walls during the first siege of 337. It may be that they were mistaken, but I prefer to believe that Shapur could have attempted the strategy twice, hoping to improve with his second attempt on what had very nearly succeeded the first time around.

Bishop Iacob – or Mar Yakob, as he is known today – was one of the early saints of the Syriac church, and supposedly led the spiritual defence of Nisibis during the first siege. An ancient baptistery dedicated to him still stands in the Turkish town of Nusaybin. Most of what we know about the sieges themselves comes from Christian sources, principally the 'Nisibene Hymns' of Iacob's disciple Ephraim. Their focus is mystical and religious; Ephraim says little about the military aspects, but implies that the city was saved by miracles brought about by the prayers of its Christian congregation and the piety of its successive bishops. We do know that it was a military commander named Lucilianus who repelled the Persian assault in 350, and quite probably other senior officers did the same in the first and second sieges. Their names are lost to history.

For obvious reasons, there has been very little archaeological exploration of the site of Nisibis, and the layout of the ancient city remains largely conjectural. My own reconstruction is based in part on Rocco Palermo's 2014 paper from the *Journal of Roman Archaeology*, 'Nisibis, Capital of the Province of Mesopotamia'. Visitors to the site in the early nineteenth century described the traces of walls still standing on the bluffs above the river, while the rest of the site was populated by 'the black tents of the Koords'. Freya Stark's *Rome on the Euphrates* was published in 1966, and while some of her conclusions may seem a little dated today her book remains a beautifully written account of the historical events, coupled with evocative literary sketches. She visited the site of Nisibis in a more tranquil time, and describes 'the walls that are now a mere blur in the cultivation, far out beyond the shabby streets that cling there like limpets to the drowned... five columns alone remain standing as pedestals for storks' nests where the fields have swallowed the vanished town.'

The battle of Narasara was one of Rome's rare victories against the Persians, but it is mentioned only briefly in a single source; other than the death of Narses during the fighting, we know almost nothing about it – the date and location are entirely obscure. Dodgeon and Lieu's *The Roman Eastern Frontier and the Persian Wars* (1991) is an invaluable compendium of original materials on the eastern campaigns of the era, while C. S. Lightfoot's thesis 'The Eastern Frontier of the Roman Empire, with special reference to the reign of Constantius II' (1982) gives a comprehensive survey of the military situation in the fourth century, backed by original research.

The events of AD 337 have been overshadowed in most historical literature by the death of Constantine himself. R. W. Burgess's 'Summer of Blood: the Great Massacre of 337 and the Promotion of the Sons of Constantine' (*Dumbarton Oaks Papers*,

2008) provides a very detailed examination of the situation surrounding the succession, and the best possible reconstruction of the chronology of the period. Study of the Sassanid Persians is hampered by a shortage of accessible written sources, but Touraj Daryaee's *Sasanian Persia, the Rise and Fall of an Empire* (2007) contains a good summary in English of the evidence for their society and warfare. Matthew Canepa's *The Two Eyes of the Earth: Art and Ritual of Kingship between Rome and Sasanian Iran* (2010) has a wealth of detail about court life, including the treatment of envoys.

For my speculative depiction of the desert tribes in this novel I have drawn on Irfan Shahid's *Byzantium and the Arabs in the Fourth Century* (1984), among other sources. It does seem that the nomadic 'Saracens', as the Romans of the later period were beginning to call them, held women in comparatively high regard – the mid-fourth century *Expositio Totius Mundi* claims that 'women are said to rule among them' – and there is a surviving inscription to a female phylarch from Syria. Imru al-Qays was a real person, who left a detailed epitaph; he apparently had a wife named Hind, but my fictional character of that name is loosely based on another historical figure: Mavia, or Mawwiya, who led the Tanukhids in a successful uprising against Rome in the AD 370s. Their 'war hymn' is derived from a Druze chant noted by Gertrude Bell in *The Desert and the Sown* (1912), while the epithet 'Mother of Dust' (*Umm Qastal*) comes from the pre-Islamic Arab poet Al-Shanfara.

I have called this series 'Twilight of Empire', although in fact the centuries-old power of Rome would not be extinguished in the west for another hundred years or more after the events of this story. It would survive in the east – as the so-called 'Byzantine' Empire – well into the Middle Ages. Historians today tend no longer to regard the later Roman era as a degraded and inferior manifestation of the classical world. In many ways the age of Constantine was a return to glory after the chaos and confusion that preceded it. It is only with the benefit of historical hindsight that we can see it as a brief respite before the slow and inevitable collapse into darkness that was to come.

Aurelius Castus, meanwhile, has reached the terminus of a journey which has taken him from wilds of northern Britain to the banks of the Tigris. As always, I am immensely grateful to all those that have helped me in the writing of these books. I would particularly like to thank my agent, Will Francis, and everyone at Janklow and Nesbit. My editor, Rosie de Courcy, has given me invaluable support and guidance in all I have done, as have the rest of the team at Head of Zeus. But most of all I am sincerely grateful to my readers, without whom these successive books would never have been written.

It has been a long road, and I thank you for following it to the end.